D1570446

THE BEST OF H. E. BATES

By H. E. Bates

SPELLA HO

FAIR STOOD THE WIND FOR FRANCE

THE CRUISE OF THE BREADWINNER

THE PURPLE PLAIN

THE JACARANDA TREE

DEAR LIFE

THE SCARLET SWORD

COLONEL JULIAN AND OTHER STORIES

LOVE FOR LYDIA

THE NATURE OF LOVE

THE FEAST OF JULY

THE SLEEPLESS MOON

THE DAFFODIL SKY

SUMMER IN SALANDAR

THE DARLING BUDS OF MAY

A BREATH OF FRENCH AIR

THE WATERCRESS GIRL AND OTHER STORIES

THE GRAPES OF PARADISE

HARK, HARK, THE LARK!

THE ENCHANTRESS AND OTHER STORIES

THE GOLDEN ORIOLE

THE BEST OF H. E. BATES

The Best of H. E. Bates

by

H. E. BATES

With a Preface by

HENRY MILLER

An Atlantic Monthly Press Book

LITTLE, BROWN AND COMPANY

BOSTON   TORONTO

Published in England under the title of
SEVEN BY FIVE

ATLANTIC—LITTLE, BROWN BOOKS
ARE PUBLISHED BY
LITTLE, BROWN AND COMPANY
IN ASSOCIATION WITH
THE ATLANTIC MONTHLY PRESS

PRINTED IN THE UNITED STATES OF AMERICA

AUTHOR'S NOTE

The earliest of these stories, *The Flame,* was first published in 1926, having been written a year earlier, when I was twenty; the latest appeared in 1961. The intervening thirty-five years, together with the thirty-five stories I have chosen from that period, therefore give this collection its title, *Seven by Five.**My aim has been to make the book as widely representative of my work as a short story writer as possible, but I have nevertheless refrained from including any of the war-time stories I wrote under the pseudonym of 'Flying Officer X', any of the stories of Uncle Silas and any *novellas,* since these all belong, in my view, to quite separate categories.

*The title of the British edition.

PREFACE BY HENRY MILLER

It was only a little over a year ago that I came across H. E. Bates' work; up until then I had never even heard his name, strange as this may sound. I blush now when I read that he is the author of forty or more books, has been translated into a dozen or more languages, and that 'his reputation in America, Australia and New Zealand equals, and in some cases surpasses, that in his own country.'

Perhaps I would never have heard of him had I not been laid up with chills and fever in the Hotel Formentor, Mallorca, where I was quartered during the Formentor Conference. Having nothing to read I asked a friend to go to the bookstore in the lobby and select something light, gay, amusing for me. My friend returned with a copy of *A Breath of French Air*. He said nothing about knowing the author until some days later when I told him how much I had enjoyed the book. A little later, at some airport, I picked up *The Darling Buds of May* and *Fair Stood the Wind for France*. The last named impressed me deeply and made me wonder why I had never heard of the author. It struck me as being the only good novel I had read about World War II.

In a way Mr Bates is the very opposite of what I look for in an author. There is certainly little relation between his manner of writing and that of Celine or Blaise Cendrars, my favourites among contemporary writers. (Both dead now, alas.) On the other hand, I do find a kinship between Bates and Jean Giono, whose work I adore. I ought to add – like whom I wish I could write.

One of the great joys for a writer is to find a fellow writer who, because he is so different, captivates and enchants him. To find a writer whose work he will read even if he is warned that it is not one of the author's best.

In general I must confess that I seldom fall for the work of a popular writer. Had I lived in Dickens' time, for example, I doubt that I would have been one of his devoted readers. As for the successful writers of our own time there is hardly one

I can think of off hand whom I have any desire to read. It demands an effort for me to read a modern novel, and an even greater one to read a short story. I make exception for the short stories of I. B. Singer, the Yiddish writer. And Mr Bates is supremely a novelist and short-story writer. He is, moreover, a rather conventional one.

After all that has been written about this author it seems rather unimportant that I add my tribute to him. Certainly he needs no further words of praise, and praise, I am afraid, is all I can summon. I assume that the reason I have been requested to write this preface to his collected short stories is because the coupling of our two names will seem highly incongruous both to Mr Bates' readers and my own. I know that I have a reputation for being highly critical of, perhaps even unfair to British authors. On the other hand, it should not be overlooked that the one author (still alive) for whom I have an undying admiration is John Cowper Powys, and that I regard his novel, *A Glastonbury Romance,* as the greatest novel in the English language.

If Mr Bates were a painter I think I could express my views about his work much better. Last night I lay awake trying to pick out the painter with whom I sought to identify his writing. No single painter whose work I know seemed suitable. I thought of Renoir and Bonnard, of Breughel the elder and others. I think that if I were to find one it would be a Flemish painter. The reason is obvious.

Whether it be the short story or the novel, Mr Bates always finds time for lengthy descriptions of nature, descriptions which in the hands of a lesser writer would seem boring or out of place. He dwells long and lovingly on things which years ago would have driven me mad. I mean such things as flowers, plants, trees, birds, sea, sky, everything in short which meets the eye and which the unskilled writer uses as so much window dressing. Indeed, it is not only the unskilled writer who is guilty of mishandling description. Some of the greatest novelists of the past were flagrantly guilty of doing just this, and more particularly British writers. With Mr Bates this fault has been made into a virtue. The reader falls upon these lengthy passages like a man athirst.

There is another virtue which goes hand in hand with the

above-mentioned one, and that is the author's feeling for women. His women are always females first and foremost. That is to say, they are fully sexed: they have all the charm, the loveliness, the attraction of the flowers he knows so well. With a few deft strokes – like a painter again – we are given their peculiar grace, character and utter femininity. Not all of them, naturally, for he can also render the other kind of woman just as tellingly.

And then there is *this* element which crops up again and again, I find – an obsession with pain. Pain stretched to the breaking point, pain prolonged beyond all seeming endurance. This element is usually called forth in connection with heroic behaviour. Perhaps it is the supreme mark of the hero, this ability to endure pain. With Mr Bates I feel that it goes beyond the point of the heroic; it carries us into some other dimension. Pain takes on the aspects of space and time, a continuum or perpetuum which one finally questions no longer.

But no matter how much one is made to suffer, one closes his books with a lasting sensation of beauty. And this sense of beauty, it seems to me, is evoked by the author's unswerving acceptance of life. It is this which makes his flowers, trees, birds, skies, whatever it be, different from those of other writers. They are not merely decorative, they are not showily dramatic: they exist, along with his characters, his thoughts, his observations, in a plenum which is spiritual as well as physical.

There is one other quality which must endear him to every reader and that is his sense of humour. It is a full, robust humour, often bawdy, which I must confess the British writer seems to have lost in the last few centuries. It is never a nasty humour, so common to American writers. It is clean and healthy, and absolutely infectious.

What surprises me most about this man's work is the fact that only one or two of his books have been made into films. Despite the abundance of descriptive passages which I spoke of, there is drama in all his work. Drama and dialogue. Good, natural dialogue which, if transferred to the screen, would need no adaptation.

I realise at this point that I have said little or nothing about the short stories themselves. Aside from a few very short ones I find them all absorbing. Meanwhile I look forward with great relish to eating my way through the thirty odd books of his

which I have yet to read, especially those containing his novellas,
a form which clearly suits him best, as it did one of my first
idols, Knut Hamsun. But I am sure that whatever Mr Bates
gives us will always please me.

HENRY MILLER
6/5/63

CONTENTS

THE BEST OF H. E. BATES

THE FLAME

'Two ham and tongue, two teas, please, Miss!'

'Yessir.'

The waitress retreated, noticing as she did so that the clock stood at six. 'Two ham and tongue, two teas,' she called down the speaking-tube. The order was repeated. She put down the tube, seemed satisfied, even bored, and patted the white frilled cap that kept her black hair in place. Then she stood still, hand on hip, pensively watching the door. The door opened and shut.

She thought: 'Them two again!'

Wriggling herself upright she went across and stood by the middle-aged men. One smiled and the other said: 'Usual.'

Down the tube went her monotonous message: 'One ham, one tongue, two teas.'

Her hand went to her hip again, and she gazed at the clock. Five past! – time was hanging, she thought. Her face grew pensive again. The first order came on the lift, and the voice up the tube: 'Two 'am an' tongue, two teas!'

'Right.' She took the tray and deposited it with a man and woman at a corner-table. On returning she was idle again, her eye still on the door. Her ear detected the sound of a bronchial wheeze on the floor above, the angry voice of a customer in the next section, and the rumble of the lift coming up. But she watched the door until the last possible second. The tray slid into her hand almost without her knowing it and the nasal voice into her ears: 'One 'am, one tongue, two teas!'

'Right.'

The middle-aged customers smiled; one nudged the other when she failed to acknowledge that salute, and chirped: 'Bright today, ain't you!'

She turned her back on him.

'Been brighter,' she said, without smiling.

She was tired. When she leant against the head of the lift she shut her eyes, then remembered and opened them again to resume her watch on the door and clock. The man in the corner

7

smacked his lips, drank with his mouth full and nearly choked. A girl in another corner laughed, not at the choking man but at her companion looking cross-eyed. The cash-register 'tinked' sharply. Someone went out: nothing but fog came in, making every one shiver at once. The man in the corner whistled three or four notes to show his discomfort, remembered himself, and began to eat ham.

The girl noticed these things mechanically, not troubling to show her disgust. Her eye remained on the door. A customer came in, an uninteresting working girl who stared, hesitated, then went and sat out of the dark girl's section. The dark girl noticed it mechanically.

The manageress came: tall, darkly dressed, with long sleeves, like a manageress.

'Have you had your tea, Miss Palmer,' she asked.

'No.'

'Would you like it?'

'No, thank you.'

'No? Why not?'

'It's my night off. I'm due out at half-past.'

She walked away, took an order, answered a call for 'Bill!' and found that the order got mixed with the bill, and that the figures wouldn't add. It seemed years before the 'tink' of the register put an end to confusion. The customer went out: fog blew in: people shivered. The couple in the corner sipped their tea, making little storms in their tea-cups.

She put her head against the lift. The clock showed a quarter past: another quarter of an hour! She was hungry. As if in consequence her brain seemed doubly sharp and she kept thinking: 'My night out. Wednesday. Wednesday. He said Wednesday! He said – '

'Bill! Bill!'

She went about mechanically, listened mechanically, executed mechanically. A difficult bill nearly sent her mad, but she wrote mechanically, cleaned away dirty platter, brushed off crumbs – all mechanically. Now and then she watched the clock. Five minutes more! Would he come? Would he? Had he said Wednesday?

The waitress from the next section, a fair girl, came and said:

'Swap me your night, Lil? Got a flame comin' in. I couldn't

get across to tell you before. A real flame – strite he is – nice, quiet, 'andsome. Be a dear? You don't care?'

The dark girl stared. What was this! She couldn't! Not she! The clock showed three minutes to go. She couldn't!

'Nothing doing,' she said and walked away.

Every one was eating contentedly. In the shadow near the lift she pulled out his note and read: 'I will come for you, Wednesday evening, 6.'

Six! Then, he was late! Six! Why should she think half-past? She shut her eyes. Then he wasn't coming!

A clock outside struck the half-hour. She waited five minutes before passing down the room, more mechanically than ever. Why hadn't he come? Why hadn't he come?

The fair girl met her. 'Be a dear?' she pleaded. 'Swap me your night. He's a real flame – 'struth he is, nice, quiet!'

Thirty-five minutes late! The dark girl watched the door. No sign! It was all over.

'Right-o,' she said.

She sent another order down. The door opened often now, the fog was thicker, she moved busily. She thought of him when a man ordered a brandy and spilt it over her hand because his own shivered with cold. He wasn't like that, she thought, as she sucked her fingers dry.

For the first time in five minutes she looked at the door. She felt her heart leap.

He had come at last. Yes, there he was. He was talking to the fair girl. The little doll was close to him. Yes, there he was, nice, quiet handsome. Their voices crept across to her.

'Two seats? two seats?' she heard.

'Yes.'

'Oh! I say! And supper?'

'Of course. And supper.'

The dark girl could not move as they went out.

The door shut hard. 'Two seats?' 'And supper?' 'Nice quiet, 'andsome.' The dark girl dreamed on.

'Miss! Miss!'

She obeyed. She was sad, hungry, tired.

'Yessir?' They were middle-aged men again!

'Two teas, two tongues,' said one.

'Two seats and supper?' she whispered.

'Whaaat? Two teas! two tongues! Can't you hear?'

'Yessir. Two teas, two tongues. Thank you, sir.'

She moved slowly away.

'You can never make these blooming gals understand,' said one man to the other.

A FLOWER PIECE

The blackthorn tree stooped over the high bank above the road. Its branches were clouded with white blossom and the spring sunlight threw lace-like patterns on the earth that had been trodden bare underneath the tree. The grass of the bank was scattered with big, pale-blue violets and stars of coltsfoot and daisies very like chance blackthorn blossoms that the wind had shaken down. In the hedge behind the blackthorn were companies of pale-green lords-and-ladies that had thrust up their unfurled hoods through a thicket of dog's-mercury. They looked cold and stately. The sunlight was sharp and brilliant and against the blue of the sky the blackthorn tree was whiter than a summer cloud.

On the road below stood a row of cottages and in the back gardens wives were beating carpets and gossiping. A clergyman rode by on a bicycle, carrying *The Times* and a bunch of daffodils. A blackbird squawked and dipped across the road and vanished into a spinney of hazels as he passed.

A girl of seven or eight was sitting under the blackthorn. The tree was so twisted and stooping that she sat there in a kind of room, shut in by a roof and walls of blossoming branches. It was very sweet and snug there on the dry floor in the freckling sunlight. She had taken off her pinafore and had spread it across the earth and had set in the centre of it a tin that had once held peaches. In the tin she was arranging flowers among ivy leaves and grasses. She had put in celandines and dog-violets and coltsfoot and a single dandelion, with a spray or two of blackthorn. She arched her fingers very elegantly and sat back to admire the effects. She had fair, smooth hair, and she had made a daisy chain to bind round her forehead. It gave her a very superior and ladylike air which was not lost on her.

Presently she ceased arranging the flowers and began to smooth her dress and polish her finger-nails on her palms, lingering over them for a long time. At last there was a move-

11

ment in a hawthorn bush a little distance away and a voice called quietly:

'Do I have to come in now?'

The girl looked up in the direction of the voice.

'You have to wait till I tell you,' she whispered sharply.

And then in a totally strange voice, very high-pitched and affected, like the voice of a stage duchess, she sang out:

'I'm at my toilet, my dear. An awful nuisance. Do excuse me.'

'I see.'

'Only a moment! I'm still in my *déshabillé.*'

She began to make hurried imaginary movements of slipping in and out of garments. Finally she undid two buttons at the bodice of her dress and turned back the bodice of her dress, revealing her naked chest. She looked down at herself in admiration, breathing heavily once or twice, so that her bosom rose and fell very languidly and softly. She gave one last touch to the flowers in the peach-tin and then whispered:

'You can come in now. Act properly.'

Another child came out of hiding and stood outside the hawthorn tree. She was a brown, shy, unassuming creature, about six or seven, with beautiful dark eyes that reflected the dazzling whiteness of the sloe blossom so perfectly that they took fresh light from it. Her voice was curiously soft and timid and whispering.

'Do I have to come straight in?' she said.

'You have to be in the garden first. You look at the flowers and then you ring and the servant comes.'

'Oh! what lovely may,' said the other child, talking softly to herself.

'It's not may! It's lilac.'

'Oh! What lovely lilac. Oh! dear, what lovely lilac.'

She pulled down a branch of blossom and caressed it with her cheek. It was very sweet and she sighed. She acted very charmingly, and finally she rang the bell and the servant came.

'May I see Mrs Lane?'

'Not Mrs Lane,' came an awful whisper. 'Lady Constance. You're Mrs Lane.'

'Is Lady Constance in?'

'Will you go into the drawing-room?'

She stooped and went through a space in the blackthorn

branches. The fair child for a moment did not notice her. She had broken off a thorn and she was absorbed in stitching imaginary embroideries very delicately. Suddenly she glanced up with a most perfect exclamation of well-mannered surprise.

'My dear Mrs Lane! It is Mrs Lane, isn't it?'

'Yes.'

'How sweet of you to come. Won't you sit down? I'll ring for tea. You must be tired.' Ting-a-ling-a-ling! 'Oh! Jane, will you bring tea at once, please? Thank you. Oh! do sit down, won't you?'

'Where do I sit?' said the brown child.

'On the floor, silly!' whispered the fair girl. 'Oh! do take the settee, won't you?'

'I was admiring your lovely may,' said the brown child.

'The lilac? Oh! yes, wouldn't you like to take some?'

'Oh! Yes. May I?'

She began to crawl through the break in the branches again. Instantly the fair child was furious.

'You don't have to do that until I tell you,' she whispered. 'Come back and sit down now. Oh! yes, of course,' she said aloud. 'I'll tell the gardener to cut you some.'

The brown-eyed child crept back under the tree and sat down. She looked very meek and solemn and embarrassed, as though she were really in a drawing-room and did not know what to do with her hands. The fair child was acting superbly, not one accent or gesture out of place. The maid arrived with the tea and the fair one said with perfect sweetness:

'Milk and sugar?'

The dark child had become busy with hidden knots, her frock uplifted, and she did not hear. The fair-haired child took one look at her and became furious again.

'Put your clothes down,' she whispered terribly. 'You're showing all you've got.'

'I can't help it. It's my knickers. I want some new elastic.'

'But you mustn't do it. Not in the drawing-room. We're ladies!'

'Ladies do it.'

'Ladies don't do it! Ladies have to sit nice and talk nice and behave themselves.'

The brown-eyed child surrendered. She looked as though she

were bored and bewildered by the affectations of the fair child
and by the prospect of being a lady. She was constantly glancing with an expression of quiet longing at the blackthorn
blossom, the blue sky and the flowers arranged in the peach-tin.

'Milk and sugar?' repeated the fair child.

'Oh! yes please.'

There were no teacups, but the fair child had gathered a heap
of stones for cakes. The brown child sat with a stone in her
hand. The other took a cake between her finger-tips and made
elegant bites and munched with a sweetish smile. She made
small talk to perfection, and when she drank her tea she extended
her little finger. Finally she observed that the dark child was
neither eating nor drinking. She looked at her as if she had
committed unpardonable sins in etiquette.

'Aren't you having any tea?' she said icily.

The brown-eyed child looked startled and then declared
timidly:

'I don't want to play this game.'

'Why don't you want to play?'

The brown child did not answer. All the dignity of the fair
child at once vanished. She made a gesture as though it were
difficult to bear all the shortcomings of the younger child.

'All because you can't act,' she said tartly.

'Let's go out and get violets and be real people.'

'We are real people. You play so silly. You aren't old enough
to understand.'

The brown-eyed child looked acutely depressed. Suddenly she
dropped the stone and began to creep out disconsolately from
under the blackthorn tree. The fair child adopted a new,
cajoling tone.

'It's easy,' she said. 'You only have to put it on a bit and
you're a lady. We can start again and you can be a duchess.
Come on.'

The dark child looked back for a moment very dubiously, as
though it were too much to believe, and then walked away up the
bank. The other child sniffed and tossed her head with fierce
pride and called out:

'You needn't think you can come back here now you've gone.'

Without answering, the brown-eyed child walked away behind
the hawthorn trees and by the hedge at the top of the bank. She

became lost in a world of dog's-mercury and budding hawthorn and pale violets. She came upon primrose buds and finally a cluster of opened primroses and a bed of white anemones. Talking to herself, she gathered flowers and leaves and put them in her hair, as the fair girl had done.

The fair child crept out from under the blackthorn tree. She had tucked her frock in her pale blue knickers and she stood upright on her toes, like a ballet-dancer. She broke off a spray of blackthorn and held it with both hands above her head and then twirled on her toes and did high kicks and waltzed majestically round and round the blackthorn tree. Now and then she broke out and sang to herself. She introduced a stage vibrato into her voice and she danced about the blackthorn tree to the tune she made, acting perfectly.

Finally the brown-haired child came down the bank again. She saw the fair child dancing and she suddenly conceived a desire to dance too. She stood by the tree and waited. The fair girl saw her.

'You needn't come here!' she sneered.

A spasm of sadness crossed the face of the dark child. She turned and descended the bank very slowly, sometimes pausing and looking backward and then edging unwillingly away. Finally, with the primroses and the single anemone still shining in her hair, she reached the road and walked slowly away and disappeared.

When she had gone there was nothing left to interrupt the gaiety of the dancing child, the flowers about the earth and the blackthorn tree scattering its shower of lovely stars.

THE MOWER

In the midday heat of a June day a farm-boy was riding down a deserted meadow-lane, straddling a fat white pony. The blossoms of hawthorn had shrivelled to brown on the tall hedges flanking the lane and wild pink and white roses were beginning to open like stars among the thick green leaves. The air was heavy with the scent of early summer, the odour of the dying hawthorn bloom, the perfume of the dog-roses, the breath of ripening grass.

The boy had taken off his jacket and had hooked it over the straw victual-bag hanging from the saddle. There were bottles of beer in the bag and the jacket shaded them from the heat of the sun. The pony moved at walking-pace and the boy rode cautiously, never letting it break into a trot. As though it was necessary to be careful with the beer, he sometimes halted the pony and touched the necks of the bottles with his fingers. The bottlenecks were cool, but the cloth of his jacket was burning against his hand.

He presently steered the pony through a white gate leading from the lane to a meadow beyond. The gate was standing open and he rode the pony straight across the curving swathes of hay which lay drying in the sun. It was a field of seven or eight acres and a third of the grass had already been mown. The hay was crisp and dry under the pony's feet and the flowers that had been growing in the grass lay white and shrivelled in the sunshine.

Over on the far side of the field a man was mowing and a woman was turning the rows of grass with a hay rake. The figure of the man was nondescript and dark, and the woman was dressed in a white blouse and an old green skirt that had faded to the yellowish colour of the grass the man was mowing. The boy rode the pony towards them. The sunshine blazed down fierce and perpendicular, and there was no shade in the field except for the shadow of an ash tree in one corner and a group of willows by a cattle-pond in another.

16

Everywhere was silence and the soft sound of the pony's feet in the hay and the droning of bees in the flowers among the uncut grass seemed to deepen the silence.

The woman straightened her back and, leaning on her rake, shaded her face with her hand and looked across at the boy as she heard him coming. The man went on mowing, swinging the scythe slowly and methodically, his back towards her.

The woman was dark and good-looking, with a sleek swarthy face and very high, soft red cheek-bones, like a gipsy, and a long pigtail of thick black hair which she wore twisted over her head like a snake coiled up asleep. She herself was rather like a snake also, her long body slim and supple, her black eyes liquid and bright. The boy rode up to her and dismounted. She dropped her rake and held the pony's head and ran her fingers up and down its nose while he slipped from the saddle.

'Can he come?' she said.

The boy had not time to answer before the man approached, wiping the sweat from his face and neck with a dirty red handkerchief. His face was broad and thick-lipped and ponderous, his eyes were grey and simple, and the skin of his face and neck and hands was dried and tawny as an Indian's with sun and weather. He was about forty, and he walked with a slight stoop of his shoulders and a limp of his left leg, very slowly and deliberately.

'See him?' he said to the boy.

'He was up there when I got the beer,' the boy said.

'In the Dragon? What did he say?'

'He said he'd come.'

The woman ceased stroking the pony's nose and looked up.

'He said that yesterday,' she said.

'Ah! but you can't talk to him. He's got to have his own way,' said the man. 'Was he drunk?' he asked.

'I don't think so,' said the boy. 'He was drunk yesterday.'

The man wiped his neck impatiently and made a sound of disgust and then took out his watch. 'Half the day gone – and a damn wonder if he comes,' he muttered.

'Oh! if Ponto says he'll come,' said the woman slowly, 'he'll come. He'll come all right.'

'How do you know? He does things just when he thinks he will – and not until.'

'Oh! He'll come if he says he'll come,' she said.

The boy began to lead the pony across the field towards the ash tree. The woman stood aside for him and then kicked her rake on a heap of hay and followed him.

The sun had crossed the zenith. The man went back to his scythe and slipped his whetstone from his pocket and laid it carefully on the mown grass. As he put on his jacket he turned and gazed at the white gate of the field. He could see no one there, and he followed the woman and the boy across the field to the ash tree.

Under the ash tree the boy was tethering the horse in the shade and the woman was unpacking bread and cold potatoes and a meat pie. The boy had finished tethering the horse as the man came up and he was covering over the bottles of beer with a heap of hay. The sight of the beer reminded the man of something.

'You told him the beer was for him?' he asked.

'He asked me whose it was and I told him what you said,' the boy replied.

'That's all right.'

He began to unfold the sack in which the blade of his scythe had been wrapped. He spread out the sack slowly and carefully on the grass at the foot of the ash trunk and let his squat body sink down upon it heavily. The boy and the woman seated themselves on the grass at his side. He unhooked the heavy soldier's knife hanging from his belt, and unclasped it and wiped it on his trousers knee. The women sliced the pie. The man took his plateful of pie and bread and potatoes on his knee, and spitting his sucking-pebble from his mouth began spearing the food with the point of his knife, eating ravenously. When he did not eat with his knife he ate with his fingers, grunting and belching happily. The woman finished serving the pie, and sucking a smear of gravy from her long fingers, began to eat too.

During the eating no one spoke. The three people stared at the half-mown field. The curves of the scythed grass were beginning to whiten in the blazing sunshine. The heat shimmered and danced above the earth in the distance in little waves.

Before long the man wiped his plate with a piece of bread and swilled down his food with long drinks of cold tea from a blue can. When he had finished drinking, his head lolled back against the ash tree and he closed his eyes. The boy lay flat on his belly, reading a sporting paper while he ate. The air was stifling and warm even under the ash tree, and there was no sound in the noon stillness except the clink of the horse's bit as it pulled off the young green leaves of the hawthorn hedge.

But suddenly the woman sat up a little and the drowsy look on her face began to clear away. A figure of a man had appeared at the white gate and was walking across the field. He walked with a kind of swaggering uncertainty and now and then he stopped and took up a handful of mown grass and dropped it again. He was carrying a scythe on his shoulder.

She watched him intently as he skirted the standing grass and came towards the ash tree. He halted at last within the shade of the tree and took a long look at the expanse of grass, thick with buttercups and tall bull-daises, scattered everywhere like a white and yellow mass of stars.

'By Christ,' he muttered softly.

His voice was jocular and tipsy. The woman stood up.

'What's the matter, Ponto?' she said.

'This all he's cut?'

'That's all.'

'By Christ.'

He laid his scythe on the grass in disgust. He was a tall, thin, black-haired fellow, about thirty, lean and supple as a stoat; his sharp, dark-brown eyes were filled with a roving expression, half dissolute and half cunning; the light in them was sombre with drinking. His soft red lips were full and pouting, and there was something about his face altogether conceited, easy-going and devilish. He had a curious habit of looking at things with one eye half closed in a kind of sleepy wink that was marvellously knowing and attractive. He was wearing a dark slouch hat which he had tilted back from his forehead and which gave him an air of being a little wild but sublimely happy.

Suddenly he grinned at the woman and walked over to where the man lay sleeping. He bent down and put his mouth close to his face.

'Hey, your old hoss's bolted!' he shouted.

The man woke with a start.

'Your old hoss's bolted!'

'What's that? Where did you spring from?'

'Get up, y' old sleepy guts. I wanna get this grass knocked down afore dark.'

The man got to his feet.

'Knock this lot down afore dark?'

'Yes, my old beauty. When I mow I do mow, I do.' He smiled and wagged his head. 'Me and my old dad used to mow twenty-acre fields afore dark – and start with the dew on. Twenty-acre fields. You don't know what mowin' is.'

He began to take off his jacket. He was slightly unsteady on his feet and the jacket bothered him as he pulled it off and he swore softly. He was wearing a blue-and-white shirt and a pair of dark moleskin trousers held up by a wide belt of plaited leather thongs. His whetstone rested in a leather socket hanging from the belt. He spat on his hands and slipped the whetstone from the socket and picked up his scythe and with easy, careless rhythmical swings began to whet the long blade. The woman gazed at the stroke of his arm and listened to the sharp ring of the stone against the blade with a look of unconscious admiration and pleasure on her face. The blade of the scythe was very long, tapering and slender, and it shone like silver in the freckles of sunlight coming through the ash leaves. He ceased sharpening the blade and took a swing at a tuft of bull-daisies. The blade cut the stalks crisply and the white flowers fell evenly together, like a fallen nosegay. His swing was beautiful and with the scythe in his hand the balance of his body seemed to become perfect and he himself suddenly sober, dignified, and composed.

'Know what my old dad used to say?' he said.

'No.'

'Drink afore you start.'

'Fetch a bottle of beer for Ponto,' said the man to the boy at once. 'I got plenty of beer. The boy went up on the nag and fetched it.'

'That's a good job. You can't mow without beer.'

'That's right.'

'My old man used to drink twenty pints a day. God's truth. Twenty pints a day. He was a bloody champion. You can't mow without beer.'

The woman came up with a bottle of beer in her hand. Ponto took it from her mechanically, hardly looking at her. He uncorked the bottle, covered the white froth with his mouth and drank eagerly, the muscles of his neck rippling like those of a horse. He drank all the beer at one draught and threw the empty bottle into the hedge, scaring the pony.

'Whoa! damn you!' he shouted.

The pony tossed his head and quietened again. Ponto wiped his lips, and taking a step or two towards the boy, aimed the point of the scythe jocularly at his backside. The boy ran off and Ponto grinned tipsily at the woman.

'You goin' to turn the rows?' he said.

'Yes,' she said.

He looked her up and down, from the arch of her hips to the clear shape of the breasts in her blouse and the coil of her black pigtail. Her husband was walking across the field to fetch his scythe. She smiled drowsily at Ponto and he smiled in return.

'I thought you'd come,' she said softly.

His smile broadened and he stretched out his hand and let his fingers run down her bare brown throat. She quivered and breathed quickly and laughed softly in return. His eyes rested on her face with mysterious admiration and delight and he seemed suddenly very pleased about something.

'Good old Anna,' he said softly.

He walked past her and crossed the field to the expanse of unmown grass. He winked solemnly and his fingers ran lightly against her thigh as he passed her.

The woman followed him out into the sunshine and took up her rake and began to turn the rows that had been cut since early morning. When she glanced up again the men were mowing. They seemed to be mowing at the same even, methodical pace, but Ponto was already ahead. He swung his scythe with a long light caressing sweep, smoothly and masterfully, as though his limbs had been born to mow. The grass was shaved off very close to the earth and was laid in a tidy swathe that curved gently behind him like a thick rope. On the backward stroke the grass and the butter-cups and the bull-daisies were pressed gently backwards, bent in readiness to meet the forward swing that came through the grass with a soft swishing sound like the sound of indrawn breath.

The boy came and raked in the row next to the woman. Together they turned the rows and the men mowed in silence for a long time. Every time the woman looked up she looked at Ponto. He was always ahead of her husband and he moved with a kind of lusty insistence, as though he were intent on moving the whole field before darkness fell. Her husband mowed in a stiff, awkward fashion, always limping and often whetting his scythe. The boy had taken some beer to Ponto, who often stopped to drink. She would catch the flash of the bottle tilted up in the brilliant sunshine and she would look at him meditatively as though remembering something.

As the afternoon went on, Ponto mowed far ahead of her husband, working across the field towards the pond and the willows. He began at last to mow a narrow space of grass behind the pond. She saw the swing of his bare arms through the branches and then lost them again.

Suddenly he appeared and waved a bottle and shouted something.

'I'll go,' she said to the boy.

She dropped her rake and walked over to the ash tree and found a bottle of beer. The flies were tormenting the horse and she broke off an ash bough and slipped it in the bridle. The sun seemed hotter than ever as she crossed the field with the beer, and the earth was cracked and dry under her feet. She picked up a stalk of buttercups and swung it against her skirt. The scent of the freshly-mown grass was strong and sweet in the sunshine. She carried the beer close by her side, in the shadow.

Ponto was mowing a stretch of grass thirty or forty yards wide behind the pond. The grass was richer and taller than in the rest of the field and the single swathes he had cut lay as thick as corn.

She sat down on the bank of the pond under a willow until he had finished his bout of mowing. She had come up silently, and he was mowing with his back towards her, and it was not until he turned that he knew she was there.

He laid his scythe in the grass and came sidling up to her. His face was drenched in sweat and in his mouth was a stalk of totter-grass and the dark red seeds trembled as he walked. He looked at Anna with a kind of sleepy surprise.

'Good old Anna,' he said.

'You did want beer?' she said.

He smiled and sat down at her side.

She too smiled with a flash of her black eyes. He took the bottle from her hand and put one hand on her knee and caressed it gently. She watched the hand with a smile of strange, wicked, ironical amusement. He put the bottle between his knees and unscrewed the stopper.

'Drink,' he said softly.

She drank and gave him the bottle.

'Haven't seen you for ages,' she murmured.

He shrugged his shoulders and took a long drink. His hand was still her knee and as she played idly with the stalk of buttercups, her dark face concealed its rising passion in a look of wonderful preoccupation, as though she had forgotten him completely. He wetted his lips with his tongue and ran his hand swiftly and caressingly from her knees to her waist. Her body was stiff for one moment and then it relaxed and sank backwards into the long grass. She shut her eyes and slipped into his embrace like a snake, her face blissfully happy, her hand still clasping the stalk of buttercups, her whole body trembling.

Presently across the field came the sound of a scythe being sharpened. She whispered something quickly and struggled and Ponto got to his feet. She sat up and buttoned the neck of her blouse. She was flushed and panting, and her eyes rested on Ponto with a soft, almost beseeching look of adoration.

Ponto walked away to his scythe and picked it up and began mowing again. He mowed smoothly and with a sort of aloof indifference as though nothing had happened, and she let him mow for five or six paces before she too stood up.

'Ponto,' she whispered.

'Eh?'

'I'll come back,' she said.

She remained for a moment in an attitude of expectancy, but he did not speak or cease the swing of his arms, and very slowly she turned away and went back across the field.

She walked back to where she had left her rake. She picked up the rake and began to turn the swathes of hay again, following the boy. She worked for a long time without looking up. When at last she lifted her head and looked over towards the pond, she saw that Ponto had ceased mowing behind the pond and was cutting the grass in the open field again. He was mowing with the same easy, powerful insistence and with the same beautiful swaggering rhythm of his body, as though he could never grow tired.

They worked steadily on and the sun began to swing round behind the ash tree and the heat began to lessen and twilight began to fall. While the two men were mowing side by side on the last strip of grass, the woman began to pack the victual-bags and put the saddle on the horse under the ash tree.

She was strapping the girth of the saddle when she heard feet in the grass and a voice said softly:

'Any more beer?'

She turned and saw Ponto. A bottle of beer was left in the bag and she brought it out for him. He began drinking, and while he was drinking she gazed at him with rapt admiration, as though she had been mysteriously attracted out of herself by the sight of his subtle, conceited, devilish face, the memory of his embrace by the pond and the beautiful untiring motion of his arms swinging the scythe throughout the afternoon. There was something altogether trustful, foolish and abandoned about her, as though she was sublimely eager to do whatever he asked.

'Think you'll finish?' she said in a whisper.

'Easy.'

He corked the beer and they stood looking at each other. He looked at her with a kind of careless, condescending stare, half smiling. She stood perfectly still, her eyes filled with half-happy, half-frightened submissiveness.

He suddenly wiped the beer from his lips with the back of his hand and put out his arm and caught her waist and tried to kiss her.

'Not now,' she said desperately. 'Not now. He'll see. Afterwards. He'll see.'

He gave her a sort of half-pitying smile and shrugged his shoulders and walked away across the field without a word.

'Afterwards,' she called in a whisper.

She went on packing the victual-bags, the expression on her face lost and expectant. The outlines of the field and the figures of the mowers became softer and darker in the twilight. The evening air was warm and heavy with the scent of the hay.

The men ceased mowing at last. The boy had gone home and the woman led the horse across the field to where the men were waiting. Her husband was tying the sack about the blade of his scythe. She looked at Ponto with a dark, significant flash of her eyes, but he took no notice.

'You'd better finish the beer,' she said.

He took the bottle and drank to the dregs and then hurled the bottle across the field. She tried to catch his eye, but he was already walking away over the field, as though he had never seen her.

She followed him with her husband and the horse. They came to the gate of the field and Ponto was waiting. A look of anticipation and joy shot up in her eyes.

'Why should I damn well walk?' said Ponto. 'Eh? Why should I damn well walk up this lane when I can sit on your old hoss? Lemme get up.'

He laid his scythe in the grass and while the woman held the horse he climbed into the saddle.

'Give us me scythe,' he asked. 'I can carry that. Whoa! mare, damn you!'

She picked up the scythe and gave it to him and he put it over his shoulder. She let her hand touch his knee and fixed her eyes on him with a look of inquiring eagerness, but he suddenly urged the horse forward and began to ride away up the lane.

She followed her husband out of the field. He shut the gate and looked back over the darkening field at the long black swathes of hay lying pale yellow in the dusk. He seemed pleased and he called to Ponto:

'I don't know what the Hanover we should ha' done without you, Ponto.'

Ponto waved his rein-hand with sublime conceit.

'That's nothing,' he called back. 'Me and my old dad used to mow forty-acre fields afore dark. God damn it, that's nothing. All in the day's work.'

He seized the rein again and tugged it and the horse broke into a trot, Ponto bumping the saddle and swearing and shouting as he went up the lane.

The woman followed him with her husband. He walked slowly, limping, and now and then she walked on a few paces ahead, as though trying to catch up with the retreating horse. Sometimes the horse would slow down into a walk and she would come almost to within speaking distance of Ponto, but each time the horse would break into a fresh trot and leave her as far behind again. The lane was dusky with twilight and Ponto burst into a song about a girl and a sailor.

'Hark at him,' said the husband. 'He's a Tartar. He's a Tartar.'

The rollicking voice seemed to echo over the fields with soft, deliberate mocking. The woman did not speak: but as she listened her dark face was filled with the conflicting expression of many emotions, exasperation, perplexity, jealousy, longing, hope, anger.

TIME

Sitting on an iron seat fixed about the body of a great chestnut tree breaking into pink-flushed blossom, two old men gazed dumbly at the sunlit emptiness of a town square.

The morning sun burned in a sky of marvellous blue serenity, making the drooping leaves of the tree most brilliant and the pale blossoms expand to fullest beauty. The eyes of the old men were also blue, but the brilliance of the summer sky made a mockery of the dim and somnolent light in them. Their thin white hair and drooping skin, their faltering lips and rusted clothes, the huddled bones of their bodies had come to winter. Their hands tottered, their lips were wet and dribbling, and they stared with a kind of earnest vacancy, seeing the world as a stillness of amber mist. They were perpetually silent. The deafness of one made speech a ghastly effort of shouting and mis-interpretation. With their worn sticks between their knees and their worn hands knotted over their sticks they sat as though time had ceased to exist for them.

Nevertheless every movement across the square was an event. Their eyes missed nothing that came within sight. It was as if the passing of every vehicle held for them the possibility of catastrophe; the appearance of a strange face was a revolution; the apparitions of young ladies in light summer dresses gliding on legs of shell-pink silk had on them something of the effect of goddesses on the minds of young heroes. There were, sometimes, subtle changes of light in their eyes.

Across the square they observed an approaching figure. They watched it with a new intensity, exchanging also, for the first time, a glance with one another. For the first time also they spoke.

'Who is it?' said one.

'Duke, ain't it?'

'Looks like Duke,' the other said. 'But I can't see that far.'

Leaning forward on their sticks, they watched the approach of this figure with intent expectancy. He, too, was old. Beside

27

him, indeed, it was as if they were adolescent. He was patriarchal. He resembled a biblical prophet, bearded and white and immemorial. He was timeless.

But though he looked like a patriarch he came across the square with the haste of a man in a walking race. He moved with a nimbleness and airiness that were miraculous. Seeing the old men on the seat he waved his stick with an amazing gaiety at them. It was like the brandishing of a youthful sword. Ten yards away he bellowed their names lustily in greeting.

'Well Rueben boy! Well Shepherd!'

They mumbled sombrely in reply. He shouted stentoriously about the weather, wagging his white beard strongly. They shifted along the seat and he sat down. A look of secret relief came over their dim faces, for he had towered above them like a statue in silver and bronze.

'Thought maybe you warn't coming,' mumbled Rueben.

'Ah! been for a sharp walk!' he half-shouted. 'A sharp walk!'

They had not the courage to ask where he had walked but in his clear brisk voice he told them, and deducing that he could not have travelled less than six or seven miles they sat in gloomy silence, as though shamed. With relief they saw him fumble in his pockets and bring out a bag of peppermints, black-and-white balls sticky and strong from the heat of his strenuous body, and having one by one popped peppermints into their mouths they sucked for a long time with toothless and dumb solemnity, contemplating the sunshine.

As they sucked, the two old men waited for Duke to speak, and they waited like men awaiting an oracle, since he was, in their eyes, a masterpiece of a man. Long ago, when they had been napkinned and at the breast, he had been a man with a beard, and before they had reached their youth he had passed into a lusty maturity. All their lives they had felt infantile beside him.

Now, in old age, he persisted in shaming them by the lustiness of his achievements and his vitality. He had the secret of a devilish perpetual youth. To them the world across the square was veiled in sunny mistiness, but Duke could detect the swiftness of a rabbit on a hillside a mile away. They heard the sounds of the world as though through a stone wall, but he could hear the crisp bark of a fox in another parish. They were condemned to an existence of memory because they could not read, but Duke devoured the papers. He had an infinite knowledge of the world and the freshest affairs of men. He brought them, every morning, news of earthquakes in Peru, of wars in China, of assassinations in Spain, of scandals among the clergy. He understood the obscurest movements of politicians and explained to them the newest laws of the land. They listened to him with the devoutness of worshippers listening to a preacher, regarding him with awe and believing in him with humble astonishment. There were times when he lied to them blatantly. They never suspected.

As they sat there, blissfully sucking, the shadow of the chestnut-tree began to shorten, its westward edge creeping up, like a tide, towards their feet. Beyond, the sun continued to blaze with unbroken brilliance on the white square. Swallowing the last smooth grain of peppermint Reuben wondered aloud what time it could be.

'Time?' said Duke. He spoke ominously. 'Time?' he repeated. They watched his hand solemnly uplift itself and vanish into his breast. They had no watches. Duke alone could tell them the passage of time while appearing to mock at it himself. Very slowly he drew out an immense watch, held it out at length on its silver chain, and regarded it steadfastly.

They regarded it also, at first with humble solemnity and then with quiet astonishment. They leaned forward to stare at it. Their eyes were filled with a great light of unbelief. The watch had stopped.

The three old men continued to stare at the watch in silence. The stopping of this watch was like the stopping of some perfect automaton. It resembled almost the stopping of time itself. Duke shook the watch urgently. The hand moved onward for a second or two from half-past three and then was dead again. He lifted the watch to his ear and listened. It was silent.

For a moment or two longer the old man sat in lugubrious contemplation. The watch, like Duke, was a masterpiece, incredibly ancient, older even than Duke himself. They did not know how often he had boasted to them of its age and efficiency, its beauty and pricelessness. They remembered that it had once belonged to his father, that he had been offered incredible sums for it, that it had never stopped since the battle of Waterloo.

Finally Duke spoke. He spoke with the mysterious air of a man about to unravel a mystery. 'Know what 'tis?'

They could only shake their heads and stare with the blankness of ignorance and curiosity. They could not know.

Duke made an ominous gesture, almost a flourish, with the hand that held the watch. 'It's the lectric.'

They stared at him with dim-eyed amazement.

'It's the lectric,' he repeated. 'The lectric in me body.'

Shepherd was deaf. 'Eh?' he said.

'The lectric,' said Duke significantly, in a louder voice.

'Lectric?' They did not understand and they waited.

The oracle spoke at last, repeating with one hand the ominous gesture that was like a flourish.

'It stopped yesterday. Stopped in the middle of me dinner,' he said. He was briefly silent. 'Never stopped as long as I can remember. Never. And then stopped like that, all of a sudden, just at pudden-time. Couldn't understand it. Couldn't understand it for the life of me.'

'Take it to the watch maker's?' Reuben said.

'I did,' he said 'I did. This watch is older'n me, I said, and it's never stopped as long as I can remember. So he squinted at it and poked it and that's what he said.'

'What?'

'It's the lectric, he says, that's what it is. It's the lectric – the lectric in your body. That's what he said. The lectric.'

'Lectric light?'

'That's what he said. Lectric. You're full o' lectric, he says. You go home and leave your watch on the shelf and it'll go again. So I did.'

The eyes of the old men seemed to signal intense questions. There was an ominous silence. Finally, with the watch still in his hand, Duke made an immense flourish, a gesture of serene triumph.

'And it went,' he said, 'It went!'

The old men murmured in wonder.

'It went all right. Right as a cricket! Beautiful!'

The eyes of the old men flickered with fresh amazement. The fickleness of the watch was beyond the weakness of their ancient comprehension. They groped for understanding as they might have searched with their dim eyes for a balloon far up in the sky.

Staring and murmuring they could only pretend to understand.

'Solid truth,' said Duke. 'Goes on the shelf but it won't go on me. It's the lectric.'

'That's what licks me,' said Reuben, 'the lectric.'

'It's me body,' urged Duke. 'It's full of it.'

'Lectric light?'

'Full of it. Alive with it.'

He spoke like a man who had won a prize. Bursting with glory, he feigned humility. His white beard wagged lustily with pride, but the hand still bearing the watch seemed to droop with modesty.

'It's the lectric,' he boasted softly.

They accepted the words in silence. It was as though they began to understand at last the lustiness of Duke's life, the nimbleness of his mind, the amazing youthfulness of his patriarchal limbs.

The shadow of the chestnut-tree had dwindled to a small dark circle about their seat. The rays of the sun were brilliantly perpendicular. On the chestnut-tree itself the countless candelabra of blossoms were a pure blaze of white and rose. A clock began to chime for noon.

Duke, at that moment, looked at his watch, still lying in his hand.

He started with instant guilt. The hands had moved miraculously to four o'clock and in the stillness of the summer air he could hear the tick of wheels.

With hasty gesture of resignation he dropped the watch into his pocket again. He looked quickly at the old men, but they were sunk in sombre meditation. They had not seen or heard.

Abruptly he rose. 'That's what it is,' he said. 'The lectric.' He made a last gesture as though to indicate that he was the victim of some divine manifestation. 'The lectric,' he said.

He retreated nimbly across the square in the hot sunshine and the old men sat staring after him with the innocence of solemn wonder. His limbs moved with the haste of a clockwork doll and he vanished with incredible swiftness from sight.

The sun had crept beyond the zenith and the feet of the old men were bathed in sunshine.

THE MILL

I

A Ford motor-van, old and repainted green with *Jos. Hartop, greengrocer, rabbits,* scratched in streaky white lettering on a flattened-out biscuit tin nailed to the side, was slowly travelling across a high treeless stretch of country in squally November half-darkness. Rain hailed on the windscreen and periodically swished like a sea-wave on the sheaves of pink chrysanthemums strung on the van roof. Jos. Hartop was driving: a thin angular man, starved-faced. He seemed to occupy almost all the seat, sprawling awkwardly; so that his wife and their daughter Alice sat squeezed up, the girl with her arms flat as though ironed against her side, her thin legs pressed tight together into the size of one. The Hartops' faces seemed moulded in clay and in the light from the van-lamps were a flat swede-colour. Like the man, the two women were thin, with a screwed-up thinness that made them look both hard and frightened. Hartop drove with great caution, grasping the wheel tightly, braking hard at the bends, his big yellowish eyes fixed ahead, protuberantly, with vigilance and fear. His hands, visible in the faint dashboard light, were marked on the backs with dark smears of dried rabbits' blood. The van fussed and rattled, the chrysanthemums always swishing, rain-soaked, in the sudden high wind-squalls. And the two women sat in a state of silent apprehension, their bodies not moving except to lurch with the van their clayish faces continuously intent, almost scared, in the lamp-gloom. And after some time Hartop gave a slight start, and then drew the van to the roadside and stopped it.

'Hear anything drop?' he said. 'I thought I heard something.'

'It's the wind,' the woman said. 'I can hear it all the time.'

'No, something dropped.'

They sat listening. But the engine still ticked, and they could hear nothing beyond it but the wind and rain squalling in the dead grass along the roadside.

'Alice, you git out,' Hartop said.

32

The girl began to move herself almost before he had spoken.
'Git out and see if you can see anything.'

Alice stepped across her mother's legs, groped with blind instinct for the step, and then got out. It was raining furiously. The darkness seemed solid with rain.

'See anything?' Hartop said.

'No.'

'Eh? What? Can't hear.'

'No!'

Hartop leaned across his wife and shouted: 'Go back a bit and see what it was.' The woman moved to protest, but Hartop was already speaking again: 'Go back a bit and see what it was. Something dropped. We'll stop at Drake's Turn. You'll catch up. I know something dropped.'

'It's the back-board,' the woman said. 'I can hear it all the time. Jolting.'

'No, it ain't. Something dropped.'

He let in the clutch as he was speaking and the van began to move away.

Soon, to Alice, it seemed to be moving very rapidly. In the rain and the darkness all she could see was the tail-light, smoothly receding. She watched it for a moment and then began to walk back along the road. The wind was behind her; but repeatedly it seemed to veer and smash her, with the rain, full in the face. She walked without hurrying. She seemed to accept the journey as she accepted the rain and her father's words, quite stoically. She walked in the middle of the road, looking directly ahead, as though she had a long journey before her. She could see nothing.

And then, after a time, she stumbled against something in the road. She stooped and picked up a bunch of pink chrysanthemums. She gave them a single shake. The flower-odour and the rain seemed to be released together, and then she began to walk back with them along the road. It was as though the chrysanthemums were what she had expected to find above all things. She showed no surprise.

Before very long she could see the red tail-light of the van again. It was stationary. She could see also the lights of houses, little squares of yellow which the recurrent rain on her lashes transformed into sudden stars.

When she reached the van the back-board had been unhooked. Her mother was weighing out potatoes. An oil lamp hung from the van roof, and again the faces of the girl and her mother had the appearance of swede-coloured clay, only the girl's bleaker than before.

'What was it?' Mrs Hartop said.

The girl laid the flowers on the back-board. 'Only a bunch of chrysanthemums.'

Hartop himself appeared at the very moment she was speaking.

'Only?' he said, 'Only? What d'ye mean by only? Eh? Might have been a sack of potatoes. Just as well. Only! What next?'

Alice stood mute. Her pose and her face meant nothing, had no quality except a complete lack of all surprise: as though she had expected her father to speak like that. Then Hartop raised his voice:

'Well, don't stand there! Do something. Go on. Go on! Go and see who wants a bunch o' chrysanthemums. Move yourself!'

Alice obeyed at once. She picked up the flowers, walked away and vanished, all without a word or a change of that expression of unsurprised serenity.

But she was back in a moment. She began to say that there were chrysanthemums in the gardens of all the houses. Her voice was flat. It was like a pressed flower, a flat faint impression of a voice. And it seemed suddenly to madden her father:

'All right, all right. Christ, all right. Leave it.'

He seized the scale-pan of potatoes and then walked away himself. Without a word the girl and her mother chained and hooked up the back-board, climbed up into the driving seat, and sat there with the old intent apprehension, staring through the rain-beaded windscreen, until the woman spoke in a voice of religious negation, with a kind of empty gentleness:

'You must do what your father tells you.'

'Yes,' Alice said.

Before they could speak again Hartop returned, and in a moment the van was travelling on.

When it stopped again the same solitary row of house-lights as before seemed to appear on the roadside and the Hartops seemed to go through the same ritual of action: the woman unhooking the back-board, the man relighting the oil lamp, and then the girl and the woman going off in the rain to the backways of the houses. And always, as they returned to the van, Hartop grousing, nagging:

'Why the 'ell don't you speak up? Nothing? Well, say it then, say it!'

Finally the girl took a vegetable marrow from the skips of potatoes and oranges and onions, carried it to the houses and then returned with it, and Hartop flew into a fresh rage:

'I'd let 'em eat it if I was you, let 'em eat it. Take the whole bloody show and let 'em sample. Go on. I'm finished. I jack up. I've had a packet. I jack up.'

He slammed down the scale-pan, extinguished the oil lamp, began to chain up the back-board. On the two women his rage had not even the slightest effect. Moving about in the rain, slowly, they were like two shabby ducks, his rage rolling off the silent backs of their minds like water.

And then the engine, chilled by the driving rain, refused to start. Furious, Hartop gave mad jerks at the starting handle. Nothing happened. The two women, silently staring through the windscreen, never moved. They might even have been in another world, asleep or dead.

Swinging viciously at the starting handle Hartop shouted: 'When I swing, shove that little switch forward. *Forward!* Christ. *Forward!* I never seen anything to touch it. Never. *Forward!* Now try. Can't you bloody well hear?'

'Yes.'

'Then act like it. God, they say there's no peace for the wicked. *Forward!*'

Then when the engine spluttered, fired, and at last was revolving and the van travelling on and the women were able to hear again, Hartop kept repeating the words in a kind of comforting refrain. No peace for the wicked. No bloody peace at all. He'd had enough. Just about bellyful. What with one thing – Christ, what was the use of talking to folks who were deaf and dumb? Jack up. Better by half to jack up. Bung in. No darn peace for the wicked.

And suddenly, listening gloomily to him, the woman realized that the road was strange to her. She saw trees, then turns and gates and hedges that she did not know.

'Jos, where are we going?' she said.

Hartop was silent. The mystery comforted him. And when at

last he stopped the van and switched off the engine it gave him
great satisfaction to prolong the mystery, to get down from the
van and disappear without a word.

Free of his presence, the two women came to life. Alice half
rose from the seat and shook her mackintosh and skirt and said,
'Where have we stopped?' Mrs Hartop was looking out of the
side window, peering with eyes screwed-up. She could see nothing. The world outside, cut off by blackness and rain, was
strange and unknown. Then when Mrs Hartop sat down again
the old state of negation and silence returned for a moment until
Alice spoke. It seemed to Alice that she could hear something, a
new sound, quite apart from the squalling of wind and rain; a
deeper sound, quieter, and more distant.

The two women listened. Then they could hear the sound
distinctly, continuously, a roar of water.

Suddenly Mrs Hartop remembered. 'It's the mill,' she said.
She got up to look through the window again. 'We've stopped at
Holland's Mill.' She sat down slowly. 'What's he stopped here
for? What've we — ?'

Then she seemed to remember something else. Whatever it
was seemed to subdue her again, sealing over her little break of
loquacity, making her silent once more. But now her silence had
a new quality. It was very near anxiety. She would look quickly
at Alice and then quickly away again.

'Is there any tea left?' Alice said.

Mrs Hartop bent down at once and looked under the seat. She
took out a thermos flask two tea-cups and an orange. Then Alice
held the cups while her mother filled them with milky tea. Then
Mrs Hartop peeled and quartered the orange and they ate and
drank, warming their fingers on the tea-cups.

They were wiping their juice-covered fingers and putting away
the tea-cups when Hartop returned. He climbed into the cab,
slammed the door, and sat down.

'What you been to Hollands' for?' the woman said.

Hartop pressed the self-starter. It buzzed, but the engine was
silent. The two women waited. Then Hartop spoke.

'Alice,' he said, 'you start in service at Hollands' Monday
morning. His wife's bad. He told me last Wednesday he
wanted a gal about to help. Five shillin' a week and all found.'

'Jos!'

But the noise of the self-starter and then the engine firing drowned what the women had to say. And as the van moved on she and Alice sat in silence, without a sound of protest or aquiescence, staring at the rain.

II

At night, though so near, Alice had seen nothing of the mill, not even a light. On Monday morning, from across the flat and almost treeless meadows, she could see it clearly. It was a very white three-storeyed building, the whitewash dazzling, almost incandescent, against the wintry fields in the morning sunshine.

Going along the little by-roads across the valley she felt extraordinarily alone, yet not lonely. She felt saved from loneliness by her little leather bag; there was comfort in the mere changing of it from hand to hand. The bag contained her work-apron and her nightgown, and she carried it close to her side as she walked slowly along, not thinking. 'You start in good time,' Hartop had said to her, 'and go steady on. The walk'll do you good.' It was about five miles to the mill, and she walked as though in obedience to the echo of her father's command. She had a constant feeling of sharp expectancy, not quite apprehension, every time she looked up and saw the mill. But the feeling never resolved itself into thought. She felt also a slight relief. She had never been, by herself, so far from home. And every now and then she found herself looking back, seeing the house she had left behind, the blank side-wall gas-tarred, the wooden shack in the back-yard where Hartop kept the motor-van, the kitchen where she and her mother bunched the chrysanthemums or sorted the oranges. It seemed strange not to be doing those things: she had sorted oranges and had bunched whatever flowers were in season for as long as she could remember. She had done it all without question, with instinctive obedience. Now, suddenly, she was to do something else. And whatever it was she knew without thinking that she must do it with the same unprotesting obedience. That was right. She had been brought up to it. It was going to be a relief to her father, a help. Things were bad and her going might better them. And then – five shillings a week. She thought of that with recurrent spasms of wonder and incredulity. Could it be true? The question crossed her mind more often than her bag crossed from hand to hand, until it was mechanical and unconscious also.

She was still thinking of it when she rapped at the back door of the mill. The yard was deserted. She could hear no sound of life at all except the mill-race. She knocked again. And then, this time, as she stood waiting, she looked at the yard more closely. It was a chaos of derelict things. Everything was derelict: derelict machinery, old iron, derelict motor cars, bedsteads, wire, harrows, binders, perambulators, tractors, bicycles, corrugated iron. The junk was piled up in a wild heap in the space between the mill-race and the backwater. Iron had fallen into the water. Rusty, indefinable skeletons of it had washed up against the bank-reeds. She saw rust and iron everywhere, and when something made her look up to the mill-windows she saw there the rusted fly-wheels and crane-arms of the mill machinery, the whitewashed wall stained as though with rusty reflections of it.

When she rapped on the door again, harder, flakes of rust, little reddish wafers, were shaken off the knocker. She stared at the door as she waited. Her eyes were large, colourless, fixed in vague penetration. She seemed to be listening with them. They were responsive to sound. And they remained still, as though of glass, when she heard nothing.

And hearing nothing she walked across the yard. Beyond the piles of rusted iron a sluice tore down past the mill-wall on a glacier of green slime. She stooped and peered down over the stone parapet at the water. Beyond the sluice a line of willows were shedding their last leaves, and the leaves came floating down the current like little yellow fish. She watched them come and surge through the grating, and then vanish under the water-arch. Then, watching the fish-like leaves, she saw a real fish, dead, caught in the rusted grating, thrown there by the force of descending water. Then she saw another, and another. Her eyes registered no surprise. She walked round the parapet, and then, leaning over and stretching, she picked up one of the fish. It was cold, and very stiff, like a fish of celluloid, and its eyes were like her own, round and glassy. Then she walked along the path, still holding the fish and occasionally looking at it. The path circled the mill pond and vanished, farther on, into a bed of osiers. The mill-pond was covered in duck-weed, the green crust split into blackness here and there by chance currents of wind or water.

The osiers were leafless, but quite still in the windless air. And standing still, she looked at the tall osiers for a moment, her eyes reflecting their stillness and the strange persistent absence of all sound.

And then suddenly she heard a sound. It came from the osiers. A shout:

'You lookin' for Mus' Holland?'

She saw a man's face in the osiers. She called back to it: 'Yes.'

'He ain't there.'

She could think of nothing to say.

'If you want anythink, go in. She's there. A-bed.' A shirt-sleeve waved and vanished. 'Not that door. It's locked. Round the other side.'

She walked back along the path, by the sluice and the machinery and so past the door and the mill-race to the far side of the house. A stretch of grass, once a lawn and now no more than a waste of dead grass and sedge, went down to the back-water from what she saw now was the front door.

At the door she paused for a moment. Why was the front door open and not the back? Then she saw why. Pushing upen the door she saw that it had no lock; only the rusty skeleton pattern of it remained imprinted on the brown sun-scorched paint.

Inside, she stood still in the brick-flagged passage. It seemed extraordinarily cold; the damp coldness of the river air seemed to have saturated the place.

Finally she walked along the passage. Her lace-up boots were heavy on the bricks, setting up a clatter of echoes. When she stopped her eyes were a little wider and almost white in the lightless passage. And again, as outside, they registered the quietness of the place, until it was broken by a voice:

'Somebody there? Who is it?' The voice came from upstairs. 'Who is it?'

'Me.'

A silence. Alice stood still, listening with wide eyes. Then the voice again:

'Who is it?'

'Me. Alice.'

Another silence, and then:

'Come up.' It was a light voice, unaggressive, almost friendly. 'Come upstairs.'

The girl obeyed at once. The wooden stairs were steep and carpetless. She tramped up them. The banister, against which she rubbed her sleeve, was misted over with winter wetness. She could smell the dampness everywhere. It seemed to rise and follow her.

On the top stairs she halted. 'In the end bedroom,' the voice called. She went at once along the wide half-light landing in the direction of the voice. The panelled doors had at one time been painted white and blue, but now the white was blue and the blue the colour of greenish water. The doors had old-fashioned latches of iron and when she lifted the end latch she could feel the first thin leaf of rust on it ready to crumble and fall. She hesitated a moment before touching the latch, but as she stood there the voice called again and she opened the door.

Then, when she walked into the bedroom, she was almost surprised. She had expected to see Mrs Holland in bed. But the woman was kneeling on the floor, by the fireplace. She was in her nightgown. The gown had come unbuttoned and Alice could see Mrs Holland's drooping breasts. They were curiously swollen, as though by pregnancy or some dropsical complaint. The girl saw that Mrs Holland was trying to light a fire. Faint acrid paper-smoke hung about the room and stung her eyes. She could hear the tin-crackle of burnt paper. There was no flame. The smoke rose up the chimney and then, in a moment, puthered down again, the paper burning with little running sparks that extinguished themselves and then ran on again.

'I'm Alice,' the girl said. 'Alice Hartop.'

She stared fixedly at the big woman sitting there with her nightgown unbuttoned and a burnt match in her hands and her long pigtail of brown hair falling forward over her shoulders almost to the depths of her breasts. Her very largeness, her soft dropsical largeness, and the colour of that thick pigtail were somehow comforting. They were in keeping with the voice she had heard, the voice which spoke to her quite tenderly again now :

'I'm so glad you've come, Alice, I am so glad.'

'Am I late?' Alice said. 'I walked.'

Then she stopped. Mrs Holland had burst out laughing. The girl stood vacant, at a loss, her mouth fallen open. The woman gathered her nightgown in her hands and held it tight against her breasts, as though she feared that the laughter might suddenly flow out of them like milk. And the girl stared until the woman could speak:

'In your hand! Look, look. In your hand. Look!'

Then Alice saw. She still had the fish in her hand. She was clutching it like a little silver-scaled purse.

'Ohdear! ohdear!' she said. She spoke the words as one word: a single word of unsurprised comment on the unconscious folly of her own act. Even as she said it Mrs Holland burst out laughing again. And as before the laughter seemed as if it must burst liquidly or fall and run over her breasts and hands and her nightgown. The girl had never heard such laughter. It was far stranger than the fish in her own hand. It was almost too strange. It had a strangeness that was only a shade removed from hysteria, and only a little further from inanity. 'She's a bit funny,' the girl thought. And almost simultaneously Mrs Holland echoed her thought:

'Oh! Alice, you're funny.' The flow of laughter lessened and then dried up. 'Oh, you are funny.'

To Alice that seemed incomprehensible. If anybody was funny it was Mrs Holland, laughing in that rich, almost mad voice. So she continued to stare. She still had the fish in her hand. It added to her manner of uncomprehending vacancy.

Then suddenly a change came over her. She saw Mrs Holland shiver and this brought back at once her sense of almost subservient duty.

'Hadn't you better get dressed and let me light the fire?' she said.

'I can't get dressed. I've got to get back into bed.'

'Well, you get back. You're shivering.'

'Help me.'

Alice put down her bag on the bedroom floor and laid the fish on top of it. Mrs Holland tried at the same moment to get up. She straightened herself until she was kneeling upright. Then she tried to raise herself. She clutched the bedrail. Her fat, almost transparent-fleshed fingers would not close. They were like thick sausages, fat jointless lengths of flesh which could not bend. And there she remained in her helplessness, until Alice put her arms about her and took the weight of her body.

'Yes, Alice, you'll have to help me. I can't do it myself any longer. You'll have to help me.'

Gradually Alice got her back to bed. And Alice, as she helped her, could feel the curious swollen texture of Mrs Holland's flesh. The distended breasts fell out of her unbuttoned nightgown, her heavy thighs lumbered their weight against her own, by contrast so weak and thin and straight. And then when Mrs Holland was in bed, at last, propped up by pillows, Alice had time to look at her face. It had that same heavy water-blown brightness of flesh under the eyes and in the cheeks and in the soft parts of the neck. The gentle dark brown eyes were sick. They looked out with a kind of gentle sick envy on Alice's young movements as she straightened the bed-clothes and then cleaned the fireplace and finally as she laid and lighted the fire itself.

And then when her eyes had satisfied themselves Mrs Holland began to talk again, to ask questions.

'How old are you, Alice?'

'Seventeen.'

'Would you rather be here with me than at home?'

'I don't mind.'

'Don't you like it at home?'

'I don't mind.'

'Is the fire all right?'

'Yes.'

'When you've done the grate will you go down and git the taters ready?'

'Yes.'

'It's cold mutton. Like cold mutton, Alice?'

'I don't mind.'

Then, in turn, the girl had a question herself.

'Why ain't the mill going?' she asked.

'The mill? The mill ain't been going for ten years.'

'What's all that iron?'

'That's the scrap. What Fred buys and sells. That's his trade. The mill ain't been worked since his father died. That's been ten year. Fred's out all day buying up iron like that, and selling it. Most of it he never touches, but what he don't sell straight off comes back here. He's gone off this morning. He won't be back till night-time. You'll have to get his tea when he comes back.'

'I see.'

'You must do all you can for him. I ain't much good to him now.'

'I see.'

'You can come up again when you've done the taters.'

Downstairs Alice found the potatoes in a wet mould-green sack and stood at the sink and pared them. The kitchen window looked out on the mill-stream. The water foamed and eddied and kept up a gentle bubbling roar against the wet stone walls outside. The water-smell was everywhere. From the window she could see across the flat valley: bare willow branches against bare sky, and between them the bare water.

Then as she finished the potatoes she saw the time by the blue tin alarum clock standing on the high smoke-stained mantelpiece. It was past eleven. Time seemed to have flown by her faster than the water was flowing under the window.

III

It seemed to flow faster than ever as the day went on. Darkness began to settle over the river and the valley in the middle afternoon: damp, still November darkness preceded by an hour of watery half-light. From Mrs Holland's bedroom Alice watched the willow trees, dark and skeleton-like, the only objects raised up above the flat fields, hanging half-dissolved by the winter mist, then utterly dissolved by the winter darkness. The afternoon was very still; the mist moved and thickened without wind. She could hear nothing but the mill-race, the everlasting almost mournful machine-like roar of perpetual water, and then, high above it, shrieking, the solitary cries of sea-gulls, more mournful even than the monotone of water. They were sounds she had heard all day, but had heard unconsciously. She had had no time for listening, except to Mrs Holland's voice calling downstairs its friendly advice and desires through the open bedroom door: 'Alice, have you put the salt in the taters? You'll find the onions in the shed, Alice. The oil-man calls to-day, ask him to leave the usual. When you've washed up you can bring the paper up, Alice, and read bits out to me for five minutes. Has the oil-man been? Alice, I want you a minute, I want you.' So it had gone on all day. And the girl, gradually, began to like Mrs Holland; and the woman, in turn, seemed to be transported into a state of new and stranger volatility by Alice's presence. She was garrulous with joy. 'I've been lonely. Since I've been bad I ain't seen nobody, only Fred, one week's end to another. And the doctor. It's been about as much as I could stan'.' And the static, large-eyed, quiet presence of the girl seemed to comfort her extraordinarily. She had someone to confide in at last. 'I ain't had nobody I could say a word to. Nobody. And nobody to do nothing for me. I had to wet the bed one day. I was so weak I couldn't get out. That's what made Fred speak to your dad. I couldn't go on no longer.'

So the girl had no time to listen except to the voice or to think or talk except in answer to it. And the afternoon was gone and the damp moving darkness was shutting out the river and the bare fields and barer trees before she could realise it.

'Fred'll be home at six,' Mrs Holland said. 'He shaves at night. So you git some hot water ready about a quarter to.'

'All right.'

'Oh! and I forgot. He allus has fish for his tea. Cod or something. Whatever he fancies. He'll bring it. You can fry it while he's shaving.'

'All right.'

'Don't you go and fry that roach by mistake!'

Mrs Holland, thinking again of the fish in Alice's hand, lay back on the pillows and laughed, the heavy ripe laughter that sounded as before a trifle strange, as though she were a little mad or hysterical in the joy of fresh companionship.

Mrs Holland and Alice had already had a cup of tea in the bedroom. That seemed unbelievably luxurious to Alice, who for nearly five years had drunk her tea from a thermos flask in her father's van. It brought home to her that she was very well off: five shillings a week, tea by the fire in the bedroom, Mrs Holland so cheerful and nice, and an end at last to her father's ironic grousing and the feeling the she was a dead weight on his hands. It gave her great satisfaction. Yet she never registered the emotion by looks or words or a change in her demeanour. She went about quietly and a trifle vaguely, almost in a trance of detachment. The light in her large flat pellucid eyes never varied. Her mouth would break into a smile, but the smile never telegraphed itself to her eyes. And so with words. She spoke, but the words never changed that expression of dumb content, that wide and in some way touching and attractive stare straight before her into space.

And when she heard the rattling of a motor-van in the mill-yard just before six o'clock she looked suddenly up, but her expression did not change. She showed no flicker of apprehension or surprise.

About five minutes later Holland walked into the kitchen.

"Ullo,' he said.

Alice was standing at the sink, wiping the frying pan with a dishcloth. When Holland spoke and she looked round at him her eyes blinked with a momentary flash of something like surprise. Holland's voice was very deep and it seemed to indicate that Holland himself would be physically very large and powerful.

Then she saw that he was a little man, no taller than herself, and rather stocky, without being stiff or muscular. His trousers hung loose and wide, like sacks. His overcoat, undone, was also like a sack. The only unloose thing about him was his collar. It was a narrow stiff celluloid collar fixed with a patent ready-made tie. The collar was oilstained and the tie, once blue, was soaked by oil and dirt to the appearance of old *crêpe*. The rest of Holland was loose and careless and drooping. A bit of an old shack, Alice thought. Even his little tobacco-yellowed moustache drooped raggedly. Like his felt hat, stuck carelessly on the back of his head, it looked as though it did not belong to him.

"Ullo,' he said. 'You *are* e're then. I see your dad. D'ye think you're going to like it?'

'Yes.'

'That's right. You make yourself at 'ome.' He had the parcel of fish under his arm and as he spoke he took it out and laid it on the kitchen table. The brown paper flapped open and Alice saw the tail-cut of a cod. She went at once to the plate-rack, took a plate and laid the fish on it.

'Missus say anythink about the fish?' Holland said.

'Yes.'

'All right. You fry it while I git shaved.'

'I put the water on,' she said.

Holland took off his overcoat, then his jacket, and finally his collar and tie. Then he turned back the greasy neck-band of his shirt and began to make his shaving lather in a wooden bowl at the sink, working the brush and bowl like a pestle and mortar. Alice put the cod into the frying-pan and then the pan on the oil-stove. Then as Holland began to lather his face, Mrs Holland called downstairs: 'Fred. You there, Fred? Fred!' and Holland walked across the kitchen, still lathering himself and dropping spatters of white lather on the stone flags as he went, to listen at the stairs door.

'Yes, I'm 'ere, Em'ly. I'm – Eh? Oh! all right.'

Holland turned to Alice. 'The missus wants you a minute upstairs.'

Alice ran upstairs, thinking of the fish. After the warm kitchen she could feel the air damper than ever. Mrs Holland was lying down in bed and a candle in a tin holder was burning on the chest of drawers.

'Oh! Alice,' Mrs Holland said, 'you do all you can for Mr Holland, won't you? He's had a long day.'

'Yes.'

'And sponge his collar. I want him to go about decent. It won't get done if you don't do it.'

'All right.'

Alice went downstairs again. Sounds of Holland's razor scraping his day-old beard and of the cod hissing in the pan filled the kitchen. She turned the cod with a fork and then took up Holland's collar and sponged it with the wetted fringe of her pinafore. The collar came up bright and fresh as ivory, and when finally Holland had finished shaving at the sink and had put on the collar again it was as though a small miracle had been performed. Holland was middle-aged, about fifty, and looked older in the shabby overcoat and oily collar. Now, shaved and with the collar cleaned again, he looked younger than he was. He looked no longer shabby, a shack, and a bit nondescript, but rather homely and essentially decent. He had a tired, rather stunted and subservient look. His flesh was coarse, with deep pores, and his greyish hair came down stiff over his forehead. His eyes were dull and a little bulging. When Alice put the fried fish before him he sat low over the plate, scooped up the white flakes of fish with his knife and then sucked them into his mouth. He spat out the bones. Every time he spat out a bone he drank his tea, and when his cup was empty, Alice, standing by, filled it up again.

None of these things surprised the girl. She had never seen anyone eat except like that, with the knife, low over the plate, greedily. Her father and mother ate like it and she ate like it herself. So as she stood by the sink, waiting to fill up Holland's cup, her eyes stared with the same abstract preoccupation as ever. They did not even change when Holland spoke, praising her:

'You done this fish all right, Alice.'

'Shall I git something else for you?'

'Git me a bit o' cheese. Yes, you done that fish very nice, Alice. Very nice indeed.'

Yet, though her eyes expressed nothing, she felt a sense of reassurance, very near to comfort, at Holland's words. It was not deep: but it was enough to counteract the strangeness of her surroundings, to help deaden the perpetual sense of the mill-race, to drive away some of the eternal dampness about the place.

But it was not enough to drive away her tiredness. She went to bed very early, as soon as she had washed Holland's supper things and had eaten her own supper of bread and cheese. Her room was at the back of the mill. It had not been used for a long time; its dampness rose up in a musty cloud. Then when she lit her candle and set it on the washstand she saw that the wallpaper, rotten with dampness, was peeling off and hanging in ragged petals, showing the damp-green plaster beneath. Then she took her nightgown out of her case, undressed and stood for a moment naked, her body as thin as a boy's and her little lemon-shaped breasts barely formed, before dropping the nightgown over her shoulders. A moment later she had put out the candle and was lying in the little iron bed.

Then, as she lay there, curling up her legs for warmth in the damp sheets, she remembered something. She had said no prayers. She got out of bed at once and knelt down by the bed and words of mechanical supplication and thankfulness began to run at once through her mind: 'Dear Lord, bless us and keep us. Dear Lord, help me to keep my heart pure,' little impromptu gentle prayers of which she only half-understood the meaning. And all the time she was kneeling she could hear a background of other sounds: the mill-race roaring in the night, the wild occasional cries of birds from up the river, and the rumblings of Holland and his wife talking in their bedroom.

And in their room Holland was saying to his wife: 'She seems like a good gal.'

'She is. I like her,' Mrs Holland said. 'I think she's all right.'

'She done that fish lovely.'

'Fish.' Mrs Holland remembered. And she told Holland of how Alice had brought up the roach in her hand, and as she told him her rather strange rich laughter broke out again and Holland laughed with her.

'Oh dear,' Mrs Holland laughed. 'She's a funny little thing when you come to think of it.'

'As long as she's all right,' Holland said, 'that's all that matters. As long as she's all right.'

IV

Alice was all right. It took less than a week for Holland to see that, although he distrusted a little Alice's first showing with his fish. It seemed too good. He knew what servant girls could be like: all docile, punctual and anxious to please until they got the feeling of things, and then haughty and slovenly and sulky before you could turn round. He wasn't having that sort of thing. The minute Alice was surly or had too much lip she could go. Easy get somebody else. Plenty more kids be glad of the job. So for the first few nights after Alice's arrival he would watch her reflection in the soap-flecked shaving-mirror hanging over the sink while he scraped his beard. He watched her critically, tried to detect some flaw, some change, in her meek servitude. The mirror was a big round iron-framed concave mirror, so that Alice, as she moved slowly about with the fish-pan over the oil-stove, looked physically a little larger, and also vaguer and softer, than she really was. The mirror put flesh on her bony arms and filled out her pinafore. And looking for faults, Holland saw only this softening and magnifying of her instead. Then when he had dried the soap out of his ears and had put on the collar Alice had sponged for him he would sit down to the fish, ready to pounce on some fault in it. But the fish, like Alice, never seemed to vary. Nothing wrong with the fish. He tried bringing home different sorts of fish, untried sorts, tricky for Alice to cook; witch, whiting, sole and halibut, instead of his usual cod and hake. But it made no difference. The fish was always good. And he judged

Alice by the fish: if the fish was all right Alice was all right. Upstairs, after supper, he would ask Mrs Holland: 'Alice all right to-day?' and Mrs Holland would say how quiet Alice was, or how good she was, and how kind she was, and that she couldn't be without her for the world. 'Well, that fish was lovely again,' Holland would say.

And gradually he saw that he had no need for suspicion. No need to be hard on the kid. She was all right. Leave the kid alone. Let her go on her own sweet way. Not interfere with her. And so he swung round from the suspicious attitude to one almost of solicitude. Didn't cost no more to be nice to the kid than it did to be miserable. 'Well, Alice, how's Alice?' The tone of his evening greeting became warmer, a little facetious, more friendly. 'That's right, Alice. Nice to be back home in the dry, Alice.' In the mornings, coming downstairs, he had to pass her bedroom door. He would knock on it to wake her. He got up in darkness, running downstairs in his stockinged feet, with his jacket and collar and tie slung over his arm. And pausing at Alice's door he would say 'Quart' t' seven, Alice. You gittin' up, Alice?' Chinks of candlelight round and under the door-frame, or her sleepy voice, would tell him if she were getting up. If the room were in darkness and she did not answer he would knock and call again. 'Time to git up, Alice. Alice!' One morning the room was dark and she did not answer at all. He knocked harder again, hard enough to drown any sleepy answer she might have given. Then, hearing nothing and seeing nothing, he opened the door.

At the very moment he opened the door Alice was bending over the washstand, with a match in her hands, lighting her candle. 'Oh! Sorry, Alice, I din't hear you.' In the moment taken to speak the words Holland saw the girl's open nightgown, and then her breasts, more than ever like two lemons in the yellow candlelight. The light shone straight down on them, the deep shadow of her lower body heightening their shape and colour, and they looked for a moment like the breasts of a larger and more mature girl than Holland fancied Alice to be.

As he went downstairs in the winter darkness he kept seeing the mirage of Alice's breasts in the candlelight. He was excited. A memory of Mrs Holland's large dropsical body threw the young girl's breasts into tender relief. And time seemed to sharpen the comparison. He saw Alice bending over the candle, her nightgown undone, at recurrent intervals throughout the day. Then in the evening, looking at her reflection in the shaving-mirror, the magnifying effect of the mirror magnified his excitement. And upstairs he forgot to ask if Alice was all right.

In the morning he was awake a little earlier than usual. The morning was still like night. Black mist shut out the river. He went along the dark landing and tapped at Alice's door. When there was no answer he tapped again and called, but nothing happened. Then he put his hand on the latch and pressed it. The door opened. He was so surprised that he did not know for a moment what to do. He was in his shirt and trousers, with the celluloid collar and patent tie and jacket in his hand, and no shoes on his feet.

He stood for a moment by the bed and then he stretched out his hand and shook Alice. She did not wake. Then he put his hand on her chest and let it rest there. He could feel the breasts unexpectedly soft and alive, through the nightgown. He touched one and then the other.

Suddenly Alice woke.

'All right, Alice. Time to git up, that's all,' Holland said. 'I was trying to wake you.'

v

'I 'spect you want to git home week-ends, don't you, Alice?' Mrs Holland said.

Alice had been at the mill almost a week. 'I don't mind,' she said.

'Well, we reckoned you'd like to go home a' Sundays, anyway. Don't you?'

'I don't mind.'

'Well, you go home this week, and then see. Only it means cold dinner for Fred a' Sundays if you go.'

So after breakfast on Sunday morning Alice walked across the flat valley and went home. The gas-tarred house, the end one of a row on the edge of the town, seemed cramped and a little strange after the big rooms at the mill and the bare empty fields and the river.

'Well, how d'ye like it?' Hartop said.

'It's all right.'

'Don't feel homesick?'

'No, I don't mind.'

Alice laid her five shillings on the table. 'That's my five shillings,' she said. 'Next Sunday I ain't coming. What shall I do about the money?'

'You better send it,' Hartop said. 'It ain't no good to you there if you keep it, is it? No shops, is they?'

'I don't know. I ain't been out.'

'Well, you send it.' Then suddenly Hartop changed his mind. 'No, I'll tell you what. You keep it and we'll call for it a' Friday. We can come round that way.'

'All right,' Alice said.

'If you ain't coming home,' Mrs Hartop said, 'you'd better take a clean nightgown. And I'll bring another Friday.'

And so she walked back across the valley in the November dusk with the nightgown wrapped in brown paper under her arm, and on Friday Hartop stopped the motor-van outside the mill and she went out to him with the five shillings Holland had left on the table that morning. 'I see your dad about the money, Alice. That's all right.' And as she stood by the van answering in her flat voice the questions her father and mother put to her, Hartop put his hand in his pocket and said:

'Like orange, Alice?'

'Yes,' she said. 'Yes, please.'

Hartop put the orange into her hand. 'Only mind,' he said. 'It's tacked. It's just a bit rotten on the side there.' He leaned out of the driver's seat and pointed out the soft bluish rotten patch on the orange skin. 'It's all right. It ain't gone much.'

'You gittin' on all right, Alice?' Mrs Hartop said. She spoke from the gloom of the van seat. Alice could just see her vague clay-coloured face.

'Yes. I'm all right.'

'See you a' Friday again then.'

Hartop let off the brake and the van moved away simultaneously as Alice moved away across the millyard between the piles of derelict iron. Raw half-mist from the river was coming across the yard in sodden swirls and Alice, frozen, half-ran into the house. Then, in the kitchen, she sat by the fire with her skirt drawn up above her knees, to warm herself.

She was still sitting like that, with her skirt drawn up to her thighs and her hands outstretched to the fire and the orange in her lap, when Holland came in.

'Hullo, Alice,' he said genially. 'I should git on top o' the fire if I was you.'

Alice, wretched with the cold, which seemed to have settled inside her, scarcely answered. She sat there for almost a full minute longer, trying to warm her legs, before getting up to cook Holland's fish. All the time she sat there Holland was looking at her legs, with the skirt pulled up away from them. The knees and the slim thighs were rounded and soft, and the knees and the legs themselves a rosy flame-colour in the firelight. Holland felt a sudden agitation as he gazed at them.

Then abruptly Alice got up to cook the fish, and the vision of her rose-coloured legs vanished. But Holland, shaving before the mirror, could still see in his mind the soft firelight on Alice's knees. And the mirror, as before, seemed to magnify Alice's vague form as it moved about the kitchen, putting some flesh on her body. Then when Holland sat down to his fish Alice again sat down before the fire and he saw her pull her skirt above her knees again as though he did not exist. And all through the meal he sat looking at her. Then suddenly he got tired of merely looking at her. He wanted to be closer to her. 'Alice, come and 'ave a drop o' tea,' he said. 'Pour yourself a cup out. Come on. You look starved.' The orange Hartop had given Alice lay on the table, and the girl pointed to it. 'I'm going to have that orange,' she said. Holland picked up the orange. 'All right, only you want summat. Here, I'm going to throw it.' He threw the orange. It fell into Alice's lap. And it seemed to Holland that its fall drew her dress a little higher above her knees. He got up. 'Never hurt you, did I, Alice?' he said. He ran his hands over her shoulders and arms, and then over her thighs and knees. Her knees were beautifully warm, like hard warm apples. 'You're starved though. Your knees are like ice.' He began to rub her hands a little with his own, and the girl, her flat expression never changing, let him do it. She felt his fingers harsh on her bloodless hands and then on her shoulders. 'Your chest ain't cold, is it?' Holland said. 'You don't want to git cold in your chest.' He was feeling her chest, above the breasts. The girl shook her head. 'Sure?' Holland said. He kept his hands on her chest. 'You put something on when you go out to that van again. If you git cold on your chest . . .' And as he was speaking his hands moved down until they covered her breasts. They were so small that he could hold them easily in his hands. 'Don't want to git cold in *them,* do you?' he said. 'In your nellies?' She stared at him abstractedly, not knowing the word, wondering what he meant. Then suddenly he was squeezing her breasts, in a bungling effort of tenderness. The motion hurt her. 'Come on, Alice, come on. I shan't do nothing. Let's have a look at you, Alice. I don't want to do nothing, Alice. All right. I don't want to hurt you. Undo your dress, Alice.' And the girl, mechanically, to his astonishment, put her hands to the buttons. As they came undone he put his hands on her chest and then on her bare breasts in clumsy and agitated efforts to caress her. She sat rigid, staring, not fully understanding. Every time Holland squeezed her he hurt her. But the mute and fixed look on her face and the grey flat as though motionless stare in her eyes never changed. She listened only vaguely to what Holland said.

'Come on, Alice. You lay down. You lay down on the couch. I ain't going to hurt you, Alice. I don't want to hurt you.'

For a moment she did not move. Then she remembered, flatly, Mrs Holland's injunction: 'You do all you can for Mr Holland,' and she got up and went over to the American leather couch.

'I'll blow the lamp out,' Holland said. 'It's all right. It's all right.'

VI

'Don't you say nothing, Alice. Don't you go and tell nobody.'

Corn for Mrs Holland's chickens, a wooden potato-tub of maize and another of wheat, was kept in a loft above the mill itself, and Alice would climb the outside loft-ladder to fill the chipped enamel corn-bowl in the early winter afternoons. And standing there, with the bowl empty in her hands, or with a scattering of grain in it or the full mixture of wheat and maize, she stared and thought of the words Holland said to her almost every night. The loft windows were hung with skeins of spider-webs, and the webs in turn were powdered with pale and dark grey dust, pale flour-dust never swept away since the mill had ceased to work, and a dark mouse-coloured dust that showered constantly down from the rafters. The loft was always cold. The walls were clammy with river damp and the windows misty with wet. But Alice always stood there in the early afternoons and stared through the dirty windows across the wet flat valley. Seagulls flew wildly above the floods that filled the meadows after rain. Strings of wild swans flew over and sometimes came down to rest with the gulls on the waters or the islands of grass. They were the only moving things in the valley. But Alice stared at them blankly, hardly seeing them. She saw Holland instead; Holland turning out the lamp, fumbling with his trousers, getting up and relighting the lamp with a tight scared look on his face. And she returned his words over and over in her mind. 'Don't you say nothing. Don't you say nothing. Don't you go and tell nobody.' They were words not of anger, not threatening, but of fear. But she did not see it. She turned his words slowly over and over in her mind as she might have turned a ball or an orange over and over in her hands, over and over, round and round, the surface always the same, the shape the same, for ever recurring, a circle with no end to it. She reviewed them without surprise and without malice. She never refused Holland. Once only she said, suddenly scared: 'I don't want to, not to-night. I don't want to.' But Holland cajoled, 'Come on, Alice come on. I'll give you something. Come on. I'll give y' extra six-pence with your money, Friday, Alice. Come on.'

And after standing a little while in the loft she would go down the ladder with the corn-bowl to feed the hens that were cooped up behind a rusty broken-down wire-netting pen across the yard, beyond the dumps of iron. 'Tchka! Tchka! Tchka!' She never varied the call. 'Tchka! Tchka!' The sound was thin and sharp in the winter air. The weedy fowls, wet-feathered, scrambled after the yellow corn as she scattered it down. She watched them for a moment, staying just so long and never any longer, and then went back into the mill, shaking the corn-dust from the bowl as she went. It was as though she were religiously pledged to a ritual. The circumstances and the day never varied. She played a minor part in a play which never changed and seemed as if it never could change. Holland got up, she got up, she cooked breakfast. Holland left. She cleaned the rooms and washed Mrs Holland. She cooked the dinner, took half up to Mrs

Holland and ate half herself. She stood in the loft, thought of Holland's words, fed the fowls, then ceased to think of Holland. In the afternoon she read to Mrs Holland. In the evening Holland returned. And none of it seemed to affect her. She looked exactly as she had looked when she had first walked across the valley with her bag. Her eyes were utterly unresponsive, flat, never lighting up. They only seemed if anything greyer and softer, a little fuller if possible of docility.

And there was only one thing which in any way broke the ritual; and even that was regular, a piece of ritual itself. Every Wednesday, and again on Sunday, Mrs Holland wrote to her son.

Or rather Alice wrote. 'You can write better 'n me. You write it. I'll tell you what to put and you put it.' So Alice sat by the bed with a penny bottle of ink, a steel pen and a tissue writing tablet, and Mrs Holland dictated. 'Dear Albert.' There she stopped, lying back on the pillows to think. Alice waited. The pen dried. And then Mrs Holland would say: 'I can't think what to put. You git th' envelope done while I'm thinking.' So Alice wrote the envelope:

'Pte Albert Holland, 94167, B Company, Fifth Battalion 1st Rifles, British Army of Occupation, Cologne, Germany.'

And then Mrs Holland would begin, talking according to her mood: 'I must say, Albert, I feel a good lot better. I have not had a touch for a long while.' Or: 'I don't seem to get on at all somehow. The doctor comes every week and says I got to stop here. Glad to say though things are well with your Dad and trade is good and he is only waiting for you to come home and go in with him. There is a good trade now in old motors. Your Dad is very good to me I must say and so is Alice. I wonder when you will be home. Alice is writing this.'

All through the winter Alice wrote the letters. They seemed always to be the same letters, slightly changed, endlessly repeated. Writing the letters seemed to bring her closer to Mrs Holland. 'I'm sure I don't know what I should do without you, Alice.' Mrs Holland trusted her implicity, could see no wrong in her. And it seemed to Alice as if she came to know the soldier too, since she not only wrote the letters which went to him but read those which came in return.

'Dear Mum, it is very cold here and I can't say I shall be very sorry when I get back to see you. Last Sunday we . . .'

It seemed almost as if the letters were written to her. And though she read them without imagination, flatly, they gave her a kind of pleasure. She looked forward to their arrival. She shared Mrs Holland's anxiety when they did not come. 'It seems funny about Albert, he ain't writ this week.' And they would sit together in the bedroom, in the short winter afternoons, and talk of him and wonder.

Or rather Mrs Holland talked. Alice simply listened, her large grey eyes very still with their expression of lost attentiveness.

VII

She began to be sick in the early mornings without knowing what was happening to her. It was almost spring. The floods were lessening and vanishing and there was a new light on the river and the grass. The half-cut osier-bed shone in the sun like red corn, the bark varnished with light copper. She could dimly feel the change in the life about her: the new light, the longer days, thrushes singing in the willows above the mill-water in the evenings, the sun warm on her face in the afternoons.

But there was no change in her own life. Or if there was a change she did not feel it. There was no change in Mrs Holland's attitude to her and in her own to Mrs Holland. And only once was there a change in her attitude to Holland himself. After the first touch of sickness she could not face him. The life had gone out of her. 'I ain't well,' she kept saying to Holland. 'I ain't well.' For the first time he went into a rage with her. 'It ain't been a week since you said that afore! Come on. Christ! You ain't goin' to start that game.' He tried to put his arms round her. She struggled a little, tried to push him away. And suddenly he hit her. The blow struck her on the shoulder, just above the heart. It knocked her silly for a moment and she staggered about the room, then sat on the sofa, dazed. Then as she sat there the room was suddenly plunged into darkness. It was as though she had fainted. Then she saw that it was only Holland. He had put out the lamp.

After that she never once protested. She became more than

ever static, a neutral part of the act in which Holland was always the aggressor. There was nothing in it for her. It was over quickly, a savage interlude in the tranquil day-after-day unaltered life of Mrs Holland and herself. It was as regular almost as the sponging of Holland's collar and the cooking of his fish, or as the Friday visit of her mother and father with the van.

'How gittin' on? You don't look amiss. You look as if you're fillin' out a bit.' Or 'This is five and six! Is he rised you? Mother, he give her a rise. Well, well, that's all right, that is. That's good, a rise so soon. You be a good gal and you won't hurt.' And finally: 'Well, we s'll ha' to git on. Be dark else,' and the van would move away.

She was certainly plumper: a slight gentle filling of her breasts and her face were the only signs of physical change in her. She herself scarcely noticed them; until standing one day in the loft, gazing across the valley, holding the corn-bowl pressed against her, she could feel the bowl's roundness hard against the hardening roundness of her belly. Then she could feel something wrong with herself for the first time. And she stood arrested, scared. She felt large and heavy. What was the matter with her? She stood in a perplexity of fear. And finally she put the corn-bowl on the loft floor and then undid her clothes and looked at herself. She was round and hard and shiny. Then she opened the neck of her dress. Her breasts were no longer like little hard pointed lemons, but like half-blown roses. She put her hand under them, and under each breast, half in fear and half in amazement, and lifted them gently. They seemed suddenly as if they would fall if she did not hold them. What was it? Why hadn't she noticed it? Then she had suddenly something like an inspiration. It was Mrs Holland's complaint. She had caught it. Her body had the same swollen shiny look about it. She could see it clearly enough. She had caught the dropsy from Mrs Holland.

For a time she was a little frightened. She lay in bed at night and touched herself, and wondered. Then it passed off. She went back into the old state of unemotional neutrality. Then the sickness began to get less severe; she went for whole days without it; and finally it ceased altogether. Then there were days when the heaviness of her breasts and belly seemed a mythical thing, when she did not think of it. And she would think that the sickness and the heaviness were passing off together, things dependent on each other.

By the late spring she felt that it was all right, that she had nothing to fear. Summer was coming. She would be better in summer. Everybody was better in the summer.

Even Mrs Holland seemed better. But it was not the spring weather or the coming of summer that made her so, but the letters from Germany. 'I won't say too much, Mum, in case. But very like we shall be home afore the end of this year.'

'I believe I could git up, Alice, if he come home. I believe I could. I should like to be up,' Mrs Holland would say. 'I believe I could.'

And often, in the middle of peeling potatoes or scrubbing the kitchen bricks, Alice would hear Mrs Holland calling her. And when she went up it would be, 'Alice, you git the middle bedroom ready. In case Albert comes,' or 'See if you can find Albert's fishing-tackle. It'll be in the shed or else the loft. He'll want it,' or 'Tell Fred when he comes home I want him to git a ham. A whole 'un. In case.' And always the last flickering desire: 'If I knowed when he was coming I'd git up. I believe I *could* git up.'

But weeks passed and nothing happened. Mid-summer came, and all along the river the willow-leaves drooped or turned, green and silver, in the summer sun and the summer wind. And the hot still days were almost as uneventful and empty as the brief damp days of winter.

Then one afternoon in July Alice, standing in the loft and gazing through the dusted windows, saw a soldier coming up the road. He was carrying a white kitbag and he walked on rather splayed flat feet.

She ran down the loft steps and across the dump-yard and up into Mrs Holland's bedroom.

'Albert's come!'

Mrs Holland sat straight up in bed, as though by a miracle, trembling.

'Get me out, quick, let me get something on. Get me out. I want to be out for when he comes. Get me out.'

The girl took the weight of the big woman as she half slid out of bed, Mrs Holland's great breasts falling out of her nightgown, Alice thinking all the time, 'I ain't got it as bad as her, not half as bad. Mine are little side of hers. Mine are little.' She had never realised how big Mrs Holland was. And she had never seen her so distressed – distressed by joy and anticipation and her own sickness. Tears were flowing from her eyes. Alice struggled with her desperately. But she had scarcely put on her old red woollen dressing-jacket and helped her to a chair before there was a shout:

'Mum!'

Alice was at the head of the stairs before the second shout came. She could see the soldier in the passage below looking up. His tunic collar was unbuttoned and thrown back from his sunred neck.

'Where's mum?'

'Up here.'

Albert came upstairs. Alice had expected a young man, very young. Albert seemed about thirty-five, perhaps older. His flat feet, splayed out, and his dark loose moustache gave him a slightly old-fashioned countrified look, a little stupid. He was very like Holland himself. His eyes bulged, the whites glassy.

'Where is she?' he said.

'In the bedroom,' Alice said. 'In there.'

Albert went past her and along the landing without another word, scarcely looking at her. Alice could smell his sweat, the pungent sweat-soaked smell of khaki, as he went by. In another moment she heard Mrs Holland's cries of delight and his voice in answer.

From that moment she began to live in a changed world. Albert's coming cut her off at once from Mrs Holland; she was pushed aside like an old love by a new. But she was prepared for that. Not consciously, but by intuition, she had seen that it must come, that Albert would usurp her place. So she had no surprise when Mrs Holland scarcely called for her all day, had no time to talk to her except of Albert, and never asked her to sit and read to her in the bedroom as she had always done in the past. She was prepared for all that. What she was not prepared for at all was to be cut off from Holland himself too. It had not occurred to her that in the evenings Albert might sit in the kitchen, that there might be no lying on the sofa, no putting out of the light, no doing as Holland wanted.

She was so unprepared for it that for a week she could not

believe it. Her incredulity made her quieter than ever. All the time she was waiting for Holland to do something: to come to her secretly, into her bedroom, anywhere, and go on as he had always done. But nothing happened. For a week Holland was quiet too. He did not speak to her. Every evening Alice fried a double quantity of fish for Holland and Albert, and after tea the two men sat in the kitchen and talked, or walked through the osier-bed to the meadows and talked there. Holland scarcely spoke to her. They were scarcely ever alone together. Albert was an everlasting presence, walking about aimlessly, putteeless, his splayed feet shuffling on the bricks, stolid, comfortable, not speaking much.

And finally when Holland did speak to her it was with the old words: 'Don't you say nothing! See?' But now there was not only fear in the words, but anger. 'You say half a damn word and I'll break your neck. See? I'll smash you. That's over. Done with. Don't you say a damn word! See?'

The words, contrary to their effect of old, no longer perturbed or perplexed her. She was relieved, glad. It was all over. No more putting out the lamp, lying there waiting for Holland. No more pain.

VIII

Outwardly she seemed incapable of pain, even of emotion at all. She moved about with the same constant large-eyed quietness as ever, as though she were not thinking or were incapable of thought. Her eyes were remarkable in their everlasting expression of mute steadfastness, the same wintry grey light in them as always, an unreflective, almost lifeless kind of light.

And Albert noticed it. It struck him as funny. She would stare at him across the kitchen, dishcloth in hand, in a state of dumb absorption, as though he were some entrancing boy of her own age. But there was no joy in her eyes, no emotion at all, nothing. It was the same when, after a week's rest, Albert began to repair the chicken-coop beyond the dumps of old iron. Alice would come out twice a day, once with a cup of tea in the morning, once when she fed the hens in the early afternoon, and stand and watch him. She hardly ever spoke. She only moved to set down the tea-cup on a box or scatter the corn on the ground. And standing there, hatless, in the hot sunlight, staring, her lips gently

parted, she looked as though she were entranced by Albert. All
the time Albert, in khaki trousers, grey army shirt, a cloth
civilian cap, and a fag-end always half burning his straggling
moustache, moved about with stolid countrified deliberation. He
was about as entrancing as an old shoe. He never dressed up,
never went anywhere. When he drank, his moustache acted as a
sponge, soaking up a little tea, and Albert took second little
drinks from it, sucking it in. Sometimes he announced, 'I don't
know as I shan't go down Nenweald for half hour and look
round,' but further than that it never went. He would fish in the
mill-stream instead, dig in the ruined garden, search among the
rusty iron dumps for a hinge or a bolt, something he needed for
the hen-house. In the low valley the July heat was damp and
stifling, the willows still above the still water, the sunlight like
brass. The windless heat and the stillness seemed to stretch away
infinitely. And finally Albert carried the wood for the new hen-
house into the shade of a big cherry-tree that grew between the
river and the house, and sawed and hammered in the cherry-tree
shade all day. And from the kitchen Alice could see him. She
stood at the sink, scraping potatoes or washing dishes, and
watched him. She did it unconsciously. Albert was the only new
thing in the square of landscape seen from the window. She had
nothing else to watch. The view was even smaller than in winter
time, since summer had filled the cherry-boughs, and the tall
river reeds had shut out half the world.

It went on like this for almost a month, Albert tidying up the
garden and remaking the hen-house, Alice watching him. Until
finally Albert said to her one day:

'Don't you ever git out nowhere?'

'No.'

'Don't you want to git out?'

'I don't mind.'

The old answer: and it was the same answer she gave him,
when, two days later, on a Saturday, he said to her: 'I'm a-going
down Nenweald for hour. You git ready and come as well. Go
on. You git ready.'

She stood still for a moment, staring, not quite grasping it all.

'Don't you wanna come?'

'I don't mind.'

'Well, you git ready.'

She went upstairs at once, taking off her apron as she went, in mute obedience.

Earlier, Albert had said to Mrs Holland: 'Don't seem right that kid never goes nowhere. How'd it be if I took her down Nenweald for hour?'

'It's a long way. How're you going?'

'Walk. That ain't far.'

'What d'ye want to go down Nenweald for?' A little sick petulant jealousy crept into Mrs Holland's voice. 'Why don't you stop here?'

'I want some nails. I thought I'd take the kid down for hour. She can drop in and see her folks while I git the nails.'

'Her folks don't live at Nenweald. They live at Drake's End.'

'Well, don't matter. Hour out'll do her good.'

And in the early evening Albert and Alice walked across the meadow paths into Nenweald. The sun was still hot and Albert, dressed up in a hard hat and a blue serge suit and a stand-up collar, walked slowly, with grave flat-footed deliberation. The pace suited Alice. She felt strangely heavy; her body seemed burdened down. She could feel her breasts, damp with heat, hanging heavily down under her cotton dress. In the bedroom, changing her clothes, she could not help looking at herself. The dropsy seemed to be getting worse. It was beyond her. And she could feel the tightly swollen nipples of her breasts rubbing against the rather coarse cotton of her dress.

But she did not think of it much. Apart from the heaviness of her body she felt strong and well. And the country was new to her, the fields strange and the river wider than she had ever dreamed.

It was the river, for some reason, which struck her most. 'Don't it git big?' she said. 'Ain't it wide?'

'Wide,' Albert said. 'You want to see the Rhine. This is only a brook.' And he went on to tell her of the Rhine. 'Take you quarter of hour to walk across. And all up the banks you see Jerry's grapes. Growing like twitch. And big boats on the river, steamers. I tell you. That's the sort o' river. You ought to see it. Like to see a river like that, wouldn't you?'

'Yes.'

'Ah, it's a long way off. A thousand miles near enough.'

Alice did not speak.

'You ain't been a sight away from here, I bet, 'ave you?'
Albert said.

'No.'

'How far?'

'I don't know.'

'What place? What's the farthest place you bin?'

'I don't know. I went Bedford once.'

'How far's that? About ten miles, ain't it?'

'I don't know. It seemed a long way.'

And gradually they grew much nearer to each other, almost
intimate. The barriers of restraint between them were broken
down by Albert's talk about the Rhine, the Germans, the war,
his funny or terrible experiences. Listening, Alice forgot herself.
Her eyes listened with the old absorbed unemotional look, but in
reality with new feelings of wonder behind them. In Nenweald
she followed Albert through the streets, waited for him while
he bought the nails or dived down into underground places or
looked at comic picture post-cards outside cheap stationers. They
walked through the Saturday market, Albert staring at the sweet
stalls and the caged birds, Alice at the drapery and the fruit
stalls, remembering her old life at home again as she caught the
rich half-rotten fruit smells, seeing herself in the kitchen at
home, with her mother, hearing the rustle of Spanish paper
softly torn from endless oranges in the kitchen candlelight.

Neither of them talked much. They talked even less as they
walked home. Albert had bought a bag of peardrops and they
sucked them in silence as they walked along by the darkening
river. And in silence Alice remembered herself again: could feel
the burden of her body, the heavy swing of her breasts against
her dress. She walked in a state of wonder at herself, at Albert,
at the unbelievable Rhine, at the evening in the town.

It was a happiness that even Mrs Holland's sudden jealousy
could not destroy or even touch.

Suddenly Mrs Holland had changed. 'Where's that Alice!
Alice! Alice! Why don't you come when I call you? Now just
liven yourself, Alice, and git that bedroom ready. You're gettin'
fat and lazy, Alice. You ain't the girl you used to be. Git on, git
on, do. Don't stand staring.' Alice, sackcloth apron bundled
loosely round her, her hair rat-tailed about her face, could only
stare in reply and then quietly leave the bedroom. 'And here!'

Mrs Holland would call her back. 'Come here. You ain't bin talking to Albert, 'ave you? He's got summat else to do 'sides talk to you. You leave Albert to 'isself. And now git on. Bustle about and git some o' that fat off '

The jealousy, beginning with mere petulancy, then rising to reprimand, rose to abuse at last.

'Just because I'm in bed you think you can do so you like. Great slommacking thing. Lazy ain't in it. Git on, do!'

And in the evenings:

'Fred, that Alice'll drive me crazy.'

'What's up?' Holland's fear would leap up, taking the form of anger too. 'What's she bin doing? Been saying anything?'

'Fat, slommacking thing. I reckon she hangs round our Albert. She don't seem right, staring and slommacking about. She looks half silly.'

'I'll say summat to her. That fish ain't very grand o' nights sometimes.'

'You can say what you like. But she won't hear you. If she does she'll make out she don't. That's her all over. Makes out she don't hear. But she hears all right.'

And so Holland attacked her:

'You better liven yourself up. See? Act as if you was sharp. And Christ, you ain't bin saying nothing, 'ave you? Not to her?'

'No.'

'Not to nobody?'

'No.'

'Don't you say a damn word. That's over. We had a bit o' fun and now it's finished with. See that?'

'Yes.' Vaguely she wondered what he meant by fun.

'Well then, git on. Go on, gal, git on. Git on! God save the King, you make my blood boil. Git on!'

The change in their attitude was beyond her: so far beyond her that it created no change in her attitude to them. She went about as she had always done, very quietly, with large-eyed complacency, doing the dirty work, watching Albert, staring at the meadows, her eyes eternally expressionless. It was as though nothing could change her.

Then Albert said, 'How about if we go down Nenweald again Saturday? I got to go down.'

She remembered Mrs Holland, stared at Albert and said nothing.

'You git ready about five,' Albert said. 'Do you good to git out once in a while. You don't git out half enough.' He paused, looking at her mute face. 'Don't you want a come?'

'I don't mind.'

'All right. You be ready.'

Then, hearing of it, Mrs Holland flew into a temper of jealousy:

'You'd take a blessed gal out but you wouldn't stay with me, would you? Not you. Away all this time, and now when you're home again you don't come near me.'

'All right, all right. I thought'd do the kid good, that's all.'

'That's all you think about. Folks'll think you're kidnappin'!'

'Ain't nothing to do with it. Only taking the kid out for an hour.'

'Hour! Last Saturday you'd gone about four!'

'All right,' Albert said, 'we won't go. It don't matter.'

Mrs Holland broke down and began to weep on the pillow.

'I don't want a stop you,' she said. 'You can go. It don't matter to me. I can stop here be meself. You can go.'

And in the end they went. As before they walked through the meadows, Albert dressed up and hot, Alice feeling her body under her thin clothes as moist and warm as a sweating apple with the heat. In Nenweald they did the same things as before, took the same time, talked scarcely at all, and then walked back again in the summer twilight, sucking the peardrops Albert had bought.

The warm air lingered along by the river. The water and the air and the sky were all breathless. The sky was a soft green-lemon colour, clear, sunless and starless. 'It's goin' to be a scorcher again tomorrow,' Albert said.

Alice said nothing. They walked slowly, a little apart decorously. Albert opened the towpath gates, let Alice through, and then splay-footed after her. They were like some countrified old fashioned couple half-afraid of each other.

Then Albert, after holding open a towpath gate and letting Alice pass, could not fasten the catch. He fumbled with the gate, lifted it, and did not shut it for about a minute. When he walked on again Alice was some distance ahead. Albert could see her plainly. Her pale washed-out dress was clear in the half light. Albert walked on after her. Then he was struck all of a sudden by the way she walked. She was walking thickly, clumsily, not exactly as though she were tired, but heavily, as though she had iron weights in her shoes.

Albert caught up with her. 'You all right, Alice?' he said.

'I'm all right.'

'Ain't bin too much for you? I see you walking a bit lame like.'

Alice did not speak.

'Ain't nothing up, Alice, is there?'

Alice tried to say something, but Albert asked again: 'Ain't bin too hot, is it?'

'No. It's all right. It's only the dropsy.'

'The what?'

'What your mother's got. I reckon I catched it off her.'

'It ain't catchin', is it?'

'I don' know. I reckon that's what it is.'

'You're a bit tired, that's all 'tis,' Albert said. 'Dropsy. You're a funny kid, no mistake.'

They walked almost in silence to the mill. It was dark in the kitchen, Holland was upstairs with Mrs Holland, and Albert struck a match and lit the oil-lamp.

The burnt match fell from Albert's fingers. And stooping to pick it up he saw Alice, standing sideways and full in the lamp-light. The curve of her pregnancy stood out clearly. Her whole body was thick and heavy with it. Albert crumbled the match in his fingers, staring at her. Then he spoke.

'Here kid,' he said. 'Here.'

She looked at him.

'What'd you say it was you got? Dropsy?'

'Yes. I reckon that's what it is I caught.'

'How long you bin like it?'

'I don't know. It's bin coming on a good while. All summer.'

He stared at her, not knowing what to say. All the time she stared too with the old habitual muteness.

'Don't you know what's up wi' you?' he said.

She shook her head.

When he began to tell her she never moved a fraction. Her face was like a lump of unplastic clay in the lamplight.

'Don't you know who it is? Who you bin with? Who done it?'

She could not answer. It was hard for her to grapple not only with Albert's words but with the memory of Holland's: 'You tell anybody and I'll smash you. See?'

'You better git back home,' Albert said. 'That's your best place.'

'When?'

'Soon as you can. Git off to-morrow. You no business slaving here.'

And then again:

'Who done it? Eh? Don't y' know who done it? If you know who done it he could marry you.'

'He couldn't marry me.'

Albert saw that the situation had significance for him.

'You better git off to bed quick,' he said. 'Go on. And then be off in the morning.'

In the morning Alice was up and downstairs soon after sunlight, and the sun was well above the trees as she began to walk across the valley. She walked slowly, carrying her black case, changing it now and then from one hand to another. Binders stood in the early wheatfields covered with their tarpaulins, that were in turn covered with summer dew. It was Sunday. The world seemed empty except for herself, rooks making their way to the cornfields, and cattle in the flat valley. She walked for long periods without thinking. Then when she did think, it was not of herself or the mill or what she was doing or what was going to happen to her, but of Albert. An odd sense of tenderness rose up in her simultaneously with the picture of Albert rising up in her mind. She could not explain it. There was something singularly compassionate in Albert's countrified solidity, his slow voice, his flat feet, his concern for her. Yet for some reason she could not explain, she could not think of him with anything like happiness. The mere remembrance of him sawing and hammering under the cherry-tree filled her with pain. It shot up in her breast like panic. 'You better git back home.' She could hear him saying it again and again.

And all the time she walked as though nothing had happened. Her eyes had the same dull mute complacency as ever. It was as though she were only half-awake.

When she saw the black gas-tarred side of the Hartop's house it was about eight o'clock. She could hear the early service bell.

The sight of the house did not affect her. She went in by the yard gate, shut it carefully, and then walked across the yard to the back door.

She opened the door and stood on the threshold. Her mother and her father, in his shirt-sleeves, sat in the kitchen having breakfast. She could smell tea and bacon. Her father was sopping up his plate with bread, and seeing her he paused with the bread half to his lips. She saw the fat dripping down to the plate again. Watching it, she stood still.

'I've come back,' she said.

Suddenly the pain shot up in her again. And this time it seemed to shoot up through her heart and breast and throat and through her brain.

She did not move. Her face was flat and blank and her body static. It was only her eyes which registered the suddenness and depths of her emotions. They began to fill with tears.

It was as though they had come to life at last.

THE STATION

For thirty seconds after the lorry had halted between the shack and the petrol pumps the summer night was absolutely silent. There was no wind; the leaves and the grass stalks were held in motionless suspense in the sultry air. And after the headlights had gone out the summer darkness was complete too. The pumps were dead white globes, like idols of porcelain; there was no light at all in the station. Then, as the driver and his mate alighted, slamming the cabin doors and grinding their feet on the gravel, the light in the station came suddenly on: a fierce electric flicker from the naked globe in the shack, the light golden in one wedge-shaped shaft across the gravel pull-in. And seeing it the men stopped. They stood for a moment with the identical suspense of the grass and the trees.

The driver spoke first. He was a big fellow, quite young, with breezy blue eyes and stiff untrained hair and a comic mouth. His lips were elastic: thin bands of pink india-rubber that were for ever twisting themselves into grimaces of irony and burlesque, his eyes having that expression of comic and pained astonishment seen on the painted faces of Aunt Sallies in shooting galleries.

His lips twisted to the shape of a buttonhole, so that he whispered out of the one corner. 'See her? She heard us come. What'd I tell you?'

The mate nodded. He too was young, but beside the driver he was boyish, his checks smooth and shiny as white cherries, his hair yellow and light and constantly ruffled up like the fur of a fox-cub. And unlike the driver's, his lips and eyes were quite still; so that he had a look of intense immobility.

He could see the woman in the shack. Short white casement curtains of transparent lace on brass rods cut across the window, but above and through them he could see the woman clearly. She was big-shouldered and dark, with short black hair, and her face was corn-coloured under the light. She seemed about thirty; and that surprised him.

69

'I thought you said she was young,' he said.

'So she is.' The driver's eyes flashed white. 'Wait'll you git close. How old d'ye think she is?'

'Thirty. More.'

'Thirty? She's been here four year. And was a kid when she was married, not nineteen. How's that up you?'

'She *looks* thirty.'

'So would you if you'd kept this bloody shack open every night for four year. Come on, let's git in.'

They began to walk across the gravel, but the driver stopped.

'And don't forget what I said. She's bin somebody. She's had education. Mind your ups and downs.'

When they opened the door of the shack and shuffled in, the driver first, the mate closing the door carefully behind him, the woman stood behind the rough-carpentered counter with her arms folded softly across her chest, in an attitude of unsurprised expectancy. The counter was covered with blue-squared oilcloth, tacked down. By the blue alarum clock on the lowest of the shelves behind it, the time was four minutes past midnight. At the other end of the shelf a flat shallow kettle was boiling on an oil-stove. The room was like an oven. The woman's eyes seemed curiously drowsy, as though clouded over with the steam and the warm oil-fumes. And for half a minute nothing happened. She did not move. The men stood awkward. Then the driver spoke. His india-rubber mouth puckered comically to one side, and his eye flicked in a wink that was merely friendly and habitual.

'Well, here we are again.'

She nodded; the drowsiness of her eyes cleared a little. All the same there was something reserved about her, almost sulky.

'What would you like?' she said.

'Give me two on a raft and coffee,' the driver said.

'Two on a raft and coffee,' the woman said. She spoke beautifully, without effort, and rather softly. 'What's your friend going to have?'

The mate hesitated. His eyes were fixed on the woman, half-consciously, in admiration. And the driver had to nudge him, smiling his india-rubber smile of comic irony, before he became aware of all that was going on.

'Peck up,' the driver said.

'That'll do me,' the mate said.

'Two on a raft twice and coffee,' the woman said. 'Is that it?'

Though the mate did not know it for a moment, she was addressing him. He stood in slight bewilderment, as though he were listening to a language he did not understand. Then as he became aware of her looking at him and waiting for an answer the bewilderment became embarrassment and his fair cherry-smooth cheeks flushed very red, the skin under the short golden hairs and his neck flaming. He stood dumb. He did not know what to do with himself.

'I'm afraid I don't know your friend's name or his tastes yet,' the woman said. 'Shall I make it two poached twice and coffee?'

'Just like me. Forgot to introduce you,' the driver said. His mouth was a wrinkle of india-rubber mocking. 'Albie, this is Mrs Harvey. This is Albert Armstrong. Now mate on Number 4, otherwise Albie.'

The woman smiled and in complete subjection and fascination the boy smiled too.

'Are you sure that's all right?' she said. 'Poached and coffee? It sounds hot to me.'

'Does me all right,' the driver said.

'I could make you a fresh salad,' she said. And again she was speaking to the mate, with a kind of soft and indirect invitation. 'There would be eggs in that.'

'I'll have that,' the mate said.

'What?' the driver said. His eyes were wide open, his mouth wide also in half serious disgust, as though the mate had committed a sort of sacrilege. 'You don' know what's good.'

'So you'll have the salad?' the woman said.

'Yes, please.'

'I can give you the proper oil on it, and vinegar. You can have fruit afterwards if you'd like it.'

'Fruit?' the driver said. 'What fruit?'

She took the kettel from the oil-stove and poured a little hot water into the coffee-pot and then a little into each of the egg-poachers. 'Plums,' she said.

'Now you're talking,' the driver said. 'Plums. Some sense. Now you *are* talking.'

'Go and get yourself a few if you like them so much.'

'Show me. Show me a plum tree within half a mile and I'm off.'

'Go straight down the garden and it's the tree on the left. Pick as many as you like.'

The driver opened the door, grinning. 'Coming, Albie?'

'You're not afraid of the dark, are you?' the woman said.

This time she was speaking to the driver. And suddenly as he stood there at the door, grimacing with comic irony at her, his whole head and face and neck and shoulders became bathed in crimson light, as though he had become the victim of a colossal blush. Startled, he lifted up his face and looked up at the shack from the outside. The bright electric sign with the naked letters saying simply *The Station* was like a fire of scarlet and white. At intervals it winked and darkened, on and out, scarlet to darkness, *The Station* to nothing. The driver stood with uplifted face, all scarlet, in surprised admiration.

'Blimey, that's a winner. When'd you get that?'

'It's new this week.'

'It's a treat. It makes no end of a difference. How's it you didn't have it on when we came in?'

'I keep forgetting it. I'm so used to sitting here in the dark I can't get used to it. It's a bit uncanny.'

The driver went down the shack steps, into the night. The woman, busy with the eggs, and the boy, leaning against the counter, could see him standing back, still faintly crimson, in admiration of the eternal winking light. And for a minute, as he stood there, the station was completely silent, the August darkness like velvet, the sultry night air oppressing all sound except the soft melancholy murmur of the simmering kettle. Then the woman called:

'You'd better get your plums. The eggs won't be two minutes.'

The driver answered something, only barely audible, and after the sound of his feet crunching the gravel the silence closed in again.

It was like a stoke-room in the shack. The smells of coffee and eggs and oil were fused into a single breath of sickening heat. Like the driver, the boy stood in his shirt-sleeves. He stood still, very self-conscious, watching the woman breaking the eggs and stirring the coffee and finally mixing in a glass bowl the salad for himself. He did not know what to do or say. Her thin white dress was like the silky husk of a seed-pod, just bursting open. Her ripe breasts swelled under it like two sun-swollen seeds. And he could not take his eyes away from them. He was electrified. His blood quivered with the current of excitement. And all the time, even though she was busy with the eggs on the stove, and the mixing of the salad, very often not looking at him, she was aware of it. Looking up sometimes from the stove or the salad she would look past him, with an air of arrested dreaminess, her dark eyes lovely and sulky. The deliberation of it maddened him. He remembered things the driver had said as they came along the road. The words flashed in his mind as though lit up by the electricity of his veins. 'She's a peach, Albie. But I'll tell you what. One bloody wink out o' place and you're skedaddled. She won't have it. She's nice to the chaps because it's business, that's all. See what I mean, Albie? She'll look at you fit to melt your bleedin' heart out, but it don't mean damn all. She wants to make that station a success, that's all. That's why she runs the night shack. Her husband runs the day show and she's second house, kind of. It's her own idea. See?'

And suddenly his thoughts broke off. The lights in his brain, as it were, went out. His mind was blank. She was looking at him. He stood transfixed, his veins no longer electric but relapsed, his blood weak.

'Like it on the lorry?' she said.

'Yes.' He hardly spoke.

She had finished making the salad and she pushed the bowl across the counter towards him before speaking again.

'You're not very old for the job, are you?'

'I'm eighteen.'

'Get on with old Spike?'

'Yes.'

'Isn't it lonely at first? They all say it's lonely when they first begin.'

'I don't mind it.'

'What's your girl say to it?'

It was as though the electric sign had been suddenly turned on him as it had been turned on the driver. He stood helpless, his face scarlet.

'I ain't got a girl.'

'What? Not a nice boy like you?' She was smiling, half in mockery. 'I know you must have.'

'No.'

'Does she love you much?' She looked at him in mock seriousness, her eyes lowered.

'I ain't got one.'

'Honest?' She pushed the bottles of oil and vinegar across the counter towards him. 'I'll ask Spike when he comes in.'

'No, don't say anything to Spike,' he begged. 'Don't say nothing. He's always kidding me about her, anyway.'

'You said you hadn't got a girl.'

'Well –'

She took two plates from the rack behind the counter and then knives and forks from the drawer under the counter and then laid them out.

'Does she hate it when you're on nights?' she said.

'Yes.'

'What's she like – dark or fair?'

'Dark.'

'Like me?'

He could not answer. He only gazed straight at her in mute embarrassment and nodded. Every word she uttered fired him with passionate unrest. The current in his blood was renewed again. He felt himself tightened up. And she could see it all.

'You'd better call Spike,' she said. 'The eggs are ready.'

He moved towards the door. Then he turned and stopped. 'Don't say nothing,' he said.

'All right.'

He stood at the door, his face scarlet under the winking sign, and called out for Spike, singing the word, 'Spi-ike!' And he could hear the sound echoing over the empty land in the darkness. There was a smell of corn in the air, stronger and sweeter even than the smell of the heat and cooking in the shack. It came in sweet waves from across the invisible fields in the warm night air.

'I know how you feel,' she said.

He turned sharply. 'How?'

'Come and eat this salad and cool down a bit.'

He came from the door to the counter in obedience, pulling out a stool and sitting on it.

'Oil and vinegar?' she said. 'The coffee will be ready by the time Spike comes.'

'How do I feel? What do you mean?'

'You know.'

'Yes, but how do you know?'

'I've felt like it myself.'

She stood with her arms folded and resting on the counter edge, and leaning slightly forward, so that he could see her breasts beneath the open dress. She looked at him with a kind of pity, with tenderness, but half-amused. He saw the breasts rise and fall with the same slow and almost sulky passion as she looked at him. He stared from her breasts to her face, and she stared back, her eyes never moving. And they stood like that, not moving or speaking, but only as it were burning each other up, until suddenly Spike came in.

The woman stood up at once. Spike's cupped hands were full of plums.

'They're green,' the woman said.

'By God, if I didn't think they was tart.'

'Didn't you find the right tree? On the left?'

'I couldn't see a blamed thing.'

'Eat your eggs. I'll get a torch and we'll go down and get some ripe ones before you go.'

'Eggs look good an' all,' Spike said.

The men ate in silence, the woman busy with bread and coffee. The boy put vinegar on his salad, but not oil, and once, noticing it, she unstoppered the oil bottle and pushed it across to him. It was her only sign towards him. The old manner of pity and intimacy had vanished. She was the proprietress; they were the drivers come in to eat. She stood almost aloof, busy with odd things at the far end of the counter. And the boy sat in fresh bewilderment, at a loss, and in wonder about her.

They each drank two cups of coffee and when the cups were finally empty she said:

'If you're ready we can go down and get the plums. But I don't want to hurry you.'

'I'm fit,' Spike said. 'And my God the eggs were a treat. You missed a treat Albie, not having eggs.'

'The salad was all right.'

'I'll get the torch,' the woman said. 'You go out that door and I'll meet you round the back.'

She went out of the shack by a door behind the counter, and the boy followed Spike through the front door, under the electric sign. Outside, behind the shack, the sweet smell of ripened corn and night air seemed stronger than ever. At the side of the shack and a little behind it, the bungalow stood out darker than the darkness. And after a minute the torch appeared from the bungalow and began to travel towards the men. The boy could see it shining white along the cinder path and on the woman's feet as she came along.

'You walk down the path,' she said. 'I'll show the light.'

Spike began to walk down the path, the boy following him, and then the woman. The shadows strode like giants over the garden and were lost beyond the yellow snake fence in the dark land. The garden was short, and in a moment they all three stood under the plum tree, the woman shining the torch up into the branches, the tree turned to an immense net of green and silver.

'I'll shine, Spike,' she said. 'You pick them. If they're soft and they lift off they're ripe.'

'This is better,' Spike said. His mouth was already full of plums. 'I struck one match to every blamed plum when I came down.'

The woman stood a little away from the tree, shining the torch steadily, making a great ring of white light across which little moths began to flutter like casual leaves. The boy stood still, not attempting to move, as though he were uninvited.

'What about you?' she said.

And again he could feel the old softness of sympathy and pity and insinuation in her voice, and again his blood leapt up.

'I'm about full up,' he said.

'Take some for the journey.'

He stood still, electrified.

'Take some to eat on the way. Look here, come round the other side. They're riper.'

She moved round the tree, shining the torch always away from her. He followed her in silence, and then in silence they stood against the plum branches, in the darkness behind the light. He saw her stretch up her arm into the silver leaves, and then lower it again.

'Where's your hand?' she was whispering. 'Here. It's a beauty.' The soft ripe plum was between their hands. Suddenly she pressed it hard against his hands, and the ripe skin broke and the juice trickled over his fingers. 'Eat it, put it in your mouth,' she said. He put the plum into his mouth obediently, and the sweet juice trickled down over his lips and chin as it had already trickled over his hands.

'Was that nice?' she said softly.

'Lovely.'

'Sweet as your girl?'

It seemed suddenly as if his blood turned to water. She was touching him. She took his hand and laid it softly against her hip. It was firm and strong and soft. It had about it a kind of comforting maturity. He could feel all the sulky strength and passion of her whole body in it. Then all at once she covered his hand with her own, stroking it up and down with her fingers, until he stood helpless, intoxicated by the smell of corn and plums and the night warmth and her very light, constant stroking of his hand.

'Shine the light,' Spike called. 'I can't see for looking.'

'I'm shining,' she said. 'Albie wants to see too.'

'Getting many, Albie?'

'He's filling his pockets.'

She began to gather plums off the tree with her free hand as she spoke, keeping her other hand still on his, pressing it against her by an almost mechanical process of caressing. He reached up and tore off the plums too, not troubling if they were ripe, filling one pocket while she filled the other, the secrecy and passion of her movements half demoralizing him, and going on without interruption until Spike called:

'Albie! Plums or no plums, we shall have to get on th' old bus again.'

'All right.'

The boy could hardly speak. And suddenly as the woman took her hand away at last he felt as if the life in him had been cut off, the tension withdrawn, leaving his veins like dead wires.

He stumbled up the path behind Spike and the woman and the light. Spike was gabbling:

'Sweetest plums I ever tasted. When we come back I'll take a couple of pounds and the missus'll pie 'em.'

'When will you be back?'

'The night after to-morrow.'

'There'll be plenty,' she said.

She said nothing to the boy, and he said nothing either.

'Let's pay you,' Spike said.

'A shilling for you, and ninepence for the salad,' she said.

'Salad's cheaper,' Spike said. 'I'll remember that. What about the plums?'

'The plums are thrown in.'

They paid her. Then she stood on the shack steps while they crunched across the pull-in and climbed up into the cab, the bright red sign flashing above her.

'That sign's a treat,' Spike called. 'You could see it miles off.'

'I'm glad you like it,' she called. 'Good night.'

'Good night!'

Spike started up, and almost before the boy could realise it the lorry was swinging out into the road, and the station was beginning to recede. He sat for some moments without moving. Then the lorry began to make speed and the smell of corn and plums and the summer land began to be driven out by the smells of the cab, the petrol and oil and the heat of the engine running. But suddenly he turned and looked back.

'The light's out,' he said.

Spike put his head out of the cab and glanced back. The sign was still flashing but the shack itself was in darkness.

'She's sitting in the dark,' he said. 'She always does. She says it saves her eyes and the light and she likes it better.'

'Why?'

'Better ask her.' Spike put a plum in his mouth. 'I don't know.'

'What's her husband doing, letting her run the place at night, and sit there in the dark?'

'It's her own idea. It's a paying game an' all, you bet your life it is.'

The boy took a plum from his pocket and bit it slowly, licking the sweet juice from his lips as it ran down. He was still trembling.

And glancing back again he could see nothing of the station but the red sign flashing everlastingly out and on, scarlet to darkness, *The Station* to nothing at all.

THE KIMONO

It was the second Saturday of August, 1911, when I came to London for the interview with Kersch and Co. I was just twenty-five. The summer had been almost tropical.

There used to be a train in those days that got into St Pancras, from the North, about ten in the morning. I came by it from Nottingham, left my bag in the cloakroom and went straight down to the City by bus. The heat of London was terrific, a white dust heat, thick with the smell of horse dung. I had put on my best suit, a blue serge, and it was like a suit of gauze. The heat seemed to stab at me through it.

Kersch and Co. were very nice. They were electrical engineers. I had applied for a vacancy advertised by them. That morning I was on the short list and Mr Alexander Kersch, the son, was very nice to me. We talked a good deal about Nottingham and I asked him if he knew the Brownsons, who were prominent Congregationalists there, but he said no. Everyone in Nottingham, almost, knew the Brownsons, but I suppose it did not occur to me in my excitement that Kersch was a Jew. After a time he offered me a whisky and soda, but I refused. I had been brought up rather strictly, and in any case the Brownsons would not have liked it. Finally, Mr Kersch asked me if I could be in London over the week-end. I said yes, and he asked me at once to come in on Monday morning. I knew then that the job was as good as settled and I was trembling with excitement as I shook hands and said good-bye.

I came out of Kersch and Co. just before twelve o'clock. Their offices were somewhere off Cheapside. I forget the name of the street. I only remember, now, how very hot it was. There was something un-English about it. It was a terrific heat, fierce and white. And I made up my mind to go straight back to St Pancras and get my bag and take it to the hotel the Brownsons had recommended to me. It was so hot that I didn't want to eat. I felt that if I could get my room and wash and rest it would be

enough. I could eat later. I would go up West and do myself
rather well.

Pa Brownson had outlined the position of the hotel so well,
both in conversation and on paper, that when I came out of St
Pancras with my bag I felt I knew the way to the street as well as
if it had been in Nottingham. I turned east and then north and
went on turning left and then right, until finally I came to the
place where the street with the hotel ought to have been. It
wasn't there. I couldn't believe it. I walked about a bit, always
coming back to the same place again in case I should get lost.
Then I asked a baker's boy where Midhope Street was and he
didn't know. I asked one or two more people, and they didn't
know either. 'Wade's Hotel,' I would say, to make it clearer, but
it was no good. Then a man said he thought I should go back
towards St Pancras a bit, and ask again, and I did.

It must have been about two o'clock when I knew that I was
pretty well lost. The heat was shattering. I saw one or two other
hotels but they looked a bit low class and I was tired and
desperate.

Finally I set my bag down in the shade and wiped my face.
The sweat on me was filthy. I was wretched. The Brownsons had
been so definite about the hotel and I knew that when I got back
they would ask me if I liked it and all about it. Hilda
would want to know about it too. Later on, if I got the Kersch
job, we should be coming up to it for our honeymoon.

At last I picked up my bag again. Across the street was a little
sweet shop and café showing ices. I went across to it. I felt I had
to have something.

In the shop a big woman with black hair was tinkering with
the ice-cream mixer. Something had gone wrong. I saw that at
once. It was just my luck.

'I suppose it's no use asking for an ice?' I said.

'Well, if you wouldn't mind *waiting*.'

'How long?'

'As soon as ever I get this nut fixed on and the freezer going
again. We've had a breakdown.'

'All right. You don't mind if I sit down?' I said.

She said no, and I sat down and leaned one elbow on the tea-
table, the only one there was. The woman went on tinkering with
the freezer. She was a heavy woman, about fifty, a little swarthy,

and rather masterful to look at. The shop was stifling and filled with a sort of yellowish-pink shade cast by the sun pouring through the shop blind.

'I supposed it's no use asking you where Midhope Street is?' I said.

'Midhope Street,' she said. She put her tongue in her cheek, in thought. 'Midhope Street, I ought to know that.'

'Or Wade's Hotel.'

'Wade's Hotel,' she said. She wriggled her tongue between her teeth. They were handsome teeth, very white. 'Wade's Hotel. No. That beats me.' And then: 'Perhaps my daughter will know. I'll call her.'

She straightened up to call into the back of the shop. But a second before she opened her mouth the girl herself came in. She looked surprised to see me there.

'Oh, here you are, Blanche! This gentleman here is looking for Wade's Hotel.'

'I'm afraid I'm lost,' I said.

'Wade's Hotel,' the girl said. She too stood in thought, running her tongue over her teeth, and her teeth too were very white, like her mother's. 'Wade's Hotel. I've seen that somewhere. Surely?'

'Midhope Street.' I said.

'Midhope Street.'

No, she couldn't remember. She had on a sort of kimono, loose, with big orange flowers all over it. I remember thinking it was rather fast. For those days it was. It wouldn't be now. And somehow, because it was so loose and brilliant, I couldn't take my eyes off it. It made me uneasy, but it was an uneasiness in which there was pleasure as well, almost excitement. I remember thinking she was really half undressed. The kimono had no neck and no sleeves. It was simply a piece of material that wrapped over her, and when suddenly she bent down and tried to fit the last screw on to the freezer the whole kimono fell loose and I could see her body.

At the same time something else happened. Her hair fell over her shoulder. It was the time of very long hair, the days when girls would pride themselves that they could sit on their pig tails, but hers was the longest hair I had ever seen. It was like thick jet-black cotton-rope. And when she bent down over the freezer the pig-tail of it was so long that the tip touched the ice.

'I'm so sorry,' the girl said. 'My hair's always getting me into trouble.'

'It's all right. It just seems to be my unlucky day, that's all.'

'I'm so sorry.'

'Will you have a cup of tea?' the woman said. 'Instead of the ice? Instead of waiting?'

'That's it, Mother. Get him some tea. You *would* like tea, wouldn't you?'

'Very much.'

So the woman went through the counter-flap into the back of the shop to get the tea. The girl and I, in the shop alone, stood and looked at the freezer. I felt queer in some way, uneasy. The girl had not troubled to tighten up her kimono. She let it hang loose, anyhow, so that all the time I could see part of her shoulder and now and then her breasts. Her skin was very white, and once when she leaned forward rather farther than usual I could have sworn that she had nothing on at all underneath.

'You keep looking at my kimono,' she said. 'Do you like it?'

'It's very nice,' I said. 'It's very nice stuff.'

'Lovely stuff. Feel of it. Go on. Just feel of it.'

I felt the stuff. For some reasons, perhaps it was because I had had no food, I felt weak. And she knew it. She must have known it. 'It's lovely stuff. Feel it. I made it myself.' She spoke sweetly and softly, in invitation. There was something electric about her. I listened quite mechanically. From the minute she asked me to feel the stuff of her kimono I was quite helpless. She had me, as it were, completely done up in the tangled maze of the orange and green of its flowers and leaves.

'Are you in London for long? Only to-day?'

'Until Monday.'

'I suppose you booked your room at the hotel?'

'No. I didn't book it. But I was strongly recommended there.'

'I see.'

That was all, only 'I see.' But in it there was something quite maddening. It was a kind of passionate veiled hint, a secret invitation.

'Things were going well,' I said, 'until I lost my way.'

'Oh?'

'I came up for an interview and I got the job. At least I think I got the job.'

'A bit of luck. I hope it's a good one?'

'Yes,' I said. 'It is. Kersch and Co. In the City.'

'Kersch and Co?' she said. 'Not really? Kersch and Co.?'

'Yes,' I said. 'Why, do you know them?'

'Know them? Of course I know them. Everybody knows them. That *is* a bit of luck for you.'

And really I was flattered. She knew Kersch and Co.! She knew that it was a good thing. I think I was more pleased because of the attitude of the Brownsons. Kersch and Co. didn't mean anything to the Brownsons. It was just a name. They had been rather cold about it. I think they would have liked me to get the job, but they wouldn't have broken their hearts if I hadn't. Certainly they hadn't shown any excitement.

'Kersch and Co.,' the girl said again. 'That really *is* a bit of luck.'

Then the woman came in with the tea. 'Would you like anything to eat?'

'Well, I've had no dinner.'

'Oh! No wonder you look tired. I'll get you a sandwich. Is that all right?'

'Thank you.'

So the woman went out to get the sandwich, and the girl and I stayed in the shop again, alone.

'It's a pity you booked your room at the hotel,' she said.

'I haven't booked it,' I said.

'Oh! I thought you said you'd *booked* it. Oh! My fault. You *haven't* booked it?'

'No. Why?'

'We take people in here,' she said. 'Over the café. It's not central of course. But then we don't charge so much.'

I thought of the Brownsons. 'Perhaps I ought to go to the hotel,' I said.

'We charge three and six,' she said. 'That isn't much, is it?'

'Oh, no!'

'Why don't you just come up and see the room?' she said. 'Just come up.'

'Well—'

'Come up and see it. It won't eat you.'

She opened the rear door of the shop and in a moment I was going upstairs behind her. She was not wearing any stockings. Her bare legs were beautifully strong and white. The room was over the café. It was a very good room for three and six. The new wall-paper was silver-leaved and the bed was white and looked cool.

And suddenly it seemed silly to go out into the heat again and wander about looking for Wade's Hotel when I could stay where I was.

'Well, what do you think of it?' she said.

'I like it.' She sat down on the bed. The kimono was drawn up over her legs and where it parted at her knees I could see her thighs, strong and white and softly disappearing into the shadow of the kimono. It was the day of long rather prim skirts and I had never seen a woman's legs like that. There was nothing between Hilda and me beyond kissing. All we had done was to talk of things, but there was nothing in it. Hilda always used to say that she would keep herself for me.

The girl hugged her knees. I could have sworn she had nothing on under the kimono.

'I don't want to press you,' she said, 'but I do wish you'd stay. You'd be our first let.'

Suddenly a great wave of heat came up from the street outside, the fierce, horse-smelling, dust-white heat of the earlier day, and I said:

'All right. I'll stay.'

'Oh, you angel!'

The way she said that was so warm and frank that I did not know what to do. I simply smiled. I felt curiously weak with pleasure. Standing there, I could smell suddenly not only the heat but the warmth of her own body. It was sweetish and pungent, the soft odour of sweat and perfume. My heart was racing.

Then suddenly she got up and smoothed the kimono over her knees and thighs.

'My father has just died, you see,' she said. 'We are trying this for a living. You'll give us a start.'

Somehow it seemed too good to be true.

II

I know now that it was. But I will say more of that later, when the time comes.

That evening I came down into the shop again about six o'clock. I had had my tea and unpacked my things and rested. It was not much cooler, but I felt better. I was glad I had stayed.

The girl, Blanche, was sitting behind the counter, fanning herself with the broken lid of a sweet-box. She had taken off her kimono and was wearing a white gauzy dress with a black sash. I was disappointed. I think she must have seen that, because she pouted a bit when I looked at her. In turn I was glad she pouted. It made her lips look full-blooded and rich and shining. There was something lovely about her when she was sulky.

'Going out?' she said.

'Yes,' I said. 'I thought of going up West and celebrating over Kersch and Co.'

'Celebrating? By yourself?'

'Well,' I said. 'I'm alone. There's no one else.'

'Lucky you.'

I knew what she meant in a moment. 'Well,' I said, almost in a joke, 'why don't you come?'

'Me?' she said, eyes wide open. 'You don't mean it. Me?'

'I do,' I said. 'I do mean it.'

She got up. 'How long can you wait? I'll just change my dress and tell mother.'

'No hurry at all,' I said, and she ran upstairs.

I have said nothing about how old she was. In the kimono she looked about twenty, and in the white dress about the same age, perhaps a little younger. When she came down again that evening she looked nearer twenty-six or twenty-seven. She looked big and mature. She had changed from the white dress into a startling yellow affair with a sort of black coatee cut away at the hips. It was so flashy that I felt uneasy. It was very tight too: the skirt so tight that I could see every line of her body, the bodice filled tight in turn with her big breasts. I forget what her hat was like. I rather fancy I thought it was rather silly. But later she took it off.

'Well, where shall we go?' she said.

'I thought of going up West and eating and perhaps dropping in to hear some music.'

'Music. Isn't that rather dull?'

'Well, a play then.'

'I say,' she said, 'don't let's go up West. Let's go down to the East End instead. We can have some fun. It'll do you good to see how the Jews live. If you're going to work for a firm of Jews you ought to know something about them. We might have some Jewish food. I know a nice place.'

So we took a bus and went. In the Mile End Road we had a meal. I didn't like it. The food didn't smell very nice. It was spiced and strong and rather strange to eat. But Blanche liked it. Finally she said she was thirsty. 'Let's go out of here and have a drink somewhere else,' she said. 'I know a place where you can get beautiful wine, cheap.' So we went from that restaurant to another. We had some cheese and a bottle of wine – asti, I think it was. The place was Italian. The evening was stifling and everywhere people were drinking heavily and fanning themselves limply against the heat. After the wine I began to feel rather strange. I wasn't used to it and I hardly knew what I was doing. The cheese was rather salt and made me thirsty. I kept drinking almost unconsciously and my lips began to form syllables roundly and loosely. I kept staring at Blanche and thinking of her in the kimono. She in turn would stare back and we played a kind of game, carrying on a kind of conversation with glances, burning each other up, until at last she said:

'What's you name? You haven't told me yet.'

'Arthur,' I said. 'Arthur Lawson.'

'Arthur.'

The way she said it set my heart on fire. I just couldn't say anything: I simply sat looking at her. There was an intimacy then, at that moment, in the mere silences and glances between us, that went far beyond anything I had known with Hilda.

Then she saw something on the back of the menu that made her give a little cry.

'Oh, there's a circus! Oh, let's go! Oh, Arthur, you must take me.'

So we went there too. I forget the name of the theatre and really, except for some little men and women with wizened bird faces and beards, there is nothing I remember except one thing. In the middle of the show was a trapeze act. A girl was swinging backwards and forwards across the stage in readiness to somersault and the drum was rolling to rouse the audience to excitement. Suddenly the girl shouted 'I can't do it!' and let loose. She crashed down into the stalls and in a minute half the audience were standing up in a pandemonium of terror.

'Oh! Arthur, take me out.'

We went out directly. In those days women fainted more often and more easily than they do now, and I thought Blanche would faint too. As we came out into the street she leaned against me heavily and clutched my arm.

'I'll get a cab and take you home,' I said.

'Something to drink first.'

I was a bit upset myself. We had a glass of port in a public house. It must have been about ten o'clock. Before long, after the rest and the port, Blanche's eyes were quite bright again.

Soon after that we took the cab and drove home. 'Let me lean against you,' she said. I took her and held her. 'That's it,' she said. 'Hold me. Hold me tight.' It was so hot in the cab that I could hardly breathe and I could feel her face hot and moist too. 'You're so hot,' I said. She said it was her dress. The velvet coatee was too warm. 'I'll change it as soon as I get home,' she said. 'Then we'll have a drink. Some ice-cream in lemonade. That'll be nice.'

In the cab I looked down at her hair. It was amazingly black. I smiled at it softly. It was full of odours that were warm and voluptuous. But it was the blackness of it that was so wonderful and so lovely.

'Why do they call you Blanche? I said. 'When you're so black. Blanche means white.'

'How do you know I'm not white underneath?' she said.

I could not speak. No conversation I had ever had with a woman had ever gone within miles of that single sentence. I sat dazed, my heart racing. I did not know what to do. 'Hold me tight,' she said. I held her and kissed her.

I got out of the cab mechanically. In the shop she went straight upstairs. I kept thinking of what she had said. I was wild with a new and for me a delicious excitement. Downstairs the shop was in darkness and finally I could not wait for her to come down again. I went quietly upstairs to meet her.

She was coming across the landing as I reached the head of the stairs. She was in the kimono, in her bare feet.

'Where are you?' she said softly. 'I can't see you.' She came a second later and touched me.

'Just let me see if mother has turned your bed back,' she whispered.

She went into my bedroom. I followed her. She was leaning over the bed. My heart was racing with a sensation of great longing for her. She smoothed the bed with her hands and, as she did so, the kimono, held no longer, fell right apart.

And as she turned again I could see, even in the darkness, that she had nothing on underneath it at all.

III

On the following Monday morning I saw Kersch and Co. again and in the afternoon I went back to Nottingham. I had been given the job.

But curiously, for a reason I could not explain, I was no longer excited. I kept thinking of Blanche. I suppose, what with my engagement to Hilda Brownson and so on, I ought to have been uneasy and a little conscience-stricken. I was uneasy, but it was a mad uneasiness and there was no conscience at all in it. I felt reckless and feverish, almost desperate. Blanche was the first woman I had known at all on terms of intimacy, and it shattered me. All my complacent values of love and women were smashed. I had slept with Blanche on Saturday night and again on Sunday and the effect on me was one of almost catastrophic ecstasy.

That was something I had never known at all with Hilda: I had never come near it. I am not telling this, emphasising the physical side of it and singling out the more passionate implications of it, merely for the sake of telling it. I want to make clear that I had undergone a revolution: a revolution brought about, too, simply by a kimono and a girl's bare body underneath it. And since it was a revolution that changed my whole life it seems to me that I ought to make the colossal effect of it quite clear, now and for always.

I know, now, that I ought to have broken it off with Hilda at once. But I didn't. She was so pleased at my getting the Kersch job that to have told her would have been as cruel as taking away a doll from a child. I couldn't tell her.

A month later we were married. My heart was simply not in it. I wasn't there. All the time I was thinking of and, in imagination, making love to Blanche. We spent our honeymoon at Bournemouth in September. Kersch and Co. had been very nice and the result was that I was not to take up the new appointment until the twenty-fifth of the month.

I say appointment. It was the word the Brownsons always used. From the very first they were not very much in love with my going to work in London at all and taking Hilda with me. I myself had no parents, but Hilda was their only child. That put what seemed to me a snobbish premium on her. They set her on a pedestal. My job was nothing beside Hilda. They began to dictate what we should do and how and where we ought to live, and finally Mrs Brownson suggested that we all go to London and choose the flat in which we were to live. I objected. Then Hilda cried and there was an unpleasant scene in which Pa Brownson said that he thought I was unreasonable and that all Mrs Brownson was trying to do was to ensure that I could give Hilda as good a home as she had always had. He said something else about God guiding us as He had always guided them. We must put our trust in God. But God or no God, I was determined that if we were going to live in a flat in London the Brownsons shouldn't choose it. I would choose it myself. Because even then I knew where, if it was humanly possible, I wanted it to be.

In the end I went to London by myself. I talked round Hilda, and Hilda talked round her mother, and her mother, I suppose, talked round her father. At any rate I went. We decided on a flat at twenty-five shillings a week if we could get it. It was then about the twentieth of September.

I went straight from St Pancras to Blanche. It was a lovely day, blue and soft. It was a pain for me merely to be alive. I got to the shop just as Blanche was going out. We almost bumped into each other.

'Arthur!'

The way she said it made me almost sick with joy. She had on a tight fawn costume and a little fussy brown hat. 'Arthur! I was just going out. You just caught me. But mother can go instead. Oh! Arthur.' Her mother came out of the back room and in a minute Blanche had taken off her hat and costume and her mother had gone out instead of her, leaving us alone in the shop.

We went straight upstairs. There was no decision, no asking, no consent in it at all. We went straight up out of a tremendous equal passion for each other. We were completely in unison, in desire and act and consummation and everything. Someone came in the shop and rang the bell loudly while we were upstairs, but it made no difference. We simply existed for each other. There was no outside world. She seemed to me then amazingly rich and mature and yet sweet. She was like a pear, soft and full-juiced and overflowing with passion. Beside her Hilda seemed like an empty eggshell.

I stayed with the Hartmans that night and the next. There were still three days to go before the Kersch job began. Then I stayed another night. I telegraphed Hilda, "Delayed. Returning certain to-morrow.'

I never went. I was bound, heart and soul, to Blanche Hartman. There was never any getting away from it. I was so far gone that it was not until the second day of that second visit that I noticed the name Hartman at all.

'I'm going to stay here,' I said to Blanche. 'Lodge here and live with you. Do you want me?'

'Arthur, Arthur.'

'My God,' I said. 'Don't.' I simply couldn't bear the repetition of my name. It awoke every sort of fierce passion in me.

Then after a time I said: 'There's something I've got to tell you.'

'I know,' she said. 'About another girl. It doesn't matter. I don't want to hear. I could tell you about other men.'

'No, but listen,' I said. 'I'm married.' I told her all about Hilda.

'It doesn't matter,' she said. 'It makes no difference. You could be a Mormon and it wouldn't matter.'

And after that, because it mattered nothing to her, it mattered nothing to me. There is no conscience in passion. When I did think of Hilda and the Brownsons it was like the squirt of a syphon on to a blazing furnace. I really had no conscience at all. I walked out of one life into another as easily as from one room into another.

The only difficulty was Kersch and Co. It was there that Hilda would inquire for me as soon as I failed to turn up.

Actually I got out of the Kersch difficulty as easily as I got out of the rest. I didn't go back there either.

IV

I went on living with Blanche until the war broke out. I got another job. Electrical engineers were scarcer in those days. Then, as soon as the war broke out, I joined up.

In a way it was almost a relief. Passion can go too far and one can have too much of it. I was tired out by a life that was too full of sublimity. It was not that I was tired of Blanche. She remained as irresistible to me as when I had first seen her in the green and orange kimono. It was only that I was tired of the constant act of passion itself. My spirit, as it were, had gone stale and I needed rest.

The war gave it me. As soon as I came home for my first leave I knew it was the best thing that could have happened to me. Blanche and I went straight back to the almost unearthly plane of former intimacy. It was the old almost catastrophic ecstasy.

I say almost catastrophic. Now, when I think of it, I see that it was really catastrophic. One cannot expect a woman to feed off the food of the gods and then suddenly, because one man among a million is not there, to go back on a diet of nothing at all. I am trying to be reasonable about this. I am not blaming Blanche. It is the ecstasy between us that I am blaming. It could not have been otherwise than catastrophic.

I always think it odd that I did not see the catastrophe coming before it did. But perhaps if I had seen it coming it would have ceased to be a catastrophe. I don't know. I only know that I came home in 1917, unexpectedly, and found that Blanche was carrying on with another man.

I always remembered that Mrs Hartman looked extraordinarily scared as I walked into the shop that day. She was an assured, masterful woman and it was not at all like her to be scared. After a minute or so I went upstairs and in my bedroom a man was just buttoning up his waistcoat. Blanche was not there, but I understood.

I was furious, but the fury did not last. Blanche shattered it. She was a woman to whom passion was as essential as bread. She reminded me of that. But she reminded me also of something else. She reminded me that that I was not married to her.

'But the moral obligation!' I raged.

'It's no good,' she said. 'I can't help it. It's no more than kissing to me. Don't be angry, honey. If you can't take me as I am you're not bound to take me at all.'

And in the end she melted my fury. 'What's between us is different from all the rest,' she said. I believed her and she demonstrated it to me too. And I clung to that until the end of the war.

But when I came home finally it had gone farther than that. There was more than one man. They came to the shop, travellers in the sweet-trade, demobilised young officers with cars. They called while I was at my job.

I found out about it. This time I didn't say anything. I did something instead. I gave up what the Brownsons would have called my appointment.

'But what have you done that for?' Blanche said.

'I can't stand being tied by a job any more,' I said. 'I'll work here. We'll develop the shop. There's money in it.'

'Who's going to pay for it?'

'I will.'

Just before I married Hilda I had nearly a hundred and fifty pounds in the bank. I had had it transferred to a London branch and it was almost all of it still there. I drew it out and in the summer of 1919 I spent nearly £80 of it on renovating the Hartman's shop. Blanche was delighted. She supervised the decorations and the final colour scheme of the combined shop and café was orange and green.

'Like your kimono,' I said. 'You remember it? That old one?'

'Oh! Arthur. I've got it.'

'Put it on,' I said.

She went upstairs and put it on. In about a minute I followed her. It was like old times. It brought us together again.

'Tell me something,' I said. 'That first day, when I came in. You hadn't anything on underneath, had you?'

'No,' she said. 'I'd just had a bath and it was all I had time to slip on.'

'By God, kiss me.'

She kissed me and I held her very tight. Her body was thicker and heavier now, but she was still lovely. It was all I asked. I was quite happy.

Then something else happened. I got used to seeing men in the shop. Most of them shot off now when they saw me, but one day when I came back from the bank there was a man in the living-room.

He was an oldish chap, with pepper and salt hair cut rather short.

'Hello,' I said, 'what's eating you?' I got to be rather short with any man I saw hanging about the place.

'Nothing's eating me,' he said. 'It's me who wants something to eat.'

'Oh! Who are you?'

'My name's Hartman,' he said.

I looked straight at his hair. It was Blanche's father. And in a minute I knew that he was out of prison.

I don't know why, but it was more of a shock to me than Blanche's affairs with other men. Blanche and I could fight out the question of unfaithfulness between ourselves, but the question of a criminal in the house was different.

'He isn't a criminal,' Blanche said. 'He's easily led and he was led away by others. Be kind to him, honey.'

Perhaps I was soft. Perhaps I had no right to do anything. It was not my house, it was not my father. Blanche was not even my wife. What could I possibly do but let him stay?

That summer we did quite well with the new café. We made a profit of nine and very often ten or eleven pounds a week. Hartman came home in May. In July things began to get worse. Actually, with the summer at its height, they ought to have been better. But the takings dropped to six and even five pounds. Blanche and her mother kept saying that they couldn't understand it.

But I could. Or at least I could after a long time. It was Hartman. He was not only sponging on me, but robbing the till too. All the hard-earned savings of the shop were being boozed away by Hartman.

I wanted to throw him out. But Blanche and her mother wouldn't hear of it. 'He's nothing but a damned scoundrel,' I shouted.

'He's my father,' Blanche said.

That was the beginning of it. I date the antagonism between us and also the estrangement between us from that moment. It was never the same afterwards. I could stand Blanche being nothing more or less than a whore, but it was the thought of the old man and the thought of my own stupidity and folly that enraged me and finally almost broke me up.

Perhaps I shouldn't have written the word whore, and I wouldn't have done if it wasn't for the fact that, as I sit here, my heart is really almost broken.

v

I am sitting in what used to be my bedroom. We have changed it into a sitting-room now. We ought to have it done up. We haven't had new paper on it for seven or eight years.

I am just fifty. I think Blanche is just about fifty, too. She is out somewhere. It's no use thinking where. Passion is still as essential to her as bread. It means no more to her and I have long since given up asking where she goes. And somehow – and this is the damnable part of it all – I am still fond of her, but gently and rather foolishly now. What I feel for her most is regret. Not anger and not passion. I couldn't keep up with her pace. She long since outdistanced me in the matter of emotions.

Mrs Hartman is dead. I am sorry. She was likeable and though sometimes I didn't trust her I think she liked me. Hartman still hangs on. I keep the till-money locked up, but somehow he picks the locks, and there it is. He's too clever for me and I can't prove it. I feel as if, now, I am in a prison far more complete than any Hartman was ever in. It is a bondage directly inherited from that first catastrophic passion for Blanche. It's that, really, that I can't escape. It binds me irrevocably. I know that I shall never escape.

Last night, for instance, I had a chance to escape. I know of course that I'm a free man and that I am not married to Blanche and that I could walk out now and never come back. But this was different.

Hilda asked for me. I was in the shop, alone, just about six c'clock. I was looking at the paper. We don't get many people in the café now, but I always have the evening paper, in case. This district has gone down a lot and the café of course has gone

down with it. We don't get the people in that we did. And as I
was reading the paper the wireless was on. At six o'clock, the
dance band ended and in another moment or two someone was
saying my name.

'Will Arthur Lawson, last heard of in London twenty-five
years ago, go at once to the Nottingham Infirmary, where his
wife, Hilda Lawson, is dangerously ill.'

That was all. No one but me, in this house I mean, heard it.
Afterwards no one mentioned it. Round here they think my
name is Hartman. It was as though it had never happened.

But it was for me all right. When I heard it I stood stunned,
as though something had struck me. I almost died where I stood,
at the foot of the stairs.

Then after a bit I got over it enough to walk upstairs to the
sitting-room. I did not know quite what I was doing. I felt faint
and I sat down. I thought it over. After a minute I could see that
there was no question of going. If it had been Blanche – yes. But
not Hilda. I couldn't face it. And I just sat there and thought
not of what I should do but what I might have done.

I thought of that hot day in 1911, and the Kersch job and how
glad I was to get it. I thought about Hilda. I wondered what she
looked like now and what she had done with herself for twenty-
five years and what she had suffered. Finally I thought of that
catastrophic ecstasy with Blanche, and then of the kimono. And
I wondered how things might have gone if the Hartmans' ice-
cream freezer had never broken and if Blanche had been dressed
as any other girl would have been dressed that day.

And thinking and wondering, I sat there and cried like a
child.

BREEZE ANSTEY

The two girls, Miss Anstey and Miss Harvey, had been well educated; but it was another matter getting a job. They first came together one summer, quite casually, and in the August of the same year, having no prospects, began farming together. In this they felt shrewd; their farm was to be so different. Not a common farm, with pigs or corn, sheep or poultry, but a farm for herbs. 'Where you will find', they said a 'thousand people farming the ordinary things, you won't find one farming herbs.' There was something in this. But in their hearts they liked it because they felt it to be different, a little poetical, charged with some unspecified but respectable romance. They had ideals. And that autumn, when they rented a small cottage in Hampshire, with an acre of land, on the edge of the forest, they felt existence for the first time very keenly; they felt independent; they had only to stretch out and pick up handfuls of sweetness and solitude.

The forest opened into a clearing where their house stood, and oak and rhododendron and holly pressed in and down on them and their land, securing their world. The plot was already cultivated, and they intended to grow the herbs, at first, in small lots, taking variety to be salvation. For the first year they would work hard, cultivating; after that they would advertise; after that sell. They divided responsibility. Miss Harvey, the practical one, took charge of the secretarial work and kept accounts and made plans. Miss Anstey had imagination and knew a little botany; she could talk of carpel and follicle, of glandulosa and hirsutum. In late August, in a world still warm and dark and secure in leaf, the first bundles of herbs began to arrive; and pressing out the small rare sweetnesses and joyfully smelling each other's hands, they felt sure of everything. Above all, they felt very sure of each other.

From the first they were devoted. Miss Anstey was the younger, twenty-three. Miss Harvey was twenty-eight. They called each other Breeze and Lorn. No one seemed clear about the origins and reasons of Miss Anstey's name, which did not express her small, slimmish, very compact and not at all volatile figure. Her hair was almost white; her nostrils were rather arched; she looked Scandinavian. She had a beautiful way of smiling at nothing, absently. She had another way of smiling at Miss Harvey, chiefly when she was not looking. It was a kind of mouse smile, furtive and timid, not fully expressed. It had in it the beginnings of adoration.

Miss Harvey was heavily built with thick eye-brows and black short hair. She was very strong and wore no stockings and her legs went red, really ham-coloured, in the sun. She was attractive in a full-blooded, jolly way. She was like some heavy, friendly mare, with her black mane falling over her face and her thick strong thighs and her arched way of walking with her shoulders back. Nothing was too much trouble for her; nothing daunted or depressed her.

The two girls at first worked hard, scorning outside help, happy together. They began with three hundred pounds. Breeze said: 'We should be very strict and apportion everything out and pay weekly.' They did this. Rent would cost them fifty a year, so they opened a new account at the bank, paid in a year's rent and signed a banker's order. That settled, they hoped to live on a hundred a year, the two of them. That left a hundred and fifty for seeds and plants, expenses and saving. 'We should save seventy-five,' Lorn said. All this was theory. In practice it did not turn out so well.

It was a long time, almost a whole winter and a spring, before they noticed it. In autumn they were pre-occupied. The autumn went on, that year, a long time, drawn up into some too-dreamy twilight of mild airs and leaves that hung on and kept out the low sunlight like blankets of dark leaf-wool. August and September were hot. Planted too soon, their first plants died. In a panic they ordered more, then kept the water bucket going. Their well got low. That was a real problem. They could not bathe. Lorn made little portable tents of lath and newspaper to shade the plants, and by September they had learnt to wash hair, face and feet in one kettle of water. Up to that time they had not worn stockings, and often not shoes. They had to give that up. They wore shoes and washed their feet twice a week. That was real hardship.

But they were not troubled about it. They liked it. It was part of the new life, more still of the new independence. It was fun. It was hardship only by comparison. Instinctively they felt that cleanliness and godliness were one, perhaps, after all. They longed for water, not seeing until then how much life might depend on it.

Then Breeze made a discovery. They felt it to be miraculous. Wandering off the forest path to look for sweet chestnuts, she came upon a pond, not a hundred yards from the house. Shaded by trees, it was quite deep. Round it marsh and sedge were dry, the earth cracked in thick crust blisters, and she could see where wild ponies had broken it up, coming down to drink. She fetched Lorn, who said: 'We could fetch twenty buckets in an hour and then bathe.' Breeze got some water in her hands. 'Why carry it?' she said. The water was brownish, leaf-stained, but clear. 'Why take the mountain to Mahomed? We could come down here and bathe.'

'Not in daylight.'

'Why shouldn't we? We would have costumes on. Who's to say anything?'

'Nobody. But this is the forest. You know people are always wandering about.'

'All right. Then we could come when the sun's gone down. It's warm enough.'

It was too good to miss. After sunset they took soap and towels and costumes and went into what was already half darkness under the trees. The pond was black, unreflective, and there was some sense, under the pitch dark roof of forest branches, of peculiar secrecy. As she took off her clothes, Breeze said: 'I'm going in without anything on.' She stood undressing, feet in the water. 'It's warm,' she said. 'It's wonderfully warm. Don't put anything on. It's warm and like silk. It would be wicked to put anything on.'

She went in naked, swam round and looked back to Miss Harvey. She was putting her costume on.

'Oh! Don't!'

'What do you think I am?' Lorn said. 'Venus?'

'Yes, but it's the feeling. It's wonderful. And it's quite warm.'

'Is it swimmable?'

'It's about four feet. Look.'

She swam off, turning, breasting back. When she stood
up again she saw Lorn knee-deep in water. She had nothing on.
Looking at her the girl was struck by an odd spasm of pleasure.
It ran up her legs like a hot current of blood and pounded up,
finally, in her chest. She felt, for about a second, strange and
weak. There was aroused in her an unconscious exquisite
capacity for pain and she did not know what to do with it. It was
like a shock.

'I thought you said it was warm?'

'Go under.'

It was all she could say. She did not know why, but the sight
of Lorn filled her with a queer excitement. Lorn was bigger than
she had imagined, more mature, more ripe. She felt absurdly
young beside her. She looked at her large brown-nippled breasts
and saw in them the potential beauty of motherhood. The thick
smooth flesh of the whole body had some beautiful power
to attract and comfort. Lorn went under, up to her neck. She
came up heavily, dripping, to stand in water up to her knees. The
girl looked at her again, in a spell of adoration.

'It's muddy!' Lorn said.

'No. Not here. Come over here. It's lovely. Like sand. Why
don't you swim?'

'I'll walk. I'm not certain of it.'

She took heavy water-bound strides across the pond, arms
folded under breasts.

'Shall we wash each other?' Breeze said.

'Puzzle, find the soap.'

'I brought it.'

'Good. Wash me. Wash my sins away. Wash my back.'

The younger girl stood with her habitual absent smile of
adoration, rubbing the soap in her hands. 'Swim round while I
get some lather.'

Lorn swam, heavy and white, in a ponderous circle, then came
back to Breeze. The water was up to their middles. The young
girl's hands were white with the lather. Lorn bent her back. She
put her hands on her knees and the girl began to soap her back,
absently tender.

'Oh! that's lovely. Lovely. Wash up as far as possible and
down as far possible. Why is it so nice to have your back
rubbed?'

'I don't know, why is it? Have the soap and rub your front.'

Lorn made lather and rubbed it over her chest, until her breasts were snow bubbles with the brown mouth of nipple alone uncovered. Then she turned, and Breeze stared at her.

'What are you looking at?'

'You're so big. I didn't think you were so big, Lorn.'

'Well, I like that! Big. You mean fat.'

'No. Lorn, I like it. You look like a woman. Not half of one. Look at me. You could hold what there is of me in one hand.'

She looked down at her small, almost stiff breasts, her slight figure.

'I ought to wear more support,' Lorn said. 'I shall be all over the place. Look at you. You're the ideal of every female in Christendom. All you need wear is half a yard of silk. Turn round and let me scrub you, child.'

Breeze turned, bent her back and Lorn rubbed her with large soap-soft hands. The sensation of the soft drawn-down palms was something exquisite, physically thrilling to the girl.

'Harder. I want to get really clean. Harder. Wash me all over. Everywhere.'

'Anything else, Madam?'

'Your hands are bigger than mine. Soap me all over.'

'Extra charge.' They both laughed. 'Front portion extra. Owing to my sensibility, Madam.'

'Oh! Lorn, you're a dear. It's a grand feeling to be washed again.'

She stood with arms over her head, hands clasped on her hair, and turned round, and Lorn soaped her chest and shoulders. Her hands took wide strong sweeps across and down the girl's body. The soap covered the small almost absurd bust in snow froth.

'Oh! it's grand, Lorn. Lovely!'

'We must get out.'

'Oh! must we? Need we?'

'I can hardly see you. It must be awfully late.'

'It's nice in the twilight. It's warm. That's all that matters. One swim.'

She swam round the darkening pond. Above, when she turned and floated, she could see the autumn evening sky colourless beyond the forest branches. The trees seemed very near, the sky correspondingly far off. She felt extraordinarily happy, her mind quiet, the exquisite sensation of shock gone. She floated serenely on the memory of emotions. She could smell the forest, dampish, closed-in, the sweetish odour of living and falling leaves, and she felt almost like crying.

Then she stood in shallow water and, looking up, saw that Lorn was out. She saw the white flap of the towel. Something made her hurry out too, some sudden and not quite conscious impulse to be near her.

She ran out, splashing. She stood quivering on the cracked mud among the sedge, and got her towel. She looked at Lorn and in a moment the sensation of physical shock, like some electric start of nerves, struck her again. She rubbed her body hard, trembling.

'I feel wonderful,' Lorn said.

Lorn put her skirt over her head. It was pale pink, almost colourless in the tree twilight. Breeze did not speak. She felt nearer to Lorn, at that moment, than she had ever done to anyone in her life. It was an attachment not only of emotion, but of body. She felt drawn to Lorn physically, in a beautiful way, by some idealised force of attraction. It elated her and, for a second or two, stupefied her with its strength and gentleness.

It was only when Lorn said at last, 'Come on, Breezy, cover your shame, child, do, and get a stitch or two on,' that she came back to her normal self. Even then she did not speak. She wanted to speak and she stood trying to speak, to frame some words to express at least a hint of her affection, but nothing came.

In five minutes she was dressed. The forest was then almost dark, and looking up at the fragments of sky above the heavy mass of trees she felt some kind of balm in them. She felt completely herself, at rest again.

II

'Lorn,' Breeze said, 'you must have been in love, sometime?'

It was early January, and now they had nothing to do, on the long winter nights, except read and talk and evolve unrealised theories about the future, the farm, the world, themselves and men. They argued hard, quarrelled a little; but the central core of affection between them was never soured or shaken. It was

dark south-west weather, wild warm days of rain followed by
black nights, when they could do very little outside. They settled
down after tea and read books, had supper at eight and generally
talked till ten. 'The less we go out, the less we spend,' they said.

'Yes,' Lorn said.

'But when was it? You never told me. You never said anything.'

'I should have told you if I'd ever told anybody.'

'Did it go on long?'

'Two years. If you can call that long.'

'Did you – did it ever come to anything?'

'Yes.'

Breeze had wanted to know this. She felt somehow that it
concerned her, was important. She had felt, sometimes, that it
might distress her. Now she felt almost indifferent, only curious.
As something in the past, it hardly touched her.

'Only once?'

'No. A lot. Almost every time we saw each other. Almost
whenever we could.'

'It must be a long time ago, or you couldn't talk about it.'

'Three or four years. Four years.'

'Who wanted it most? Did he, or you?'

'Both of us. We both did. We couldn't go on without it. It
wouldn't have meant anything.'

Breeze did not speak. She wanted to ask something else. Lorn
said :

'Why this sudden discussion of my affairs, young lady?'

'We swore we'd have no secrets.'

'Well, I've told you now.'

'Lorn,' Breeze said, 'what's it like? The loving part. The
proper loving.'

'Sometimes there's nothing there.'

'And others?'

'You must know. I can't explain. It's something you can't tell.'

'Like some electric shock?'

'No.'

'What then?'

'Partly electric. But more a fulfilment. You take something
from each other, and something in you is fulfilled.'

'That doesn't make sense.'

'I know. It's a thing that doesn't make sense. Why should it?'
Breeze said earnestly: 'Does it change you?'

'Yes.'

'How? Physically?'

'Partly. It must do. But I don't think you'd notice it anyway, whatever it does.'

'Not till afterwards?'

'No.' Lorn got up. 'I don't think you do till afterwards. Till you must do without it.'

She went into the kitchen, gathered plates and knives and forks from the dresser, and came back to lay supper. Breeze looked at her with an absent smile, and said:

'Why is it all over?'

Lorn flacked the cloth, smoothed it, her eyes looking down flat on its dead whiteness.

'I never said it was all over.'

Breeze could not speak. She felt it instantly, for some reason, to be something between them. She felt the minute beginnings of a queer jealousy. It was not active; it moved in her consciousness like a remote pain, pricking her.

When it faded, in a moment, and she was able to speak, she said: 'I don't see what you mean. How do you mean, it's not all over?'

'Oh! Just that. We had a pact and parted, but very shortly he'll be home again, and then – '

'Home?'

'He's in India.'

'India? A soldier?'

'An army doctor.'

'Let me make the cocoa,' Breeze said.

She bent down before the fire, pushed the kettle against the logs. The kettle sang a little. She straightened up, mixed cocoa and milk in the two cups, on the table, while Lorn cut bread. Breeze felt strangely anxious, as though Lorn had told her she was ill or was going away. Remote, not fully conscious, her anxiety pricked her, as the jealousy had done, like a small pain. The kettle boiled and she made cocoa, half looking at Lorn. How very strong Lorn was: big wind-cut arms, solid neck, such friendly strength, so warm. She stood absently fascinated, the small pain dying away.

'It was a question of finishing his period of service,' Lorn said 'He wanted to go back.'

'He wanted to go back more than he wanted you.'

'No. He wanted to go back. I understood that all right. I wanted him to go back. I was only twenty-three, just out of college.'

'What difference did that make? If it was all you say it was?'

'That was just it. We wanted to see if it made a difference. If it made a difference, well, there it was. If it didn't, then he could come back, and we'd get married.'

They sat by the fire, with cocoa and bread and cheese, Lorn with her skirts up, warming her knees.

'I think that's awful,' Breeze said. 'For all it mattered, you were married. Nothing could alter that.'

'I don't see it. We'd made love. But that was something we couldn't help. We could help marriage, if we ever got to it. Hence the arrangement.'

'It was like making a business of it,' Breeze said. She was upset, trembling. 'It's a hateful thing. It was like making a business of it, it was like making a business of it! It was awful!'

'Breeze, Breeze.'

'You don't deny it, do you?'

'Breeze.'

'Who proposed it, he or you?'

'He did. He was older.'

'Then he wasn't worthy of you! How could he be? Proposing that. Proposing an awful thing like that. He wasn't worthy of you!'

'Breeze. I can't bear to hear it.'

The words were too much for the girl. She began to cry, deeply, with shame and some unhappiness she could not define. She set her cocoa on the hearth, could not see for tears, and spilt it. Lorn put her cup down beside it and put her arms round Breeze's neck. 'You're not to cry. Why are you crying? Breeze. It's silly to cry.' She held her, strongly, against the warm resilient bulk of her large body. They sat like mother and child, bound by grief and comfort. 'You hear me? You're not to cry.'

'It does me good,' Breeze said. 'I shall feel better. Hold me. I shall feel better.'

'I'm holding you,' Lorn said. 'I've got you.'
'Hold me tighter.'

III

By April things had begun to move. The rows of herbs began
to look vigorous and full of promise. Turned over and hoed, the
earth was sweet and black. The two girls planted fresh supplies
of plants, new varieties, and sowed seeds. They got up early and
worked on into the bright spring evenings, and in the evenings,
after a warm day, they could smell the forest, the strong,
vigorous and yet almost drowsy odour of a great mass of trees
breaking into leaf. They were enchanted by the new life, by an
existence in which, as never before, they felt they had a purpose.
They lived physically. Tired out, earth-stained, they came indoors as darkness came on and sat down in the little kitchen-
sitting-room in the cottage and sat on without speaking and
watched the fading out of the primrosy twilights, their minds
dumbly content. Too tired to talk, they ate supper, went to bed
early and were up again at six.

They spent energy needlessly. Lorn did the digging : she had a
large four-pronged fork and used it bravely, like a weapon,
knocking the soil about, throwing out every stone. She had some
strenuous ambition to see the land as smooth as sand, without
stones, immaculate. She did a man's work, and her body got to
have some kind of male awkwardness about it : a longer stride,
cruder grasp, a way of straddling as she stood. Close to her every
day, Breeze did not notice it. She did the hoeing, generally, and
the labelling and sowing, and the little artistic things : she would
have a little rock-garden by the back door, on the south side,
with patches of purple horned viola and winey primulas and
then lavender hedges down the paths, giving vistas. 'You and
your vistas,' Lorn said. But vistas were important; they had
the effect of making things seem, to Breeze, not quite as they
were, and the illusion was precious. She felt the beauty of
things keenly; she could not bear ugliness, and spring drove her
into small inexpressible ecstasies. Beauty was everything. It
impinged upon her sharply, with pain, so that she felt something
immensely precious and personal about the spring. It was for her
and she could not share it. Unlike Lorn, she worked in a kind of

semi-consciousness, not bravely, but with a kind of absent per-
sistence. She spent greater energy of spirit, dreaming as she
worked, and it seemed as if the spring days sucked her up, body
and spirit and all, leaving her at times almost crying with weari-
ness. She did not understand this supreme tiredness at all. She
worked harder to overcome it, splashing her hoe crudely with
clenched hands, forcing herself into the full consciousness of the
act, breaking down her dreamy passivity. All the time, and all
through spring and summer, it seemed to get worse. The great
massed ring of forest seemed to shut out life sometimes, so that
she felt imprisoned by a wall of wood and leaf, sucked by a
beauty that was almost parasitic into an awful listlessness of
spirit that she could not understand. All the time, in contrast to
Lorn, she seemed to get more and not less feminine: much
slighter, very brown and delicate, with a light detached beauty
and an almost irritating remoteness of spirit. It was as though she
needed waking up; as though the best of her were not alive.

Then Lorn noticed it. By the end of May the oaks were in full
flower and the forest stood like an olive cloud. The great polished
bushes of rhododendron split pinkly into blossom, and the rare
sweet-scented wild azaleas, pale yellow. The forest breathed out
its enormous but not quite tangible sweetness and sucked back,
in turn, the still more enormous breath of the life about it. There
were days when, under the shelter of the too-close trees, life was
utterly stupefied.

'I get so tired,' Lorn said. 'How is it? Do you get tired?'

'Yes. I didn't want to say anything about it. I thought it was
just myself.'

'But how is it? What's the reason for it?'

'I feel there's no air.'

'Possibly we need a change,' Lorn said. 'We might have been
working too hard.'

'But it's not the work. I'm tired if I sit still.'

'Even so, a change would do us no harm.'

So they went, for three days, to London. For economy they
stayed at a little scrubby hotel off Guildford Street. They ate
cheaply; saw films cheaply. London tired them, but in a new
way; it stripped off the old lassitude like a heavy skin. They had
a double room with one bed, and they stayed in bed, every morning, as late as they dare. And at night, when Lorn took the

younger girl in her arms and mothered her down to sleep, Breeze felt a tender and inexplicable restful transfusion of strength take place. She lay close to Lorn and felt again, still not with full consciousness, that queer stirring of remote affection that was like a small pain. It was beautiful, but it was also reassuring, a very wonderful comfort, a strength against trouble. One night Breeze woke up with a start, frightened, not knowing where she was, feeling alone in a strange place. She started wildly up in bed, and said: 'What is it? I don't want it! I don't want it to come, please! I don't want it,' but in a moment Lorn stretched out her arms and took her back, saying, 'Silly kid, silly kid,' in a voice of strong but amused tenderness.

'What made you wake up in the night?' she said next morning.

'I was in trouble,' Breeze said. 'It was you I wanted. I was all right when I'd got you.'

That afternoon they went to see a woman, the secretary of an organisation specialising in the distribution of rural products. Lorn had heard of her and had written, asking for an interview. This woman made them see various new aspects of things. She raised hopes. Where they had seen, vaguely, that some day they must organise distribution in order to keep going, they now began to see, rationally, how such organisation must be planned, how far ahead it must be planned, how little they had done. They would need, in time, packers, a mail-order system, expert knowledge on this, that and the other. Miss Wills, the secretary, wore light amber rimmed spectacles and spoke in a voice of vinegar and treacle which both Breeze and Lorn disliked. But they felt, beyond the voice and the spectacles, a shrewd, clever, no-nonsense personality. 'You're on a good thing, you girls, if you'll work hard, and come to me whenever you're stuck. But don't try to be elegant. You're amateurs and you can't afford to be amateurs. We're in touch with all kinds of markets here and we can take all your stuff, if it's good, on a commission basis. You've got to look at things rationally, Miss Harvey, without a lot of sticky romance. When shall you be ready for production?'

Lorn told her. 'We hope to be in a position to do something next year. That's what we thought.'

'All right. Up to date, what have you done? I mean regarding organisation?'

'Not much.'

'Then you must start. I think it might be as well if I came down to see you. Discuss things. I could come' – she looked up a diary, marked it off in blue pencil – 'in a fortnight. That is, after Whitsun. I'll say the week-end of June 5. Let me know if that suits you. Drop me a card: yes or no. That'll be enough.'

They went away full of hope, excited. They saw the thing in rational outline at last, no longer some cloudy embryo of romance. They saw that they must work hard, plan, think, that it was not enough to waste an energy of body and spirit. They saw that by working in the dark, they had worked for nothing; they had given themselves up, wholeheartedly, to emptiness.

'I think that's what made us so tired,' Lorn said. 'Working and working and not knowing quite where we were going.'

'Oh! let's get home, Lorn. I want to be back, doing something. I don't want to be away any longer.'

They went back on the following day, excitement still strong, their whole hopes concentrated on the pole of the ideal pointed out by the secretary. 'I didn't like her,' Breeze said. 'She was too sweet and too sure, but she knew what was what. Oh! Lorn, I'm glad we went. We've *got* something now. We can look forward to something.'

When they arrived back at the cottage, in the late afternoon, they found a slip on the front door-mat: a cable awaited Lorn at the post office. She at once got on her bicycle and rode with excitement into Lyndhurst. She was back in half an hour. By that time Breeze had tea laid. Lorn laid the cable on the table, for Breeze to read. The cable had been handed in at Port Said, two days previously, and it said:

Expect arrive London Friday telegraph me Grosvenor Hotel when and where possible meet you have plans for future: Vernon.

'He's coming home,' Lorn said. She stood in silence for a moment, and then began to cry. Her strength seemed to vanish at once, she stood weak and in some way foolish, womanish, miserable with joy. All the time Breeze stood apart from her, repelled by some unaccountable feeling of dislike, not knowing what to do.

IV

She was caught up, from that moment, by the force of a peculiar jealousy. She got fixed in her mind, as though by some fierce and abrupt photographic flash, a fully realised picture of the man who was coming. He was about thirty, an easy sociable being, with large, cold medical hands, a man of assurance, with the blond aloof sobriety of the English middle class. She saw also, for some reason, his mother in the background. Why, she did not know, but she saw the mother as some skinny and also aloof halo behind the man. She was holding a cablegram too, and smiling, with indulgent proud stretched lips, like some absurd filmic emblem of maternity and sacrifice: the brave waiting for the brave. She felt that she hated her too.

She saw the change in Lorn with identical clarity. Emotion sharpened her before she knew it. With quiet derision she saw Lorn get on her bicycle, the next morning, to bike off to send her wire. She was not prepared for the sudden switch over from adoration to contempt. She had not time to consider it or defend herself from it when it came. It hit her, striking from within, before she had time to think. 'Lorn looks so silly, rushing off. Rushing off like a school-kid.' Lorn, getting on her bicycle in a hurry, had got her skirt bundled beneath her, showing the laddered and worn tops of her working stockings. She looked, for a second, ungainly, heavily ridiculous. The darned stockings and the gap of bare red flesh above them looked ugly. 'Her legs are ugly. Why doesn't she pull her skirts down?' She rode off with excited haste, her thick legs pounding on the bicycle pedals. 'She's got the saddle too low. She hasn't raised it since I used it. Her knees stick out.' The impressions were instinctive, having no incentive from the conscious self. She could not control them.

Lorn was gone an hour. Breeze worked, meanwhile, on the plot, hoeing among rows of thyme and parsley. It was warm, heavy weather; weeds were coming fast. Breeze kept looking towards the house. She heard at last Lorn's bicycle bell and, looking up, saw Lorn herself pushing the bicycle up the path: pushing heavily, panting, excited, thick legs lumping down on the path, head forward, mouth open. Instinctively the impression leapt to mind: 'She thumps her feet down like a horse. Why doesn't she hold herself straight?' Lorn was untidy, hot from the ride. 'Her face looks awful. Like raw meat. Has she been to

Lyndhurst and back like that?' Lorn almost flung the bicycle against the water-butt at the house corner and thumped into the house, catching her foot against the step, stumbling. 'She looks as though she doesn't know what she's doing. She looks stupid. Only half there.'

She went on hoeing. Lorn did not come out of the house. For a time Breeze did not take much notice; then half an hour passed, an hour, and it was almost noon. Breeze began to get more and more impatient, hoeing fiercely, chopping the hoe hard against the soft dry earth, raising dust. What was Lorn doing? Why didn't she come out, just to say Hullo? Hungry, Breeze remembered then that it was Lorn's turn to cook. That explained it. Even so, she felt inexplicably and persistently angry, against her will. She hoed until her shoes and legs were soot-powdered with dust and her body muck-sweaty and her insides weak with hunger.

Then at twelve-thirty she dropped the hoe and went into the house. She registered, at once, a number of unpleasant impressions: no smell of dinner, no table laid, no Lorn, nothing. Wherever was Lorn? She wrenched open the stairs door and shouted her name.

'Lorn! Lorn! For goodness sake!'

And at once Lorn replied, easily, almost sweetly: 'Yes? Want anything?'

In vacant fury, Breeze stood at the foot of the stairs. 'I thought it was your turn to cook? What have you been doing? You've been back from Lyndhurst hours.'

'I know. Come up a second. I want to tell you something.'

Breeze went upstairs, into Lorn's bedroom. Lorn was sitting at her dressing-table in new peach-coloured slip and knickers, making up. She had a clean huckaback towel over her shoulders and was rubbing a white skin-cream over her face; then, as Breeze came in, she took the towel off her shoulders and wiped her hands and, very carefully, her lips. Bare again, her shoulders looked heavy and coarse, without grace. Breeze stood still, at the door; she could see Lorn's face in the mirror. She did not know what to do or say or what to make of it. Emotion and face-cream had made Lorn's face somehow shining and puffed. It looked faintly gross: not Lorn's face at all, but the face of some absurd obese stranger.

'What's come over you?' Breeze said.

'He's coming down this afternoon,' Lorn said, 'by the four o'clock.'

'How do you know? I thought you telegraphed.'

'I telephoned. I telephoned the hotel instead. I spoke to him.'

'Is that why you were gone so long?'

'Not altogether. I had to get something.' She was unscrewing a cylinder of lipstick. 'She doesn't know how to hold it,' Breeze thought. 'She holds it like a stick of kid's rock. What's come over her?'

Lorn's thick strong fingers grasped the lipstick crudely and she began to rub it clumsily, to and fro, on her lips. 'She uses it like an india rubber. She's got no idea. She's never done it before.' The lips grew orange, greasy. 'She's got the wrong colour. She's daubing it on. She can't know. She's like a kid.' All of this continual creation of impressions was unconscious, in some way against her will. It ceased when Lorn said:

'Then I had to order the taxi.'

'Taxi?'

'He said order a taxi. It could call for me here, then bring us both back from the station. He said he didn't fancy a tramp with luggage.'

'He's staying?'

'Well, I should think so.' She was pushing out her lips towards the mirror, in an orange pout; she drew them back, pursed them; she twitched the corners, smiling a little. The lips seemed enamelled, brittle, like snakeskin. Satisfied, Lorn set them in what she felt was a line of tenderness, naturally. 'She looks hopeless, awful,' Breeze thought. 'She looks pathetic. She's got pimples on her face. She can't know how awful she looks.' Suddenly she could not bear it. 'Lorn, let me do it,' she said. 'Let me touch it up. You're too heavy.'

She took the lipstick: the tinfoil was warm and sweaty where Lorn had held it in her hot hands, the stick already soft beneath.

'What made you get orange?'

'He likes it.'

'It's not your colour.'

'I know. I wanted cerise. But he likes flame. He always liked it.'

Breeze looked at the stick. Flame-coloured, kiss-proof, it was a symbol of some kind of fatuous hope. She wiped Lorn's lips, until they were clean again except for fissures of orange in the cracks of the skin; then she began all over again, painting them delicately, bringing the mouth into softer, longer line. All the time Lorn was trembling.

v

That afternoon, while Lorn had gone to the station in her taxi, there was a storm. It broke with warm stickiness and a great beat of thick rain that flashed white against the summery dark background of forest. It drove Breeze indoors. She sat miserable, waiting and listening for the taxi beyond the sound of rain and the huge sudden blunderings of thunder. The air was hot and oppressive and the rain, smashing down grass and plants and flowers, made small floods among the flattened rows of herbs. By mid-afternoon the garden looked a desolation, its grace gone, its colours washed out, the forest beyond it a gloomy wall of solid leaf and rain. Waiting, miserable, she felt it to be almost the worst thing that could have happened. The place looked mean and small and dead.

The taxi came at half-past three. Going to the window to watch, Breeze had in her mind her pre-conceived picture of the man: blond, aloof, coldly medical, about thirty, with the skinny and aloof halo of his mother shining, inexplicably, in the background. She had waited for his arrival with a kind of remote arrogance, in a determination to be aloof also, her preconceived image part of a preconceived hatred.

Looking across the garden, to the gate, she had a great shock. There appeared with Lorn, under her grey umbrella, a man of more than fifty. She could not believe it. She stood and stared at him in a conflict of pain: the pain of unbelief, amazement and the shock of a momentary and stupid terror. Her image of him went black, like a fused light, the halo of the mother fluttering out behind it like a silly candle.

She had not time to think. In a moment he was standing before her, grey-haired, lean, flesh yellow with sun, with the air of some decaying and dictatorial professor, nose slightly askew, eyes having some curious affliction of twitching, so that she could not look at him.

'So this', he said, shaking hands with her, 'is Breeze Anstey?'

His voice was nasal, meticulous, a little superior. It was a voice accustomed to speaking obliquely, in innuendoes. She did not trust it. Hearing it, she felt the conception of her hatred of him harden more firmly than ever. At that moment it was the only thing of which she felt quite sure.

Foolishly she said: 'I'm sorry it rained like this – I mean in this tropical way.'

'Tropical. This?' He was very amused. Greatly. Tropical? Very, very funny. Did she understand, dear young lady, quite what tropical meant? He looked at her with oblique superiority, with a maddening amusement and a thin nasal sneer which she was to discover, later, was habitual.

Explaining to her what tropical rain was really like, he addressed her again as 'Dear young lady.' She felt furious. She stared at him with crude dislike, openly. All the time Lorn was smiling, open-mouthed, teeth gay and white against her absurd lipstick. It was a smile in which there was something like a giddiness of adoration: the smile of utterly silly, uncritical feminine delight. She was in heaven.

It went on all through tea. It was like the functioning of some cheap machine into which Lorn kept pressing unseen coins in order to keep it working. To Breeze it was incomprehensible. It could not be genuine. She could not conceive of it as anything else but forced, the desperate mechanical reaction to the occasion.

The doctor talked. To Breeze he was an old man. He framed his sentences with the slow care of experience, searching for his words, as though engaged on some careful and perpetual diagnosis.

'When I first had – er – intimation of – of this – this project of yours, my dear, I had – er – some notion that you had taken – taken a place of some size.'

'It doesn't *look* big, dear,' Lorn said, 'but you try to work it and see.'

'But you said – you said a farm.'

'Well?'

'But this is – just a garden.'

'We call it a farm. It couldn't very well be bigger because of the forest.'

'The – the forest?'

He looked out of the window with a kind of amazed contempt, at their small confined and now rain-flattened plot of earth, with the barricade of trees beyond and the heavy English sky pressing down on it all and giving it some air of civilised meanness. He looked in silence. Then he began laughing. It was, to Breeze, an extraordinary laugh, almost silent, impersonal and yet selfish, as though the joke were for himself alone and yet on them. He laughed for fully two minutes before finally saying anything. Then he repeated 'Forest, forest', in the tone of a man who, though knowing everything, has a little pity for the rest of the world.

Breeze understood. She caught the accent, almost the sneer, of pity: pity for them, pity for their so-called farm, for their ideals, for two silly too-earnest Englishwomen with their pretence of ambition. Without saying it, he hinted that there were lives of which they knew nothing, forests beside which their own miserable affair was a shrubbery. He seemed to say: 'You may believe in it, but is it worth believing in? It can't be serious. It can't mean anything. And now that I've come it can't go on.'

Almost as though she heard it, Breeze said, frankly:

'You came home in a hurry, Dr Bentley.'

He looked at her, then at Lorn, obliquely. 'I had business,' he said. He kept looking at Lorn, still obliquely, with a soft and almost crafty smile of adoration, until Lorn at last lifted her eyes and smiled back in a confusion of happiness. Their eyes, in silence, telegraphed secrets which were not secrets at all. 'Yes,' the doctor said, 'I had business. It's not – not for me to say how – important – it is. But I had business. That is so – eh, Lorn?'

The system of telegraphy, once begun, went on. After tea, and on into the misty heavy evening, the doctor and Lorn sat about in the little sitting-room and, whenever Breeze was there, sent each other messages of what was almost adolescent adoration. They spoke in riddles: restless, obvious riddles of which they were only too anxious that Breeze should know the meaning. They held out their love to her, as it were, on a plate, like some piece of juicy steak, inviting her to admire and, while indicating that it was not for her, to envy. She responded by muteness. She did not know what to say. Dumbly she sat and waited for the time when she could decently go to bed.

'Tempus fugit,' the doctor said, once.

'Yes, but slowly,' Lorn said, 'when you're waiting.'

'Everything comes,' the doctor said, 'to him who waits.'

At eight Breeze pleaded excuses and went up to bed. After lying awake, listening to the slow summer drip of rain from the branches outside, she heard, at nine, the shutting and locking of doors, footsteps on the stairs, whispers, the small shufflings and rustling of retirement. She waited for Lorn to come into her, as always, to say good-night. They would sit together, talk, confide, discuss the happenings of one day and their plans for another. She cherished the moment jealously.

She waited. Nothing happened. Then, towards ten, she heard a door, footsteps. They approached and went past. She heard the opening and shutting of another door, then silence.

She listened for a long time. There was no other sound. The rain had ceased and she could hear the silence, could feel it as something hard and tangible about her, as a crystallisation of emptiness into solidity, into something as light and sharp as a knife, cutting her off from Lorn completely.

VI

By innuendoes, half-phrases, gestures of superiority, and above all by the sly oblique smile of pity, the doctor poured contempt on the little farm. For almost a week Lorn, bewildered by the pull of opposing emotions, wavered between the man and the ideal she and Breeze had set themselves. As though aware of it, the doctor said, at last:

'I suppose you two – young things know that this – this place – isn't healthy? It isn't doing either of you any good.'

This was a shock; and Breeze at once resented it.

'Who said it wasn't healthy?'

The doctor was patient: which aroused her still more. She detested the assured enamel superiority of the man. Honest, decent anger, resentment, bitterness, had no place in his make-up. He presented only an assured too-smooth egg-like coldness. Her own anger, like some feeble Lilliputian pin, could not even scratch the iron shell of his supreme priggishness. It was all hopelessly beyond her. Lorn and this man, this man for a lover.

Another time he said to her: 'Do you feel well?'

'Yes,' she said. 'As well as I ever did.'

'Which means?' He paused, waiting for a reply which did not come. 'You feel tired?'

'No.'

'Sleepy? No – no energy?'

'No.'

'Oppressed?'

'No.'

She was lying. He knew it and she, in a moment, knew that he was aware of it. 'Lorn tells me – quite – quite otherwise,' he said.

'I'm not Lorn,' she said.

'Lorn says you are both tired – er – continually – and can't understand it.'

'We work hard.'

'Perhaps so. But that would not account for this – this extraordinary enervation. The trouble is that there are too many trees in this place. They suck up the air.'

'That's your opinion. I like the trees.'

'May I take your pulse?' he said.

Before she could resist he had taken her hand, had his thumb on her wrist. It was as though she were held in a clasp of pure dead bone. In the feel of his hands she felt, as it were, the whole essence of his nature: hard, bony, dead, the expression of man seeing life as something to be perpetually diagnosed, the delicacy of human nature as something needing eternal probing and some ultimate interesting operation.

He dropped her hand. She felt, for a few seconds, the small cool point of the thumb's contact. She stood waiting, resentfully, in silence. What had he to do with her? Why did he trouble with her? It was beyond her, this damnable solicitude, and she did not want it.

'You'll be telling me next,' she said, 'that I've got galloping consumption.'

For a moment he did not reply. They were in the little sitting-room. Lorn had gone to cut lettuces for the evening salad. It was a sultry, still evening, breathless

'No, it's not that you've got,' he said. 'Will you sit down?'

'Why?'

'Just sit down. I want to ask you the same – er – questions as I asked Lorn.'

'What questions?'

'Well – – er – just – '

'You're going to ask me to sleep with you perhaps?' she said. She raised her voice, spoke without thinking, the words out of her mouth before she could prevent them. 'You're going to ask me to wait seven years for you perhaps? No thank you! Not to-day, thank you! No *thank* you!'

He looked at her, smiling, the small chill oblique smile of professional reticence, as one accustomed to such ill-mannered outbursts. He did not speak. She set her teeth, waiting, meaning the words she had spoken with all her heart, yet wishing, now, that she had not spoken them. She stood poised somewhere between anger and embarrassment.

At that moment Lorn came in, carrying the already dew-wet lettuces.

'Hullo, you two,' she said. 'Quarrelling?'

'Yes!' Breeze said.

'Breeze!'

'He's got as far as taking my pulse – but that isn't far enough.' Her anger quickened again, fired up in her face.

'He's not satisfied with coming here and taking you away. That isn't enough. He wants to prove the place isn't healthy. He wants to get *me* out of it.'

'Breeze, Breeze, I won't have it! I won't have it.'

'It's true. He's smashed our life.'

'You can't say it. I won't have you saying it.'

'Why isn't it true? Before he came rushing home like a love-sick boy we were quite happy here. The farm was our whole life. You know that. We'd planned and schemed and banked on it. We'd arranged for the organiser to come down. Now he comes rushing home and it all means nothing.'

'You mean you mean nothing!'

'Well, what difference? What difference whether it's me or the farm? He's trying to make you believe it's unhealthy. That means he either wants you to give me up or me to give up the farm. Well, I'll give up the farm.'

'Oh! Breeze, please. Please, not now.'

'I'll give it up, I tell you! You don't want me! What point in my staying? I'll clear out now – before I can change my mind.'

Suddenly she looked from Lorn to the man. He was smiling and the smile had that perpetual as though engraved mockery in it, the slightly oblique sneer of condescension, and she knew that he was not only laughing at her physical self, her behaviour, but her ideals, her anger and the very preciousness of her affection.

Suddenly rage burned up in her to a point when she could not control it. She went across to him and hit him full across the face. For a moment nothing happened. The smile did not change. It remained, like some rotten and yet imperishable engraving of his whole nature. Beside herself, almost crying, she struggled with a terrific desire to hit it again, to smash it out of existence. Then, suddenly, the smile, the rage, the reason for it all had no meaning. She went very weak. She had just strength enough to lift her voice and half shout:

'I'll get out in the morning. I'll go! There's not room for all of us.'

Lorn would have spoken, but Breeze ran out of the room. She was already crying. In the second before the door slammed she heard the faint condescending breath of a laugh from the doctor.

She lay in bed and cried with anguish and comfort. She waited for Lorn to come, clinging to the hope of reconciliation. It must have been about eight o'clock, and she lay for two hours, until darkness, before she heard a sound from below. Sounds came, then, and went, but nothing happened. She lay in silence and could not sleep. She thought of Lorn. She saw Lorn, physically, as a constant presence, comforting, large, so soft and maternal. She ached for her. She saw her as she had seen her in the forest, bathing, and she was caught up, unexpectedly, by a return of the same singular moment of acute anguish, almost pain, that had shot through her at the first sight of Lorn's body.

Then, for the first time, she understood herself. She knew, suddenly, what it was she resented, what exactly it was she had wanted, what she was so extraordinarily afraid of losing.

She sat up in bed. She had ceased crying and she felt, now, like a rag that has been wrung out. The cold realisation of her feeling for Lorn struck her with fear, almost terror, as though she had suddenly become aware that she was incurably ill.

Simultaneously she saw also the reason for the doctor's smile: that perpetual smile of aloof knowingness. 'No, that's not what you've got.' He knew. Unconsciously she must have known that he knew. But curiously, for all her knowing, her rage against him did not lessen. He had struck so hard at her ideals, the little and now absurd farm, the business partnership, the hope of success. He had taken, and in a way destroyed Lorn.

She lay for a long time. She hoped that Lorn would come. She wanted, and for the first time consciously, to be held by Lorn, tenderly, with the same love and strength as she felt in return. Something had taught her that a love of that kind belonged to the limbo of things that were never mentioned. To her, in the full realisation of it, it seemed a beautiful thing. She cried tenderly because of it. It comforted her. There was some kind of sad inverted pleasure in the gentle pain of realisation and loss.

At one o'clock she got up, lighted her candle and packed her bag. Going to shut the window she caught the great breath of the forest, damp, profound, summer-drenched, the smell of a whole section of her life. She stood for a moment breathing it in, looking over the dark quiet earth of the garden towards the still darker mass of trees. The night was deadly still. As it hung about her, huge and intangible, with an intolerable quality of suspense and comfort, her life seemed very little and not to matter.

She shut the window. She felt, at once, back in the cramped confinement of her own affairs, where things had seemed, a moment before, to be all over, but where they seemed, now, to be just beginning.

And she knew that the rest, whatever it was, lay with herself.

THE OX

I

The Thurlows lived on a small hill. As though it were not high enough, the house was raised up, as on invisible stilts, with a wooden flight of steps to the front door. Exposed and isolated, the wind striking at it from all quarters, it seemed to have no part with the surrounding landscape. Empty ploughed lands, in winter-time, stretched away on all sides in wet steel curves.

At half-past seven every morning Mrs Thurlow pushed her great rusty bicycle down the hill; at six every evening she pushed it back. Loaded, always, with grey bundles of washing, oilcans, sacks, cabbages, bundles of old newspaper, boughs of wind-blown wood and bags of chicken food, the bicycle could never be ridden. It was a vehicle of necessity. Her relationship to it was that of a beast to a cart. Slopping along beside it, flat heavy feet pounding painfully along under mud-stained skirts, her face and body ugly with lumpy angles of bone, she was like a beast of burden.

Coming out of the house, raised up even above the level of the small hill, she stepped into a country of wide horizons. This fact meant nothing to her. The world into which she moved was very small: from six to nine she cleaned for the two retired sisters, nine to twelve for the retired photographer, twelve-thirty to three for the poultry farm, four to six for the middle-aged bachelor. She did not think of going beyond the four lines which made up the square of her life. She thought of other people going beyond them, but this was different. Staring down at a succession of wet floors, working always for other people, against time, she had somehow got into the habit of not thinking about herself.

She thought much, in the same stolid pounding way as she pushed the bicycle, of other people: in particular of Thurlow, more particularly of her two sons. She had married late; the boys

120

were nine and thirteen. She saw them realising refined ambitions, making their way as assistants in shops, as clerks in offices, even as butlers. Heavily built, with faces having her own angular boniness, they moved with eyes on the ground. She had saved money for them. For fifteen years she had hoarded the scubbing-and-washing money, keeping it in a bran bag under a mattress in the back bedroom. They did not know of it; she felt that no one, not even Thurlow, knew of it.

Thurlow had a silver plate in his head. In his own eyes it set him apart from other men. 'I got a plate in me head. Solid silver. Enough silver to make a dozen spoons and a bit over. Solid. Beat that!' Wounded on the Marne, and now walking about with the silver plate in his head, Thurlow was a martyr. 'I didn't ought to stoop. I didn't ought to do nothing. By rights. By rights I didn't ought to lift a finger.' He was a hedge cutter. 'Lucky I'm tall, else that job wouldn't be no good to me.' He had bad days and good days, even days of genuine pain. 'Me plate's hurting me! It's me plate. By God, it'll drive me so's I don't know what I'm doing! It's me plate again.' And he would stand wild and vacant, rubbing his hands through his thin black hair, clawing his scalp as though to wrench out the plate and the pain.

Once a week, on Saturdays or Sundays, he came home a little tipsy, in a good mood, laughing to himself, riding his bicycle up the hill like some comic rider in a circus. 'Eh? Too much be damned. I can ride me bike, can't I? S' long as I can ride me bike I'm all right.' In the pubs he had only one theme, 'I got a plate in me head. Solid silver,' recited in a voice challenging the world to prove it otherwise.

All the time Mrs Thurlow saved money. It was her creed. Sometimes people went away and there was no cleaning. She then made up the gap in her life by other work: picking potatoes, planting potatoes, dibbing cabbages, spudding roots, pea picking, more washing. In the fields she pinned up her skirt so that it stuck out behind her like a thick stiff tail, making her look like some bony ox. She did washing from five to six in the morning, and again from seven to nine in the evening. Taking in more washing, she tried to wash more quickly, against time. Somehow she succeeded, so that from nine to ten she had time for ironing. She worked by candlelight. Her movements were largely instinctive. She had washed and ironed for so long, in the

same way, at the same time and place, that she could have
worked in darkness.

There were some things, even, which could be done in darkness; and so at ten, with Thurlow and the sons in bed, she blew
out the candle, broke up the fire, and sat folding the clothes or
cleaning boots, and thinking. Her thoughts, like her work, went
always along the same lines, towards the future, out into the re-
splendent avenues of ambitions, always for the two sons. There
was a division in herself, the one part stolid and uncomplaining
in perpetual labour, the other fretful and almost desperate in an
anxiety to establish a world beyond her own. She had saved
fifty-four pounds. She would make it a hundred. How it was to
be done she could not think. The boys were growing; the cost of
keeping them was growing. She trusted in some obscure provi-
dential power as tireless and indomitable as herself.

At eleven she went to bed, going up the wooden stairs in darkness, in her stockinged feet. She undressed in darkness, her
clothes falling away to be replaced by a heavy grey nightgown
that made her body seem still larger and more ponderous. She
fell asleep almost at once, but throughout the night her mind,
propelled by some inherent anxiety, seemed to work on. She
dreamed she was pushing the bicycle down the hill, and then that
she was pushing it up again; she dreamed she was scrubbing
floors; she felt the hot stab of the iron on her spittled finger and
then the frozen bite of icy swedes as she picked them off un-
thawed earth on bitter mornings. She counted her money, her
mind going back over the years throughout which she had saved
it, and then counted it again, in fear, to make sure, as though
in terror that it might be gone in the morning.

II

She had one relaxation. On Sunday afternoons she sat in the
kitchen alone, and read the newspapers. They were not the newspapers of the day, but of all the previous week and perhaps of
the week before that. She had collected them from the houses
where she scrubbed, bearing them home on the bicycle. Through
them and by them she broke the boundaries of her world. She
made excursions into the lives of other people: tragic lovers,
cabinet ministers, Atlantic flyers, suicides, society beauties,

murderers, kings. It was all very wonderful. But emotionally, as she read, her face showed no impression. It remained ox-like in its impassivity. It looked in some way indomitably strong, as though little things like beauties and suicides, murderers and kings, could have no possible effect on her. About three o'clock, as she sat reading, Thurlow would come in, lumber upstairs, and sleep until about half-past four.

One Sunday he did not come in at three o'clock. It was after four when she heard the bicycle tinkle against the woodshed outside. She raised her head from the newspaper and listened for him to come in. Nothing happened. Then after about five minutes Thurlow came in, went upstairs, remained for some minutes, and then came down again. She heard him go out into the yard. There was a stir among the chickens as he lumbered about the woodshed.

Mrs Thurlow got up and went outside, and there, at the door of the woodshed, Thurlow was just hiding something under his coat. She thought it seemed like his billhook. She was not sure. Something made her say:

'Your saw don't need sharpening again a'ready, does it?'

'That it does,' he said. 'That's just what it does. Joe Woods is going to sharp it.' Thurlow looked upset and slightly wild, as he did when the plate in his head was hurting him. His eyes were a little drink-fired, dangerous. 'I gonna take it down now, so's I can git it back to-night.'

All the time she could see the saw itself hanging in the darkness of the woodshed behind him. She was certain then that he was lying, almost certain that it was the billhook he had under his coat.

She did not say anything else. Thurlow got on his bicycle and rode off, down the hill, his coat bunched up, the bicycle slightly crazy as he drove with one tipsy hand.

Something, as soon as he had gone, made her rush upstairs. She went into the back bedroom and flung the clothes off the mattress of the small iron bed that was never slept in. The money: it was all right. It was quite all right. She sat down heavily on the bed. And after a moment's anxiety her colour returned again – the solid, immeasurably passive calm with which she scrubbed, read the newspapers, and pushed the bicycle.

In the evening, the boys at church, she worked again. She darned socks, the cuffs of jackets, cleaned boots, sorted the washing for the following day. The boys must look well, respectable. Under the new scheme they went, now, to a secondary school in the town. She was proud of this, the first real stepping-stone to the higher things of the future. Outside, the night was windy, and she heard the now brief, now very prolonged moan of wind over the dark winter-ploughed land. She worked by candlelight. When the boys came in she lighted the lamp. In their hearts, having now some standard by which to judge her, they despised her a little. They hated the cheapness of the candlelight. When they had eaten and gone lumbering up to bed, like two colts, she blew out the lamp and worked by candlelight again. Thurlow had not come in.

He came in a little before ten. She was startled, not hearing the bicycle.

'You want something t' eat?'

'No,' he said. He went straight into the scullery. She heard him washing his hands, swilling the sink, washing, swilling again.

'You want the light?' she called.

'No!'

He came into the kitchen. She saw his still-wet hands in the candlelight. He gave her one look and went upstairs without speaking. For some time she pondered on the memory of this look, not understanding it. She saw in it the wildness of the afternoon, as though the plate were hurting him, but now it had in addition fear, and, above fear, defiance.

She got the candle and went to the door. The wind tore the candle flame down to a minute blue bubble which broke, and she went across the yard, to the woodshed, in darkness. In the woodshed she put a match to the candle again, held the candle up at eye level, and looked at the walls. The saw hung on its nail, but there was no billhook. She made a circle with the candle, looking for the bicycle with dumb eyes. It was not there. She went into the house again. Candleless, faintly perturbed, she went up to bed. She wanted to say something to Thurlow, but he was dead still, as though asleep, and she lay down herself, hearing nothing but the sound of Thurlow's breathing and, outside, the sound of the wind blowing across the bare land.

Asleep, she dreamed, as nearly always, about the bicycle, but this time it was Thurlow's bicycle and there was something strange about it. It had no handles, but only Thurlow's billhook where the handles should have been. She grasped the billhook, and in her dream she felt the pain of the blood rushing out of her hands, and she was terrified and woke up.

Immediately she put out her hands, to touch Thurlow. The bed was empty. That scared her. She got out of bed. 'Thurlow! Bill! Thurlow! Thurlow!'

The wind had dropped, and it was quiet everywhere. She went downstairs. There, in the kitchen, she lighted the candle again and looked round. She tried the back door; it was unlocked and she opened it and looked out, feeling the small ground wind icy on her bare feet.

'Thurlow!' she said. 'Bill! Thurlow!'

She could hear nothing, and after about a minute she went back upstairs. She looked in at the boys' bedroom. The boys were asleep, and the vast candle shadow of herself stood behind her and listened, as it were, while she listened. She went into her own bedroom. Thurlow was not there. Then she went into the back bedroom.

The mattress lay on the floor. And she knew, even before she began to look for it, that they money was gone. She knew that Thurlow had taken it.

Since there was nothing else she could do, she went back to bed, not to sleep, but to lie there, oppressed but never in despondency, thinking. The money had gone, Thurlow had gone, but it would be all right. Just before five she got up, fired the copper, and began the washing. At seven she hung it out in long grey lines in the wintry grey light, holding the pegs like a bit in her teeth. A little after seven the boys came down to wash in the scullery.

'Here, here! Mum! There's blood all over the sink!'

'Your dad killed a rabbit,' she said. 'That's all.'

She lumbered out into the garden, to cut cabbages. She cut three large cabbages, put them in a sack, and, as though nothing had happened, began to prepare the bicycle for the day. She tied the cabbages on the carrier, two oilcans on the handlebars, and then on the crossbar a small bundle of washing, clean, which she had finished on Saturday. That was all: nothing much for a Monday.

At half-past seven the boys went across the fields, by footpath, to catch the bus for school. She locked the house, and then, huge, imperturbable, planting down great feet in the mud, she pushed the bicycle down the hill. She had not gone a hundred yards before, out of the hedge, two policemen stepped into the road to meet her.

'We was wondering if Mr Thurlow was in?'

'No,' she said, 'he ain't in.'

'You ain't seen him?'

'No, I ain't seen him.'

'Since when?'

'Since last night.'

'You mind,' they said, 'if we look round your place?'

'No,' she said, 'you go on up. I got to git down to Miss Hanley's.' She began to push the bicycle forward, to go.

'No,' they said. 'You must come back with us.'

So she turned the bicycle round and pushed it back up the hill again. 'You could leave your bike,' one of the policemen said. 'No,' she said, 'I'd better bring it. You can never tell nowadays what folk are going to be up to.'

Up at the house she stood impassively by while the two policemen searched the woodshed, the garden, and finally the house itself. Her expression did not change as they looked at the blood in the sink. 'He washed his hands there last night,' she said.

'Don't touch it,' the policeman said. 'Don't touch it.' And then suspiciously, almost in implied accusation: 'You ain't touched nothing – not since last night?'

'I got something else to do,' she said.

'We'd like you to come along with us, Mrs Thurlow,' they said, 'and answer a few questions.'

'All right.' She went outside and took hold of her bicycle.

'You can leave your bicycle.'

'No,' she said. 'I'll take it. It's no naughty way, up here, from that village.'

'We got a car down the road. You don't want a bike.'

'I better take it,' she said.

She wheeled the bicycle down the hill. When one policeman had gone in the car she walked on with the other. Ponderous, flat-footed, unhurried, she looked as though she could have gone on pushing the bicycle in the same direction, at the same pace, for ever.

They kept her four hours at the station. She told them about the billhook, the blood, the way Thurlow had come home and gone again, her waking in the night, Thurlow not being there, the money not being there.

'The money. How much was there?'

'Fifty-four pounds, sixteen and fourpence. And twenty-eight of that in sovereigns.'

In return they told her something else.

'You know that Thurlow was in the Black Horse from eleven to two yesterday?'

'Yes, I dare say that's where he'd be. That's where he always is, Sundays.'

'He was in the Black Horse, and for about two hours he was arguing with a man stopping down here from London. Arguing about that plate in his head. The man said he knew the plate was aluminium and Thurlow said he knew it was silver. Thurlow got very threatening. Did you know that?

'No. But that's just like him.'

'This man hasn't been seen since, and Thurlow hasn't been seen since. Except by you last night.'

'Do you want me any more?' she said. 'I ought to have been at Miss Hanley's hours ago.'

'You realise this is very important, very serious?'

'I know. But how am I going to get Miss Hanley in, and Mrs Acott, and then the poultry farm and then Mr George?'

'We'll telephone Miss Hanley and tell her you can't go.'

'The money,' she said. 'That's what I can't understand. The money.'

III

It was the money which brought her, without showing it, to the edge of distress. She thought of it all day. She thought of it as hard cash, coin, gold and silver, hard-earned and hard-saved. But it was also something much more. It symbolised the future, another life, two lives. It was the future itself. If, as seemed possible, something terrible had happened and a life had been destroyed, it did not seem to her more terrible than the fact that the money had gone and that the future had been destroyed.

As she scrubbed the floors at the poultry farm in the late afternoon, the police telephoned for her again. 'We can send the car for her,' they said.

'I got my bike,' she said. 'I'll walk.'

With the oilcans filled, and cabbages and clean washing now replaced by newspapers and dirty washing she went back to the police station. She wheeled her bicycle into the lobby and they then told her how, that afternoon, the body of the man from London had been found, in a spinney, killed by blows from some sharp instrument like an axe. 'We have issued a warrant for Thurlow's arrest,' they said.

'You never found the money?' she said.

'No,' they said. 'No doubt that'll come all right when we find Thurlow.'

That evening, when she got home, she fully expected Thurlow to be there, as usual, splitting kindling wood with the billhook, in the outhouse, by candlelight. The same refusal to believe that life could change made her go upstairs to look for the money. The absence of both Thurlow and the money moved her to no sign of emotion. But she was moved to a decision.

She got out her bicycle and walked four miles, into the next village, to see her brother. Though she did not ride the bicycle, it seemed to her as essential as ever that she should take it with her. Grasping its handles, she felt a sense of security and fortitude. The notion of walking without it, helplessly, in the darkness, was unthinkable.

Her brother was a master carpenter, a chapel-going man of straight-grained thinking and purpose, who had no patience with slovenliness. He lived with his wife and his mother in a white-painted electrically-lighted house whose floors were covered with scrubbed coco-matting. His mother was a small woman with shrill eyes and ironed-out mouth who could not hear well.

Mrs Thurlow knocked on the door of the house as though these people, her mother and brother, were strangers to her. Her brother came to the door and she said:

'It's Lil. I come to see if you'd seen anything o' Thurlow?'

'No, we ain't seen him. Summat up?'

'Who is it?' the old woman called.

'It's Lil,' the brother said, in a louder voice. 'She says have we seen anything o' Thurlow?'

'No, an' don't want!'

Mrs Thurlow went in. For fifteen years her family had openly disapproved of Thurlow. She sat down on the edge of the chair nearest the door. Her large lace-up boots made large black mud prints on the virgin coco-matting. She saw her sister-in-law look first at her boots and then at her hat. She had worn the same boots and the same hat for longer than she herself could remember. But her sister-in-law remembered.

She sat untroubled, her eyes sullen, as though not fully conscious in the bright electric light. The light showed up the mud on her skirt, her straggling grey hair under the shapeless hat, the edges of her black coat weather-faded to a purplish grey.

'So you ain't heard nothing about Thurlow?' she said.

'No,' her brother said. 'Be funny if we had, wouldn't it? He ain't set foot in this house since dad died.' He looked at her hard. 'Why? What's up?'

She raised her eyes to him. Then she lowered them again. It was almost a minute before she spoke.

'Ain't you heard?' she said. 'They reckon he's done a murder.'

'What's she say?' the old lady said. 'I never heard her.'

Mrs Thurlow looked dully at her boots, at the surrounding expanse of coco-matting. For some reason the fissured pattern of the coco-matting, so clean and regular, fascinated her. She said: 'He took all the money. He took it all and they can't find him.'

'Eh? What's she say? What's she mumbling about?'

The brother, his face white, went over to the old woman. He said into her ear: 'One of the boys is won a scholarship, She come over to tell us.'

'Want summat to do, I should think, don't she? Traipsing over here to tell us that.'

The man sat down at the table. He was very white, his hands shaking. His wife sat with the same dumb, shaking expression of shock. Mrs Thurlow raised her eyes from the floor. It was as though she had placed on them the onus of some terrible responsibility.

'For God's sake,' the man said, 'when did it happen?'

All Mrs Thurlow could think of was the money. 'Over fifty pounds. I got it hid under the mattress. I don't know how he could have found out about it. I don't know. I can't think. It's

all I got. I got it for the boys.' She paused, pursing her lips together, squeezing back emotion. 'It's about the boys I come.'

'The boys?' The brother looked up, scared afresh. 'He ain't –
they—'

'I didn't know whether you'd have them here,' she said. 'Till
it's blowed over. Till they find Thurlow. Till things are
straightened out.'

'Then they ain't found him?'

'No. He's done a bunk. They say as soon as they find him I
shall git the money.'

'Yes,' the brother said. 'We'll have them here.'

She stayed a little longer, telling the story dully, flatly, to the
scared pairs of eyes across the table and to the old shrill eyes,
enraged because they could not understand, regarding her from
the fireplace. An hour after she had arrived, she got up to go.
Her brother said: 'Let me run you back in the car. I got a car
now. Had it three or four months. I'll run you back.'

'No, I got my bike,' she said.

She pushed the bicycle home in the darkness. At home, in the
kitchen, the two boys were making a rabbit hutch. She saw that
they had something of her brother's zeal for handling wood. She
saw that their going to him would be a good thing. He was a man
who had got on in the world: she judged him by the car, the
white-painted house, the electric light, the spotless coco-matting.
She saw the boys, with deep but inexpressible pride, going to the
same height, beyond it.

'Dad ain't been home,' they said.

She told them there had been a little trouble. 'They think your
dad took some money.' She explained how it would be better for
them, and for her, if they went to stay with her brother. 'Git to
bed now and I'll get your things packed.'

'You mean we gotta go and live there?'

'For a bit,' she said.

They were excited. 'We could plane the wood for the rabbit
hutch!' they said. 'Make a proper job of it.'

IV

That night, and again on the following morning, she looked
under the mattress for the money. In the morning the boys de-

parted. She was slightly depressed, slightly relieved by their excitement. When they had gone she bundled the day's washing together and tied it on the bicycle. She noticed, then, that the back tyre had a slow puncture, that it was already almost flat. This worried her. She pumped up the tyre and felt a little more confident.

Then, as she prepared to push the bicycle down the hill, she saw the police car coming along the road at the bottom. Two policemen hurried up the track to meet her.

'We got Thurlow,' they said. 'We'd like you to come to the station.'

'Is he got the money?' she said.

'There hasn't been time,' they said, 'to go into that.'

As on the previous morning she pushed her bicycle to the village, walking with one policeman while the other drove on in the car. Of Thurlow she said very little. Now and then she stopped and stooped to pinch the back tyre of the bicycle. 'Like I thought. I got a slow puncture,' she would say. 'Yes, it's gone down since I blowed it up. I s'll have to leave it at the bike shop as we go by.'

Once she asked the policeman if he thought that Thurlow had the money. He said, 'I'm afraid he's done something more serious than taking money.'

She pondered over this statement with dull astonishment. More serious? She knew that nothing could be more serious. To her the money was like a huge and irreplaceable section of her life. It was part of herself, bone and flesh, blood and sweat. Nothing could replace it. Nothing, she knew with absolute finality, could mean so much.

In the village she left the bicycle at the cycle shop. Walking on without it, she lumbered dully from side to side, huge and unsteady, as though lost. From the cycle-shop window the repairer squinted after her, excited. Other people looked from other windows as she lumbered past, always a pace or two behind the policeman, her ill-shaped feet painfully set down. At the entrance to the police station there was a small crowd. She went heavily into the station. Policemen were standing about in a room. An inspector, many papers in his hand, spoke to her. She listened heavily. She looked about for a sign of Thurlow. The inspector said, with kindness, 'Your husband is not here.' She felt a sense of having been cheated. 'They are detaining him at Metford. We are going over there now.'

'You know anything about the money?' she said.

Five minutes later she drove away, with the inspector and two other policemen, in a large black car. Travelling fast, she felt herself hurled, as it were, beyond herself. Mind and body seemed separated, her thoughts numbed. As the car entered the town, slowing down, she looked out of the side windows, saw posters: 'Metford Murder Arrest.' People, seeing policemen in the car, gaped. 'Murder Sensation Man Detained.'

Her mind registered impressions gravely and confusedly. People and posters were swept away from her and she was conscious of their being replaced by other people, the police station, corridors in the station, walls of brown glazed brick, fresh faces, a room, desks covered with many papers, eyes looking at her, box files in white rows appearing also to look at her, voices talking to her, an arm touching her, a voice asking her to sit down.

'I have to tell you, Mrs Thurlow, that we have detained your husband on a charge of murder.'

'He say anything about the money?'

'He has made a statement. In a few minutes he will be charged and then remanded for further inquiries. You are at liberty to see him for a few moments if you would like to do so.'

In a few moments she was standing in a cell, looking at Thurlow. He looked at her as though he did not know what had happened. His eyes were lumps of impressionless glass. He stood with long arms loose at his sides. For some reason he looked strange, foreign, not himself. It was more than a minute before she realised why this was. Then she saw that he was wearing a new suit. It was a grey suit, thick, ready-made, and the sleeves were too short for him. They hung several inches above his thick protuberant wrist bones, giving his hands a look of inert defeat.

'You got the money, ain't you?' she said. 'You got it?'

He looked at her. 'Money?'

'The money you took. The money under the mattress.'

He stared at her. Money? He looked at her with a faint expression of appeal. Money. He continued to stare at her with complete blankness. Money?

'You remember,' she said. 'The money under the mattress.'

'Eh?'

'The money. That money. Don't you remember?'

He shook his head.

After some moments she went out of the cell. She carried out with her the sense of Thurlow's defeat as she saw it expressed in the inert hands, the dead, stupefied face, and his vacant inability to remember anything. She heard the court proceedings without interest or emotion. She was oppressed by a sense of increasing bewilderment, a feeling that she was lost. She was stormed by impressions she did not understand. 'I do not propose to put in a statement at this juncture. I ask for a remand until the sixteenth.' 'Remand granted. Clear the court.'

This effect of being stormed by impressions continued outside the court, as she drove away again in the car. People. Many faces. Cameras. More faces. Posters. The old sensation of mind severed from body, of thoughts numbed. In the village, when the car stopped, there were more impressions: more voices, more people, a feeling of suppressed excitement. 'We will run you home,' the policemen said.

'No,' she said. 'I got my cleaning to do. I got to pick up my bicycle.'

She fetched the bicycle and wheeled it slowly through the village. People looked at her, seemed surprised to see her in broad daylight, made gestures as though they wished to speak, and then went on. Grasping the handles of the bicycle, she felt a return of security, almost of comfort. The familiar smooth handlebars hard against her hands had the living response of other hands. They brought back her sense of reality: Miss Hanley, the cleaning, the poultry farm, the time she had lost, the boys, the money, the fact that something terrible had happened, the monumental fact of Thurlow's face, inert and dead, with its lost sense of remembrance.

Oppressed by a sense of duty, she did her cleaning as though nothing had happened. People were very kind to her. Miss Hanley made tea, the retired photographer would have run her home in his car. She was met everywhere by tender, remote words of comfort.

She pushed home her bicycle in the darkness. At Miss Hanley's at the poultry farm, at the various places where she worked, the thought of the money had been partially set aside Now, alone again, she felt the force of its importance more strongly, with the beginnings of bitterness. In the empty house she worked for several hours by candlelight, washing, folding, ironing. About the house the vague noises of wind periodically resolved themselves into what she believed for a moment were the voices of the two boys. She thought of the boys with calm unhappiness, and the thought of them brought back with renewed force the thought of the money. This thought hung over her with the huge preponderance of her own shadow projected on the ceiling above her.

On the following Sunday afternoon she sat in the empty kitchen, as usual, and read the stale newspapers. But now they recorded, not the unreal lives of other people, but the life of Thurlow and herself. She saw Thurlow's photograph. She read the same story told in different words in different papers. In all the stories there was an absence of all mention of the only thing that mattered. There was no single word about the money.

During the next few weeks much happened, but she did not lose the belief that the money was coming back to her. Nothing could touch the hard central core of her optimism. She saw the slow evolution of circumstances about Thurlow as things of subsidiary importance, the loss of the life he had taken and the loss of his own life as things which, terrible in themselves, seemed less terrible than the loss of ideals built up by her sweat and blood.

She knew, gradually, that Thurlow was doomed, that it was all over. She did not know what to do. Her terror seemed remote, muffled, in some way incoherent. She pushed the bicycle back and forth each day in the same ponderous manner as ever, her heavy feet slopping dully beside it.

When she saw Thurlow for the last time his face had not changed, one way or the other, from its fixed expression of defeat. Defeat was cemented into it with imperishable finality. She asked him about the money for the last time.

'Eh?'

'The money. You took it. What you do with it? That money. Under the mattress.' For the first time she showed some sign of desperation. 'Please, what you done with it? That money. My money?'

'Eh?' And she knew that he could not remember.

V

A day later it was all over. Two days later she pushed the bicycle the four miles to the next village, to see her brother. It was springtime, time for the boys to come back to her. Pushing the bicycle in the twilight, she felt she was pushing forward into the future. She had some dim idea, heavily dulled by the sense of Thurlow's death, that the loss of the money was not now so great. Money is money; death is death; the living are the living The living were the future. The thought of the boys' return filled her with hopes for the future, unelated hopes, but quite real, strong enough to surmount the loss of both Thurlow and money.

At her brother's they had nothing to say. They sat, the brother, the mother, and the sister-in-law, and looked at her with eyes over which, as it were, the blinds had been drawn.

'The boys here?' she said.

'They're making a bit of a wheelbarrow.'

'They all right?'

'Yes.' He wetted his lips. His clean-planed mind had been scarred by events as though by a mishandled tool. 'They don't know nothing. We kept it from 'em. They ain't been to school and they ain't seen no papers. They think he's in jail for stealing money.'

She looked at him, dully. 'Stealing money? That's what he did do. That money I told you about. That money I had under the mattress.'

'Well,' he said slowly, 'it's done now.'

'What did he do with it?' she said. 'What d'ye reckon he done with it?'

He looked at her quickly, unable suddenly to restrain his anger. 'Done with it? What d'ye suppose he done with it? Spent it. Threw it away. Boozed it. What else? You know what he was like. You knew! You had your eyes open. You knew what—'

'Will, Will,' his wife said.

He was silent. The old lady said: 'Eh? What's that? What's the matter now?'

The brother said, in a loud voice, 'Nothing.' Then more softly: 'She don't know everything.'

'I came to take the boys back,' Mrs Thurlow said.

He was silent again. He wetted his lips. He struck a match on the warm fire-hob. It spurted into a sudden explosion, igniting of its own volition. He seemed startled. He put the match to his pipe, let it go out.

He looked at Mrs Thurlow, the dead match in his hands. 'The boys ain't coming back no more,' he said.

'Eh?' she said. She was stunned. 'They ain't what?'

'They don't want to come back,' he said.

She did not understand. She could not speak. Very slowly he said:

'It's natural they don't want to come back. I know it's hard. But it's natural. They're getting on well here. They want to stop here. They're good boys. I could take 'em into the business.'

She heard him go on without hearing the individual words. He broke off, his face relieved – like a man who has liquidated some awful obligation.

'They're my boys,' she said. 'They got a right to say what they shall do and what they shan't do.'

She spoke heavily, without bitterness.

'I know that,' he said. 'That's right. They got a right to speak. You want to hear what they got to say?'

'Yes, I want to,' she said.

Her sister-in-law went out into the yard at the back of the house. Soon voices drew nearer out of the darkness and the two boys came in.

'Hullo,' she said.

'Hello, Mum,' they said.

'Your Mum's come,' the carpenter said, 'to see if you want to go back with her.'

The two boys stood silent, awkward, eyes glancing past her.

'You want to go?' the carpenter said. 'Or do you want to stay here?'

'Here,' the elder boy said. 'We want to stop here.'

'You're sure o' that?'

'Yes,' the other said.

Mrs Thurlow stood silent. She could think of nothing to say in protest or argument or persuasion. Nothing she could say would, she felt, give expression to the inner part of herself, the crushed core of optimism and faith.

She stood at the door, looking back at the boys. 'You made up your minds, then?' she said. They did not speak.

'I'll run you home,' her brother said.

'No,' she said. 'I got my bike.'

She went out of the house and began to push the bicycle slowly home in the darkness. She walked with head down, lumbering painfully, as though direction did not matter. Whereas, coming, she had seemed to be pushing forward into the future, she now felt as if she were pushing forward into nowhere.

After a mile or so she heard a faint hissing from the back tyre. She stopped, pressing the tyre with her hand. 'It's slow,' she thought; 'it'll last me.' She pushed forward. A little later it seemed to her that the hissing got worse. She stopped again, and again felt the tyre with her hand. It was softer now, almost flat.

She unscrewed the pump and put a little air in the tyre and went on. 'I better stop at the shop,' she thought, 'and have it done.'

In the village the cycle-shop was already in darkness. She pushed past it. As she came to the hill leading up to the house she lifted her head a little. It seemed to her suddenly that the house, outlined darkly above the dark hill, was a long way off She had for one moment an impression that she would never reach it.

She struggled up the hill. The mud of the track seemed to suck at her great boots and hold her down. The wheels of the bicycle seemed as if they would not turn, and she could hear the noise of the air dying once again in the tyre.

Colonel Julian lay in the sun. By pressing down his hands so that the bony knuckles touched the dusty hot lead of the balcony floor he could raise himself up just enough to look through the openings of the stone balustrade to where the deep ring of rhododendrons broke and revealed, across fields of oak-brown corn, the line of the sea.

The balcony was built above the portico of the house, facing southward. Beyond the rhododendrons, quite flowerless now, dark without that Indian glory the Colonel loved, he could see also his only gardener cutting with a horse-mower the wild outer fringe of lawn, and he could smell the sweet, light fragrance of it drying in the August heat. The terrace, the gardener, the horse and the sun were almost all that was left to him of his life before the war. Not, he often reflected, that they were very much good to him. He could no longer ride the horse, and the gardener was a witless sort of bounder who abused him to his face and raided his tobacco jar behind his back. That left him only the terrace, and, if he were lucky, the sun. All the rest had long since been given up to what he always called the young Air Force gentlemen. They had long ago invaded the solitude, broken the silence and recoloured, sometimes excitingly, the grey privacy of a house that was, anyway, too large for one old man. All that remained to him now was a single room above the stables, and, by a purely compassionate arrangement, the terrace in the sun. The young men filled all the rest of the place with their eating and drinking, their laughter and their language that he could never quite understand, and he in turn had lain for four years in the sun, whenever there was any sun, and watched the faces of them come and go.

He had not been very lucky with the sun since invasion day. The papers were saying that it was the worst summer for forty years. Cold gales had swept down from the north in June, breaking the oats into shabby and forlorn wreckage and burning the tender leaves of the limes. The Colonel, who felt the cold easily and bitterly, lit the gas-fire in his room in the evenings, or sat on the balcony with his overcoat on and read over and over again the invasion news in the papers. After the first few days there was very little flying and he began to feel depressed by having to look so often at a sky without planes. It seemed as if the cloud was solid, unchanged by turns of wind, and dark over the whole world. Ten-tenths, the boys called it: which seemed a curious sort of arithmetical and more difficult way of saying complete, he thought.

But then he had no knowledge at all of the language of modern war; he had lost touch with its progress; at eighty-three he had fallen a long way behind. The young men who came and talked to him in the garden and even on the balcony talked to him constantly in a language which it seemed to him made no sense at all. He discovered in himself a depressing and uneasy ignorance as they talked of kites and pieces of cake, of a shaky do and a very curious situation in which they informed you that you had had it. The Colonel did not know where all this had sprung from. Language in his day had been rather a pompous affair, perhaps rather puerile, but he felt that at least you could understand it. He did not understand this other at all. He felt sometimes like a small boy left out in the cold, not yet initiated into the secret of the games of older boys.

And yet he liked talking to them. He liked it very much; perhaps more than he cared to say. On the few days when flying began again he found himself alone on the balcony all day in the sun, bored with the remote contents of newspapers, missing the immediate touch that he got from talking with men who perhaps only an hour before had been over the battlefield.

That also was a thing he could not get used to. In his day you went off to war after a series of stern farewells; you lived a life of monastic remoteness somewhere on a damnable plain in India, or you went to the northern hills and were cut off for some months at a time. Or if there were no war you went pig-hunting or you had furlough, and if you liked that sort of thing you arranged something unofficially pleasant in the way of women. You needed the hide of a pig yourself not to be affected by all this, and you did in fact come back with that sort of hide, sun-brown or yellow and as harsh as rind. You looked like a soldier. But nowadays these young fellows flew out and put the fear of

God into what they called a gaggle of Wolfers or a bunch of
tanks at four-thirty in the afternoon, and at seven they were
lying in the hay with a young woman or drinking gin in the local
bar. For some reason or other they hadn't any kind of soldierly
look about them, either. He had looked almost in vain for a
martial type. He sometimes saw instead a touch of almost
feminine dreaminess about some of them. They were very quiet
sometimes and had long-seeing eyes that seemed to be dreaming
in planetary distances. They were boyishly hilarious and laughed
fantastically behind quite impossibly unclipped moustaches.
There was none of that heroic stuff at all.

He spread out his fingers loosely in the sun. The weather had
changed at last. Now he could feel the heat stinging up through
his fingers from the lead. It was the sort of heat he loved; it
seemed to burn him to the bone. It was now about twelve o'clock
and if he were lucky one of the young night-fliers who slept all
morning would be waking up now and would come up to talk to
him before lunch. The war was going very well at last, and there
had arisen another of those curious situations in which the night-
fliers now talked of beating the daylights out of Jerry.

He sat for another ten minutes or so alone, listening to the
clap-racket of the horse-mower and the soft wind that lifted
gently up and down, in slow dark swells, the flat branches of
two cedars on the lawn. He felt the sun beating not only into his
fingers but down through the closed lids of his eyes, which
seemed transparent in the vertical light. Then he heard sounds in
the bedroom that opened out on to the balcony and the voice
of one of the young men saying 'Good morning, sir,' and he
opened his eyes to see Pallister, one of the night-pilots, standing
there quite naked except for a pink-and-white towel round his
loins.

'Ah, young fellow,' he said.

Pallister danced from one foot to another on the hot lead of
the balcony, and then dropped the towel and stood on it. His
body was brown all over, a sort of light buttery brown, except
for paler islands of skin on the inner flanks of his thighs. The
Colonel knew all about those islands. The skin from them had
been used to re-cover the burnt lids of the boy's eyes.

The Colonel watched Pallister spread out the towel and then
sit on it, cross-legged, like one of the Indian boys the Colonel so

clearly remembered. The boy sighed and screwed up his eyes and put on a pair of dark glasses.

'Too hot for you?' the Colonel said.

'I just can't have enough of that sun soak into me,' the boy said.

'It's certainly very beautiful,' the Colonel said.

He wanted to talk about the war; to get that intimate touch of fire no newspaper ever gave. But Pallister, behind dark glasses, looked remote and anonymous. He was cut off from him, and the Colonel lost for some moments the friendliness of the young face.

But after a time he got used to the dark glasses; he concentrated on the lips of the boy instead. They, too, were friendly, and unlike the eyes had never been burnt out of the shape of youth. They had sometimes a way of looking very cynical that only made them more youthful still.

'Well,' the Colonel said, 'what is it like over there?'

He supposed he always asked that. He could think of no other way of beginning.

'Oh! It's a bloody ramping mess,' the boy said. 'Looks like fair-day.'

'Even at night?' the Colonel said. He wondered how even the August moon showed this rampant detail.

'Oh! It was light already when I was coming back,' the boy said. 'There was a bit of a doings.'

'Shoot something down?'

'Up,' the boy said. 'Road stuff. And a Ju.88 down. Piece of cake.'

'Tell me about it.'

'Oh! They hadn't a clue. It was just a hell of a nice bang on the ground and hell of a nicer bang upstairs,' the boy said. 'Very smooth do.'

The boy grinned as he spoke, and the Colonel got the impression of an idol, darkly eyeless, laughing up into the sun. The severance of the lips from the black-glassed eyes was so complete as to be unreal and in a way almost hideous. The eyes in their unalive darkness were for the Colonel the symbol of the fact that there had been a time, only a summer ago, when the boy had really been eyeless and for many months nearly dead. It had happened that flak over Denmark had hit something in the Mosquito, the Colonel thought perhaps the pyrotechnics, and had driven white whirlwinds of flame down through the aircraft with terrible fury that could not be stopped. It burnt the face of the boy for a few moments as the heat of a blow-lamp burns off the skin of old paint. The boy had heard himself screaming against the death that was coming up to seize him with a terror that made a lacerating shriek throughout the whole of his body. Instantaneously he was dead but alive: the death living and torturous in a second of screaming flame before its hellish extinction of him. He knew in this awful interval what it was to be burning alive; to be dying and to be aware; to be aware and to be quite helpless. The flame leapt up for an awful and final moment of savage agony and slit the light out of his eyes and left the light of his body and the terror of his mind completely dead.

He did not know quite what happened after that. The flame went out into darkness. It seemed never to have happened; there seemed never to have been a flame. He was afterwards told that for a long time he did not utter a sound; but he had a fanciful and private impression of talking the whole time. It was also quite real; an impression of repeating to himself a frenzied catechism; 'I can see, I can see, I can see.' And then: 'I will see, I will see, God! I will see!' Then it appeared that at last he did begin talking and did amazing things in the way of instructing Jackson, his observer, to fly the aircraft. He was reported as being nervously and consciously active over the whole seaward course, and that, among other details, he kept naming the stars. He had again the private and absolute conviction that all this was nonsense. He had never talked at all. He knew that he was not even very good at naming the stars. He was quite certain about these things. And yet it was quite certain also that Jackson had flown the aircraft home and could only have done so under his advice. As he struggled afterwards to get at the truth of the long darkness that had succeeded the catastrophic moment of white flame, in which he was living and yet also dead, he fell back on the simple defence against terror that was its own dissolution. It was just one of those things.

There followed about nine months in hospitals. The Colonel, who was still staring at the boy and trying to get himself into a state when he could talk easily beyond what were always the first moments of embarrassment, knew all about that time. Sometimes the boy talked very well. Even then the Colonel got the impression that, as often as not, he did not talk to him. He lay flat on his back, perfectly naked, outstretched and very brown except for white patches on the inner flanks of his thighs, and simply talked upward to the sun. He talked quite rapidly, giving no other sign of his high-pitched nervousness except that he drummed his fingers restlessly on the lead of the balcony. It might have been, the Colonel thought, that he was sometimes very much afraid. In a laconic and careless sort of way he talked of the miracles they had done to him in hospital. The Colonel, simply by sheer repetition, got to know some part of the surgical language of them: things like scarlet mercurochrome, Tierch grafts, pre-anæsthetic injections and God knew what. He heard how those grafts had left the boy for some time looking like a young cuckoo, his face a mess of puffed sewing that had a foul baldness not yet touched by sun. He had heard of physiotherapy and occupational therapy, and how, at last, the boy had come out of it, less shocking to look at than he had feared, with the fierce light of living in him, and able to see.

Then the miracle of it all had almost been lost. It appeared from the livid language of the boy, who could out-swear a regular army sergeant without effort, that there had been a fool of a psychiatrist who had made the suggestion that he was mentally unfit to fly. It had had a violently opposite effect. It instantly brought to the surface, in a high emotional temperature, all the symptoms of the disease from which the Colonel now knew the boy was suffering. For as the Colonel lay on the terrace day after day and talked to the boy, it seemed to him that the very great differences between war as he had fought it long ago in Northern Indian hills, and as the boy fought it over the fields of France, was not a difference of time, of latitude, of speed or of weapons, but something more simple and more amazing. The Colonel had gone into war as another man might go into business; respectably, steadfastly, following his father in a line of succession. For the boy it was all quite different. Flying was a disease.

He did not know if the boy was aware of that. He had only recently become aware of it himself. You could, of course, suffer from a disease without being aware of it. It was quite certain that it was something not wholly conscious which had sent the boy into a frenzy of antagonism and scheming against all authority until at last authority had finally given way and let him fly once more.

Thinking of this, and then letting it slip away from his mind, the Colonel once again spoke to the boy. What was now happening in France interested him greatly. This war of movement was so fast that he did not know if you could any longer talk of strategy as he had once been taught it. He longed to get a picture of it, fixed and clear, as the boy might have photographed it from the air.

'Tell me about this Seine thrust,' he said. 'What do you think of it? Do you think it aims at the coast?'

'I never really trouble about what the Brown Jobs are doing,' the boy said.

The Colonel was silenced. It was not a very good morning. Once again he was up against some new term he did not understand.

'Brown Jobs?'

'Army.'

'Oh!' the Colonel said. 'Oh!' He understood now. Of course, apart from the slight contempt it was very apt, very typical.

'Yes, but it's a combined operation,' he said. 'You are all in it. You depend very much on each other.'

'Oh! I know,' the boy said: as if he did not know at all.

The Colonel did not know what to say. The astonishing realisation that the boy did not know what was happening on a general scale stupefied him. It seemed an incredible thing. It seemed to arise from a different sort of blindness, not physical, but from the blindness of this intense and narrow passion to fly. To the boy all horizons beyond these narrow limits of vision were closed. His life soared furiously and blindly between.

'Without you,' the Colonel said, 'the Brown Jobs might never force the issue.'

The boy slightly tilted his head, turning towards the Colonel a pair of black sun-glassy lenses, as if to say 'Force the issue? What the bloody hell does that mean?'

For a moment the Colonel felt that he did not know what the hell it meant himself. He lay quietly in his chair. Across the garden now the horse-mower was silent. There was no sound except the sea-sound of cedar branches gently lifting and falling on the summer wind. It seemed now to the Colonel that the battle-front, really half an hour's flight to the south, was a million miles away.

'There is no bloody issue except killing Huns,' the boy said. 'That's all that matters.' He looked straight up into the sun.

A certain essence of individual cruelty in this remark quite shocked the Colonel. It startled him so that he lifted himself up in the chair and looked at the boy. In the hot sun the face had a pure and impersonal immobility. The savagery of the remark was quite natural. To the Colonel there seemed a certain absence of ethics in the whole of this careless and calculated attitude of the boy's towards fighting. In his day, the Colonel's, there had been in fighting some sort of – well, he supposed it to be sort of ethical water-line. You kept above it. The people who sank below the water-line, who made public a private desire to kill the man on the opposite side, were not thought very much of. It was very much like a game, and all the wars in which he had played it were really, beside this one, quite small. They seemed very important then and were quite forgotten now. He supposed perhaps that that was finally the essence of it: the hugeness of the thing. The boy had in his hands, like the rest of his generation, a frightening and enormous power. It was perhaps the greatest power ever given into the hands of the individual in all time.

'Wizard day,' the boy said. As suddenly as he spoke he curved up his long legs and outstretched them again, in a slow convulsive movement of pleasure in the sun. 'Bloody wizard.' He took great breaths of the warm, noontide air and breathed them out again.

The Colonel, startled out of his reminiscence, did not speak, and the boy went on, talking as if to himself:

'Gosh, the trees,' the boy said, 'and the smell of the bloody hay and the lime trees and all that. After all those months of smelling hospital wards and ether and anæsthetics, Christ, it's good. Did I ever tell you what it was like in Normandy? I mean in the D-minus days.'

'No,' the Colonel said. He had given up.

'Not the orchards? You could see them all in blossom at night, in the full moon. Miles of them. You know how short the nights are in May. Never quite dark. You could see everything. Every puff of smoke from a train, and the rivers, and the orchards in blossom. Bloody wonderful, Colonel, I tell you. You never saw anything so lovely as the sun coming up and the moon not set and the sky half pink with sunlight and half yellowy with moon-light, and all the colour on the French orchards. I tell you, Colonel, you never saw anything so wonderful.'

So much for the passionate, impersonal cruelty of the boy, the Colonel thought. So much for the notion of calculated savagery. It now seemed quite monstrous beside the tenderness of that description of orchards in May. He could see that the boy felt it very deeply and he tried to remember if, so long ago, he too had been touched by anything like that, but he could remember only scarlet rhododendrons, in fantastic cascades, on a wild furlough trek above Darjeeling; how they fell bloodily into rocky spring valleys there and how impressed he had been and how for that reason he had planted them liberally in the garden here. But the glory of them was never quite the same. The scarlet wildness was never renewed. There was something hot and foreign and un-English about them, anyway; not like the orchards, that were so cool and cloudy, like the northern skies. It pleased him very much that the boy liked them. It seemed to make him quite human again.

Then to his dismay the boy got up. He stood quite naked, and took off his glasses and turned away from the sun. His eyes had the oddest appearance of not belonging to the rest of his body. The pale new tissue, not yet merged into the older skin of the face, seemed lividly dead. It seemed to have been grafted there from another person altogether. It aroused the instant and un-easy impression that the boy was two different people.

'Must you?' the Colonel said. 'So soon?'

'I'm as hungry as hell,' the boy said. 'I've got to get dressed and lunch is off at two.'

'Well, nice of you to come up,' the Colonel said. 'I do so appreciate it.'

'Can I send you up a can of beer, sir?' the boy said.

'No. No thanks. I don't think so.'

'A half-can? The orderly can bring it up.'

'No, thank you. Thank you all the same.' He did not want to offend the boy. The pilots were very kind to him sometimes like that, sending him up tobacco or chocolate, or a glass of beer. 'Perhaps to-morrow. Perhaps we might have a drink together. I should like that.'

'Good show,' the boy said.

'About this time?' the Colonel said.

'Yeh. I'll get the orderly to bring the beer up.'

'I'll wait for you,' the Colonel said.

The boy tucked the towel round his loins and hopped over the hot lead of the terrace into the bedroom, calling back over his shoulder something about the Colonel having a sleep, and as if in obedience the Colonel smiled and closed his eyes against the brassy midday light, the only light in which, after many years in the East, he ever felt really warm.

He lay there next day at about the same time, in much the same attitude, waiting for the boy. The strength of the grasses' sweetness had faded a little overnight. He caught it only at odd moments, in brief renewed waves, on the seaward wind. But the branches of the cedars rose and fell with the same slow placidity as the day before, and beyond them, if he raised himself up on his fleshless knuckles, he could again see across brown cornfields to the blue-grey edge of sea.

He waited for just over an hour before deciding to go down into the garden to see if he could find the boy. He was permitted to use the back-stairs, once the servants' stairs, on which now there was always a loathsome smell of stale cooking. He did not like these stairs and he was glad to be out of them, past the back entrance and the heaps of boiler coke, into the garden and the sun.

At eighty-three he walked very slowly, with a sort of deliberate majesty, keeping his head up more by habit than any effort, and it was some time before he could walk far enough across the lawns to find someone to ask about Pallister. Groups of young officers were playing croquet on the farthest lawn, and the knock of balls and the yelling of voices clapped together in the clear air.

Under one of the cedars, in shadow that was almost black, an officer in battledress was lying on the grass with a book. He had Canada on his shoulder.

'Excuse me,' the Colonel said.

'Oh! hullo, sir,' the Canadian said. 'How've you bin?'

'I was looking for Mr Pallister,' the Colonel said. 'We were to have a drink together. I thought you might have seen him somewhere.'

'I guess he bought it,' the Canadian said.

The language that he did not understand left the Colonel without a reply.

'Yeh!' the Canadian said. 'I guess he bought it. Over France last night.'

THE LIGHTHOUSE

The thin tongue of coast was so flat that it was like a scar on the sea. Nothing rose above the level of the one-storeyed shacks scattered about it like cubes of sea-worn wreckage except a light-house, standing up like a vast white candle in a wide lofty sky, so that from a distance it seemed to float in air.

By the end of September, after the heat of summer, the sea-flowers were dead. A long flat tide floated in, almost limped in, washing over and over again the same wide salt-grey waste of sand, the same bright fringe of shingle, black with fresh-strewn seaweed and sprinkled with pretty white and rose and turquoise shells. Salt dust blew on small winds from one side of the road to the other, rattling harshly on steely patches of sea-thistle and dune-grass, and then blew back again. It drifted finely against the shacks, with their sun-spent flowers, that would soon be closed for winter, and buried the steps of their porches a little deeper every day.

From the end of the peninsula it was a two-mile walk for Brand to get the papers. Every morning he walked along the cracked concrete road and bought the papers and perhaps a magazine from the shop where squat black plaice-boats, cur-tained about with kipper-coloured netting, were beached from the bay. The air was always thick with the smell of sun-dried sea-fish and gangs of swooping gulls crying about the boats, and he was always thirsty by the time he began to walk back along the shore.

Half-way back was a shack, facing the sea, that had tin-plate advertisements nailed over one side of it so that it glittered harshly, blue and green and white and red, in the sun. He noticed it first not because of the advertisements but because it had outside it a square of grass. This grass, watered all summer, was vivid green in the desert of beach and sand. In the middle of it was a white flag-pole and at the top of the flag-pole was a triangular scarlet flag, with ICES sewn across it in white letters.

He had been there nearly a week when he first went in. Sun

and sea-air had warped the jerry-built glass door so that he had to push it violently before it would open. Before he knew it he was half-thrown into the small café, against the counter.

Behind the counter stood a woman in a black fur coat and a green scarf on her head, and through a window behind her he could see the sea.

'And about time too,' she said. 'I thought you were never coming.'

She was smoking a cigarette and she did not take the cigarette from her mouth when she spoke to him. It was burning short and the smoke was curling up into her big face, crinkling the pouches under her eyes.

Suddenly, looking at him again, she burst out laughing.

'Oh! God alive, I thought it was the taxi.'

He smiled and she began coughing violently from smoke and laughter, so that grey ash spilt in a fine cloud on the black fur coat. She laughed again and did not shake it free.

'Hear that?' she called. 'Gentleman came in and I thought it was the cab.'

Behind the counter was a door and he could see a kitchen beyond it, but no one answered.

'Terribly sorry, sir.' The cigarette smoke burned straight up into her baggy colourless eyes. 'Very rude of me.' She let the ash drop on to her coat again. 'Something we can get you?'

'Glass of milk?' he said.

'Sorry, no milk. It's the drought. They cut us down.' She took the cigarette out of her mouth, coughing ash on the counter. 'Excuse me. Cuppa tea?'

'Cup of tea.'

'Haven't seen a taxi anywhere, I suppose, have you? What do you make the time?'

'Just after eleven.'

'Supposed to be here for eleven. Puts years on you.' She looked beyond him, irritated, through the glass door. 'Same with everything.'

He did not answer. She took a packet of cigarettes from the pocket of her fur coat and lit a fresh cigarette from the old, coughing again.

'Gentleman'd like a cuppa tea,' she called. 'Got one on?'

There was no answer.

'Whyn't you sit down?' she said. 'On holiday? Got a beach-hut here?'

'Up by the lighthouse.'

'Getting a bit late in the season. What d'you do with yourself all day?'

He did not know what to say; there was no point in telling her he was bored all day. Then suddenly she began coughing again, this time with excitement, spilling ash on her coat, the coarse skin of her face and neck creasing and flopping up and down; and in the same moment he heard the taxi on the road outside.

'God alive, I must fly!'

She came from behind the counter, waddling and coughing, picking up her handbag from the corner of the counter as she passed him.

'Cab's here!' she called. 'No message for Fred?'

She pulled the door open and went out across the square of grass under the flag-pole to where, on the concrete beyond, the taxi was turning round. The thin door banged loudly, shaking the walls of the shack, but there was no answer from the room behind.

He sat on one of the stools by the counter and opened the paper. Every day they were saying it was the driest, hottest summer for fifty years. There was already something boring about the sequence of dead dry days and the calm glitter of sea.

'Sugar?'

He looked up to see a girl standing at the door behind the counter. The high sea-light coming in at the window fell full on her face and made her eyes, especially, seem very large. They were dark brown eyes with extraordinary whites that were not really white at all. They were a pure pale blue, wet and shining, that made the point of the pupils almost black.

'Please,' he said.

'One or two?'

'One.'

He heard the lump of sugar clink on the spoon. She came up to the counter, carrying a cup in one hand and a teapot in the other.

'Anything in the paper?'

She poured out the tea.

'Not much.'

'Never is.' She tried for a second or two to read the paper where it was on the counter, upside down. 'Anything to eat? I forgot to ask you.'

'No,' he said. 'Just the tea.'

She gave up trying to read the paper upside down and for some moments stood with her arms folded on the counter. She had slim cream hands, the skin thin and transparent, so that the veins shone through like soft blue tendrils; and the fingers were slightly upturned as they lay on the smooth golden hairs of her forearms.

'Busy these days?' he said.

'I can be busy. Just how it takes me. Where are you?'

'Up by the lighthouse.'

She turned the paper round where it lay on the counter, turning it with one long finger, so that she could read it with her head only slightly averted. Her neck was long and deep cream under the dark brown hair.

'Ever been up there?' she said.

'No. Not me. Makes me giddy.'

'Does it?' she said. 'Funny. Never affects me.'

'Ugh,' he said.

'Got a beach-hut?'

'Yes.'

'What do you do for cooking? I hear there's no gas up there.'

'Never bother.'

'You're the sort of people who put us out of business,' she said.

He did not know what to say; he stirred his tea without drinking and remembered the woman running for the taxi.

'That your mother?'

'Don't blame me,' she said. 'She was born first. Off to London for the week while I look after the sea.'

With that curious expression she turned the paper round again, so that she could read it right way up. He found himself screwing his own head round, trying to read it as she had done, upside down, and as he did so he was aware of her body pressed against the counter. She gave him a quick glance and then went on reading; then after some moments she spoke without looking up.

'Not drinking your tea,' she said.

He sipped it gently, looking down at her over the edge of the cup.

She turned the paper over, lifting her body slightly in the act of doing so, raising her eyes, brown and casual, in the slightest flicker.

'I'll bet you think I'm rude. Reading your paper.'

'No,' he said. 'You can have it. I don't want it. Keep it and I'll call in later.'

'Come in and I'll get you a meal,' she said. 'Why don't you? You must eat sometimes.'

'I could.'

'Well, say it as if you wanted to,' she said.

He smiled.

'Nothing elaborate, just eggs or something. But say it as if you wanted to.'

She stared up at him with great brown eyes that were casual and bored but brilliant, too, with bright sea-light; he looked back at her and felt the blood beating up in his throat. He thought, too, that she knew it was beating there because she held him a little longer with that same slow bored stare.

'All right?'

'All right,' he said.

She smiled. She had a way of smiling by opening her mouth and putting her tongue slowly outward and pressing it against her teeth and then upward, casually and softly, against her lip.

'About six?' she said.

'About six.'

She pressed her tongue upward against her lips, and then, as if deliberately letting him go, lowered her eyes and folded her long creamy arms, blue with tender veins, on the paper.

'Now drink your tea,' she said.

Walking back along the sea-road, he thought of Ella. Things had not been going well with Ella. More and more she seemed to him like a peremptory bright-nosed hen decked up. She had begun to be a great one on committees. At supper, after the office, she bored him with histories of committees rather as she must, he thought, have bored the committees. Sometimes, in hasty moments, he did silly things like putting his socks on inside out, and that in turn would urge her to endless nagging resolutions, all of which he felt she had put down on the agenda of

their married differences. Whenever she came home from committees she wore the same dark brown straw hat. It was too
small for her; it sat on her head, mocking her, like a ridiculous
piece of flat stale toast. He longed to jump on it. One day he
almost did jump on it and she screamed: 'The trouble with you
is that you can't tolerate anything but yourself! You're so selfish,
so vain!' and in a fit of rage he had driven the car down to the
sea.

Back at the point, by the lighthouse, he read the papers and
watched the tide. It washed over a series of shallow corrugated
valleys, blue-grey with jelly-fish and sown with pretty rose and
white and turquoise shells. The sandy peninsula projected so far
out to sea that ships skirted it by only a hundred and fifty yards.
Sometimes liners came so close that he could see even the sparkle
of drinks in passengers' glasses in the dining-saloons or the
lounge. And sometimes passengers waved their hands.

He wondered about these passengers. Who were they all?
Among them were surely men who hated their wives because
they wore hats like slices of toast and wives who hated their hus-
bands for the monstrosity of trivial things.

He began to think of the girl in the café. Her voice, throaty
and casual, seemed to come along the seashore with the lazy softness of the tide. He thought of her hands. There was something
intensely disturbing in their creamy transparence and the blue
tendril veins. And then the extraordinary dark brown eyes, with
the whites that were really not white, but blue, like some of the
smoother pearl-like shells. And then the bored casual way of
pressing her tongue against her teeth and the bored casual way
of trying to read the paper upside down.

He swam twice during the afternoon. The sea, heavily salt and
warm, made him hungry and drowsy. The sun curved round and
shone flat on his face. He slept without realising it and woke
suddenly with the idea that one of the ships was ramming the
point. It was a liner painted white for the tropics and it seemed
for a second or two to tangle itself with the white cone of the
lighthouse and come bearing down on him where he lay.

It was past six when he woke and nearly seven o'clock by the
time he had dressed and walked along the sea-road to where the
scarlet flag was waving above the square of watered grass in the
evening sun.

The shack was closed. He started to rap on the thin glass door. The door was loose and rattled loudly, echoing across the empty beach in the warm still air.

After a moment or two he gave it up and went round to the back. The girl was lying on the sand, in a white and red-spotted cotton beach-dress, without shoes or stockings, her long blue-veined creamy legs and arms stretched out in the sun. She did not get up.

'You're a nice one,' she said.

'I went to sleep. I didn't realise—'

'I got fed up and closed. Nobody to talk to all afternoon, so I came out to look after the sea.'

Again he noticed that curious expression.

'I'm sorry,' he said.

She rolled over and lay sideways, looking up at him.

'Well: what do you fancy?'

'Anything; if it's not too late – whatever you've got.'

'It isn't what I've got, it's what you fancy.'

'Whatever you've got I'll fancy,' he said.

'Well, if that's the way you look at it.' She moved once again on the sand, turning her body. 'Can't see you. You're upside down.' He remembered how she had read the news-paper upside down and something in the turn of her body immediately electrified him, making the blood beat up in his throat.

'Oh! You're the same man. I wondered. Your voice sounded different.'

'Disappointed?'

'Oh! no. No. I just got the impression of you in my mind somehow, and I like to get the right impression' She suddenly knelt up, brushing away sand from her dress. 'Well, let's go in. The sea can look after itself for a bit.'

It struck him again as curious how she spoke, now and then, of looking after the sea. She stood up, brushing sand from first one leg and then another and then from her arms.

'Am I all sand at the back?'

'On your shoulders.'

'Brush me down, will you? It gets into everything – food and everything. Beds and everywhere.'

He brushed with both hands at the half-circle of her naked

shoulder. The skin was smooth and oily and he felt the blood
beat up into his throat again as he touched it with the sweeping
tips of his fingers under the thick brown hair.

'I'll fry you a Dover sole,' she said. 'A good fat one. How's
that?'

'It's just what I fancy.'

She had the sole ready in about half an hour. She pulled the
blinds down on that side of the café overlooking the sea-road,
and she laid him a table overlooking the sea. From there, as he
waited, he could see the lighthouse. The lamps had not begun
to burn and the tall white cylinder looked more than ever like
an unlit candle on the narrow scar of sand.

'Been up the lighthouse yet?'

She was in the kitchen and he called back: 'No. I told you.
Makes me feel –'

'You'll have to try it some day.'

'Not me,' he said.

The sole, dipped in golden breadcrumbs, was nicely fried.

'All right?' she said.

'Lovely. What about you?'

'You're a customer. Can't eat with the customers.'

'I hoped you could.'

'Well, there's no law against it. I'll have a cup of tea.'

She had changed her dress and now she was wearing a thin
frock of silky sea-bright green. It gave a smouldering candle-like
warmth to her bare arms as she crooked them on the table and
watched him eat.

'You wanted that. You were hungry,' she said.

'Didn't bother about lunch.'

She looked at the sea. It was after eight o'clock and now
suddenly, in a wonderful flash, the lamps in the lighthouse
began turning, swinging startling bars of light on darkening
water and shore.

'There she goes,' the girl said. 'I always love that. It sends a
thrill right through me. Right down. A real thrill. I watch it
every night.'

She was watching the light eagerly, her mouth parted, her
tongue touching her lip as she smiled.

As it grew slowly darker ships with star-like navigation lights
appeared across a copper-crested sea that was deep indigo under

a paler sky. After watching them for some time she turned her face and looked at him.

'Married?' she said.

'No,' he said.

'You ought to get yourself a nice wife that can cook.'

'Are you married?' he said.

'No,' she said. 'Not me.'

Who was Ella? The sudden accusing unreality of Ella forced itself on his conscience for a moment and then assumed the remoteness of one of the lights creeping slowly away to sea. His wife seemed in every way like one of those dim lights going out, going away for ever. Committees and the hat like toast, agenda of married faults and the face like a peremptory pecking hen's; there was no lie about them. They did not exist any more.

'What about Fred?' he said. He remembered the parting words of her mother.

'Oh! Fred. Fred's nobody. He's cook up there. We got another café at King's Cross. He's cook up there.' The lids of her eyes, olive and dark and gleaming, closed down smoothly as she looked at his empty cup and plate. 'More tea?'

'No, thank you.'

'Like to go outside for a breath of air?'

'If you like.'

They were already outside when she spoke once again of looking after the sea. The shack had a small railed verandah overlooking the beach. Sand had piled against it in deep smooth breasts, submerging the lower steps. She leaned against one of the posts of it. The shore was dark except for the repeated flash of the lighthouse, revolving like a wheel, and as she stared at the sea and spoke again of looking after it he said:

'Think it'll run away or something?'

'No.'

'What then?'

'Oh! nothing.'

He watched the lighthouse flashing on her face, heightening sharply every few seconds or so the candle-like warmth given by the green dress; and then he said:

'Odd. What's the idea of looking after the sea? That's one thing that'll look after itself – '

She turned on him in the moment that the lighthouse flashed.

It gave the impression of her entire body leaping into flame. All her bored casual face flared up, bright and bitter and angry.

'What else have I got to do? God, I got nothing else to do but look after it, have I? Nobody to talk to from Monday to Friday. Nothing to do, nobody to talk to. What else have I got to do but look after it? God, I feel it's all I got left – '

The act of kissing her for the first time had in it the shock of something bare and bruising and antagonistic. He had not expected it to be like that. He had wanted it to be drawn out of her sleepy languid casualness: to be one with the soft brown eyes, the way she read the paper upside down. Now she held him with both arms and the stiffened frame of her body, driving her mouth at his with the dry hunger of long boredom; and all the time the lighthouse flashed with its dazzling revolutions on her face.

After a time she was quieter and they lay down on the sand. He could hear the sea: gentle, the tide out, endless small waves licking backwards in the warm September darkness. 'If you hadn't turned up I'd have gone off my head. I thought you wouldn't turn up – I'd have gone off my head –'

He liked her more as she quietened. She seemed to grow drowsy and languid again, the frame of her body in its relaxation melting into the deep softness he wanted: the entire antithesis of Ella, the pecking hen-like face, the toast-like hat; the antidote to all his own dry boredom and rage. He found her limbs in long deep curves. Her skin had seemed so delicate, with its fine transparence and the many blue tendrils of veins, that the full discovered strength of her body surprised him. 'I wanted you like that,' she said, 'by the sea. I wanted you terribly.' The lighthouse flashed on her face, giving the brown eyes a look of transfixed dark burning. 'Be careful how you touch me. You make me feel how the lighthouse does.'

Walking home at last, after midnight, he understood her feeling about the lighthouse. It had been the flame in the drabness of her boredom: burning and flashing suddenly to excite her once a day. He was pleased to think he was like that. He was pleased to stand where he was and watch, like a fading down-channel light, the dying discordant figure of Ella and Ella's hat, the former world of committees and catechisms and the pecking hen. He felt slightly intoxicated and elated as if he stood on the top of the lighthouse, watching the minute and inconsequential light of something that had bored and angered him and would do so no longer.

He had arranged to go back for lunch next day. 'Not too early,' she said, 'because I can close up from two to five. You can swim and have a lie in the sun,' and in the morning, for the first time, he did not trouble to fetch the papers. It was enough to wait for afternoon.

But about two o'clock, after they had eaten and just as she was about to lock up, something happened. He looked out of the window and saw a wild troop of Boy Scouts invading the shore. Soon they began to invade the shack. He had dreamed so long of lying with her in warm sun, alone on the shore, that the sight of scores of small boys besieging her for ice-cream and drinks and sandwiches brought him furious frustration. She, too, looked desperate and he could have hit a ridiculous grey-haired scoutmaster who said:

'You may remember us. We dropped in last year. We remembered your flag.'

Bathing and yelling, punting footballs, littering the shore with cartons and trousers and shirts and papers, the boys stayed until six o'clock. So many of them came into the shack that finally he took off his jacket and for four hours, impotent and full of hatred of them, he helped the girl behind the counter. All afternoon there was a dry hunger in her eyes that made him think she could not wait for him.

'Well, it'll please Ma,' she said when it was all over. And then a cheerful thought: 'Anyway, we took enough so we close to-morrow and the next day. That's if there's no Boy Scouts.'

'There'll be no Boy Scouts,' he said. 'To-morrow we'll go to the lighthouse.'

'That's an idea.'

'Perhaps we could have a trip in the car.'

'I'd like that. That would be lovely.'

Again and again, in the darkness on the shore, to the sound of small consuming lapping waves, the lighthouse flashed on her face. Her long arms held him down on the soft sand and the deep brown eyes burned insatiably.

Next day, when they climbed the lighthouse, a little breeze was blowing in fitful gusts against the sun. It had the effect of ploughing the sea into furrows of brilliant white and blue. Along the coast small sails skimmed about; white gulls planed down on long air-currents about black plaice-boats and the dazzling candle of lighthouse; and the white sea-light was heady and very beautiful.

It seemed to him that the top of the lighthouse swayed. All his fear of heights rushed up through his body and he felt the irresistible paralysing terror of wanting to go over. It froze the back of his legs coldly and he was hardly conscious of the keeper, who was also a guide, saying:

'The point puts on another six feet of land every year. Can you see where it's creeping out? Ten or fifteen years and they'll have to be thinking of building another lighthouse.'

Brand could not look and the keeper pointed inland over flats of sea-thistled shingle:

'That's the old lighthouse. That shows you where the point used to be.'

All the time the girl moved carelessly from side to side of the lighthouse top, following the keeper's fingers, leaning non-chalantly over, long arms folded, staring straight down. To Brand's intense horror she hung over the side, laughing, waving to groups of people below.

'For God's sake,' he said, and felt terribly and weakly sick at the thought that a beating squall of wind might, in an awful moment, move the wrong way and take her over.

'Now if you'll follow me down, sir,' the keeper said.

They stood for a moment together, alone on the top. She held him flat against her body, her skirt flapping in the breeze against her legs, and he could have sworn that once again the lighthouse swayed.

She kissed him, holding him rigidly, but he knew the light-house rocked. For some idiotic reason he thought of the pre-carious toast-like hat perched on Ella's head, and the girl said:

'Don't be so jittery. There's nothing to be scared of – '

'I hate it. I always have hated it.'

'It's because you let it,' she said. 'If you looked down – just made yourself look down – you'd be all right.' She began laugh-ing at him: gay with the quivering exhilaration of breeze and height and sun. 'Come on – look down. Make yourself. It's better.'

Once again she leaned far over. This time she held his hand, and for the space of a second or two he looked down too, his entire body wrapped in a stiffened chrysalis of vertigo. A sinister narrowing world of shore, of boats, of faces and of kaleidoscope sea-waves seemed to draw him down and then the girl laughed at him again, mocking slightly:

'Come on. You can't take it. The keeper's waiting.'

Even fifty or sixty feet below he could still feel the horror in his legs and he said:

'Don't you feel anything? Doesn't it affect you at all?'

'Only like you,' she said. 'That nice feeling. Right through my body.'

She was pleased about the car. From the new lighthouse they drove inland, through a flat sea-beaten world of drab shingle and faded sea-poppy and steely sea-thistle, towards the old. He thought its black tarred stump looked hideous even among the cracked concrete of ruined sea-defences and shabby summer bungalows whose doorsteps were being slowly buried by autumn sand.

'Like an old lady going to a funeral or something,' the girl said.

Like every horrifying experience the cold moments at the lighthouse top afterwards exhilarated him. For each of the three following nights as he lay on the shore with the girl he felt a certain vague bravery about it all.

'I'm your lighthouse,' he would say to her. Already it was Friday, and for two nights he had not troubled to go back to sleep at the hut. 'I make you feel the same way – '

'Not after to-night,' she said.

A moment of freezing sickness, identical with all he had felt on the lighthouse, turned his stomach over.

'What are you talking about?'

'Ma comes to-morrow. Did you forget? She's down every week-end, Saturday to Monday.'

'Oh! God,' he said, 'is that all? I thought – '

'You better keep out of the way,' she said. 'Just for a night or two.'

'I could come in for a cup of tea or something,' he said, 'couldn't I? She'd never know.'

'Not Ma?' she said. 'The old gimlet. Not Ma? You never get over Ma.'

'God,' he said, 'the whole week-end – '

'There's all next week,' she said. 'Plenty of time.' He felt her reasoning sweetness express itself in one of those slow casual expanding smiles. Her tongue touched her lip and a wonderful beauty of dark eyes held him profoundly as the lighthouse flashed. He was agonised once again by the thought of giving her up, and she said: 'A rest from each other will do us good. Then we'll have all next week. What are you worrying for?'

'I want you – all the time. Terribly – '

'I'm here,' she said. He saw all the languid beauty of her long curving body as she pressed herself down into dark dry sand. 'Nobody's stopping you.'

The next day, Saturday, he did not see her at all. He could not bring himself to walk along the sea-road; he did not want the papers. Teasing him, she had said: 'You can always go up the lighthouse. You can wave from there. If I see you I'll know it's you.'

And that afternoon, in a moment of puerile anguish, he went up. A great dry loneliness, horrible as the lifeless sea-broken concrete road and the barren shingle, had held him all day. From the top of the lighthouse the tranquil bay, circled by a gigantic bracelet of sun-dried sand, was like pure glass, windless and beautiful. He stared across lines of plaice-boats and a few trippers to the shack. The red flag had not enough air to raise it from the pole; but he could see, underneath it, the spray of a water-hose, sprinkling the bright square of grass.

Presently he saw figures there. It seemed like a man and perhaps, he tried to persuade himself, the girl; but it was much too far away. He even waved his hand; but nothing happened and soon, driven by sudden misery and vertigo, he hurried down.

For the rest of that day and during Sunday his only remedy was to swim and walk westward, away from the shack, in the queer derelict half-urban, half-marsh country between the two lighthouses. He began to think of Ella. When he was with the girl all his thought of Ella was moulded in terms of an amused and tolerant pity. Poor dear old Ella: he really felt sorry for her. All the discordance about her vanished. Did she wonder about him? Had she gone round in panic circles of distress? Had it spoiled the routine of committees, the hideous respectable pose of the toast-like hat? What would she say, he thought, if she could see me now? Poor dear old Ella. The ease of that long generous body on the sand would have shocked her, would have made her realise that there were not only women who gave more pleasure than they asked, but gave it without asking questions, as beautifully as flowers.

But that day, as he tried to wear out Sunday, he did not have many amused and rather fanciful thoughts of women like flowers. Ella appeared to stand up in the flat endless day with the gauntness of the old lighthouse above the ugly marsh. She was a terrible relic, Ella; and somehow Sunday was her day. She had a great fondness for fussing about the kitchen on Sunday mornings, roasting beef, baking a particular kind of tart called Maids of Honour. What maids, he would tease her, and what honour? Her hands were floury and he ate the tarts from the stove, while they were still hot. To-day, inexplicably, between loneliness and discordance, he felt keenly the absence of these trivialities. It was not permanent; he knew that. It was just Sunday. It was less that he missed Ella than that Sunday was a day of infinite desolation when deprived of the comfort of floured hands, beef, hot tarts and long-known company. Monday would show it all to have been another example of puerile heartache; but to-day he could not bear it at all.

And finally, because he could not bear it, he walked along, about half-past seven, to the shack. Lights were burning and a few people were having supper. He walked past and got himself several drinks, a mile farther on, at a place called *The Fisherman's Arms,* before walking back again.

When he walked back lights were still burning in the shack but the place seemed empty. After a few moments he went in. The girl's mother was leaning on the counter, coughing cigarette ash down the heavy black front of her body, but there was no sign of the girl.

'Yessir?' she said.

'Too late for anything?'

'Never too late for anything. What'll it be? Coffee, tea, orange?'

'I'll take coffee.'

'You'll take coffee,' she said.

While he drank it he said:

'Remember me? I'm the fellow you mistook for the taxi-driver last Monday.'

'God alive, so it is.' Coughing and laughing, she sprayed a small cloud of cigarette ash. 'I don't know whatever you thought of me, sir.'

'Your daughter made up for it,' he said. 'Got me a nice meal that day.'

'Nice cook,' she said.

He looked round the café. 'Not here to-night?'

'Gone to the flicks with Fred.'

'Fred?' he said. He could feel a horrible tightness, cold and not unlike the vertigo he so hated and dreaded, taking hold of his body, cramping it with jealousy and fear. 'Boy friend?'

'Boy friend my foot,' she said. 'Husband.'

Monday brought, as he knew it would, the notion that to be lonely for Ella was something quite puerile. Between the thought of Ella and the thought of the girl he felt a haunting and growing sense of being cheated. Ella, he felt, had got him into this. He felt dislocated, slightly crazy, trapped. That infernally silly hen-like face, the committees and the maddening toast-like hat had manœuvred him into a trap.

It was late afternoon before he could bring himself to go along to the café. The girl had closed the café and he found her lying behind it, as he always did, on the sand. The breeze of the last few days had piled up still higher the smooth clean breasts of sand below the verandah, submerging yet another of the steps. In one of the hollows between these breasts she lay in her red beach-dress, staring at the sky.

'Oh God, I thought you were never coming. I wanted you terribly – I hated the waiting –'

He let himself be drawn down, almost sucked down, by her long arms and the tightened frame of her body, stiffly anguished as it had been when he had first kissed her.

'Did you want me?' she said.

'All the time,' he said. 'How was the week-end?'

'Oh! terrible. She talked and talked. Nothing but talk. I was bored to death. What did you do?'

'Went to the lighthouse.'

'There,' she said. 'You see. How was it?'

'I'm getting better. It's like you said. I just need practice.'

She laughed, pressing her tongue against her lips, her brown eyes brilliant and languid and burning in the shell-like whites.

'One more trip and you'll be all right,' she said.

'Might be.'

'Probably when you're all right you won't make me feel how you do,' she said. 'Had you thought of that?'

'No.'

'Make me feel like it now,' she said.

He did not speak of Fred until they lay in the sand in darkness. A twisted and crazy sort of dislocation made him keep back, until then, all he felt by way of the trap, the cheating and the jealousy. Out at sea small navigation lights floated about like stars and one of them, as before, was Ella, dying and fading away; and he hated her because of his pain.

'How was the husband?' he said.

'You don't have to speak like that,' she said. 'No need to speak like that.' Her face, in the flash from the lighthouse, was undis- turbed, casual and languid as ever.

'You didn't tell me,' he said.

'It didn't make any difference. It didn't and it doesn't now.'

'Me during the week and a change for Sundays,' he said. Rage beat at his pride with callous and lacerating strokes of pain. He felt himself drop away, crazy and blinded and embittered by acid dregs of cheating and jealousy. All the time he was aware of her moving her body with quiet suppleness deeper into the sand and that movement, too, made him ache with helpless bitterness.

'You didn't tell me either,' she said. 'But it wouldn't make any difference if you did. No difference at all.'

'I'd nothing to tell.' His voice was quiet; he could hear the tide slowly coming in across the sand.

'Well, then – who should care?' She moved in the sand again, supple and astonishingly quiet, and in distraction he found her body once again in long deep curves; the flash of the lighthouse fell on her mouth, making it glisten and then leaving it wonder- fully dark again as the light swung out to sea.

'We're just two people,' she said. 'People get so messed up about the right and wrong of things. We're just two people. What do we want with rights and wrongs? All we want is here.'

No: not here, he thought. Vainly he tried to listen to the tide;

but he was distracted by the feel of her soft body into agonies of mind that flung up thoughts of Ella and the lighthouse. He determined not to be afraid of the lighthouse any longer, and now, too, he remembered the girl, high up there, leaning over.

'Come on, kiss me; it's nothing,' she said. 'Come on; just once more like the lighthouse. In case it cures you. You never know.'

She folded him down into a body that had lost the last of its rigidity and seemed now to have the quality of burying him into itself, like the sand. The lighthouse flashed several times, across the shore and across the long, oblivious kiss, and then she freed her face and said, smiling:

'When do we go up again?'

'To-morrow?' he said.

'When do you suppose they'll put up the new lighthouse?' she said. He did not answer. His heart, at that moment, seemed to stop beating. His body lay imprisoned in its harsh chrysalis of jealousy and weakness and fear. He could not look at her face; and down on the shore there was no movement but a small wind eating at the sea and innumerable small waves casually consuming what remained of the waste of sand.

THE FLAG

'We are surrounded by the most ghastly people,' the Captain said. All across miles of unbroken pasture there was not another house.

Up through the south avenue of elms, where dead trees lifted scraggy bone against spring sky, bluebells grew like thick blue corn, spreading into the edges of surrounding grass. The wind came softly, in a series of light circles from the west. Here and there an elm had died and on either side of it young green leaves from living trees were laced about smoke-brown brittle branches. In a quadrangle of wall and grass the great house lay below.

'You never really see the beauty of the house until you get up here,' the Captain said. Though still young, not more than forty-five or so, he was becoming much too fat. His ears were like thickly-veined purple cabbage leaves unfurling on either side of flabby swollen cheeks. His mouth, pink and flaccid, trembled sometimes like the underlip of a cow.

'They have killed the elms,' he said. 'Finished them. They used to be absolutely magnificent.'

He stopped for a moment and I saw that he wanted to draw breath, and we looked back down the hill. Down beyond soldierly lines of trees, the tender lucent green broken here and there by the black of dead branches, I could see a flag waving in such intermittent and strengthless puffs of air that it, too, seemed dead. It was quartered in green and scarlet and flew from a small round tower that was like a grey pepper-box stuck in the western arm of the cross-shaped house.

Now I could see, too, that there were four avenues of elms, repeating in immense pattern the cross of the house below. As we stood there, the Captain making gargling noises in his throat, a cuckoo began calling on notes that were so full and hollow that it was like a bell tolling from the elms above us. Presently it seemed to be thrown on a gust of air from the tip of a tree, to float down-wind like a bird of grey paper.

'There she goes,' I said.

'Tank emplacements mostly,' the Captain said. His face shone lividly in the sun, his lip trembling. 'The place was occupied right, left and centre. We used to have deer too, but the last battalion wiped them out.'

The breath of bluebells was overpoweringly sweet on the warm wind.

'When we get a little higher you will see the whole pattern of the thing,' the Captain said.

Turning to renew the ascent, he puffed in preparation, his veins standing out like purple worms on his face and neck and forehead.

'Tired?' he said. 'Not too much for you? You don't mind being dragged up here?'

'Not at all.'

'One really has to see it from up here. One doesn't grasp it otherwise. That's the point.'

'Of course.'

'We shall have a drink when we get back,' he said. He laughed and the eyes, very blue but transparent in their wateriness, were sad and friendly. 'In fact, we shall have several drinks.'

It was only another fifty yards to the crown of the hill and we climbed it in silence except for the hissing of the Captain's breath against his teeth. All the loveliness of spring came down the hill and past us in a stream of heavy fragrance, and at the top, when I turned, I could feel it blowing past me, the wind silky on the palms of my hands, to shine all down the hill on the bent sweet grasses.

'Now,' the Captain said. It was some moments before he could get breath to say another word. Moisture had gathered in confusing drops on the pink lids of his eyes. He wiped it away. 'Now you can see it all.'

All below us, across the wide green hollow in which there was not another house, I could see, as he said, the pattern of the thing. Creamy grey in the sun, the house made its central cross of stone, the four avenues of elms like pennants of pale green flying from the arms of it across the field.

'Wonderful,' I said.

'Wonderful, but not unique,' he said. 'Not unique.'

Not angrily at first but wearily, rather sadly, he pointed about him with both arms. 'It's simply one of six or seven examples here alone.'

Then anger flitted suddenly through the obese watery-eyed face with such heat that the whole expression seemed to rise to a bursting fester, and I thought he was about to rush, in destructive attack at something, down the hill.

'It was all done by great chaps,' he said, 'creative chaps. It's only we of this generation who are such absolute destructive clots.'

'Oh! I don't know.'

'Won't even argue about it,' he said. His face, turned to the sun, disclosed now an appearance of rosy calm, almost boy-like, and he had recovered his breath. 'Once we were surrounded by the most frightfully nice people. I don't mean to say intellectual people and that kind of thing, but really awfully nice. You know, you could talk to them. They were on your level.'

'Yes.'

'And now you see what I mean, they've gone. God knows where but they're finished. I tell you everything is a shambles.'

Across from another avenue the cuckoo called down-wind again and over the house I saw the flag lifted in a green and scarlet flash on the same burst of breeze. I wanted to ask him about the flag, but he said:

'It's perfectly ghastly. They've been hounded out. None of them left. All of them gone – '

Abruptly he seemed to give it up. He made gestures of apology, dropping his hands:

'So sorry. Awfully boring for you, I feel. Are you thirsty? Shall we go down?'

'When you're ready. I'd like to see the house – '

'Oh! please, of course. I'd like a drink, anyway.'

He took a last wide look at the great pattern of elm and stone, breathing the deep, almost too sweet scent of the hill.

'That's another thing. These perishers don't know the elements of decent drinking. One gets invited to the dreariest cocktail parties. The drinks are mixed in a jug and the sherry comes from God knows where.' Anger was again reddening his face to the appearance of a swollen fester. 'One gets so depressed that one goes home and starts beating it up. You know?'

I said yes, I knew, and we began to walk slowly down the hill, breathing sun-warm air deeply, pausing fairly frequently for another glance at the scene below.

'How is it with you?' he said. 'In your part of the world? Are you surrounded by hordes of virgin spinsters?'

'They are always with us,' I said.

He laughed, and in that more cheerful moment I asked him about the flag.

'Oh! it's nothing much.' He seemed inclined to belittle it. I thought. 'It gives a touch of colour.'

'I must look at it.'

'Of course. We can go up to the tower. There's a simply splendid view from there. You can see everything. But we shall have a drink first. Yes?'

'Thank you.'

'My wife will be there now. She will want to meet you.'

Slowly we went down to the house. About its deep surrounding walls there were no flowers and the grass had not been mown since some time in the previous summer, but old crucified peaches, and here and there an apricot, had set their flowers for fruiting and it was hot in the hollow between the walls. At the long flight of stone steps, before the front door, the Captain said something in a desultory way about the beauty of the high windows but evidently he did not expect a reply. He leapt up the last four or five steps with the rather desperate agility of a man who has won a race at last, and a moment later we were in the house.

In the large high-windowed room with its prospect of unmown grass the Captain poured drinks and then walked nervously about with a glass in his hand. I do not know how many drinks he had before his wife appeared, but they were large and he drank them quickly.

'Forty-six rooms and this is all we can keep warm,' he said.

When his wife came in at last she was carrying bunches of stiff robin-orange lilies. She was very dark and her hands, folded about the lily stalks, were not unlike long blanched stalks of up-rooted flowers themselves. She had a hard pallor about her face, very beautiful but in a way detached and not real, that made the Captain's festering rosiness seem more florid than ever.

I liked the lilies, and when I asked about them she said:

'We must ask Williams about them. I'm frightful at names. He'll know.'

'Williams knows everything,' the Captain said.

He poured a drink without asking her what she wanted and she seemed to suck at the edge of the glass, drawing in her lips so that they made a tight scarlet bud.

'Are you keen on flowers?' she said.

I said 'Yes,' and she looked at me in a direct clear way that could not have been more formal. Her eyes had slits of green, like cracks, slashed across the black.

'That's nice,' she said.

'Has Williams done the cabbages?' the Captain said.

'What cabbages? Where?'

'He knew damn well he had cabbages to do,' the Captain said. 'I told him so.'

'How should I know what he has to do and what he hasn't to do?' she said.

'How should you know,' he said. He drank with trembling hands, trying to steady himself a little. He went to the window and stared out. The room was so large that his wife and I seemed to be contained, after his walking away, in a separate and private world bordered by the big fireless hearth and the vase where she was arranging flowers. She smiled and I looked at her hands.

'Williams will tell you the name of the flowers if you like to come along to the conservatory before you go.' She did not raise her voice; there was no sound except the plop of lily stalks falling softly into the water in the vase. 'He would like it. He likes people who are interested.'

She dropped in the last of the lilies and then took off her coat and laid it on a chair. It was black and underneath she was wearing a yellow jumper of perpendicular ribbed pattern over a black skirt. It went very well with her black hair, her white long face and her green-shot eyes.

I heard the Captain pouring himself another drink, and he said:

'What about the tower? You still want to go up?'

'I really ought to go.'

'Oh! Good God man, no. We've hardly seen a thing.'

'He's coming to see the conservatory, anyway,' his wife said.

'Is that so?' he said. 'Well, if he's to see everything you'd better get cracking.'

He made a jabbing kind of gesture against the air with his

glass and he was so close to the window that I thought for a moment he would smash one glass against another. I could not tell if he was nervous or impatient. He covered it up by pouring himself another drink, and his wife said, with acid sweetness:

'There are guests too, my dear.'

'No thanks,' I said.

'You haven't had anything,' the Captain said. 'Good God, I feel like beating it up.'

'If you still want to see the conservatory I think we'd better go,' she said.

I went out of the room with her and we had gone some way to the conservatory, which really turned out to be a hot-house of frilled Victorian pattern beyond the walls on the south side of the house, before I realised that the Captain was not with us.

'Williams,' she called several times. 'Williams.' Big scarlet amaryllis trumpets stared out through the long house of glass. 'Ted!'

Presently Williams came out of the potting shed and I thought he seemed startled at the sight of me. He was a man of thirty-five or so with thick lips and carefully combed dark brown hair that he had allowed to grow into a curly pad on his neck. There was a kind of stiff correct strength about him as he stared straight back at her.

She introduced me and said: 'We'd like to see the conservatory.'

'Yes, madam,' he said.

It was very beautiful in the conservatory. The pipes were still on and the air was moistly sweet and strangling. The big scarlet and pink and crimson-black amaryllis had a kind of golden frost in their throats. They were very fiery and splendid among banks of maidenhair, and when I admired them Williams said:

'Thank you, sir. They're not bad.'

'Don't be so modest,' she said. 'They're absolutely the best ever.'

He smiled.

'What we haven't done to get them up to this,' she said.

I walked to the far end by the house to look at a batch of young carnations, and when I turned back the Captain's wife was holding Williams by the coat-sleeve. It exactly as if she were absent-mindedly picking a piece of dust from it, yet it was also as if she held him locked, in a pair of pincers. I heard her saying something, too, but what it was I never knew, because at that moment the fiery festering figure of the Captain began shouting down the path from the direction of the house. I could not hear what he said, either.

'He's worrying to get you up to the tower,' she said. 'I'm frightfully sorry you're being dragged about like this.'

'Not at all.'

Williams opened the door for me. The cuckoo was calling up the hillside, and the Captain, more rosy than ever, was coming up the path.

'Don't want to hurry you, but it takes longer than you think to get up there.'

At the door of the conservatory his wife stretched out her hand. 'I'll say good-bye,' she said, 'in case I don't see you again.' We shook hands, and her hand, in curious contrast to the moist sweet heat of the house behind her, was dry and cool. Williams did not come to say good-bye. He had hidden himself beyond the central staging of palm and fern.

The Captain and I walked up to the tower. Once again we could see, as from the top of the hill, the whole pattern of the thing: the four avenues of elms flying like long green pennants from the central cross of the house, the quadrangle of stone below, the corn-like bluebells wind-sheaved on the hill. The Captain staggered about, pointing with unsteady fingers at the landscape, and the flag flapped in the wind.

'Curious thing is you can see everything and yet can't see a damned thing,' the Captain said. On all sides, across wide elm-patterned fields, there was still no sign of another house. Below us the conservatory glittered in the sun and it was even possible to see, huge and splendidly scarlet under the glass, the amaryllis staring back at us.

The Captain began to cry.

'You get up here and you'd never know any difference,' he said. His tears were simply moist negative oozings on the lids of his pink-lidded eyes. They might have been caused by the wind that up there, on the tower, was a little fresher than in the hollow below.

'Never know it was going to pot,' he said. 'Everything. The whole damn thing.'

I felt I had to say something and I remembered the flag.

'Oh! it's simply a thing I found in an attic,' he said. 'Just looks well. It doesn't mean a thing.'

'Nothing heraldic?'

'Oh! Good God, no. Still, got to keep the flag flying.' He made an effort at a smile.

I said I had seen somewhere, in the papers, or perhaps it was a book, I could not remember where, that heraldry was simply nothing more than a survival of the fetish and the totem pole, and he said:

'Evil spirits and that sort of thing? Is that so? Damn funny.'

Again, not angrily but sadly, biting his nails, with the trembling of his lower lip that was so like the lip of a cow, he stared at the green empty beautiful fields, and once again I felt all the warm sweetness of spring stream past us, stirring the green and scarlet flag, on tender lazy circles of wind.

Below us the Captain's wife and Williams came out of the greenhouse, and I saw them talking inside the winking scarlet roof of glass.

'Well, you've seen everything,' the Captain said. 'We'll have another snifter before you go.'

'No thanks. I really ought –'

'No?' he said. 'Then I'll have one for you. Eh? Good enough?'

'Good enough,' I said.

We climbed down from the tower and he came to the gate in the fields to say good-bye. Across the fields there were nearly two miles of track, with five gates to open, before you reached the road. The Captain's eyes were full of water and he had begun to bite his nails again and his face was more than ever like a florid fester in the sun.

There was no sign of his wife, and as I put in the gears and let the car move away he looked suddenly very alone and he said something that, above the noise of the car, sounded like:

'Cheers. Thanks frightfully for coming. Jolly glad –'

Half a mile away, as I got out to open the first of the five field gates, I looked back. There was no sign of life at all. The Captain had gone into the house to beat it up. The greenhouse was hidden by the great cross of stone. All that moved was the cuckoo blown once again from the dying elms like a scrap of torn paper, and on the tower, from which the view was so magnificent, the flag curling in the wind.

THE FRONTIER

Twice a month, going back to the tea-garden in the north, he took the Darjeeling night mail out of the heat of Calcutta; seldom without meeting on the station as he departed some returning English nurse with a basket of primroses fresh from the hills, but never, for some reason, seeing these same nurses go. Calcutta, with its vast and sticky heat, its air charged with post-war doom, shrivelled them in the moment of departure into nonentity. The hills revived and re-shaped them, so that they returned, carrying their little native baskets of yellow and pink and purple primula, shaded with fern, northern and cool as English spring, like strangers coming in from another world.

He arrived at the last junction of the broad-gauge line at six in the morning, in a cool dawn of exquisite dusty mistiness through which in the dry season the snows were rarely visible. He longed always to see these snows, cloud-like or icy-blue or at their most wonderful like vast crests of frozen sea-foam, and was disappointed whenever he stepped from the cinder-dusted night train on to a platform of seething dhotis and smoke-brown faces, to find that he could not see them in the northern sky. He envied always those travellers who were going further north and would, from their bedroom windows, see Kangchenjunga as they shaved. He thought jealously of the little nurses and the last war-ime service girls he never saw on their way to Darjeeling, but only, refreshed and snow-cool, as they came down to the Delta again, carrying their mountain flowers.

Wherever he appeared along the line, especially at the terminus where he drank a cup of milkless tea before driving out in the lorry the sixty miles to the tea-garden, there was a respect for him that was friendly. He had been travelling up and down there, in the same way, for twenty years. He had a long lean figure and a pale face, rather dreamy and prematurely grey and in very hot weather blue-lipped, that had become almost Indian-ised, giving him a look of Asiatic delicacy. He had learned, very early, that in the East time is an immensity that does not matter;

that it is better not to get excited; that what does not happen to-day will happen to-morrow and that death, it is very probable, will come between. His chief concern was not to shout, not to worry, not to get excited, but to grow and manufacture a tolerably excellent grade of tea.

There was a clubhouse at the junction, deliciously shaded with large palms and peepul trees, an old white house with exceptionally lofty open rooms through which birds flew freely, where he sometimes shaved in the mornings after the more hideous train journeys and then had a quick breakfast before driving on to the plantation. There was also an army station near, and during the war the club had become a mere transit camp, with both English and Indian officers piling bedrolls in the doorway, and rather noisy behaviour in the compounds. There were often girls there too, and once he had seen an Indian girl, in khaki uniform, of the very highest type, having cocktails with a bunch of wartime subalterns who belonged to some dismal section of army accountancy and were in consequence behaving like abandoned invaders. It upset him a little. He looked at her with envious deep feeling for a long time. She had a pale, aloof, high-cheeked beauty, with smoky brown shadows of the eyes and purple depth of hair, that he had never grown used to; and he longed to talk to her. But she, too, was going southward at a moment when he was coming north; she was simply one of those entrancing, maddening figures that war threw up for a few illuminating seconds before it snuffed them out again; and in the end he went on to the plantation alone.

He always went on to the plantation alone. In the misty distances of the Dooar country there was a curious tranquillity and it entranced and bored him at the same time. It entranced him by the beauty of its remoteness. It had the strange tenseness, amplified in daylight by heat haze and at night by the glow of forest fires in the Bhutan hills, of a country at the foot of great mountains that were themselves a frontier. There was an intense and overshadowed hush about it. He felt always, both on the long truck journey across recurrent dried or flooded river beds and then on the green orderly tea plantation itself, that something wonderful and dramatic was about to happen there.

And nothing ever did. His boredom sprang from a multitude of cheated moments. The place was a great let-down. It was like coming down to a meal, day after day, year in, year out, and finding the same tablecloth, impeccably ironed and spread, white in perfect invitation. There was about to be a wonderful meal on it, and there never was.

His visits to the plantation were like that. He expected something wonderful to dramatise itself out of the hazy fire-shot hills, the uneasy nearness of a closed frontier, the deep Mongol distances lost so often in sublime sulphur haze. And he expected Kangchenjunga. The days when he saw the snows of the mountain always compensated him, in a wonderful way, for the humdrum parochial business of going the rounds of the plantation, visiting the MacFarlanes on the adjoining estate, talking of Dundee, doling out the Sunday issue of rice and oils to his workers, and eating about a dozen chickens, skinny and poorly cooked, between Friday and Monday afternoon. He also conceived that he had a sense of duty to the place. He had rather a touching pride in an estate he had taken over as derelict and that was now a place with thirty or forty miles of metalled road, with hardly a weed, and with every tea-pruning neatly burned, every bug neatly captured by yellow pot-bellied children, every worker devoted and contented. And, though he was not aware of it, he was bored by that too.

And then something upset him. One of his workers got drunk on rice-beer, ran madly about the plantation for a day, and then raped and murdered a woman over by the MacFarlane boundary.

When he got down to the plantation on his next visit the murderer, armed with a stolen rifle, was still roaming about the low bamboo-forest country along the river. Everybody was stupidly excited, and it was impossible to get the simplest accurate report. The affair had developed into a gorgeous and monstrous Indian mess, everybody at clamorous cross-purposes, sizzling with rumour and cross-rumour and revived malice, seething with that maddening Indian fatalism that sucks fun out of disaster and loves nothing better than prolonging it by lying and lamentation.

After he had organised search parties and sent out rumour-grubbing scouts, putting on a curfew for the women and children, he spent most of the week-end driving wildly about his thirty-five miles of metalled road in pursuit of false reports. In the tiring excitement of it he forgot to look for Kangchenjunga, only remembering it when he was far back in the heart of Bengal, in the hot and cinder-blackened train.

When he came back on his next visit, a week earlier than normal, the murderer had not been found. He was worried about it all and did not sleep well in the hot train, with its noisy midnight dislocations. It was a blow to his pride and he was angry that it had ever happened.

Then he fell asleep, to be woken suddenly by the sound of frantic arguments. The train had stopped and he put on a light. He let down the gauze window and saw, in the light of the station outside, a mass of seething dhotis clamouring at each other with brown antennæ, like moths. He shouted angrily for everybody to shut up. A bubble of surprise among the dhotis, with explanatory sing-song inflexions, was followed by someone shouting back, in English:

'Shut up yourself! You're lucky. You've got a compartment. They won't let me on.'

'I'll be out in a moment!' he said.

'Oh! don't worry.'

He slipped his dressing-gown over his pyjamas and went out on to the platform, really no more than a length of cinder track running past the metals, and pushed his way among the fluttering dhotis. He heard the English voice again and then saw, among the crowd, under the low station lights, what seemed to him an incredibly unreal thing.

Standing there was one of the nurses he had so often seen coming back to Calcutta on the south-bound train. She was very young and she was waving angry hands.

'Something I can do?' he said.

'Yes, you can shut these people up!'

Her eyes had the dark brightness of nervous beetles. Her hair, parted in the middle, was intensely black and smoothed.

'May I look at your ticket?'

'Oh! I suppose so.'

He took her ticket, looking at it for a moment under the station lights.

'This isn't a sleeper ticket. This is just a –'

'Oh! I know, I know. It's the wrong ticket. I know. That comes of not getting it yourself! My bearer got it. In this country if you want a thing done, do it yourself. I know.'

'Where are you going?'

'Darjeeling. On leave.'

'I've a compartment. I'm not sleeping. You can share with me.'

'That makes me feel pretty small. Getting so excited.'

'Oh, everybody in India gets excited. It's nothing. It's the thing.'

'I'm awfully sorry,' she said.

He called a porter for her luggage; the moth-like dhotis floated away under the station lights; and together they got on the train.

He always had plenty of food and ice-water and beer and fruit packed up in neat travelling baskets, and the rest of the night he and the girl sat opposite each other on the bunks, eating ham and bread and bananas and drinking beer. He was fascinated by her hunger and thirst. They were the hunger and thirst of the very young, and it seemed to him that she talked all night with her mouth full.

'Ever been to Darjeeling before?' he said.

'No. They say it's wonderful and it stinks,' she said.

'You're lucky. You'll see Kangchenjunga.'

She had not the faintest idea what Kangchenjunga was, and he talked of it for some time as a man talks of a pet grievance, a pet memory, or an old campaign. He told her several times how wonderful it was, and then he knew that she was bored.

'Oh! I'm sorry,' he said. 'The trouble is that I like mountains. I'm rather in love with mountains.'

'Really?' She sat cross-legged on the bunk, eating a fourth banana, her shoes off, her knees rounded and smoothly silken, her skirt pulled tightly above.

'Don't you care for mountains?'

'Not terribly.'

'Then why Darjeeling? That's why people go there.'

'You've got to go somewhere,' she said.

He knew suddenly that she was going there simply because it was a place, a thing, a convention; because she had a piece of time to be killed; because she was bored. She was going to a place whose identity did not matter, and suddenly he was aware of wanting to say something to her; to make, as casually as he could, a desperate suggestion.

He began to make it, and then he found himself trembling unexpectedly and with immense diffidence, so that all he could say was:

'I – I – I – '

She took another banana and began to peel it very slowly, as if indifferently.

'What were you going to say?'

'Oh! it was an idea. But then I remembered it wouldn't – it wasn't possible.'

'What was it?' she said; and when he did not answer she looked at him with delightful black eyes, teasing him a little, mock serious. 'Please.'

'Well,' he said. 'Well – I was going to suggest you spent the week-end on the estate with me. Oh! you could go on to Darjeeling afterwards.'

She began laughing, her mouth full of banana, so that she hung her head. He saw then that her very black hair was parted in a rigid wonderful white line straight down the middle and he had the first of many impulses to bend down and touch it with his hands.

Just as he felt he could no longer keep himself from doing this she lifted her head sharply and said:

'I thought you were going to ask me something terribly serious. You know, like – '

He was shocked.

'Oh! but it is serious. The reason I didn't ask you the first time was because there's a murderer running about the place.'

'What possible difference could that make?'

'I'll have to spend most of the week-end trying to catch him,' he said. 'It wouldn't be fair to you. You'd have to entertain yourself.'

'Entertain my foot,' she said. 'I should come with you.'

He discovered very soon that she accepted everything in that same way: without fuss, offhand but rather bluntly, as if things like riding on night trains with strange men, changing her plans and hunting native murderers in remote places were all things of the most casual account to her.

It troubled and attracted him so much that he forgot, in the morning confusion at the junction, to take his customary look for the snows in the north. He did not remember it until he had been driving for ten or fifteen miles along the road to the estate.

And then he remembered another simple and curious thing at the same time. He had stupidly forgotten to ask her name; and he had neglected, still more stupidly, to tell her his own.

The three of them, his Indian driver, himself and the girl, were pressed together in the driving cab of a Ford truck. In the back of the truck were a dozen huddled Indians who wanted to be dropped off at hamlets along the road. It was impossible to speak in the roaring, jolting open-sided cabin, in the trembling glare of dust, and it was only when the truck stopped at last to let four or five villagers alight that he said:

'You can't see the snows this morning. Awful pity. It's the haze. By the way, my name's Owen.'

She took it indifferently and it struck him that possibly she had known it all the time.

'Mine's Blake,' she said.

'What else?'

'Oh! just Blake. I get used to it,' she said.

All along the road, for the next hour, he watched for the slightest dispersal, northward, of the vaporous glare that hid all of the mountains except the beginnings of forested foothills. These first hills, deceptively distant in the dusty glare of sun, were like vast lines of sleeping elephants, iron-grey and encrusted with broken forest, above tea-gardens that now began to line the road.

And then, thirty miles from the station, they came to the river. He had been looking forward to it as an important event he wanted to show her. He had spoken of it several times at village stopping-places. At bridges over smaller streams he had shouted above the noise of the motor: 'Not this one. This isn't it. A bit further yet. You'll see.'

And then they were there. The sight of the broad, snow-yellow stream running splendidly down with furious and intricate currents between flat banks of sun-whitened sand, of lines of ox-wagons standing on dusty bamboo traverses waiting to be ferried across, of the ferry being madly poled by sweating and singing men against the powerful snow-flood: all of it filled him with a pride and excitement that he wanted somehow to convey to her. He felt in a way that it was his own river; that the water was from his own snows; and that the snows were from his own mountains. This was his country and his pride in it all was parochial and humble. It was inadequate and he could not put it into words.

He simply stood on the deck of the slowly-crossing ferry, crowded now with ox-carts, many peasants, a single car and his own truck, and stared at the wide sweeping waters.

'Wonderful, isn't it? Don't you think so? Don't you think it's a wonderful river?'

'Reminds me of one I saw in Burma,' she said.

'Burma?' he said. He felt himself once again brought up sharp by the casual bluntness of her way of speaking. 'Burma? Were you there?'

'The whole caboodle,' she said.

He suddenly felt small and crushed. The river and all it meant for him, and had so long meant, shrivelled into insignificance. He stared round for some moments at the scraggy oxen on the ferry. The carts, he noticed, were overloaded, and the oxen, as they always were, underfed, their thighs raw and bloody from struggling against each other and against the ill-balanced pole of the shafts. He felt angry at the stupidity of drivers who drove them with such savage lack of thought. The suffering of the grey moon-eyed creatures standing in the glare of sun, staring at the water, depressed him, and the miserable little songs of the ferrymen, in a dialect he did not understood, might have been, in their primitive whining, the voices of cattle themselves, whimpering in pain.

And then the girl said:

'Who are those people?'

'Oh! just peasants.'

'No,' she said. 'The people with the car.'

He looked up to see, on the other side of the ferry, a family of educated Indians, a man in a European suit and soft white hat, a woman in a blue sari, two pig-tailed girls in cotton frocks. They belonged, he saw, to the Chevrolet saloon.

'They're Indians,' he said. 'An educated family.'

'I want to get myself a sari like that,' she said. 'I want to take one home.'

'Home?' he said. He felt suddenly and brutally pained. 'When do you go home?'

'Soon.'

He looked at the Indians standing by the car. He felt the

collective pain of his thoughts about the oxen, the river, and of the girl leaving India abruptly increased by the thought that he himself had not much longer to remain. 'Quit India,' the curt and shabby slogan that one had seen for so many years chalked up on walls and bridges and decaying tenements in cities, everywhere, meant him too. In a year, perhaps in a few months, he, too, would have to go.

They reached the estate, with its pleasant two-storey bungalow of white-railed verandahs, its little plantation of pineapples, its papaia trees and its garden of orange and rose and crimson gerbera daisies, purple petunias and now fading sweet peas, about forty minutes later. He showed it her with pride. Its windows faced a view of lawn and flowers, of thousands of tea-bushes in the gardens, neatly shaped under high and slender trees of shade, and beyond it all the line of elephantine mountains, smouldering in morning haze.

'Over there,' he said, 'is Bhutan. This is the frontier.'

'What is Bhutan?'

'It's a state. A closed state. You can't get in there.'

'Why not?'

'You just can't,' he said. 'The mountains are the frontier and they'd keep you out if nothing else did.'

'Just like Burma,' she said. 'Only they didn't keep us out.'

He did not know what to say.

'Awfully good place for your murderer,' she said. 'Once he's in there you've had it. It's all over.'

'Yes,' he said.

He had hoped she would not mention the murder. She had changed after her bath into a white dress with scarlet candy stripes, sleeveless and fresh, with a simple belt. Diagonal lines of scarlet met down the centre line of her body, continuing the line of her hair. Each time she lowered her head, to bend over her plate, he saw this line with increasingly aggravated impulses, aching to touch it. Then when she stood up from the table, after breakfast, he was aware of the line running down through the whole length of her body. It was the division between her breasts; it went on, in a series of scarlet arrowheads, to the tip of her skirt; it divided her brown sun-warm legs, fascinating him.

'What would you like to do?' he said.

'Hunt the murderer,' she said, 'of course. Isn't that what I came for?'

They drove most of that day about the estate. It was quite hot, but she did not rest in the afternoon. Some of the excitement about the murder had died down, and now there was a stillness of heat about the long avenues of tea-bushes, under the delicate high shade trees, that was enchanting. Bougainvilleas flamed on roofs seen through far sun-washed openings of the gardens. Delicious small winds stirred in the forest of bamboo. He showed her all of it with pride: the good new roads, the tea manufactory, the cool office where he paid his workers, the yellow slant-eyed children solemnly squatting with their tea-bugs spread out like patterns of dominoes, waiting for them to be counted. He let her pluck from the bushes a few leaves of tea.

'All we needed to make a perfect day of it was a pot at the murderer,' she said.

After dinner they sat on the north verandah, facing the hills. In the darkness smouldering hill fires seemed at intervals to be fanned by sudden winds. They flared with golden tips and then died for a moment, deep red, before they flamed and ran again.

She was fascinated by these fires, and he explained them to her. They were the fires of itinerant hill-people, clearing sections of forest, burning them and then moving on. They were like beacons on the frontier, far-off and unattainable, mysterious and lovely in the tense night air.

And in the sudden lighter fannings of flame, as he turned to speak to her, he saw the light of them on her face. It accentuated the line of her scalp so vividly that he could hardly bear to sit there, an arm's length away, and not touch her. He longed to run his fingers down this line and tenderly down its lovely continuations.

Suddenly he knew that she was aware of this. She stirred in her chair, her legs stretched outward. He saw her black eyes turn and fix themselves fully on him, and he felt the beating undercurrent of their dark excitement. He put out his hands. In the hills a furious moment of fire leapt up and flooded her face with crimson light and he saw her lips, wet and soft, parting themselves slowly, ready to accept him.

A moment later he heard the voice of MacFarlane calling

across the verandah, in the broad Dundee Scots that he had always faintly loathed:

'Hi there, Owen, where are you hidin' ye'self, man?'

For the rest of the evening the fierce parochialism of MacFarlane filled the chair between them. MacFarlane, tall and angular and stiff, spoke volubly of other Scots, of Scotland, of Scottish compounds in Calcutta. He bloomed with Scottish pride.

'Miss Blake, that's a Scots name, surely?'

'As English as –'

'I'd no be so sure o' that. I'd no be so sure, Miss Blake. I'd no be so sure.'

'Well—'

'Better be true Scot than half English,' MacFarlane said. Something about his discovery of the two of them on the verandah, together with the astonishing fact of Miss Blake being there at all, seemed to fill him with a hostile desire to taunt their secrecy. 'Ye're like Owen here. He's a Welsh name. Ye've a Scots name. The pair of ye claim to be English and a' the damn time neither one of you knows where y'are!'

MacFarlane took ferocious sips of whisky and Owen felt all the delicacy, the tension and the beauty of the day crumble in his hands. The girl lay in her chair, full length, black eyes dreaming, her body quiet and bored, and stared at the hills and their gigantic bursting flowers of fire.

But once, before MacFarlane finally got up and staggered off across the garden down the path hidden from the house by groves of banana, she was moved to taunt him back:

'And when is Scotland going to capture the murderer?'

'Ah, he's about. He's about yet. We'll have him yet.'

'That'll be a brave day for Scotland.'

'Not a damn bit braver than any other!'

MacFarlane waved proud, extravagant, tipsy hands and Owen hated him. He looked across at the girl, catching the light of her dark eyes for a second, and felt that she, too, waited for the time when the moment of shattered secrecy between them could be renewed. He felt his body once again ache for the line of her hair, and then MacFarlane said:

'Ah weel, I'll bid ye good night, ye damn' Sassenachs. We'll be glad to gie ye tea to-morrow if ye care to run over. 'Phone us up.'

'Miss Blake hasn't much time,' Owen said. 'She's leaving India. Going home. To England.'

'England!' MacFarlane said. ' Wha'ever said England was home!'

'Good night,' Owen said.

'Good night,' MacFarlane said. 'Sleep well.' He began to stagger away, across the garden, towards the banana grove, from which he called with final dour triumph: 'Not that ye will!'

When he had gone there was no sound in the garden except the occasional turning, like the slow page of a book, of banana leaves twisting in soft air. It was a sound that gave the impression, now and then, of being part of the echo of distant fires splintering fresh paths into dark forests along the hills.

On the still verandah Owen felt his own emotions bursting forward in just such sudden flaring spurts of exploration into the darkness where the girl lay stretched in her chair. He waited for a few moments after MacFarlane had gone and then he went over to her and did what he had wanted to do ever since she had ridden with him in the train that morning. He smoothed his hands down the parted flanks of her hair. She did not stir. After dinner she had put on a house-gown of dark blue silk and the metal zip down the front of it ended in a tassel of blue cord. He wanted to pull gently at this cord; he wanted the gown to fall away like the dark shell of a nut, leaving her naked body pale with rounded bowls of shadow underneath it. He wanted to watch the colour of the fire from the hills on her face and see it grow rosy on the pale skin of her breasts, on her shoulders and on the intensely black divisions of her hair. But he did not do anything; he was paralysed suddenly by withering shyness; and suddenly he stood away.

'I just wanted to say that it was sweet of you to come,' he said. 'Awfully sweet, and I'm grateful.'

In the morning they drove across the estate again. He took his rifle in the back of the car. On the hills, above the fresh green gardens, so like orchards of privet, there was nothing to be seen, in the glistening haze of dust, of the fires of the night before: except here and there dead scars of burning, like black scabs, across brown serrations of shale. The great fires were lost, like the smoulderings of matches, in the vaster substance of mountains, and the light of them had become extinguished by sun.

He wanted to drive her out beyond the gardens, through the first fringes of bamboo forest and on to the deep reaches of grass-swamp where, by the river, there were rhinoceros. On the narrow sandy track of the forest, like a white gulley between tall olive stalks of bamboo, they passed a running Indian, naked except for a small loincloth, with his bow and arrows.

'A Sunday morning hunter,' he said. 'It's the same the world over.'

'Except here they hunt the murderer,' she said. 'They're probably all murderers, anyway.'

'I think we can give that up,' he said. 'They're really wonderful people.'

'Give up nothing,' she said. 'It's what I came for.'

'He's probably up there,' he said. He could not tell if she were teasing him or not, and he pointed to the hills.

'Then let's chase him,' she said. 'Let's get up there.'

'It's impossible,' he said. 'You can't get in there. And even if you could get in there it would mean a jungle trek, an expedition.'

'Then let's have an expedition. I've got a week with nothing to do. It would be fun.'

'You simply don't understand,' he said. 'There are some things you just can't do.'

'They said that about Burma,' she said.

Then as they drove on through the deep dry grasses of river swamp, dusty and withered and only partly green now after the dry season, he stopped the car sometimes to point out the things he thought would interest her: a clearing where he had shot an elephant before the war, tunnels bored in the grasses by rhinoceroses, the dried tributary of a stream with its carefully built fin-like breakwaters of stone, his own enterprise and invention, to prevent the sweeping erosion of monsoons.

Whenever he stopped the car and stood up and pointed about the swamp she did not stir. She sat in the seat next to his own as she had sat in the chair on the verandah, the night before, dreamy and quiet but with bright warm black eyes, so that it was hard to tell if she was bored or not by all he said.

'We'll see the other river in five minutes,' he said.

Then she said an unexpected thing.

'By the way, did you come to my room last night?'

'You were fast asleep,' he said.

'I was awake and I heard you.'

'I came to see if you had a mosquito net, that's all,' he said. 'Some people come here and because it's high they think a net isn't necessary. They think there are no mosquitoes. But there are. They come from the swamp here. You need a net.'

'I never have a net,' she said. 'In Burma for four years and I never had a net. I hate them. I feel they stifle me. I can't sleep with them.'

'That was silly. It was dangerous,' he said.

'In wartime,' she said, 'you get used to that.'

He did not speak; but as they drove on again he felt overwhelmed by his own inadequacy. He had been doing the same two trips a month out of Calcutta, by the night mail, for twenty years; pottering round the estate; fussing over improvements; finicking and praying over it as a parish priest finicks and prays over the little eddies and whirls of a parochial pond. War had come and swept disastrously over the East like an awful flood and had left him as he was.

And now it was Quit India. Riots were beginning in Calcutta. The English – Scots like MacFarlane did not seem to him of the same account – were going at last. There would be great rejoicing. People who did not know India and did not understand and did not care would say it was a wonderful thing, a great step forward, a revolutionary thing. Perhaps for some people it was. But to him it was a pace backward: the birth of another nationalism in a world diseased by nationalism, the creation of yet another frontier.

He was glad when they reached the river. He got out and ran round the front of the car and helped the girl jump down into the sand. She was wearing a pure white dress of smooth linen that buttoned down the front, and once again he was shaken by impulses to touch the line of her hair and the deep fine thread, down through her body, of its continuation.

'This river comes from the Himalayas,' he said. 'It's Himalayan snow.'

'It's like the other,' she said.

The river, very wide at that point, melted on the far side into forests of yellow haze. Strong green currents broke across it from all directions like quivering muscles. In that way it was like the river of the previous day, except that now there was no ferry to the other side.

The girl bent down and put her hand in the water.

'Icy,' she said. 'Wonderful and icy.'

'This is the best view of Kangchenjunga you can get,' he said. 'Straight through there.' He pointed upstream, squinting against the sun. 'That's the spot exactly, although you can't see it today.'

'The water's wonderful,' she said. 'Why didn't you tell me it was so marvellous? I'd have brought a costume.'

'There are terrible currents,' he said.

She stood looking at the shore of monsoon-washed sand, white and fine as a seashore in brilliant sun between the river edge and the grasses of the swamp. In its icy clearness there were great egg-like stones, whiter than the sand.

He saw her begin to take off her shoes.

'What are you going to do?' he said.

'Paddle.' She lifted the edges of her dress and unrolled her stockings, peeling them down her brown smooth legs. 'Come on.' The dark eyes flashed. 'You too.'

'No,' he said. 'I'll sit here. I'll watch you.'

Standing in the water, holding her dress above her knees, she bent her head, looking down at her feet, and he felt himself quiver, once again, because of the line of her hair.

As she turned and began to walk slowly upstream, in the shallow edge of water, swishing her feet, he saw her head, vividly black above the white dress, move slowly into the line of mountains, where Kangchenjunga should have been.

'Don't go too far,' he called.

'No,' she said. 'If I don't come back you'll know I'm swimming.'

'No,' he said. He was agitated. 'Don't do that! It's dangerous. Don't do that.'

'Have a nap,' she called. 'It'll do you good!'

He stood watching her for a moment or two longer. As she stepped away on big white stones he saw water and sun gleam on the bare skin of her legs and arms. Then as she poised to balance herself he saw the line of her body going down, white and brown, with her reflection, to the bottom of the pools she was crossing. He watched her go like this, seventy or eighty yards upstream, past the first elbow of sand and rock, and then he sat down to wait for her by the car.

When the rifle shot came out of the swamp edge, also from upstream, and hit him full in the chest, he did not fall. The suddenness of it seemed simply to paralyse him from the waist upwards. For some seconds he did not even stagger. He stood acutely watching the white river shore, the water, the swamp edge, the running Indian figure with the rifle disappearing into low bamboo.

For a few moments longer he seemed to hold these objects briefly focused with the most painless calm and brilliance and then he fell backwards, choking.

As he lay there the girl came running to him over soft sand. He kept his eyes open with terrible difficulty, waiting for her to arrive. When she did arrive she had taken off her dress, and once again there was her face, white but calm; her black hair with its tormenting central line; her naked breast and shoulders as she bent down.

'That was your murderer all right,' she said. 'That was one of your wonderful people.'

He lay on the sand, burned by sun, his mouth open, and tried to answer. He could not speak. All the life of his body, borne on a great torrent of blood, was flowing back to his head, choking with hideous congestion his sight and breath. He made weak and frantic signs that he wanted to sit up.

She put her arms about him, holding him upright for a few seconds longer. He whimpered in a great struggle to hold his weakness, his terror and the flow of blood.

'Don't worry,' she said. 'It's all right. I'm with you. Try not to move.'

He made another tortured effort to speak but he could make no sound. His mouth slowly slobbered blood. Everything he wanted to say seemed to become compressed, in a final glittering moment, into his eyes. She saw them convulsedly trying to fix themselves on herself, the sky and the mountains. This convulsion, calming down at last, gave way to a startling flash of reflected light. It leapt into the dying retina with such brilliance that she turned and instinctively looked behind her, towards the swamp and the mountains, as if for a second he had seen the murderer coming back.

But when she turned there was no one there; and when she looked back at his eyes she saw that all sight of sky, the mountains and the haze that hid the further mountains had been extinguished too.

Now only herself remained.

A CHRISTMAS SONG

She gave lessons in voice-training in the long room above the music shop. Her pupils won many examinations and were afterwards very successful at local concerts and sometimes in giving lessons in voice-training to other pupils. She herself had won many examinations and everybody said how brilliant she was.

Every Christmas, as this year, she longed for snow. It gave a transfiguring gay distinction to a town that otherwise had none. It lifted up the squat little shops, built of red brick with upper storeys of terra-cotta; it made the roofs down the hill like glistening cakes; it even gave importance to the stuffy gauze-windowed club where local gentlemen played billiards and solo whist over meagre portions of watered whisky. One could imagine, with the snow, that one was in Bavaria or Vienna or the Oberland, and that horse-drawn sleighs, of which she read in travel guides, would glide gracefully down the ugly hill from the gasworks. One could imagine Evensford, with its many hilly little streets above the river, a little Alpine town. One could imagine anything. Instead there was almost always rain and long columns of working-class mackintoshes floating down a street that was like a dreary black canal. Instead of singing Mozart to the snow she spent long hours selling jazz sheet-music to factory workers and earned her reward, at last, on Christmas Eve, by being bored at the Williamsons' party.

Last year she had sung several songs at the Williamson's party. Some of the men, who were getting hearty on mixtures of gin and port wine, had applauded in the wrong places, and Freddy Williamson had bawled out 'Good old Clara!'

She knew the men preferred Effie. Her sister was a very gay person although she did not sing; she had never passed an examination in her life, but there was, in a strange way, hardly anything you felt she could not do. She had a character like a chameleon; she had all the love affairs. She laughed a great deal, in rippling infectious scales, so that she made other people begin

192

laughing, and she had large violet-blue eyes. Sometimes she laughed so much that Clara herself would begin weeping.

This year Clara was not going to the Williamsons' party; she had made up her mind. The Williamsons were in leather; they were very successful and had a large early Edwardian house with bay-windows and corner cupolas and bathroom windows of stained glass overlooking the river. They were fond of giving parties several times a year. Men who moved only in Rotarian or golf circles turned up with wives whose corset suspenders could be seen like bulging pimples under sleek dresses. About midnight Mrs Williamson grew rowdy and began rushing from room to room making love to other men. The two Williamson boys, George and Freddy, became rowdy too, and took off their jackets and did muscular and noisy gymnastics with the furniture.

At four o'clock she went upstairs to close the windows of the music-room and pull the curtains and make up the fire. It was raining in misty delicate drops and the air was not like Christmas. In the garden there were lime trees and their dark red branches, washed with rain, were like glowing veins in the deep blue air.

As she was coming out of the room her sister came upstairs.

'Oh! there you are. There's a young man downstairs who wants a song and doesn't know the name.'

'It's probably a Danny Kaye. It always is.'

'No it isn't. He says it's a Christmas song.'

'I'll come,' she said. Then half-way downstairs she stopped; she remembered what it was she was going to say to Effie. 'By the way, I'm not coming to the party,' she said.

'Oh! Clara, you promised. You always come.'

'I know; but I'm tired, and I don't feel like coming and there it is.'

'The Williamsons will never let you get away with it,' her sister said. 'They'll drag you by force.'

'I'll see about this song,' she said. 'What did he say it was?'

'He says it's a Christmas song. You'll never get away with it. They'll never let you.'

She went down into the shop. Every day people came into the shop for songs whose names they did not know. 'It goes like this,' they would say, 'or it goes like that.' They would try humming a few notes and she would take it up from them; it was always something popular, and in the end, with practice, it was never very difficult.

A young man in a brown overcoat with a brown felt hat and an umbrella stood by the sheet-music counter. He took off his hat when she came up to him.

'There was a song I wanted—'

'A carol?' she said.

'No, a song,' he said. 'A Christmas song.'

He was very nervous and kept rolling the ferrule of the umbrella on the floor linoleum. He wetted his lips and would not look at her.

'If you could remember the words?'

'I'm afraid I can't.'

'How does it go? Would you know that?'

He opened his mouth either as if to begin singing a few notes or to say something. But nothing happened and he began biting his lip instead.

'If you could remember a word or two,' she said. 'Is it a new song?'

'You see, I think it's German,' he said.

'Oh,' she said. 'Perhaps it's by Schubert?'

'It sounds awfully silly, but I simply don't know. We only heard it once,' he said.

He seemed about to put on his hat. He ground the ferrule of the umbrella into the linoleum. Sometimes it happened that people were too shy even to hum the notes of the song they wanted, and suddenly she said:

'Would you care to come upstairs? We might find it there.'

Upstairs in the music room she sang the first bars of one or two songs by Schubert. She sat at the piano and he stood respectfully at a distance, leaning on the umbrella, too shy to interrupt her. She sang a song by Brahms and he listened hopefully. She asked him if these were the songs, but he shook his head, and finally, after she had sung another song by Schubert, he blurted out:

'You see, it isn't actually a Christmas song. It is, and it isn't. It's more that it makes you think of Christmas—'

'Is it a love song?'

'Yes.'

She sang another song by Schubert; but it was not the one he wanted; and at last she stood up. 'You see, there are so many love songs—'

'Yes, I know, but this one is rather different somehow.'

'Couldn't you bring her in?' she said. 'Perhaps she would remember?'

'Oh! no,' he said. 'I wanted to find it without that.'

They went downstairs and several times on the way down he thanked her for singing. 'You sing beautifully,' he said. 'You would have liked this song.'

'Come in again if you think of it,' she said. 'If you can only think of two or three bars.'

Nervously he fumbled with the umbrella and then quickly put on his hat and then as quickly took it off again. He thanked her for being so kind, raising his hat a second time. Outside the shop he put up the umbrella too sharply, and a breeze, catching it, twisted him on the bright pavement and bore him out of sight.

Rain fell gently all evening and customers came in and shook wet hats on bright pianos. She walked about trying to think of the song the young man wanted. Songs by Schubert went through her head and became mixed with the sound of carols from gramophone cubicles and she was glad when the shop had closed.

Effie began racing about in her underclothes, getting ready for the party. 'Clara, you can't mean it that you're not coming.'

'I do mean it. I'm always bored and they really don't want me.'

'They love you.'

'I can't help it. I made up my mind last year. I never enjoy it, and they'll be better without me.'

'They won't let you get away with it,' Effie said. 'I warn you they'll come and fetch you.'

At eight o'clock her father and mother drove off with Effie in the Ford. She went down through the shop and unbolted the front door and let them out into the street. 'The stars are shining,' her mother said. 'It's getting colder.' She stood for a second or two in the doorway, looking up at the stars and thinking that perhaps, after all, there was a touch of frost in the air.

'Get ready!' Effie called from the car. 'You know what the Williamsons are!' and laughed with high infectious scales so that her mother and father began laughing too.

After the car had driven away she bolted the door and

switched off the front shop bell. She wnt upstairs and put on
her dressing-gown and tried to think once again of the song the
young man had wanted. She played over several songs on the
piano, singing them softly.

At nine o'clock something was thrown against the sidestreet
window and she heard Freddy Williamson bawling:

'Who isn't coming to the party? Open the window.'

She went to the window and pulled back the curtain and stood
looking down. Freddy Williamson stood in the street below and
threw his driving gloves at her.

'Get dressed! Come on!'

She opened the window.

'Freddy, be quiet. People can hear.'

'I want them to hear. Who isn't coming to whose party? I
want them to hear.'

He threw the driving gloves up at the window again.

'Everybody is insulted!' he said. 'Come on.'

'Please,' she said.

'Let me in then!' he bawled. 'Let me come up and talk to
you.'

'All right,' she said.

She went downstairs and let him in through the shop and he
came up to the music room, shivering, stamping enormous feet.
'Getting colder,' he kept saying. 'Getting colder.'

'You should put on an overcoat,' she said.

'Never wear one,' he said. 'Can't bear to be stuffed up.'

'Then don't grumble because you're starved to death.'

He stamped up and down the room, a square-boned young
man with enormous lips and pink flesh and small poodle-like
eyes, pausing now and then to rub his hands before the fire.

'The Mater sends orders you're to come back with me,' he
said, 'and she absolutely won't take no for an answer.'

'I'm not coming,' she said.

'Of course you're coming! I'll have a drink while you get
ready.'

'I'll pour you a drink,' she said, 'but I'm not coming. What will
you have?'

'Gin,' he said. 'Clara, sometimes you're the most awful bind.'

She poured the drink, not answering. Freddy Williamson lifted
the glass and said:

'Sorry, didn't mean that. Happy Christmas. Good old Clara.'

'Happy Christmas.'

'Good old Clara. Come on, let's have one for Christmas.'

Freddy Williamson put clumsy hands across her shoulders, kissing her with lips rather like those of a heavy wet dog.

'Good old Clara,' he said again. 'Good old girl.'

Songs kept crossing and recrossing her mind, bewildering her into moments of dreamy distraction. She had the feeling of trying to grasp something that was floating away.

'Don't stand there like a dream,' Freddy Williamson said. 'Put some clothes on. Come on.'

'I'm going to tie up Christmas presents and then go to bed.'

'Oh! Come on, Clara, come on. Millions of chaps are there, waiting.'

She stood dreamily in the centre of the room, thinking of the ardent shy young man who could not remember the song.

'You're such a dream,' Freddy Williamson said. 'You just stand there. You've got to snap out of yourself.'

Suddenly he pressed himself against her in attitudes of muscular, heavier love, grasping her about the waist, partly lifting her from the floor, his lips wet on her face.

'Come on, Clara,' he kept saying, 'let the blinds up. Can't keep the blinds down for ever.'

'Is it a big party?'

'Come on, let the blinds up.'

'How can I come to the party if you keep holding me here?'

'Let the blinds up and come to the party too,' he said. 'Eh?'

'No.'

'Well, one more kiss,' he said. He smacked at her lips with his heavy dog-like mouth, pressing her body backwards. 'Good old Clara. All you got to do is let yourself go. Come on – let the blinds up. Good old Clara.'

'All right. Let me get my things on,' she said. 'Get yourself another drink while you're waiting.'

'Fair enough. Good old Clara.'

While she went away to dress he drank gin and stumped about the room. She came back in her black coat with a black and crimson scarf on her head and Freddy Williamson said: 'Whizzo. That's better. Good old Clara,' and kissed her again, running clumsy ruffling hands over her face and neck and hair.

When they went downstairs someone was tapping lightly on the glass of the street door. 'Police for the car,' Freddy Williamson said. 'No lights or some damn thing,' but when she opened the door it was the young man who could not remember the song. He stood there already raising his hat:

'I'm terribly sorry. Oh! you're going out. Excuse me.'

'Did you remember it?' she said.

'Some of it,' he said. 'The words.'

'Come in a moment,' she said.

He came in from the street and she shut the door. It was dark in the shop, and he did not seem so nervous. He began to say: 'It goes rather like this – I can't remember it all. But something like this – *Leise flehen meine Lieder – Liebchen, komm zu mir–*'

'It is by Schubert,' she said.

She went across the shop and sat down at one of the pianos and began to sing it for him. She heard him say, 'That's it. That's the one,' and Freddy Williamson fidgeted with the latch of the shop door as he kept one hand on it, impatient to go.

'It's very beautiful,' the young man said. 'It's not a Christmas song, but somehow –'

Freddy Williamson stamped noisily into the street, and a second or two later she heard him start up the car. The door-catch rattled where he had left it open and a current of cold air blew into the dark shop.

She had broken off her singing because, after the first verse, she could not remember the words. *Softly fly my songs – Loved one, come to me –* she was not sure how it went after that.

'I'm sorry I can't remember the rest,' she said.

'It's very kind of you,' he said,' The door irritated her by banging on its catch. She went over and shut it and out in the street Freddy Williamson blew impatiently on the horn of the car.

'Was it the record you wanted?' she said. 'There is a very good one – '

'If it's not too much trouble.'

'I think I can find it,' she said. 'I'll put on the light.'

As she looked for the record and found it, she sang the first few bars of it again. 'There is great tenderness in it,' she began to say. 'Such a wonderful tenderness,' but suddenly it seemed as if the young man was embarrassed. He began fumbling in his pocket-book for his money, but she said, 'Oh! no. Pay after Christmas. Pay any time,' and at the same moment Freddy Williamson opened the door of the shop and said:

'What goes on? After hours, after hours. Come on.'

'I'm just coming,' she said.

'I'll say good night,' the young man said. 'I'm very grateful. I wish you a Happy Christmas.'

'Happy Christmas,' she said.

Outside the stars were green and sharp in a sky without wind; the street had dried except for dark prints of frost on pavements.

'Damn cool,' Freddy Williamson kept saying. 'Damn cool.'

He drove rather fast, silent and a little sulky, out towards the high ground overlooking the river. Rain had been falling everywhere through all the first weeks of December and now as the car came out on the valley edge she could see below her a great pattern of winter floodwater, the hedgerows cutting it into rectangular lakes glittering with green and yellow lights from towns on the far side.

'I'd have told him to go to hell,' Freddy Williamson said. 'I call it damn cool. Damn cool.'

'See the floods,' she said. 'There'll be skating.'

'The damn cheek people have,' Freddy Williamson said. 'Damn cheek.'

He drove the car with sulky abandon into the gravel drive of the big Edwardian house. Dead chestnut leaves swished away on all sides, harsh and brittle, and she could see frost white on the edges of the big lawn.

'One before we go in,' Freddy Williamson said. She turned away her mouth but he caught it with clumsy haste, like a dog seizing a bird. 'Good old Clara. Let the blinds up. It's Christmas Eve.'

'Put the car away and I'll wait for you,' she said.

'Fair enough,' he said. 'Anything you say. Good old Clara. Damn glad you come.'

She got out of the car and stood for a few moments looking down the valley. She bent down and put her hands on the grass. Frost was crisp and hard already, and she could see it sparkling brightly on tree branches and on rain-soaked stems of dead flowers. It made her breath glisten in the house-lights coming across the lawn. It seemed to be glittering even on the long wide floodwaters, so that she almost persuaded herself the valley was one great river of ice already, wonderfully transformed.

Standing there, she thought of the young man, with his shy ardent manner, his umbrella and his raised hat. The song he had not been able to remember began to go through her head again – *Softly fly my songs – Loved one, come to me –* ; but at that moment Freddy Williamson came blundering up the drive and seized her once again like a hungry dog.

'One before we go in,' he said. 'Come on. Good old Clara. One before we go in. Good show.'

Shrieks of laughter came suddenly from the house as if some-one, perhaps her sister, had ignited little fires of merriment that were crackling at the windows.

'Getting worked up!' Freddy Williamson said. 'Going to be good!'

She felt the frost crackling under her feet. She grasped at something that was floating away. *Leise flehen meine Lieder – Oh! my loved one –* how did it go?

THE MAJOR OF HUSSARS

That summer we lived in the hotel on the lake below the mountains, and Major Martineau, the Major of Hussars, lived on the floor below us, in a room with a eucalyptus tree on the balcony.

The weather was very hot and in the sunlight the lake sparkled like crusty golden glass and in the late afternoon the peaks of the Blumlisalp and the whole range about the Jungfrau glistened in the fine mountain air with fiery rosy snow. The major was very interested in the mountains, and we in turn were very interested in the major, a spare spruce man of nearly sixty who wore light shantung summer suits and was very studious of his appearance generally, and very specially of his smooth grey hair. He also had three sets of false teeth, of which he was very proud: one for mornings, one for evenings, and one for afternoons.

We used to meet the major everywhere: on the terrace, where lunch was served under a long pergola of crimson and yellow roses, and from which you got a magnificent view of the snow caps; and then under the dark shade of chestnut trees on the lake edge, where coffee was served; and then at the tram terminus, where the small yellow trams started their journeys along the hot road by the lake; and then on the white steamers that came up and down the lake, calling at all the little towns with proud peeps of the funnel whistle, several times a day. At all of these places there was the major, very spruce in cool shantung and always wearing the correct set of false teeth for the time of day, looking very correct, very English, and, we thought, very alone.

It must have been at the second or third of these meetings that he told us of his wife. 'She'll be out from England any day now.' And at the fifth or sixth that he told us of his false teeth. 'After all, one has several suits. One has several pairs of shoes. All excellent for rest and change. Why not different sets of teeth?' It did not occur to me then that the teeth and his wife had anything to do with each other.

201

Sometimes as we walked along the lake we could see a figure marching briskly towards us in the distance.

'The major,' I would say.

'It can't be,' my wife would say. 'It looks much too young.'

But always, as he came nearer, we could see that it was the major, sparkling and smart and spruce with all the shine and energy of a younger man. 'Sometimes you'd take him for a man of forty,' my wife would say.

Whenever we met on these occasions we would talk briefly of the major's wife; then of the lake, the food, the delicious summer weather, the alpine flowers, the snow on the mountains and how we loved Switzerland. The major was very fond of them all and we got the impression, gradually, that his wife was very fond of them too.

'Ah!' he would say, 'she will adore all this. She will simply adore it.' His correct blue eyes would sparkle delightfully.

'And when do you expect her?'

'Well,' he would say, 'in point of fact she was to have been here this week. But there seems to have been some sort of hitch somewhere. Bad staff work.'

'I hope she'll soon be able to come.'

'Oh! any day now.'

'Good. And oh! by the way,' I said, 'have you been up to the Jungfrau yet? The flowers are very lovely now on the way up.'

'The Virgin?' the major said. 'Oh! not yet. I'm leaving all the conquest of that sort of thing till my wife gets here,' and he would laugh very heartily at the joke he made.

'It's just as well,' I said.

But the next day, on the steamer, we saw the major making a conquest of the girl who brought the coffee. She had a beautiful Swiss head, with dark coiled hair, and she was wearing a very virginal Bernese bodice in black and white and a skirt striped in pink and blue. She was very young and she laughed very much at whatever it was the major was saying to her. On the voyage the major drank eight cups of coffee and ate four ham rolls. There was so much ham in the rolls that it hung over the side like spaniel's ears, and the major had a wonderful time with his afternoon false teeth, his best pair, champing it in.

'The major is conquering the Jungfrau,' I said.

'You take a very low view of life,' my wife said. 'He's alone and he's simply being friendly.'

'Queer how he doesn't notice us to-day.'

The major, in fact, did not notice us; he did not notice us in fact for two days, and I wondered if I had said something to offend him. But when at last we met him again under the chest-nut trees at noon, with a glass of lager at his table in the shade, he seemed more friendly, more sparkling and more cheerful than ever. The yellow beer, the light shantung suit and the gleaming white teeth were all alight with the trembling silver reflections that sprang from the sunlight on the water.

'Any news of your wife?' we said.

'Coming to-day!'

We said we were very pleased. 'What time?'

'Coming by the afternoon boat. Gets in at three.'

He looked at the lake, the roses on the terrace, the blue-grey eucalyptus tree shining on the balcony of his room and then at the vast snows towering and glistening beyond the lake. 'I can't tell you how she will adore all this,' he said. 'I can't tell you.'

'I'm sure she will,' we said. 'You must be very excited.'

'Just like a kid with a toy!' he said. 'You see, I came out first to arrange it all. Choose the place. Choose the hotel. Choose everything. She doesn't know what she's coming to. You see? It's all going to be a great surprise for her.'

'Don't forget you have to conquer the Jungfrau,' I said. 'The soldanella are wonderful above the Scheidegg now.'

'Of course, ' he said. 'Well, I must go. Perhaps you'd join us for an *apéritif* about six? I do very much want you to meet her.'

We said we should be delighted and he went singing away up to the hotel.

'Your remark about the Jungfrau was very pointed,' my wife said.

'I saved it with the soldanella,' I said.

'Anyway,' she said, 'be careful what you say to-night.'

From the lower terrace we could watch the steamers come and go. The afternoon was very hot and we stayed under the dark shade of the chestnut trees to watch the three o'clock boat come in. Among the hotel porters with their green and plum-coloured and scarlet and brown caps and uniforms the major stood out, in cool spruce shantung, as a very English, very conspicuous visitor on the quay.

When the white steamer came up the lake at last, tooting in the hot afternoon air, the major had taken up his stand in front of all the porters, by the water's edge. I got up and leaned on the railings of the terrace to get a better view.

The steamer came swinging in with a ring of engine-room bells, with six or seven passengers waiting by the gangway.

'There she is,' I said.

'Where?' My wife had come to stand beside me.

'The lady with the green case,' I said. 'Standing by the captain. She looks about the major's age and about as English.'

'She looks rather nice – yes,' my wife said, 'it could be.'

The steamer bounced lightly against the quay and the gangway came down. The hotel porters adjusted their caps and the passengers began to come ashore. In his eagerness the major almost blocked the gangway.

To my astonishment the lady with the green case came down the gangway and went straight past the major, and the porter from the *Hôtel du Lac* raised his green and gold cap and took the case away from her. The major was looking anxiously up the gangway for the figure of his wife, but in less than two minutes all the passengers had come down. When the steamer moved away again the major was standing on the quay alone, still staring anxiously and still waiting for the wife who had not come.

That evening we went down to the terrace for the *apéritif* with the major. 'For goodness' sake don't make that joke about the Jungfrau,' my wife said. 'He'll be in no mood for that.' The five o'clock steamer had come in, but the major's wife had not arrived.

'It's his joke,' I said. 'Not mine.'

'You twist it round,' she said.

On the terrace the major, dressed in a dark grey suit and with his evening false teeth in, had a surprising appearance of ebullient gaiety. He had a peculiar taste in drinks and drank four or five glasses of Kirsch because there was no whisky and after it he did not seem so tired.

'Met a friend in Paris,' he explained to us. 'Amazing coincidence.' He kept waving a rather long telegram about in front of us. 'Hadn't seen this friend for years, and then suddenly ran into her. Of course, it's only a night. She'll be here on Thursday.'

Three weeks went past, but the major's wife did not arrive. The best of the roses by that time were over on the terrace and long salmon-scarlet lines of geraniums were blooming there instead. In the beds behind the chestnut trees there were purple petunias with interplantings of cherry-pie and in the hot still evenings the scent of them was delicious against the cool night odour of water. 'It's a pity for her to be missing all this,' we said.

Now when we met the major we avoided the subject of his wife. We went on several excursions to the mountains and some-times on the steamers the major was to be seen on the first-class deck champing with his false teeth at the spaniel-eared ham sandwiches and drinking many cups of coffee. As he talked to the Swiss girl who served him he laughed quite often. But I did not think he laughed so much. I thought in a way he seemed not only less happy and less laughing, but more alone. He had stopped making explanations, and I thought he seemed like a man who had given up hoping.

And then it all began again. This time she was really coming. There had really been some awful business of a hold-up about her visa. It had taken a long time. It was all over now.

'She'll be here on Sunday,' the major said. 'Absolutely certain to be on the boat that gets in at three.'

The Sunday steamers were always crowded, their decks gay with Swiss families going up the lake for the day, with tourists going to Interlaken. The little landing stages at the lakeside resorts were always crowded too. There were many straw hats and Bernese bodices and much raising of caps by hotel porters.

So when the steamer arrived this time there was no picking out Mrs Martineau. Crowds of Sunday holiday-makers stood on the steamer deck and pushed down the gangway and more crowds stood on the quay waiting to go on board. Under the trimmed lime trees of the quayside restaurant the Sunday orchestra was playing, and people at little gay white tables were drinking wine and coffee. It was a very simple, very laughing, very bourgeois, very noisy afternoon.

On the quay the major waited in his bright shantung suit, with his best teeth in.

'There she is,' I said.

'You said that last time,' my wife said.

'You can see her waving, and the major is waving back.'

'Several people are waving.'

'The lady in the grey costume,' I said. 'Not the one with the sun-glasses. The one waving the newspaper.'

At the steamer rails an amiable, greyish English-woman of sixty was waving in a nice undemonstrative sort of way to some-one on shore. Each time she waved I thought the major waved back.

'Anyway,' my wife said, 'let's go round and meet her.'

We walked up through the hotel gardens and across the bridge over the stream that came down and fed the lake with green snow-water from the mountains. It was very hot. The sun-blinds in the hotel were like squares of red and white sugar candy in the sun, and in the hot scented gardens under the high white walls almost the only thing that seemed cool was the grey eucalyptus tree growing on the balcony of the major's room. I had always rather envied the major the eucalyptus tree. Even the steamer whistle seemed stifled as it peeped the boat away.

'Now mind what you say,' my wife said. 'No references to any Jungfrau.'

'If she's that very English lady with the newspaper I shall like her,' I said.

Just at that moment we turned the corner of the kiosk that sold magazines and postcards of alpine flowers, and the lady with the newspaper went past us, arm in arm with another English lady carrying a wine-red parasol.

My wife did not take advantage of this situation. At that moment she became, like me, quite speechless.

Up from the landing-stage the major was coming towards us with his wife. She staggered us. She was a black-haired girl of twenty-five, wearing a very smart summer suit of white linen with scarlet cuffs and revers, with lipstick of the same colour. I do not know what it was about her, but even from that distance I could tell by the way she walked, slightly apart from the major and with her head up, that she was blazingly angry.

'A Jungfrau indeed,' I said.

'Be quiet!' my wife said. 'They're here.'

A moment or two later we were face to face with them. The

major had lost his habitual cool spruceness, I thought, and looked harassed and upset about something and seemed as if he would have gone past us, if possible, without speaking.

Instead, he stopped and raised his hat. His manners were always very correct and charming, and now they seemed painfully so.

'May I present Mrs Martineau?' he said.

Across the narrow roadway the orchestra on the restaurant terrace was playing at full blast, with sour-sharp violins and a stinging trumpet. Mingled with the noise came the sound of guitars played on the steamer as it drew away.

We both shook hands with Mrs Martineau and said we were glad to meet her. She smiled at us in a politely savage sort of way and the major said:

'Had an exhausting journey. Going to get her some tea and let her lie down.'

'Not exhausting, darling,' she said. 'Just tiresome.'

'I thought you said you were exhausted, dear.'

'I did not say I was exhausted. I am not exhausted.'

'Sorry, dear, I thought you did.'

'You shouldn't think,' she said. 'I am not exhausted. The last thing I am is exhausted.'

I could see by the way she looked over her shoulder at the restaurant orchestra that she already hated the place.

'Perhaps you will join us this evening for an *apéritif*?' the major said.

We said we should be delighted, but Mrs Martineau did not speak, and together, walking apart, she and the major went on to the hotel.

'Oh! dear,' I said.

'You sum people up so quickly,' my wife said. 'Too quickly.'

'I didn't say a word.'

'Then what was behind that oh! dear?'

'She makes up too much,' I said.

I really didn't know what lay behind that oh! dear. It may have been that Mrs Martineau was very tired; it may have been that she was one of those women who, though young, get fretful and unsociable and angered by the trials of a journey alone; it may have been that she was a person of sensitive temperament and ear who could not bear without pain the terrace orchestras of Swiss Sunday afternoons. I did not know. I only knew that she was less than half the major's age and that the major, when he walked beside her, looked like a sorrowful old dog that had just been beaten.

'They didn't say any time for the *apéritif*,' my wife said. 'Or where.'

It was about six o'clock that same evening and it was still very warm as we went downstairs.

'The major always has his on the terrace,' I said. 'We'll wait there.'

We waited on the terrace. The red and white sun-blinds were still down, casting a rosy-yellow sort of light, and I asked the waiter to pull them up so that we could see the mountains. When he raised the blinds the whole range of the Jungfrau and the Blümlisalp shone, icily rose and mauve above the mountain-green waters of the lake, and in the gardens below us the flowers were rose and mauve too, tender in the evening sun.

It always seemed to me that you could sit there on the terrace for a long time and do nothing more than watch the changing colours of the lake, the flowers and the mountains.

'The major's late,' I said.

From across the lake the smaller of the white steamers was coming in, and as it came nearer I could hear once again the sound of the guitars that were played by two Italian Swiss who travelled on the lake every Sunday, playing gay little peasant melodies from the south, earning a glass of beer or a coffee as they played on the boat or at the cafés of the landing-places.

The sound of the guitars over the water was very gay and charming in the still air.

And then suddenly as we sat listening to it the major came hurrying down.

'So sorry.' He seemed agitated and begged several times that we should forgive him. 'She'll be down in a moment. Waiter! Very exhausted after that journey. Awful long way. Waiter – ah! there you are.'

The major insisted on ordering drinks. He drank very rapidly and finished four or five glasses of Kirsch before Mrs Martineau came down.

'I've been waiting for hours in the lounge,' she said. 'How was I to know?'

'Let me get you something to drink,' I said. 'What will it be?'

'Whisky,' she said, 'if I may.'

'There's never any whisky,' the major said.

'Good grief!' she said.

I got up. 'I think it'll be all right,' I said.

I walked to the end of the terrace and found the waiter. The hotel had a bad brandy that tasted spirituous and harsh like poor whisky, and I arranged with the waiter to bring a double one of that.

When I got back to the table my wife and Mrs Martineau were talking of the mountains. My wife was trying to remember the names of those you could see from the terrace, but she was never very clear as to which they were.

'I think that's Eiger,' she said.

'No,' the major said, 'that's Finsteraarhorn.'

'Then which is the one with pigeons on top?' she said, and I knew she was trying to avoid the question of the Jungfrau. 'It has bits of snow on all summer that look like white pigeons,' she explained.

'You can't see it from here.'

'The one straight across,' the major said, 'the big one is the Jungfrau.'

My wife looked at me. Mrs Martineau looked very bored.

'There's a railway goes almost to the top,' my wife said. 'You must really go up while you're here.'

I knew the major did not think very much of climbing mountains by rail. 'I don't think you'd find it very exciting crawling up in that cold little train.'

'Oh! don't you?' Mrs Martineau said. 'I think it would be awful fun.'

'No sense of conquest that way,' the major said.

'Who wants a sense of conquest? The idea is to get to the top.'

'Well, in a way ——'

'Oh! don't be so vague. Either you want to get to the top or you don't go.'

I said something very pointed about the mountain being called the Jungfrau, but it made no impression on her.

'Have you been up there yet?' she said.

'No,' I said, 'we're always meaning to go. We've been as far as Wengen, that's all.'

'Why don't we all go up together?' my wife said. 'I think it
would be lovely.'

'Marvellous idea,' Mrs Martineau said.

'It means being up very early,' the major said. 'Have to be up
by six. Not quite your time.'

'Don't be so rude, darling,' she said.

'Anyway, you'll be tired to-morrow.'

'I shall not be tired. Why do you keep saying I'm tired? I'm
not tired. I simply don't know the first thing about being tired,
and yet you keep saying so. I can certainly be up by six if you
can.'

I could see that she was very determined to go. The major
drank three more glasses of Kirsch and looked more than ever
like a beaten dog. The sound of the guitars came faintly over the
lake and Mrs Martineau said, 'What is that ghastly row?' and
we ended up by arranging to go to the Jungfrau the following
morning, and then went in to dinner.

The train to Jungfraujoch goes very slowly up through lovely
alpine valleys rich in spring and summer with the flowers of the
lower meadows, violet salvia and wild white daisy and pink
lucerne and yellow burnished trollius, and peasants everywhere
mow the flowery grass in thick sweet swathes. There is a smell of
something like clover and butter in the bright snow-lit air. As the
train goes higher the flowers by the track grow shorter and finer
until on the slopes about Scheidegg there are thousands of white
and pale mauve crocus, with many fragile purple soldanellas, and
sharp fierce blue gentians among yellow silken anemones everywhere about the short snow-pressed grass.

As we rode up in the little train that morning under the
dazzling snow-bright peak, the major was very interested in the
flowers and kept asking me what they were. He was quite
dazzled by the blueness of the gentians, and kept saying, 'Look
at that blue, darling, look at it,' but I had never seen anyone
quite so bored as Mrs Martineau. Gradually we climbed higher
and nearer the snow until at last the air was white with the
downward reflection of snow-light from the great peaks above;
so that the powder on her cheeks, too heavy and thick for a
young girl, looked scaly and blue and dead, and the scarlet of her
lips had the flakiness of thin enamel wearing away.

'God, I simply loathe tunnels,' she said.

Above the Scheidegg the train goes into the mountain and climbs darkly and coldly inside, with funereal creakings and clankings every yard or so, for a long time. Mrs Martineau was furious every yard of that cold gloomy climb.

In the half-darkness she said she could not think why the hell the major had not told her it was this kind of train.

'I did tell you,' he said. 'I said it would be no fun.'

'You said absolutely nothing of the kind.'

'My dear, indeed I did. Did you expect the train would climb outside the mountain all the time?'

'How the hell did I know what to expect, darling, if you didn't say a word?'

'I said—'

'The whole trouble is, darling, you haven't a clue.'

'It isn't far to the top, anyway,' he said.

'It seems a hell of a way to me!' she said. She looked terribly restless and shouted something about claustrophobia.

So we climbed up in the cold gloom of the tunnel, with Mrs Martineau growing more and more furious, exclaiming more and more of claustrophobia, and all the time calling the major darling more often, as her anger grew. In the queer unwordly coldness of the clanking little train it was hard to believe in the pleasant heat of summer shining on the lake below. Mrs Martineau shivered and stamped her feet at the halts where we changed carriages and in her white and scarlet suit, with her scarlet lips and her white lamb-skin coat thrown over her shoulders she looked like a cold angry animal pacing up and down.

But if she hated the journey up in the wearying little train under the mountain, she hated even more the hotel at the terminus on top.

The hotel was bright and warm and flooded with the brilliant sunlight of high places, snow-sharp as it leapt off the glacier below. There was a pleasant smell of food, and the menu said *potage parmentier* and escallops of veal with spaghetti. But Mrs Martineau said she was height-sick and did not want to eat.

'In any case I loathe spaghetti!' she said.

'All right, dear,' the major said. He had been quite gentle, in an almost frightened way, under the most trying circumstances in the train. 'Have the veal alone.'

'I'm not so frightfully fond of veal, either. I'm not hungry.'

'Try it, dear.'

'Why should I try it if I hate it, darling? Why should I eat if I'm not hungry?'

The major looked terribly embarrassed for us and did not know what to do.

'Well, can't you get the waiter, the manager or something? At least we could order a drink!' she said.

The major sent for the manager.

The manager was a very pleasant fat man with glasses who was amiably running about the large pinewood dining-room with two or three bottles of wine in each hand. There was a great popping of corks everywhere and in the high alpine sunlight, with the smell of food and pine-wood and sun-warmed air, nothing could have been more pleasant than to eat and drink and talk and watch that amiable man.

In a few moments he spared the time to come over to us. The major explained how Mrs Martineau did not like the menu. Wasn't there something else? he said.

'It would mean waiting,' the manager said. 'The veal is very good.' He pronounced it weal instead of veal.

'She doesn't like veal. What else could you do?'

'It would mean waiting.'

'Isn't there a steak or something?' Mrs Martineau said.

'A steak, yes.'

'All right, dear, if you'd like a steak?'

'Or I could do you a *fritto misto*,' the manager said.

'What is that?' Mrs Martineau said. 'What is *fritto misto*?'

The manager explained what *fritto misto* was. I am exceedingly fond of *fritto misto* myself; I like the spaghetti, and the delicate morsels of fried meat of various kinds, including, as the manager said, the small tender escallops of weal. It was, after all, a refined and more poetical version, with Italian variations, of the dish already on the menu.

'It sounds wonderful,' Mrs Martineau said. 'I'll have that.'

The manager did not smile. 'And something to drink? Some wine?'

'Two bottles of the Dôle,' the major said.

The manager smiled very nicely and went away.

'These people are always the same,' Mrs Martineau said. 'They don't do a damn thing until you tear the place down.'

The one thing it is not necessary to do in Switzerland in order to eat is to tear the place down. And when the *fritto misto* arrived, fifteen minutes late and looking not very different from the escallops of veal we had eaten with so much pleasure, I thought Mrs Martineau ate them with great gusto for a woman who hated spaghetti and veal and was height-sick and not hungry.

Before the train took us back down the mountain the major drank four more glasses of Kirsch after the wine. He drank them too fast; he also had a cognac with his coffee. And by the time we went upstairs to the men's room he was a little stupid and unsteady from the Kirsch, the wine, the cognac and the rarefied Jungfrau air.

In the men's room he took out his false teeth. I had forgotten all about them. He was a little unsteady. And without his teeth he did not look like the spruce proud man we had first known at the hotel on the lake below. The toothless mouth had quite an aged, unhappy, empty look of helplessness.

Swaying about, he wrapped his morning teeth in a small chamois leather bag and then took his afternoon teeth from an identical bag. Both sets were scrupulously clean and white. I had often wondered why he changed his teeth three times a day and now he told me.

'Gives me a feeling of keeping young,' he said. 'Renews me. One gets stale, you see, wearing the same teeth. One loses a feeling of freshness.'

He put his afternoon teeth into his mouth very neatly, and I could understand, seeing him now with the fresh bright teeth, how much younger, fresher and more sprightly he might feel.

'You have your own teeth?' he said.

'Yes.'

'It's the one thing I'm awfully sensitive about. Really awfully sensitive. That's why I change them. I am very self-conscious about feeling a little old. You understand?

I said it was a good idea.

He said he was glad I thought so. For a moment he swayed about in a confidential lugubrious sort of way, so that I thought he might cry. 'It would have to be something really frightfully bad to make me forget to change them,' he said.

We rumbled down the mountain in the train all afternoon.

Slowly out of the dark tunnel we came down into the dazzling flowery light of the Scheidegg, and once again Mrs Martineau, altogether oblivious of the scenery and the flowers, was height-sick as we waited on the station for the lower train. All the way down through the lovely meadows of high summer grass, rosy with lucerne, the major had a much needed nap, sleeping in the corner of the carriage with his mouth open, so that I thought once or twice that his teeth would fall out. Mrs Martineau did not speak and the major woke with a start at Interlaken. He looked about him open-mouthed, like a man who had woken in another world, and then he looked at Mrs Martineau. She looked young enough to be a reprimanding daughter.

'Really, darling. Honestly,' she said.

The major worked his teeth up and down as if they were bothering him, or like a dog that has nothing left to bite on.

We parted at the hotel.

'Oh! dear,' I said to my wife, and this time she did not ask what lay behind it. She, too, had rather given up. It was one of those excursions on which enemies are made for life, and for some reason or other I thought that neither the major nor Mrs Martineau would ever speak to us again.

It was Saturday, in fact, five days later, before we came near enough to them to exchange another word. Somehow we always saw them from a distance. We saw the major running back to the hotel with Mrs Martineau's bag; we saw them on the steamers, where the major no longer enjoyed the pink-eared ham sandwiches or made eye-love to the waitress; we saw them shopping in the town. Mrs Martineau wore many new dresses; she seemed to go in very particularly for short-skirted, frothy things, or day-frocks with sailor stripes of scarlet and blue, so that she looked more than ever like a young bright girl and the major more than ever like a father too painfully devoted.

On Saturday came the affair of the eucalyptus tree. It was one of those trees that the Swiss are fond of for courtyards and bal-conies in summer; it was three or four feet high and it had soft tender blue-grey leaves that I always thought looked charming against the red pot on the major's sunny balcony.

At half-past five that afternoon we heard the most awful crash on the floor below. I went to the balcony and looked down. The eucalyptus tree lay shattered in the courtyard below,

and on the balcony the major, looking very unspruce and dis-
hevelled and shattered himself, was standing in his undervest and
trousers, staring down. For a moment I could not tell whether
the major had thrown the eucalyptus tree down there in a
terrible fit of despair, or whether Mrs Martineau had thrown it
at him in an equally terrible fit of anger.

A waiter in a white jacket and then the manager came running
out of the hotel to see what had happened and at the same
moment Mrs Martineau shouted from the bedroom: 'Come
inside you decrepit old fool! Stop making an exhibition of yourself, for God's sake!'

'Please!' I heard the major say. 'People are coming.'

'Well, let them come!' she shouted. 'If you've no more sense
than to take a room with a eucalyptus tree when you know I
loathe eucalyptus, when you know I've a phobia about
eucalyptus—'

'It isn't that sort of eucalyptus,' the major whispered.

'Any kind of eucalyptus is eucalyptus to me!' she shouted.

'Please,' the major said. He leaned over the balcony and called
down to the waiter and the manager below.

'An accident! I will pay!'

'Oh! for God's sake come inside!' she shouted. 'What's it
matter?'

'I will pay!' the major shouted down again.

Back in the room Mrs Martineau began throwing things.
'You're always fussing!' I heard her shout, and then there was
the enraged dull noise of things like books and shoes being
thrown.

'Please, darling, don't do that,' the major said. 'Don't do it
please.'

'Oh! shut up!' she said. 'And these damn things too!'

I heard the most shattering crash as if a glass tumbler had
been thrown.

'Oh! not my teeth!' the major said. 'Please, darling. Not my
teeth! For God's sake, not both sets, please!'

He rushed into the bedroom. I went back into my own.

'Whatever in the world?' my wife said.

'Just the eucalyptus tree,' I said. 'The major will pay.'

The following afternoon the major and Mrs Martineau went
away. On the lake the steamers were very crowded and under the

lime trees, at the restaurant by the landing-stage, the Sunday orchestra played very loudly to crowds of visitors in the hot afternoon. It was glorious weather, and on the four o'clock steamer as it came in there were crowds of happy Sunday-laughing people.

On the landing-stage neither Mrs Martineau nor the major looked very happy. The hotel porter with his scarlet cap stood guarding their luggage, three trunks, two brown hide suitcases, a military-looking khaki grip, a pigskin hat-box and a shooting-stick, and the major, who was no longer wearing his spruce shantung but a suit of grey tweed, did not see us on the quay. Beside us the two Italian Swiss with their guitars were waiting to catch the steamer too.

When the boat came in there was some difficulty about getting the major's luggage aboard. The trunks were fairly large and the porters grew hot and excited and everyone stared. But at last it was all finished, and on the landing-stage the hotel porter raised his scarlet cap in polite farewell.

As the steamer moved away the major stood by the rail, watching the shore. I could not see Mrs Martineau. Somewhere behind him the two Italian Swiss struck up with their guitars and began to play their little hungry-sweet gay tune.

At that moment the major saw us. He lifted his hand in recognition, and almost eagerly, I thought, in sudden good-bye. He opened his mouth as if to say something, but the steamer was already too far away and his mouth remained open and empty, without a sound. And in that moment I remembered something. I remembered the eucalyptus tree falling from the balcony and the crash of the major's teeth on the bedroom wall.

'How beautiful the Jungfrau is to-day,' my wife said.

From the steamer the major, with his wrong teeth in, gave the most painful sort of smile, and sweetly from across the lake came the gay sound of the guitars.

'I suppose the fact is men are more sentimental about them,' she said. 'Wouldn't you think that was it?'

'No,' he said.

Her face, underneath a little hat of striped brown and white fur, was like that of a pretty tigress that did not smile.

'But don't they have them at Oxford?' she said. 'Isn't it one of those things there?'

'How can having them at Oxford possibly have anything to do with it?' he said.

'I don't know. I just thought,' she said.

As the train rushed forward into spring twilight I could see, everywhere on the rainy green cuttings, pale eyes of primroses winking up from among parallel reflections of carriage lights. Above and beyond the cuttings many apple orchards were in thick wide pink bloom.

'Then what is it you don't like about them?' she said.

'In the first place they're messy. They're not like pansies,' he said. 'They don't have the flower on a stem. That's what repulses me. They're messy.'

'Repulses,' she said. 'What a word.'

His hair, a weak brandy brown, was shredded like tobacco into short separated curls that hung untidily down over the fiery flesh of his neck. His lips were full and pettish. When motionless they were like a thick slit in a red indiarubber ball. In the soft fat face the eyes were like blue glass marbles that did not quite fit into their sandy lidded slots and I sometimes got the impression that they would suddenly drop out as he gazed at her.

At this moment she hid behind her newspaper and in the darkening glass of the train windows, across the carriage, we exchanged reflections. I half expected her to smile. Instead I saw the last of the paling primrose reflections sow themselves lightly across a pair of dark still eyes that were almost expressionless.

'Another thing is that the smell absolutely nauseates me.'

'Why?' she said. 'It's so delicious.'

'Not to me.'

'Oh! that's fantastic,' she said. 'That heavenly scent. Everybody thinks so.'

'I don't happen to be everybody,' he said.

She had lowered her newspaper as she spoke. Now, sharply, she raised it up again. As she did so she pulled up, very slightly, the skirt of her dress, so that I could see for a moment or two her small pretty knees.

'Who was it who made that remark about pansies being one side of Leicester Square and wallflowers on the other?' she said.

'That was Elaine.'

'I knew it was somebody.'

'Thank you.'

This time I knew she would smile at me and I got ready to smile back at her dark steady reflection in the glass. But to my surprise she did not smile. She sat transfixed, staring at me as if I were transparent and she could see through and beyond me into the mass of fading apple orchards sailing past in the brilliant blue evening above the cuttings.

'What sort of day did you have?' she said. 'What did you do?'

'I had a very bad, tiring day.'

'All bad days are tiring,' she said. 'That's why they're bad.'

'Don't be trite.'

He began to fuss with a brief-case, taking out first papers, then books, sorting them over and putting them back again. Between his knees he held a walking-stick of thick brown cane, the colour something more than a shade or two paler than the hairs that crawled down the flanks of his face. In the confusion he let the walking-stick slip and it fell with a clatter on the carriage floor and as he leaned forward to pick it up I saw his hands. They were pink and puffy, as if the flesh had been lightly boiled.

'Why don't you put it on the rack?' she said.

'Because I prefer it here.'

'You didn't ask me what I did today,' she said.

'If it had been interesting you'd have told me all about it,' he said.

After that the girl and I stared at each other for a long time from behind the evening papers, first directly and then, when I could not bear the steady smileless dark eyes looking straight at me any longer, obliquely through the darkening glass. Now and then she moved her body slightly and I could see once again the rounded pretty knees. Then when she saw me looking at the knees she would cover them up again, not quickly, but dreamily, slowly, almost absent-mindedly, fixing me always with the steady eyes from under the tigress hat.

All the time I expected her to smile at me but all this time there was no sign of a smile. I had begun to wonder how long this strange exchange could go on, first the direct stare, then the stare that was like something between two apparitions on two smoky photographic plates, and then the knees uncovering themselves and her hands slowly covering them up again, when she said:

'I think this is frightfully funny. Look at this.'

She leaned forward and gave him the evening paper. He took it with puffy casual hands and for the first time I saw her smile. The parting of her lips, revealing her teeth, produced exactly the same effect as the parting of her skirt when it revealed her knees. They were very pretty teeth and he did not notice them either.

'Why funny?' he said.

He gave her back the paper.

'Don't you think it's funny? I do.'

'In what way?'

'Well, I don't know – I just think it's funny.'

'You mean it's funny because you think it is or you think it's funny because it really is?'

'I just think it's funny – that's all. Don't you?'

'No.'

The smile, as it went from her face, reminded me of a flame turned off by a tap. Abruptly she turned it on again; and again the teeth were white and pretty and he did not notice them.

'You can't have looked at the right piece,' she said.

She gave him back the paper.

'It made me laugh —— '

'It's exactly like the wallflowers,' he said. 'Just because you think they're sweet it doesn't mean to say they are. That doesn't make it a fact. Don't you see?'

'No.'

Furiously he threw the evening paper back in her face. She caught it in silence and held it rigidly in front of her. In this painful moment there was nothing for me to do but to hide behind my own. By this time the evening was fully dark outside and in place of primroses and orchards of apple bloom, candescent in the twilight, I could see only the rolling phantom lights of little country stations.

For some time I watched these lights. Then there was a long stretch of line with no lights at all and presently from behind my paper I looked at her face again. To my astonishment the smile was still there. It was not only still there but she appeared, it seemed to me, to be nursing it. It was like a light or a piece of fire she did not want to go out.

When she caught me looking at her again she seemed to do the trick of turning the tap again. The pretty teeth were suddenly hidden behind the tight lips. Only the pretty knees remained exposed, delicate and pale and rounded, until with the dreamy absent movement she covered them up again.

Then she began to talk to him from behind her paper.

'Did you have dinner?' she said.

He moved savagely among his books and papers and did not answer.

'With Elaine?'

He did not answer.

'How was Elaine?' she said.

Her voice had raised itself a little. She looked at me hard from behind the paper.

The train screamed through a little station beyond which were woods that were torn with long shrill echoes. I shaded my face with my hand and squinted out and pretend to search among the flashing little old-fashioned station lamps for a name, but darkness rushed in and tall spring woods crowded the sky.

'Dear Elaine,' she said.

He suddenly got up and snatched a suitcase from the rack. He banged on its locks as if they were jammed and she said:

'She's a dear. I like her. Did she have her lily-of-the-valley hat on?'

The suitcase yawned open and he began to try to press into it the brief-case with its books and papers. There was not room for it and he banged at it for some time with his podgy fingers like an angry baker pummelling dough.

'Or was it wallflowers? or doesn't she like them?'

He wrestled with the two cases. In a moment or two he gave up the idea of putting one into the other and threw the brief-case on to the seat. Then he shut down the locks of the larger case in two swift metallic snaps and said:

'You take the brief-case. I'll take the two suitcases. We're nearly there.'

From behind her newspaper she had nothing to say. Her knees with their delicate rounded prettiness were exposed again, with a naked effect of pure smooth skin but he did not notice them as he leaned forward and said in a voice of slow, cold, enamelled articulation:

'I said would you take the brief-case? Do you mind? I'll take the suitcases. I have only one pair of hands.'

'What a funny thing to talk to a woman about,' she said. 'The scent of wallflowers.'

'We shall be there in two minutes,' he said.

He reached up for the second suitcase. It was cumbersome, of old shiny worn leather that slipped too easily down through his hands. He prevented its fall with clumsiness and as he did so she stared at me again, full face this time, unsmiling, the dark bright eyes giving that uneasy effect of trying to transfix and penetrate me.

And when she spoke again it was again in a slightly louder voice, gazing straight at me:

'I told you it was because men were more sentimental about them. They always are about flowers.'

From the rack he took down a large brown dufflecoat, struggling fatly into it, submerging everything of himself except the untidy mass of brandy brown hair. I could see by this time the lights of the town and I could hear the train brakes grinding on. Sharply he slid back the corridor door but she made no sign of getting up. He did not look at her either. He was unaware of the pretty knees, the uplifted face, the little tigress hat. He was consumed by the struggle to get two suitcases through the door at once. Then the train lurched over points and the sudden motion seemed to throw himself, the suitcases and the heavy walking-stick in one clattering mass into the corridor outside.

'Don't forget anything,' he said.

A moment later he had disappeared along the corridor. The train stopped and I heard him banging on an outer door to open

it. I saw him lurch forward under the station lights, grossly out
of balance, head forward, puffing.

She got up and began to gather up her things. I waited behind
her so that she could leave the carriage first and it was only then
that I realised how much he had left for her to carry. She was
trying to gather up an umbrella, a handbag, three parcels, the
brief-case and the evening paper.

'May I help?' I said.

She stared past me coldly.

'No, thank you.'

'It's no trouble.'

She stared into me this time, rather as she had done so many
times on the journey. For a second or two her eyes were,
I thought, less chilly. I fancied there was perhaps a little relaxing
in the lips. For another second or two I thought of the way she
had exposed her knees and how attractive they were and how
pretty. I thought too of the wallflowers, of Elaine, of the lily-of-
the-valley hat and of how there were pansies on one side of
the square and wallflowers on the other. Most of all I remembered how men were sentimental about them.

'Are you quite sure?' I said.

'Quite sure.'

'It's absolutely no trouble. I have nothing to carry and if—'

'Good night,' she said.

Outside, in the station yard, a light rain was falling. As I stood
unlocking the door of my car a sudden wind seemed to throw
her out of the station. She came out without dignity, as if lost,
clutching parcels and brief-case and umbrella and newspaper,
and she could not put up the umbrella against the rain.

Thirty yards ahead he was striding out, oblivious, still grossly
out of balance, brandy-coloured head down against the rain.

When she saw him she gave a little cry and began running. I
could see her pretty legs flickering under the lights of the station
yard, white against the black spring rain.

'Darling,' she called after him. 'Darling. Couldn't you wait for
me?'

THE DAFFODIL SKY

As he came off the train, under a sky dusky yellow with spent thunder, he turned instinctively to take the short cut, over the iron footbridge. You could cut across allotment grounds that way and save half a mile to the town. He saw then that the footbridge had been closed. A notice painted in prussian blue, blocking the end of it, saying *Bridge Unsafe. Keep off. Trespassers will be prosecuted,* told him more than anything else how much the town had changed.

It was some time, the long way, down the slope and under the other bridge, before you got clear of the coalyards. The street was narrow and torrents of thunder-rain had flooded the granite setts with tides that left in the gutters patches of black sand that gave off oily glinting rainbows in the hot wet air.

Beyond the coal-yards, where sheds spanned strips of railway track like huge black bats in the gaping sky, there was a pub that he remembered well because, many years before, he often stopped at it as he came down from the country to market, bringing his plums or peas or broccoli or apples or, in early spring, his daffodils. In those days he had started first of all with a horse and trap, then a motor bike with a large flat side-car that he had made himself. He had good, powerful hands. In the year he had met Cora Whitehead he had saved enough for his first car. He was twenty-two then, and that was the year he had begun to go ahead.

The brick walls of the pub were red-black with old smoke from passing trains. Just beyond it another road bridge, blackened too, spanned the tracks, and the lights of buses passing over it were a strange sharp green under the unnatural stormy glare of sky.

The lights in the pub were burning too. They touched the cut-glass pattern of foaming jug and bottle in the glass door with outer stencillings of silver that the light of sky, in turn, impressed with a stormy copper glow.

'I'll have a double whisky with water,' he said.

Two railwaymen were playing darts in one corner of the saloon, perching pint jugs of dark beer on the mahogany curve of the counter. Another man was shooting a pin-table, making the little lights come up with jumping, yellow fires.

There had never been a pin-table in the old days. That too showed how things had changed. The barman too was a stranger.

'How much is that?'

'Three and six.'

'Have something for yourself?'

'Well, thank you,' the barman said. 'I'll have a brown.'

'I'm looking for a Miss Whitehead,' he said.

The barman drew himself an overflowing small ale in a glass. He set it on the counter and then picked it up again and wiped away, with a cloth, the circle of froth it had made.

'You mean in here?'

'No. She used to come in here. She used to live in Wellington Street.'

'Wellington Street? When would that be?'

'Before the war. She used to work in the stocking factory.'

'That's been a minute,' the barman said. 'They built a new one ten year ago. Outside the town.'

'She was a big girl. Brown hair – a lot of it. Turning red. She used to come in here in Jack Shipley's time.'

'Jack Shipley – that's been a minute,' the barman said. 'Jack's been dead eight year – nine year. That's been a minute.'

The shorter of the two railwaymen stood with a dart in his hand, poised forward on the balls of his feet, in readiness to throw.

'You mean Cora Whitehead?' he said.

'That's her.'

'She's still in Wellington Street. Her old dad works at the furnaces. He was a plate-layer once – then he went to the furnaces when they started up again.'

'That's been a minute,' the barman said.

'Thanks,' he said.

He drained his glass and set it down. There was no point in waiting. He went outside and heard, almost immediately, from beyond the coal-yards, a new peal of thunder. It seemed to roll back, in an instant, the entire discoloured space of sky above

him, leaving it pure and clear as it had been on the morning he
had first called in, many years ago, with the idea of giving his
horse a bucket of water and having a pint of Black Boy for himself. He remembered that day as if, in the way the barman said,
it had been a minute ago. His cart was piled with daffodils. Like
the sky where the storm had ripped it open in the west they were
fresh and brilliant, shot through with pale green fire. The morning was one of those April mornings that break with pure blue
splendour and then are filled, by ten o'clock, with coursing
western cloud. A spatter of hail caught him unawares on the
bridge. He had no time to put the tarpaulin up and he gave the
horse a lick instead and came down into the pub-yard with the
hail cutting his face like slugs of steel. He drove the cart under a
shed at the back and then ran through the yard to the saloon
door and by that time the hail was big and spaced and glistening
as snow in the sun.

'Don't knock me flat,' she said. 'Somebody might want me tomorrow.'

Running with head down, he had reached the door at the same
time as she did. He blundered clumsily against her shoulders.
She had a morning off that day and she had started out in a thin
dress with no sleeves, thinking that summer had come. The
funny thing was that he couldn't remember the colour of the
dress. It might have been anything: black or white or blue or
cream. He didn't remember. He remembered only the shoulders
and the bare arms, the big fleshy arms cold and wet with
splashes of hail, the big soft lips, the masses of heavy red-brown
hair and the brown eyes set into whites that were really a kind
of greyish china-blue.

Then the door stuck and he could not open it. A final whip of
hail lashed along the pub-wall as he tried to twist the loose wet
brass knob. She began laughing and the laugh was strong and
friendly and yet low in key. A moment later the sun flashed out.
The glare of it was white and blinding after the shadow of hail
and he felt it hot on his face and neck, burning the skin where
hail had cut him.

'You're as good as an umbrella on a wet day,' she said.

Then the door opened and they were inside the pub. It was
simpler in those days: just a beer-house where railwaymen called

as they came up from the yards and a farmer or two like himself from across the valley. There was a big triangle of cheese
under a glowing brown cheese-dish on the counter and a white
round spittoon on the sawdust floor. You could smell steam-
coal smoke and stale beer and cheap strong cheese, but she said
almost at once:

'There's a smell of flowers or something. Can't you smell it?'
and he saw her nostrils widen and quiver as she breathed at the
scent of daffodils.

'I got a load of 'em,' he said. 'Been gathering them since six
this morning. It's the scent on my hands.'

Almost unconsciously he lifted his hands and she took them
and held them against her face.

'That's it,' she said. 'That's lovely.'

She smiled and drank Black Boy with him. It was early and
there was no one else in the pub. Once as she lifted the black
foaming glass of stout she laughed again and pretended to wince
and said:

'I believe you bruised my arm. My drinking arm at that.'

'I always been big and clumsy,' he said. 'I can't help it.'

'Then somebody will have to teach you better, won't they? she
said. 'Can you see any bruise?'

He looked down at her arm, the upper part soft and fleshy and
bruiseless, and he felt the flame of her go through him for the
first time.

'Farmer?' she said, and he told her yes, sort of, hardly knowing what he said, feeling only the racing flame running hot
through his blood and choking his thinking. She asked him a lot
of questions, all about himself, how he was getting on, how many
acres he had, what his plans were, and she seemed somehow to
talk with the enormous glistening brown eyes rather than with
her lips. At least that was how he remembered it: the big brown
eyes always widening and transfixing him, bold and warm and
apparently still and yet not still, drawing him down in fascination
until he could hardly trust himself to look at her.

He had wanted to be early at market that day. The trade in
Midland market-squares didn't begin till afternoon but he had
reckoned on being there by twelve o'clock. He stayed drinking
with her until nearly two. They ate most of the cheese from the
big dish on the bar counter and he began to feel his eyes crossing

and rolling as he looked at her. He thought several times of the daffodils in the cart and the drink of water he ought to be giving to his horse. He worried about it for a time and then it didn't matter. Hail seemed to spring and lash at the windows every time he made up his mind that he ought to go, and then the fierce, flashing daffodil sun was out again and the railyards were steaming in the cutting below.

'You'll be all right,' she said. 'Nobody gets up to market-hill yet awhile. It's Friday. Take it easy. You'll catch folks as they come from the factories. You'll be lucky.'

'I ought to go – I got a lot to unpack—'

'You'll be lucky,' she said. 'You're the sort. You'll get on. Your sort always does.'

'How do you know?'

'I'm lucky for them,' she said. 'I always am.'

Presently that was how it turned out; all that day and other days the luck was with him. Hail closed in again that afternoon, rattling white bullets across the black setts of the market square, but the evening was clear and fine, with a bright yellow-green frosty April sky. People came late to buy under the orange paraffin flares. The daffodils shone a deeper yellow in the oily glow. Everything was good and the luck was with him.

The motor-bike followed the cart. He had thought about it already and decided he couldn't afford it. Then it turned out she knew a man named Frankie Corbett who had a Beardmore combination that he was willing to sell very cheap and that she could even get for less than that, she thought. He made the sidetruck himself from packing cases, with a detachable tarpaulin hood for wet days. It was a natural step from that to the car.

'You see I'm lucky for you,' she would say. 'Like I told you. I'm lucky. I always am.'

That summer he began to go to the house in Wellington Street. Her mother was dead and her father worked a night-shift at the furnaces. That made it easy to spend the nights with her. Her body was like her face: big and frank and bold, running against him like a brassy flame. In exactly the way that she always seemed to speak to him through her large brown eyes rather than her lips so all her thoughts about him did not come from her mind but through the pores of her skin.

'You know what?' she would say. 'I know when you turn the corner by the bridge. I feel it. That's how I feel. I can tell you're there.'

He rented his land, five acres of it, from an elderly man named Osborne who kept chickens and geese on an adjoining ten acres, most of it an orchard of apples and plums where the daffodils grew thick and almost wild in spring. 'I'm gittin' old,' Osborne would say. 'I'm gittin' past it, boy.' He had a room with Osborne in a square wooden bungalow surrounded by a cart-hovel and a few disused pig-sties and a stack of hay that was taken every year from the orchard. Osborne pottered about the place with a scythe or a feed-bucket or a basket of eggs. At certain times of the year the house seemed full of geese-feathers. In wet weather the yard was sloppy and green with web-flattened droppings.

'I'm gittin' past it,' Osborne said. 'If you could raise the money I'd git out and be glad on it. I'll go and live with my sister. Raise part on it, boy. You'll git on. Raise part on it and pay me later.'

He remembered the day, most of all the evening, Osborne had told him that. Suddenly all his life seemed to pull him forward like a bounding dog on a leash. It seemed to tear at the socket of his mind with a terrible excitement. He was going to own his own land, his own house, his own poultry or heifers or bullocks or whatever it was he wanted. He was going to have his feet on his own piece of earth.

He drove her out that evening across the valley, along a backwater of the river, not much more than a wide ditch after the heat of summer, where meadowsweet and willow-herb and thick red burnet with a smell of cucumber made a deep barrier that hid the two of them from the road. They lay down by the backwater and it was so still that he could hear young pike rising below him, making soft sounds like blobs of summer rain in the warm pools. He took off his coat and lay on his back and stared at the sky and spoke of his plans. He was for rushing in and fixing it up at once, before there could be any hitch in things, but it was she who held him back.

'Very like this Osborne is crafty. They're always the same. They seem simple and then they've got something up their sleeves.'

'Osborne's all right. He's as straight as the day is long.'

'Yes, and some days are longer than others,' she said. 'Don't forget that.'

She lay on her back too, staring with brown eyes at the August sky, giving the impression once again that her words flowed sleepily out of them.

'You get it right from the beginning,' she said. 'Then you'll know it's right. How much money have you got?'

He had saved a hundred and fifty pounds. He thought the farm could make him three hundred a year. 'I seen the bills for eggs. That's more than a hundred,' he said.

'You'll put your hundred and fifty down as deposit and then what've you got?' she said.

'I got all the stock. The geese and the hens. The fruit – there's a lot of fruit. The goodwill.'

'What's goodwill?' she said.

'You know what it is. Every business has got goodwill.'

'So has your grandmother,' she said.

She lay for some time longer staring at the sky. Then she shut her eyes. Dusky olive, the lids seemed to throb softly and steadily under the evening heat, and suddenly she turned with closed eyes and put her mouth against his face, finding his own mouth with instinct, without mistake or clumsiness, the first time. Her way of kissing was in long, soft strokes of her lips, from side to side, each as if it were the last, as if she could not bear it and must break away.

After a long time she broke away. She seemed to have been thinking and she opened her eyes.

'What if I came in with you?'

He felt he needed only something like that for the completion of his plan and his happiness.

'I've got fifty saved up,' she said. 'What does he want for the place?'

'A thousand for the bungalow and everything in.'

'That's two hundred we've got. Could you raise any more?'

'I don't know where from.'

'I might raise it,' she said. 'Frankie Corbett might raise for us. He's got it – I've only got to talk round him somehow.'

Suddenly he was leaning over her, holding her face in his hands.

'We'll get married,' he said. 'You know what you said – you're lucky for me.'

'Are you asking me?' she said.

'Yes,' he said. 'Yes, I'm asking.'

'All right,' she said. 'I'm glad you asked me.'

He would never forget that day: the soft summer evening with fish plopping in the pools of the backwater, the smell of water and meadowsweet and willow-herb, the cool cucumber smell of burnet which they crushed with their bodies as they lay there; and all his green, bounding satisfaction at his luck, his success and his future, a young man with a car, a house, a farm-holding and the woman he wanted.

'And to think it all started,' he said, 'with the daffodils.'

'It's always little things like that,' she said.

Six weeks later, almost to the minute, on a rainy October evening, he was killing Frankie Corbett in a street below the bridge.

He walked slowly and deliberately up Wellington Street. The houses were all the same, long rows of flat boxes in blackened yellow brick, with gaping oblong holes for porches. It was getting darker with the swing of the storm coming back across the railway yards.

A man came up the street with two whippet dogs quiet as long-legged ferrets covered with red and yellow jackets as they trotted before him on a double leash. That was how Frankie Corbett had come up that evening, except that he had only one dog, a wire-haired white mongrel that yapped in front of him without a lead. It had been getting dark then too, with spits of rain and a cold touch of autumn in the wind, and he knew the man was Frankie Corbett because of the dog. He had to admit he had been waiting for Frankie. He was too honest not to admit it and it was the honesty of it, subsequently, that had him damned. He was simply waiting to have a word with Frankie, that was all. He knew Frankie exercised the dog every evening about the same time. That was the only thing about it he had managed with any subtlety. He had tricked Cora into telling him that. The rest was clumsy and stupid.

What he ought to have realised, and did not realise till afterwards, was that he had been blinded with the stupor of a slow-eating jealousy. First there was the way she began to call him Frankie. 'Frankie'll get the money. I'll see Frankie. I got to see Frankie tomorrow. No, I can't see you because I got to see Frankie. Of course I'm going to his house – where else would I go? You don't suppose he carries a couple o' hundred quid round with him any day?'

How long had she known this Frankie? That was the next step in his rising suspicion of her.

'Oh! years. I never knew the time when I didn't know Frankie.'

Had she been with him? She knew how he meant – that way? more than friends?

'Oh! I don't say we didn't have a bit of fun sometimes. Girls do – it's been known.'

He wasn't talking about fun. He was talking about something else. What about that?

'Oh! we courted a bit once. But we were always squabbling. We were no good for each other.'

Then why didn't she give it up? Once and for all? Why did she go on seeing him? Why did she think she had the pull with him to get the money?

'Oh! I can get round him,' she said.

Get round him? That was a damn funny expression. What did that mean?

'We want the money, don't we?' she said. 'I got to get it the best way I can, haven't I? You can't just rush in and ask for a couple of hundred quid like that, can you?'

It took a month to get the money. Long before the end of it his mind was eaten by something more than suspicion. He began to lie awake at night with his head feeling black and soft and heavy as a rotting apple, and in it a vast canker, ugly as death, slimily eating its way outward.

That was how he came to be standing in the raining October street, waiting for Frankie. His dream of the house, the farm, the little orchard with its daffodils had been eaten by the canker.

Presently, after that ugly obliteration, he knew that she was going to have a child. And somehow he felt that the child was ugly and cankerous too: that was not because he knew it was Frankie's. It was because he didn't know. And that was why, in the end, he had to have a word with Frankie.

That evening he waited for nearly half an hour in the street and there were people who passed and saw him waiting. Then the dog came, yapping, and then Frankie came, a man older than he was, with jockey legs in brown buckskin breeches and a yellow check muffler and black check cap and a cane crop in his hands.

He stopped him, and they stood on the pavement and spoke a word or two. He was trembling violently and the air was a confusion of red and black. A few heavier spits of rain came hastily down and Frankie said he was getting wet and hadn't all night to stand there jawing over trifles. 'There's no trifle about this and all I want is a straight answer.' Then the dog yapped, splashing in a gutter puddle, and Frankie began to swing the crop.

He had a sudden blind idea that the swing of the crop was meant for him. A moment later he was hitting at Frankie with a broccoli knife. It was a thin curved knife and he had sharpened it that morning on the grindstone, with Osborne turning the wheel. Then Frankie lashed at him with the crop and then in return he hit out with the knife again. At the fourth or fifth stroke Frankie fell and hit his skull against the iron lip of the gutter, and suddenly there was bright blood in the rain.

It was exactly as she had said: it was the little things that started it. The broccoli knife, the grindstone, the yapping dog, the people seeing him waiting in the rain.

And then, on top of these, his jealousy of Frankie. She had made a great deal, in the witness box, of his jealousy of Frankie. 'What sort of jealousy would you call it?' they had asked her. 'Normal jealousy? Blind jealousy? A passing sort of jealousy? What kind of jealousy did it seem to you?'

'I'd call it black,' she said.

And he knew, again, that that was true. She knew, as always, exactly how he felt about things. She was full of the uncanny instinct of the blood.

The number in Wellington Street was eighty-four. He stood for a moment outside. He felt his blood plunging and beating in his chest like a clumsy suction pump exactly as it had done the night he had waited for Frankie. If she was there what was he going to say to her? What was he going to do?

It was like an argument that for all those years had not been finished. He wanted to have the last word: perhaps another violent one, perhaps only to tell her what he thought of her, perhaps merely to ask why in God's name she had had to do a thing like that? Perhaps it was a damn fool thing to do. Perhaps he ought to have kept away. A man of his age ought to know better. He was a man of forty now; the young man with the dream of a piece of orchard land and a place of his own had long been eaten by the canker.

He rapped on the door by twice lifting the knocker above the slit of letter box. A streak of lightning went forking across the darkening brown-purple sky and seemed to be answered, a moment or so later, by the flash of a naked light in the passage of the house.

His hands were trembling and he locked them together. The door dragged on the jerry-built bottom step. He felt the same dragging sensation across his chest and then a terrified and blinding idea that if she opened the door he might not be able to restrain himself but would rush straight at her and kill her exactly as he had killed Frankie. Then he remembered that this time there would be no manslaughter about it, and he gripped his hands even harder behind his back, waiting.

When she opened the door he knew at once that she had not changed much. The light from the naked electric bulb illuminated reddishly the mass of chestnut hair. The curious thing was, he thought, that he had no agony or bitterness about her. He felt only the flame of her stab through him again exactly as it had done on the day he had run against her in hail and sun, the day of the daffodils.

'Yes?' she said.

Then he knew that the voice was not the same. It was quieter and lighter in key. And then in a quick movement she turned her face and peered at him and he knew that the face was not the same.

He knew that it was, after all, not her at all.

'I am looking for a Miss Whitehead,' he said, 'or perhaps it's Mrs Whitehead.'

'I'm Miss Whitehead,' she said. 'Mrs Whitehead isn't in.'

'Are you Cora's girl?' he said.

'Yes, that's my mother,' she said.

He began to say that he was an old friend of her mother's. He found himself clumsily using the words 'stranger in the district,' and asking when would she be back?

'Not tonight,' she said. 'She's just gone on shift. She's out at the stocking factory.'

'I see,' he said. 'Perhaps I could call again.'

'You could catch her tomorrow.'

'All right,' he said. He found he could not take his eyes off the mass of reddish, familiar, light-framed hair. 'I'll see if I can drop in tomorrow.'

'What time? What name shall I say?'

A burst of thunder seemed to fill the street with a solid spout of rain before he could answer.

'It's coming back. You'd better wait,' she said. 'You could come in and wait.'

'No. I'll get a bus back to the station,' he said.

The street was drowned in storm-white curtains.

'You'll get soaked,' she said. 'Wait till it lets up a bit.'

Overhead the thunder made a raw lash, with long overtones of echoes, and heavy rain swept in as far as his feet in the porch.

'You'd better stand in the doorway,' she said.

She pushed back the door as far as it could go and he stood with his back to the door-frame, she on the other side.

'Frightened of thunder?' he said.

'No.'

Suddenly he felt the rising steam of rain in the air, making it hotter and thicker than ever. His blood began to beat again with heavy suction strokes in his throat. She had turned her face now and she was leaning one bare shoulder on the door-frame, her arms folded across her breasts. They were the same kind of arms, full and naked and fleshy, that had inflamed him on the day he had first met her mother. He wondered suddenly if the eyes were the same, brown and large, with that strange and compelling manner of eloquence, and then a moth flew across her neck, darting for the light in the passage, and as she turned to brush it away he saw the same perfect brown depth in the pupils, the same blueness in the large whites, the same eloquence that could say things without speaking.

'It seems as if it'll never let up,' she said. 'It's been rolling round all day.'

'Perhaps I'd better make a dash for it.'

'You'll get soaked. Have you got a train to catch? If you haven't I could lend you an umbrella and you could bring it back tomorrow.'

He peered for a second out of the dripping doorway. 'It looks lighter across the yards.'

'Wait one more minute,' she said. 'Then if it doesn't let up I'll lend you the umbrella.'

He waited, watching her face, younger and lighter and finer in tone than her mother's as he remembered it, the hair soft and red, perhaps a tone or two darker, the throat moving with deep slow strokes in the naked cross-light from behind her.

'Still at school?' he said.

'Good Lord, no. Me? I'm in the hosiery too. Only they don't allow night shift till you're twenty. Lord knows why.'

He was all at once afraid of talking too much; he was scared that at any moment she might remember her unanswered question and ask his name.

'I'd better push off,' he said. 'I don't want to keep you standing here.'

'I'll get the umbrella,' she said.

She went into the house and pulled an umbrella from a round tin stand that stood in the passage. Suddenly he remembered what her mother had said, in that quick and flashing way of hers: 'You're as good as an umbrella on a rainy day,' and then the girl said:

'I'll walk as far as the bridge with you. It's letting up a bit. You can get a bus there and I can bring the umbrella back.'

'I don't like——'

'Oh! that's all right. I got nothing to do. I get bored with both of them on night shift and me sitting there waiting for bed-time. Wouldn't you? It gives you the atmospherics – like the radio.'

She laughed as they ran out together, she holding the umbrella, into the rain, and the laugh too was much like her mother's, but lighter and softer in tone. The rain was slacking a little and they walked with heads down against it and once he peered out from under the rim of the umbrella to see if the sky was growing lighter still across the yard.

'Keep your head under. You'll get soaked,' she said. 'It's com-

ing in enough as it is. This umbrella's one of mine I had as a
kid. It's only half size.'

He crouched closer under the umbrella and found himself
taking her arm. She said, 'That's better. That's more like it,' and
again he felt the flame of touching her go through him exactly as
it had done when he had touched Cora's arm, cold and wet with
hail under a fiery burst of sunshine on a spring day.

'That's better,' she said. 'Isn't it?'

'Do you like it?'

'I like it a lot,' she said. 'Do you?'

'Yes.'

'Is that why you're running so hard to catch the bus?'

He had not realised that he was running. He had not grasped
that excitement was driving him through the rain. He laughed
and slackened his pace and she said:

'The way you were going anybody would think you had to get
the Manchester express.'

'Perhaps I have.'

'Oh! go on. Where are you going? Nowhere, are you?'

'Nowhere particular.'

'I knew it all the time.'

That was like her mother too: that queer thinking through the
pores, the knowingness, the second sight about him. 'I know
when you're coming round the corner. I know when you're
there.'

By the time they had reached the bridge it was raining no
longer. The few peals of thunder might have been far-distant
wheels of freight trains thudding heavily up slow gradients to the
north. The sky beyond the black low yards was pure and empty,
almost stark, a strong green-yellow, after the swift and powerful
wash of rain.

She did not put the umbrella down. Its shadow almost com-
pleted the summer darkness so that when they halted and stood
by the bridge he could see her face only in softened outline,
under the mass of brown-red hair. Then a bus came with its
glare of strange green thundery light over the crest of the bridge
and she said:

'This is your bus. This is the one you ought to get.'

'There's no bus. There's no train. There's no nothing,' he said.
She did not speak. They let the bus go by. It flared away,

leaving behind it a darkness momentarily shot with dancing fires
of green that were also like broken after-reflections of the clearing, yellowing sky.

'It's nice being with you,' she said. 'Do you feel that about
some people? It's nice the first time you meet them. You feel it
and you know.'

'That's right,' he said.

He wanted suddenly to tell her who he was: who and why and
what and all about himself. He wanted to tell her about her
mother and the dream the canker had eaten and he wanted to
run. He knew he ought to get out. He ought to find a little farm
like Osborne's and get work on it and save money and start
again. It was getting late and he ought to find himself a bed
down by the station. Then in the morning he could get out and
start clear, over in another county, somewhere east, Norfolk perhaps, where he wasn't known. Harvest was beginning and there
was plenty of work on the farms.

Then he was aware of an awful loneliness. He felt sick with it.
His stomach turned and was slipping out. It was the feeling he
had known when they sentenced him. His stomach was black and
he was alone and terribly afraid. He looked at the haunting
yellow sky. He heard at the same time a train rushing down
through the yards from the north and he began to say:

'I suppose you——'

'What?'

The express came roaring down, double-engined, crashing and
flaring under the bridge. She waited for it to pass in its cloud of
floating orange steam before she spoke again.

'What was that you said?'

'Nothing.'

'You know what I thought you were going to say?'

'No.'

'I thought you were going to ask if I'd come out with you
again.'

'No,' he said. 'No.' His entire body was beginning to shake
again, so that he could hardly say:

'No – I was going to say I wanted a drink. That's all. I was
going to say I suppose you wouldn't have one with me.'

'Well, of course I would,' she said. 'That's easy. What could be
easier than that?'

He knew that nothing could be easier than that. He waited for a moment or two longer without speaking. He looked down at her face, not very clear in the partial shadow of the umbrella, but familiar as if he had known it a long time. The train was through the yards. It was roaring now through the station, under the old closed footbridge, and behind it, in noisy flashes, the signals were lifting to red.

'Well, what are we waiting for?' she said.

'Nothing,' he said.

Still under the umbrella, they began to walk up the gradient, by smoke-blackened walls, towards the pub. She gave the umbrella a sideways lift so that, above the yards, in the fresh light of after-storm, he could see a great space of calm, rain-washed daffodil sky.

'It's all over,' she said. 'It's fine. It'll be hot again tomorrow.'

She closed down the umbrella. She was smiling and he could not look at her face.

'We'd better get on,' he said. 'It's nearly closing-time.'

THE GOOD CORN

For twenty-five years Joe Mortimer and his wife had lived in a valley, getting a living from raising hens and geese, a few cows and calves, the fruit from half a dozen cherry trees and an acre or two of corn.

Their small red brick house, surrounded by coops of wire and low wooden sheds for chickens, stood close to a railway line, and occasionally passengers could look out and see, walking about the small grass paddock or across the bare autumn stubbles, a woman with wispy fair hair and long brown arms. Sometimes she was lovingly leading a calf by a halter; sometimes she seemed to be earnestly talking to flocks of geese and hens. At times a man was with her: a tall gaunt-framed man with close-cut hair and spare knotty muscle and water-blue eyes that slowly lifted themselves and gazed absently on the windows of passing trains. In summer there were always many children on the trains, eagerly pressing faces to the glass as they travelled down to the sea, and whenever the Mortimers caught sight of them there was a sudden brightness on their faces, a great eagerness, almost an illumination, as they smiled and waved their hands.

Every Tuesday and again on Saturday the Mortimers drove in a small black truck to market. They took with them cases of eggs, half a dozen unplucked brown chickens, a few chips of cherries in their season and odd things like bunches of turnips and onions, a brace of pigeons, a hare, and daffodils carefully tied in dozens.

In the evenings, when they came home again, they counted out their money on the kitchen table. They laid it out in little piles of silver and copper and notes, counting it several times to make sure how much they had.

Then when the counting was finished Joe Mortimer would divide the money exactly in half. Solemnly, from the very beginning of their marriage, he would put one half into a tin cash box and then push the other across to his wife, who took it from him with long, uneager hands.

'You know what that's for,' he would say, 'put that away.'

At first they were quite sure about children. It seemed as natural to think of children coming as to think of eggs in the hen-runs and calves for cows and flowers on cherry trees. It was merely a question of time before children came. Mrs Mortimer thought of children laughing and running among flocks of hens, scattering grain, tossing it among the snapping, quarrelling brown feathers. In early spring, in cold wet weather, she sometimes nursed the first yellow chicks in warm flannel, in baskets, under the kitchen stove. That was the sort of thing children always loved, she thought.

It was in summer, when the corn was ready, that Mortimer thought of them most. In imagination he saw boys riding in harvest carts or chasing rabbits among shocks of wheat and barley. He saw himself cutting them ash-plants from hedgerows or teaching them to thresh wheat in the palms of their hands. He saw them bouncing on piles of fresh light straw on threshing days.

Then gradually, as time went by and there were no children, he became resigned to it in a puzzled, absent sort of way. It did not embitter him. If there were no children there were no children, he thought. That was nature; that was how it was. You could not alter that. It turned out like that with some people. There was nothing you could do about it but hope and make the best of it.

But his wife could not see it like that. It was not simply that she wanted children; it was not merely a question of pride. It was a woman's duty to have children; it was all of a woman's life to give birth. Not to bear children, when her pride was deep, was something more to a woman than misfortune. It was a failure in her living. It was like a hen that did not lay eggs or a cow that was sterile or a tree that never came into blossom. There was no point in the existence of them.

As time went on she drew more and more into herself. With something more than injured pride she drew deep down into an isolation where she thought of nothing but the failure that came from sterility. The reproach of failure never left her; she could not grow used to the pain of it. It was like a gnawing physical disability, an ugly mark she wanted to hide.

All the time, waiting for children, the two of them worked very hard. They saved money. Chickens and eggs went to market every week; cherries brought good money in summer; there was always enough corn for the hens and enough hay for the cows and calves and plenty over.

Whenever a new calf came she cried a little. The mournful tender glassiness of a cow's big eyes after birth was something she could not bear. She liked to lift the soft wet heads of the new calves and hold them in her arms. She liked the smell of milk on their faces and the gluey suck of their mouths if she fed them from the bucket.

After they had been married twenty-five years she stood one morning in the small cow-shed at the back of the house and watched a calf die in her arms. It was a red heifer calf and she began to cry bitterly. The calf had been dropped in the meadow the previous afternoon, prematurely, while she and Mortimer were at market. A cold wet wind with hail in it was blowing from the west. The calf could not stand on its feet by the time she and Mortimer found it and there was a drift of wet hail along the side of its body.

She went on to grieve about the calf. The death of the calf became a personal thing. She found she could not sleep at night. She bit the edges of the pillow so that she could lay and cry without a sound. After a time there was a continuous pain in her chest: a great bony bolt that shot across her throat and made it difficult to swallow.

At the same time she began to despise herself.

'Don't come near me. I'm no good to you. You should have found someone else, not me. What have I done for you? What good have I ever been?'

'Don't say that. Don't talk like that,' Mortimer said. 'You're not well. You're not yourself. I'm going to get the doctor to look at you.'

The doctor spent a long time with her in the bedroom, alone, sitting on the edge of the bed, asking questions. She stared at him most of the time with pallid, boring eyes. After a time he went downstairs and gave Mortimer a pipe of tobacco and walked about the yard, among the crying geese, and talked to him.

'All she can talk about is how she's been no good to me,' Joe said. 'How I'm not to go near her. How she hates herself. How she's been a failure all the time.'

The doctor did not answer; the geese cried and squawked among the barns.

'Neither one of us is sleeping well,' Joe said. 'I can't put up with it. I can't stand it much longer.'

'Was there something that began it?'

'The calf. We lost a calf about three weeks ago. She blamed herself for that.'

'Never thought of going away from here?' the doctor said.

'Away?'

'How long have you lived here?'

'Five and twenty years. Nearly six and twenty.'

'I believe you might do well to move,' the doctor said.

'Move? Where to? What for?'

'It might be that everything here has the same association. This is where she wanted her children and this is where she never had them. She might be happier if you moved away from here.'

'She misses children. She'd have been all right with children,' Joe said.

'Think it over,' the doctor said. 'She needs a rest too. Get her to take it a little easier. Get a girl to help in the kitchen and with the hens. It'll be company for her. Perhaps she won't think of herself so much.'

'All right. It upsets me to see her break her heart like that.'

'I wish I were a farmer. If I were a farmer you know what I'd like to do?' the doctor said. 'Grow nothing but corn. That's the life. Give up practically everything but corn. With the cows and stock and birds it's all day and every day. But with corn you go away and you come back and your corn's still there. It's a wonderful thing, corn. That's what I'd like to do. There's something marvellous about corn.'

The following spring they moved to a farm some distance up the hill. All their married lives they had lived on flat land, with no view except the hedges of their own fields and a shining stretch of railway line. Now they found themselves with land that ran away on a gentle slope, with a view below it of an entire broad valley across which trains ran like smoking toys.

The girl who answered their advertisement for help was short and dark, with rather sleepy brown eyes, a thick bright complexion and rosy-knuckled hands. She called at the house with her mother, who did most of what talking there was.

'She's been a bit off colour. But she's better now. She wants to work in the fresh air for a bit. You want to work in the fresh air, don't you, Elsie?'

'Yes,' Elsie said.

'She's very quiet, but she'll get used to you,' her mother said. 'She don't say much, but she'll get used to you. She's not particular either. You're not particular, are you, Elsie?'

'No,' Elsie said.

'She's a good girl. She won't give no trouble,' her mother said.

'How old is she?' Mortimer said.

'Eighteen,' her mother said. 'Eighteen and in her nineteen. She'll be nineteen next birthday, won't you, Elsie?'

'Yes,' Elsie said.

The girl settled into the house and moved about it with unobtrusive quietness. As she stood at the kitchen sink, staring down across the farm-yard, at the greening hedgerows of hawthorn and the rising fields of corn, she let her big-knuckled fingers wander dreamily over the wet surface of the dishes as if she were a blind person trying to trace a pattern. Her brown eyes travelled over the fields as if she were searching for something she had lost there.

Something about this lost and dreamy attitude gradually began to puzzle Mrs Mortimer. She saw in the staring brown eyes an expression that reminded her of the glazed eyes of a calf.

'You won't get lonely up here, will you?' she said. 'I don't want you to get lonely.'

'No,' the girl said.

'You tell me if you get anyways lonely, won't you?'

'Yes.'

'I want you to feel happy here,' Mrs Mortimer said. 'I want you to feel as if you was one of our own.'

As the summer went on the presence of the girl seemed occasionally to comfort Mrs Mortimer. Sometimes she was a little more content; she did not despise herself so much. During daytime at least she could look out on new fields, over new distances, and almost persuade herself that what she saw was a different sky. But at night, in darkness, the gnaw of self-reproaches remained. She could not prevent the old cry from breaking out:

'Don't come near me. Not yet. Soon perhaps – but not yet. Not until I feel better about things. I will one day, but not yet.'

Once or twice she even cried: 'You could get someone else. I wouldn't mind. I honestly wouldn't mind. It's hard for you. I know it is. I wouldn't mind.'

Sometimes Mortimer, distracted too, got up and walked about the yard in summer darkness, smoking hard, staring at the summer stars.

All summer, in the afternoons, after she had worked in the house all morning, the girl helped about the yard and the fields. By July the corn was level as a mat of thick blue-green pile between hedgerows of wild rose and blackberry flower. In the garden in front of the house bushes of currant were bright with berries that glistened like scarlet pearls from under old lace curtains.

The thick fingers of the girl were stained red with the juice of currants as she gathered them. Her fingermarks were bright smears across the heavy front of her cotton pinafore.

As the two women knelt among the bushes, in alley-ways of ripe fruit, lifting the bleached creamy curtains in the July sun, Mrs Mortimer said:

'I'm glad of another pair of hands. I don't know what I should have done without another pair of hands. Your mother will miss you back home I reckon.'

'She's got six more to help,' the girl said. 'She don't need me all that much.'

'Six? Not children?'

'When I was home there was seven. Eight before the baby went.'

'Before the baby went? Whose baby? What happened to the baby?'

'It was mine. I gave it away,' the girl said. 'I didn't know what to do with it no sense, so I gave it away. My sister adopted it. They all said it was best like that. I gave it to my married sister.'

'Gave it away?' Mrs Mortimer sat on the earth, between the bushes, feeling sick. 'Gave it away? A baby? You gave it away?'

'Yes,' Elsie said. 'It's no bother to me now.'

Towards the end of the month the first corn began to ripen. The sheen of olive on the wheat began to turn pale yellow, then to the colour of fresh-baked crust on bread.

As he looked at it Mortimer remembered what the doctor had said. 'You go away and you come back and your corn's still there. It's a wonderful thing, corn. There's something marvellous about corn.'

Now as he looked at it he could not help feeling proud of the corn. It helped him too as he thought of his wife. It hurt him to hear her cry that he must keep away from her, that the pride in her was still tortured, the love in her not smoothed out. The corn helped to soothe him a little. The wind that ran darkly across it on cloudy days had a beautiful twist as if long snakes were slipping among the ears.

In the evenings, after supper, while the two women washed the dishes, he was often alone with the corn. And one evening as he stood watching it he did something he had always liked to do. He broke off an ear and began to thresh it in his hands, breaking the husk from the grain with the pressure of the balls of his thumbs.

While he was still doing this the girl came down the hillside from the house with a message that a man had called to deliver a sailcloth. Mortimer blew on the grain that lay in his cupped hands, scattering a dancing cloud of chaff like summer flies.

'I'll be up in a minute,' he said. 'Here – tell me what you think of that.'

'The wheat?' she said.

She picked a few grains of wheat from the palm of his hand. She did not toss them into her mouth but put them in one by one, with the tips of her fingers, biting them with the front of her teeth. Her teeth were surprisingly level and white and he could see the whiteness of the new grains on her tongue as she bit them.

'They're milky,' she said.

'Still want a few more days, I think,' he said.

As they walked back up the field she plucked an ear of wheat herself and began to thresh it with her hands. The corn, almost as high as the girl herself, rustled in her fingers. When she bent down to blow on the husks a small gust of wind suddenly turned and blew the chaff up into her face. She laughed rather loudly, showing her teeth again, and he said:

'Here, you want to do it like this. You want to bring your

thumbs over so that you can blow down there and make a chimney.'

'How?' she said.

A moment later he was holding her hands. He stood slightly behind her and held her hands and showed her how to cup them so that the chaff could blow out through the chimney made by her fingers.

'Now blow,' he said.

'I can't blow for laughing.'

Her mouth spluttered and a new gust of laughter blew into her hands and a dancing cloud of chaff leapt up in a spurt from her fingers. She laughed again and he felt her body shaking. A few husks of wheat blew into her mouth and a few more stuck to the moist edges of her lips as she laughed.

She pulled out her handkerchief to wipe her lips, still laughing, and suddenly he found himself trying to help her and then in a clumsy way trying to kiss her face and mouth at the same time.

'Elsie,' he said. 'Here, Elsie——'

She laughed again and said, 'We don't want to fool here. Somebody will see us if we start fooling here. Mrs Mortimer will see us. Not here.'

'You were always so quiet,' he said.

'It isn't always the loud ones who say most, is it? she said. She began to shake herself. 'Now I've got chaff down my neck. Look at me.'

She laughed again and shook herself, twisting her body in a way that suddenly reminded him of the twist of dark air running among the ripening corn. He tried to kiss her again and she said:

'Not here I keep telling you. Some time if you like but not here. Not in broad daylight. I don't like people watching me.'

'All right——'

'Some other time. It's so public here,' she said. 'There'll be another time.'

By the end of August the corn was cut and carted. The stubbles were empty except for the girl and Mrs Mortimer, gleaning on fine afternoons, and a few brown hens scratching among the straw. 'I could never quite give up the hens,' Mrs

Mortimer said. 'It would be an awful wrench to give them up. I didn't mind the cherries and I didn't even mind the calves so much. But the hens are company. I can talk to the hens.'

About the house, in the yard, bright yellow stacks stood ready for threshing, and there was a fresh clean smell of straw on the air. During summer the face of the girl had reddened with sun and air and as autumn came on it seemed to broaden and flatten, the thick skin ripe and healthy in texture.

'Soon be winter coming on, Elsie,' Mrs Mortimer said. 'You think you'll stay up here with us for the winter?'

'Well, I expect I shall if nothing happens,' Elsie said.

'Happens? If what happens?'

'Well, you never know what may happen,' Elsie said, 'do you?'

'I want you to stay if you can,' Mrs Mortimer said. 'They get a lot of snow up here some winters, but perhaps we'll be lucky. Stay if you can. I got now so as I think of you as one of our own.'

In a growing fondness for the girl Mrs Mortimer occasionally remembered and reflected on the incident of the baby. It was very strange and inexplicable to her, the incident of the baby. It filled her with mystery and wonder. It was a mystery beyond comprehension that a girl could conceive and bear a child and then, having delivered it, give it away. She felt she would never be able to grasp the reasons for that. 'You'd think it would be like tearing your own heart out to do a thing like that,' she thought.

Towards the end of November the first snow fell, covering the hillsides down to within a hundred feet of the valley. The house stood almost on the dividing line of snow, like a boat at the edge of a tide, between fields that were still fresh green with winter corn and others smooth with the first thin white fall.

'I got something to tell you,' the girl said to Mrs Mortimer. 'I don't think I'll be staying here much longer.'

'Not staying?'

'No.'

'Why not?'

'I don't think I will, that's all.'

'Is it the snow? You don't like the snow, do you? That's what it is, the snow.'

'It's not the snow so much.'

'Is it us then?' Mrs Mortimer said. 'Don't you like us no more?'

'I like you. It isn't that,' the girl said.

'What is it then, Elsie? Don't say you'll go. What is it?'

'It's the baby,' Elsie said.

'The baby?' Mrs Mortimer felt a pain of tears in her eyes. 'I somehow thought one day you'd want it back. I'm glad.'

'Not that baby,' the girl said. 'Not that one. I'm going to have another.'

Mrs Mortimer felt a strange sense of disturbance. She was shaken once again by disbelief and pain. She could not speak and the girl said:

'In the Spring. April I think it'll be.'

'How did you come to do that?' Mrs Mortimer said. 'Up here? With us——?'

'I know somebody,' the girl said. 'I got to know somebody. That's all.'

'I don't understand,' Mrs Mortimer said. She spoke quietly, almost to herself. She thought, with the old pain, of her years of sterility. She remembered how, in distraction, she had so much despised herself, how she had turned, out of pride, into isolation, away from Joe. 'I don't understand,' she said.

At night she turned restlessly in her bed. Splinters of moonlight between the edges of the curtains cut across her eyes and kept them stiffly open.

'Can't you sleep again?' Joe said.

'It's the girl,' she said. 'Elsie. I can't get her out of my mind.'

'What's wrong with Elsie?'

'She's having another baby,' she said. 'In the Spring.'

'Oh! no!' he said. 'Oh! no. No. You don't mean that? No.'

'It seems she got to know somebody. Somehow,' she said. She felt across her eyes the hard stab of moonlight. She turned and put her hand out and touched Joe on the shoulder. 'Joe,' she said. 'That doesn't seem right, does it? It doesn't seem fair.'

Joe did not answer.

'It doesn't seem fair. It's not right. It seems cruel,' she said.

The following night she could not sleep again. She heard a westerly wind from across the valley beating light squalls of rain on the windows of the bedroom. The air was mild in a sudden change and she lay with her arms outside the coverlet, listening to the rain washing away the snow.

Suddenly Joe took hold of her hands and began crying into them.

'I didn't know what I was doing. She kept asking me. It was her who kept asking me.'

She could not speak and he turned his face to the pillow.

'I didn't think you wanted me. You used to say so. I got so as I thought you didn't want me any more. You used to say——'

'I want you,' she said. 'Don't be afraid of that.'

'Did she say anything?' he said. 'Did she say it was me?'

'No. She didn't say.'

'Did you think it was me?'

'I'd begun to think,' she said. 'I thought I could tell by the way you couldn't look at her.'

She heard him draw his breath in dry snatches, unable to find words. Suddenly she was sorry for him, with no anger or reproach or bitterness, and she stretched out her long bare arms.

'Come here to me,' she said. 'Come close to me. I'm sorry. It was me. It was my fault.'

'Never,' he said. 'Never. I won't have that——'

'Listen to me,' she said. 'Listen to what I say.'

As she spoke she was aware of a feeling of being uplifted, of a depressive weight being taken from her.

'Listen, Joe, if I ask her perhaps she'll give it to us. You remember? She gave the other away.'

'No,' he said. 'You couldn't do that——'

'I could,' she said. She began smiling to herself in the darkness. 'Tomorrow I'll ask her. We could do it properly – make it legal – so that it was ours.'

'If you forgive me,' Joe said. 'Only if you do that——'

'I forgive you,' she said.

She went through the rest of the winter as if she were carrying the baby herself. 'You mustn't do that, Elsie. Don't lift that,' she would say. 'Take a lie down for an hour. Rest yourself – it'll do you the world of good to rest.' She looked forward to Spring with a strange acute sensation of being poised on a wire, frightened that she would fall before she got there.

When the baby was born she wrapped it in a warm blanket and succoured it like the early chickens she had once wrapped in flannel, in a basket, under the stove.

'And I can have him?' she said. 'You haven't changed your mind? You won't change your mind, will you?'

'No,' the girl said. 'You can have him. I don't want the bother. You can look after him.'

'We'll love him,' she said. 'We'll look after him.'

*   *   *

On a day in late April she took the baby and carried him down through the yard, in the sunshine, to where the fields began. Hedgerows were breaking everywhere into bright new leaf. Primroses lay in thick pale drifts under the shelter of them and under clumps of ash and hornbeam. In every turn of wind there was a whitening of anemones, with cowslips trembling gold about the pasture.

She lifted the baby up, in the sunshine, against the blue spring sky, and laughed and shook him gently, showing him the world of leaf and flower and corn.

'Look at all the flowers!' she said. 'Look at the corn! The corn looks good, doesn't it? It's going to be good this year, isn't it? Look at it all! – isn't the corn beautiful?'

High above her, on the hill, there was a sound of endless lark song and in the fields the young curved lines of corn were wonderfully fresh and trembling in the sun.

COUNTRY SOCIETY

All the vases in Mrs Clavering's house were filled with sprays of white forced lilac and glossy pittosporum leaves. In January the lilac was almost more expensive than she could afford. But the tall leafless sprays were very distinguished and she hoped they would not fade.

She was going to give everyone white wine to drink at the party. This was partly because she had read somewhere, in a magazine or a newspaper, that that was distinguished too; partly because at the Fanshawes' party she had heard Captain Perigo's wife complaining quite loudly of the stinking drinks you nowadays got out of jugs; and partly because at another party, the Luffingtons', at the Manor, a Colonel Arber, a newcomer to the district, had started to proclaim his intention of beating things up and had done so, rowdily, on dreadful mixtures of cider and gin. That was exactly what she wanted to avoid. She did not want rowdiness and people complaining, even if they did not mean it, that the drinks you gave them were not strong enough. She thought that nowadays everyone drank too much gin. At one time gin was nothing but a washer-woman's drink but now everyone drank it, everywhere. They tippled it down. White wine sounded so much more reserved and distinguished even if people did not like it so much. She thought too that it was bound to give tone to her attempt to get to know the Paul Vaulkhards. The Paul Vaulkhards, who were new to the county, had taken the house down the hill, and she understood that they were very distinguished too.

All day frost lingered on the trees. It drew a curtain of rimy branches, like chain armour, over the sky, shutting in the large oak-staired house, making it darker than ever, in isolation. It lingered in black ice pools about the road. At three o'clock the caterers' van should have arrived; and nervously, for an hour, Mrs Clavering paced about the house, wondering where it had got to; and it was not until after four o'clock that it arrived, with dented mudguards and one tray of *vol-au-vent* cakes smashed into crumbs, because of a skid on the frozen hill.

The three caterers' men grumbled and said the roads were worse than ever and that everyone ought to have chains. And then suddenly the western hill of beeches took away the last strips of frost green daylight too early, as it always did, and the fields became dark and unkindly, closing in. Mrs Clavering felt the awful country isolation extinguish immediately all hope about the party. She felt that no one would come. She became doubtful of the coldness of the white wine. There were people who had to come from considerable distances, such as the Blairs and Captain Perigo and the principal of the research college and his wife, very distinguished and important people too, who would certainly not risk it. She doubted even if the Luffingtons would risk it from the Manor. With fear and coldness she felt that the Paul Vaulkhards would not risk it. Nobody of distinction or importance would dare to risk it and she would be left with people like the dropsical Miss Hemshawe and her mother, with Miss Ireton and Miss Graves, who lived together and spun sheep-wool and dyed it into shades of porridge and pale autumnal lichen, and with the Reverend Perks and his elder brother: with those people whom Mr Clavering sometimes rudely called the hen-coop tribe.

'Because they cluck and fuss and scratch and make dirt and pull each other's feathers out,' Mr Clavering said.

Mrs Clavering had not succeeded in curing her husband, in thirty years, of a habit of accurate flippancy, to which he sometimes added what she felt was deliberate forgetfulness.

Mr Clavering too, like the caterers, was late coming out from his office in the town.

'You said you would be here at four!' she called from the first-floor landing. 'Wherever have you been? Did you remember the pecan nuts? But they were ready! They were telephoned for! All you had to do was to pick them up from Watsons'—'

'Nobody ate the damn things last time.'

'Of course they ate them. They were much appreciated.'

In the hall, where Mr Clavering stood taking off his homberg hat and overcoat, the telephone rang and she called:

'That's the first one. Answer it! I can't bear to—'

Mr Clavering, answering the telephone, called that it was Mrs Vaulkhard. 'She'd like to speak to you,' he said.

'This is it, this is it, this is it,' she said. In a constraint of cold-ness and fear she scurried downstairs and picked up the tele-phone, trembling, but Mrs Vaulkhard said:

'I did not want to trouble you. Oh! it was not that. It was simply to ask you – we have my niece here. We thought it would be so nice – No: she is young. Quite young. Seventeen – could we? Would it be any kind of inconvenience? – I did not want you to think—'

With joy Mrs Clavering forgot the absence of the pecan nuts and a haunting fear that the white wine was, after all, not a suitable drink for so dark and freezing a day.

'Well, *they* will come at any rate. If no one else does—'

'Everybody will come,' Mr Clavering said. 'And a few you never thought of.'

'I'm sure no one would ever think of doing that sort of thing,' she said.

'Everybody will be here,' Mr Clavering said. 'The hen-coop tribe. The horse-box tribe. The wool-spinning tribe. The medical tribe. The point-to-pointers. You didn't ask Mrs Bonnington and Battersby by any chance, did you?'

'Of course I did.'

'And Freda O'Connor?'

'Of course.'

'Charming, very charming,' he said.

'I don't know what you mean. I chose everybody very care-fully.'

Mrs Bonnington, who was dark and shapely and in her thirties, kept house for a retired naval commander who amused himself by fishing and sketching in water colour; Mr Bonnington came down from somewhere at week-ends. The naval commander had a silvery piercing beard, commanding as a stiletto, and ice-blue handsome passionate eyes. Freda O'Connor, a long brown-haired hungry-looking girl with a flaunting bust that was like two full-blown poppy-heads, had left her husband and gone to live, while really preferring horses, with a Major Battersby. In a pleasant way Major Battersby, brown and shaggy and side-whiskered and untidily muscular, was rather like a large horse himself. Miss O'Connor had succeeded Mrs Battersby. In the furies of separation Mrs Battersby, a woman of broad-hipped charm who wore slacks all day, had taken refuge with

Mrs Bonnington. On a horse she looked commanding and
taller than she was. It seemed sometimes to Mr Clavering that
Mr Bonnington arrived at week-ends simply for the purpose of
seeing Mrs Battersby, later departing only to leave Mrs Bonnington free for the naval commander. He did not know. You could
never be quite sure, in the country, about these complicated
things and he said:

'You didn't invite Major Battersby too, did you?'

'I invited all the people I thought ought to be invited. After all
one has to keep *up*,' she said, 'one has to keep *in*—'

Mr Clavering, who would have preferred to live in town,
where you could have a leisurely game of snooker or bridge in the
evenings at the Invicta Club over a quiet glass of whisky, out of
reach of women, gave a sigh of pain and said something about
not caring whether one was up or in and then added that Mrs
Clavering was wonderful.

Mrs Clavering replied that she thought Mr Clavering ought to
go and change.

'Change what?' he said.

'That suit of course! You're never coming down in that
suit!'

Mr Clavering, who could see nothing wrong with his suit,
began to go upstairs whistling. Mrs Clavering rushed suddenly
past him, remembering she had turned on the bath water. This
gave him an opportunity of saying that on second thoughts he
would have a quick snifter before the herd arrived, but Mrs
Clavering leaned swiftly over the banisters and called:

'No! Absolutely and utterly not. No snifters. If you want
to do something useful see that the lights are switched on in
the drive—' She was bullying him with affection, and he
succumbed.

Some minutes later, as he switched the lights on in the long
paved drive that led under canopies of frosted beech boughs up
to the front door of the house, he saw that darkness had fallen
completely. The lamps set all the low weeping boughs glistening
delicately under cold blue air. He stood for a moment watching
the sparkling wintry lace of frosted twigs. He thought how cold
and dark and isolated the garden beyond them seemed, and he
thought of the billiard room of the Invicta Club, where light was
coned above green warm tables in a soft silence broken only by

men's voices and the click of snooker balls. He did not really care much for country life. The house was really too big and too expensive and too difficult to keep up; there was always the tiresome problem of servants who did not want to stay. It was only for his wife's sake that he kept it up. He was easy-going. She was fond of it all; she liked country society.

'Isn't there any gin?' he said to the caterers' men in the sitting-room.

'Only the white wine, Sir,' they told him, and he said 'Good God! Wine?' and then recognised that it was another idea of his wife's designed to make the party different, to elevate and keep up its tone. He was amused by this and decided to try a glass of the wine. It was a delicate light green in colour and he thought it seemed insipid, all taste frozen out of it, and after drinking half a single frosted glass he went off to grope in the dining-room cellarette for the gin, but the usual bottle was not there, and with tolerant amusement he realised his wife had probably hidden it away.

By soon after six o'clock a dozen people were standing about in stiff cold groups in the too large hall, grasping chilled glasses of wine with chilly fingers. The owl-like eyes of the dropsical, spectacled Miss Hemshawe and her mother prowled to and fro, searching all newcomers. The Reverend Perks and his elder brother arrived, looking like two pieces of scraped shin-bone with a little beef left on, red and fierce at the edges of their ears and noses. Mrs Clavering fluttered. Some conversation went on in subdued tones, and the caterers' men advanced with trays of wine-glasses and coloured fish-bright snippets of food, eagerly seized upon by the Reverend Perks and then earnestly recommended by his brother to Miss Graves and Miss Ireton, who were clad in sheep's wool in the form of large net-like faded blotting paper.

Soon there was a clucking everywhere, as Mr Clavering said, of busy hens. There was even, in the clink of glasses, a sound of pecking in the air. Presently the hall began to be very full; people overflowed into the dining-room; and Mr Clavering found he could not see everybody, or keep track of everybody, at once. The wine seemed to him horribly cold and insipid and he hid his glass behind a vase of lilac without noticing what the sprays of naked blossom were.

Then his wife came to whisper with despair that it was nearly seven o'clock and that neither the Paul Vaulkhards nor the Perigos nor the Blairs had arrived.

'All the best people arrive last,' he said, and then looked across bubbling mole-hills of hats and heads to see Mrs Battersby standing on the threshold.

Mrs Battersby looked outraged and stunned. Her eye sockets seemed to have lost their pupils and looked like two dark empty key-holes. Mr Clavering saw that this sightless stare of dark outrage was directed at Freda O'Connor. Until that moment he had not noticed her. Now he saw that her slender skimmed figure, looking taller than ever, was bound tightly in a long skirt of black silk, with a brief bodice of white from which her bust protruded with enforced and enlarged distinction. She was talking to Colonel Arber, who was not very tall and had the advantage of not needing to alter the level of his protuberant watery eyes in order to appraise the parts of her that interested him most. Freda O'Connor looked casual and hungry and languidly, glamorously indifferent. Her body lacked the cohesive charm of Mrs Battersby's, but it seemed instead to flame. Mrs Battersby melted away somewhere into another room. Colonel Arber took another glass of wine, holding it at the trembling level of Freda O'Connor's bosom, and seemed as if about to speak with husky passion of something. He guffawed instead, and the conversation was of horses.

Gradually Mr Clavering felt that he had seen everybody. The rooms were impossibly, clamorously full. The Perigos, the Blairs, the Luffingtons had all arrived. A sound of cracked trumpets came from the turn of the baronial staircase, echoing into wall displays of copper cooking-pans, where Dr Pritchard was telling what Mr Clavering thought were probably obstetric stories to Miss Ireton and Miss Graves, who gazed at him with a kind of rough fondness, half-masculine. Dr Pritchard had an inexhaustible fund of stories drawn from the fountains of illegitimacy and the shallows of infidelity that he liked to tell for the purpose, most often, of cheering women patients waiting in labour. But maiden ladies liked them too, and sometimes pressed him to tell one rather more *risqué* than they had heard before. In consequence something infectious seemed to float from the foot of the staircase, filling the room with light and progressive laughter.

'I want you, I want you!' Mrs Clavering whispered. 'The Paul Vaulkhards are here!'

He found himself joined to her by the string of a single fore-finger that led him through the crowd of guests to where, in a corner, the Paul Vaulkhards and their niece were waiting.

Mr Vaulkhard was tall and white, and, as Mrs Clavering had hoped, as distinguished as a statue. Mrs Clavering fluttered about him, making excited note of his subdued dove-blue waistcoat, so much more élite than red or yellow, and thought that Mr Claver-ing must have one too. Mrs Vaulkhard had the loose baggy charm of a polite pelican covered in an Indian shawl of white and gold.

'Let me introduce my niece,' she said. 'Miss Dufresne. Olivia.'

Charming, distinguished name, Mrs Clavering thought; and almost before Mr Clavering had time to shake hands she said:

'Would you look after Miss Dufresne? I'm going to positively drag Mr and Mrs Paul Vaulkhard away – that is if they don't mind being dragged. Do you mind being dragged?' She gave a spirited giggle of excuse and excitement and then dragged the Vaulkhards away.

A young dark face looked out from, as it seemed to Mr Clavering, a crowd of swollen, solid cabbages. It had something of the detachment of a petal that did not belong there. He took from a passing tray a glass of wine and held it out to her, con-scious of curious feelings of elevated lightness, of simplification. Out of the constricted clamour of voices he was aware of a core of silence about her that was absorbing and tranquil.

'Are you here for long?' he said. 'Do you like the country?'

'No to one,' she said. 'Yes to the other.'

He said something about being glad about one thing and not the other, but a small cloudburst of conversational laughter split the room, drowning what he had to say, and she said:

'I'm terribly sorry, but I couldn't hear what you were saying.'

'Let's move a little,' he said.

He steered her away through the crowd, watching her light figure. She leaned by the wall at last, sipping her wine and look-ing at him.

'I don't know that it's any quieter,' he said. 'Perhaps we should lip-read?'

She laughed, and he said:

'Really instead of standing here I ought to take you round and introduce you. Is there anyone you know?'

'No.'

'Is there anyone you'd like to know?'

'What do you think?'

She gave him an engaging delicate smile, brief, almost nervous, and he felt that it was possibly because she was young and not sure of herself. He looked about the room, at the groups of cabbage heads. And suddenly he decided that he did not want to introduce her. He wanted instead to keep her, to isolate her for a little while, letting her remain a stranger.

'Haven't you ever been here before?' he said.

'No.'

'And you really like the country?'

'I love it. I think it's beautiful.'

Mr Clavering felt himself appraise the tender, uplifted quality of her voice.

'I think everything's beautiful,' the girl said.

'Everything?'

'The lilac,' she said, 'for instance. That's marvellously beautiful.'

'Lilac?'

Absurd of him, he thought, not to have noticed the lilac.

'I noticed it as soon as I came in,' she said. 'I love white things. Don't you? White flowers. I love snow and frost on the boughs and everything like that.'

At this moment Mr Clavering noticed for the first time that her dress was white too. Frilled about the neck, simply and tastefully, it too had a frosty appearance. It seemed almost to embalm her young body in a cloud of rime.

'What masses of people,' she said. 'What a marvellous party.'

'Are you at school?' he said.

'Me? School?' She gave, he thought, a little petulant toss of the wine glass as she lifted it to her mouth and sipped at it swiftly. 'Oh! don't say that. Don't say I still look like a schoolgirl. Do I?'

'No,' he said.

Across the room Major Battersby laughed, for the fourth or fifth consecutive time, like a buffalo.

'Who is the man who laughs so much?' she said.

He told her. Battersby was with Freda O'Connor and Mrs Bonnington and Colonel Arber. The factions had begun to split up. He felt he would not have been surprised to hear from the Battersby group a succession of whinnies instead of laughter. Occasionally Colonel Arber bared his teeth and Freda O'Connor tossed her hair back from her neck and throat like a mane.

'Have you a nice garden?' she said.

Yes, he supposed the garden was nice. He supposed it was pleasant. He thought if anything there were too many trees. It was a bore getting people to work in it nowadays and sometimes he would have preferred a house with a good solid courtyard of concrete all round.

'I love gardens,' she said. 'Especially gardens like yours with big old trees. I love it at night when you see the car lights on the boughs and then on the very dark trees. It looks so mysterious and wonderfully like old legends and that sort of thing. Don't you think so?'

'Yes,' he said. He had never given the slightest thought to the fact that his garden was mysterious with old legends. 'I suppose so.'

'Oh! It's lovely just to watch people,' she said. 'Marvellous to wonder who they are—'

Her remark coincided with a thought of his own that his house was full of jibbering monkeys. The rooms were strident with people clamouring with jibberish, sucking at glasses, trying to shout each other down. There was nothing but jibberish everywhere.

'I just love to stand here,' she said. 'I just love to wonder what's in their minds.'

Great God, he thought. Minds? As if hoping for an answer to it all he stared into the glittering, mocking confusion of faces and smoke and glassiness. Minds? He saw that Mrs Battersby had got together her own faction, joining herself with the Perigos and a woman named Mrs Peele, who smoked cigarettes from a long ivory holder, and a man named George Carter, who managed kennels for her at which you could buy expensive breeds of dachshunds. There was something of the piquant dachshund broodiness in the face of Mrs Peele. She was short in the body, with eyes darkly encased in coils of premature wrinkles, and the long cigarette holder gave her a grotesque touch of being top-heavy.

There was no doubt that Mrs Peele and George Carter lived together, just as there was no doubt that the dachshunds were much too expensive for anybody to buy.

'Oh! it's fascinating to watch,' the girl said. 'Don't you think so?'

A waiter tried to push his way past with a tray of snippets. With guilt Mr Clavering remembered that he had offered her nothing to eat.

'Please take something,' he said.

'Oh! yes, may I? I'm famished. Do you think wine makes you hungry?' She took several fish-filled cases while the waiter stood by, and then a moon-like round of egg. 'I adore egg,' she said. 'Don't you?' and when he did not answer simply because he felt there could be no answer:

'Am I talking too much? I'm not, am I? But the wine gives me a feeling of being gay.'

Through smoke-haze he saw his wife, pride-borne and fussy with anxiety, steering the Paul Vaulkhards from, as it were, customer to customer, as if they were sample goods for which you could place an order.

I ought to circulate too, he thought, and then found himself grasping the mild limp dropsical hand of a slightly flushed Miss Hemshawe, who with her mother had come to say good-bye. They must be toddling, Miss Hemshawe said, and under a guise of passiveness gave him a look of unresolved curiosity, because he had been talking for so long a time, alone, to so young a girl.

'Good-bye, Mr Clavering,' they fussed. 'Good-bye. Good-bye.'

'Sweet,' the girl said. She grinned as if the facial distortions of Miss Hemshawe and her mother, toothsome and expansive in farewell, were a secret only she and himself could share.

'Yes,' he said, and he knew that now he had only to be seen touching her hand, placing himself an inch or so nearer the frothy delicate rime of her dress, for someone like Miss Hemshawe to begin to build about him too a legend to which he had never given a thought.

Presently he was surrounded by other people coming to say good-bye; every few moments he heard somebody say what a wonderful party it was. His wife, they told him, was so good at these things. He was assailed by shrill voices ejected piercingly from the roar of a dynamo.

The girl pressed herself back against the wall, regarding the scene through eyes limpid with fascination, over the rim of her glass. He was aware of a fear that she would move away and that he did not want her to move away.

'Don't go,' he said, and touched her hand.

Before she had time to speak he was involved in the business of saying good-bye to a Mrs Borden and a Mr Joyce. He remembered in time that Mrs Borden was really Mrs Woodley and that she had changed her name by deed-poll in order to run away with Borden, who had then rejected her in favour of Mrs Joyce. The complications of this were often beyond him, but now he remembered in time to address her and the consolatory Mr Joyce correctly.

'Nice party, old boy,' Mr Borden said. 'Nice.'

He felt that Mrs Borden had a face like a bruised swede-turnip and that Joyce, red and crusted and staggering, was a little drunk.

'I ought to go too,' the girl said. 'I think I see them signalling me.'

He began to steer her gently through the maze of groups and factions like a man steering a boat through a series of crowded reefs and islands. As he did so he was aware of a minute exultation because, until the last, he had kept her a stranger, apart from them all.

'Oh! Clavering, must say good-bye.'

He found himself halted by a clergyman named Chalfont-Beverley, from a parish over the hill. Chalfont-Beverley was tall and young, with a taste for flamboyance that took the form of dressing-up. He was now dressed in a hacking jacket of magnified black-and-white check, with a waistcoat of magenta and a purple tie. His chest had something of the appearance of a decorated altar above which the face was a glow of rose and blue.

'Damn good party, Clavering,' he said. His hands were silky. Clavering remembered that he was given to Anglo-Catholicism and occasional appearances at afternoon services dressed in pink-cord riding breeches and spurs below sweeping robes of white and scarlet. 'Damn good. Must bear away.' There was an odour of talcum powder in the air.

By the time Clavering was free again he saw the girl being taken away, in the hall, by the Paul Vaulkhards. He reached them just in time to be able to hold her coat.

'It isn't far,' she said. 'I'll just slip it over my shoulders.'

She held the collar of the coat close about her neck, so that he felt the young delicacy of her face to be startlingly heightened.

'Good-bye,' everyone said. The Paul Vaulkhards said they thought it had been enchanting. Mr Paul Vaulkhard gave a bow of courteous dignity, holding Mrs Clavering's hand. Mrs Paul Vaulkhard said that the Claverings must come to see them too, and not to leave it too long; and he saw his wife exalted.

'Good-bye, Miss Dufresne,' he said and again, for the second time, held her hand. 'I will see you all out. It's a little tricky. There are steps—'

The Paul Vaulkhards went ahead with Mrs Clavering, and as he followed through the outer hall he said:

'Did you enjoy it? Would you care to come and see us again before you go away?'

'Oh! it was a marvellous, wonderful exquisite party,' she said. 'It was beautiful. It was vivid.'

The word lit up for him, like an unexpected flash of centralised light, all her eagerness, touching him into his own moment of reserved exultation. He walked with her for a few yards into the frosty drive, where the Paul Vaulkhards were waiting. A chain of light frozen boughs, glistening in the lamplight, seemed to obscure all the upper sky, but she lifted her face in a last gesture of excitement to say:

'Oh! All the stars are out! Look at all the stars!'

'Now remember,' he said. 'Don't forget to come and see us before you go.'

'Oh! I will, I will,' she said. She laughed with light confusion. 'I mean I will come – I mean I won't forget. I will remember.'

He watched her run into the frosty night, down the drive.

Later, in a house deserted except for the caterers' men and shabby everywhere with dirty glasses and still burning cigarettes and a mess of half-gnawed food, his wife said:

'Honestly, *did* you think it went well? *Did* you? You didn't think everybody was awfully stiff and bored?'

'I don't think so,' he said.

'Oh! Somehow I thought it never got going. It never jelled.

People just stood about in groups and glared and somehow I thought it never worked up. You know how I mean.'

'I thought it was nice,' he said.

'What about the wine? I knew as soon as we started it was a mistake. People didn't know what to make of it, did they? It was too cold. Didn't you feel they didn't know what to make of it? – it's funny how a little thing like that can go through a party.'

Disconsolately, agitatedly picking up glasses and putting them down again, she wandered about the empty rooms. The caterers' men, in their shirt-sleeves, were packing up. In the hall a spray of lilac had become dislodged from its green guard of pittosporum leaves and as Clavering passed through the hall he picked it up and put it back again.

'What do you suppose the Paul Vaulkhards made of it?' his wife called. 'Didn't you have an awful feeling they felt they were a bit above it? Not quite their class?'

Opening the front door, he was too far away to answer. He walked for a few paces down the still-lighted drive, looking up at the stars. The night in its rimy frostiness was without wind. With a tenderness he did not want to pursue into anything deeper he remembered how much the girl had liked all things that were white. He remembered how she had thought everything was beautiful.

From the frozen meadows behind the house there was a call of owls and from farther away, from dark coverts, a barking of foxes.

'How many langoustines today, Monsieur Harris?' the boy said.

Almost every day that summer there were big blue dishes of cream pink langoustine, a sort of small spidery lobster, for lunch, and all through the sunny dining-room of the hotel there was a hungry cracking of claws. A fine bristling Atlantic air blew in hot from the bay.

The small boy, Jean-Pierre, had eyes like glistening blobs of bright brown sea-weed. 'English! English! – in English, please!'

'Nine.'

'One, two, three, four, five, six, seven, eight – noine!'

'*Nine.*'

'Noine.'

'*Ninе.*'

'Please say nine!' Madame Dupont said. 'Nine, Jean-Pierre – now! No more of that noine!'

'Noine.'

'Ten now,' Harris said and even Madame Dupont, the governess, who with small beady dark eyes and neat pink jaws delicately champing had something of the look of a refined langoustine herself, laughed gaily.

'I have to laugh,' Madame Dupont said. 'It's very wrong, but I can't help it. The boy is very happy.'

Harris had begun to share a table under the window with Madame Dupont and the boy because now, in July, towards the height of the season, the hotel was quickly filling up. There were no longer any single tables for single men. Every day new French mammas and papas arrived with shrieking families and dour matriarchal grandmothers and small yapping dogs, and every day Madame Dupont, who had chosen the table in the corner because it was secluded and strategic, squinted finely through her small gold spectacles so that she could see them better.

'That's a family named Le Brun who were here last year. They are from Lyons. He is in the Sûreté.'

'How many langoustines now, Monsieur Harris?'

'One dozen.'

'Dozen, dozen, dozen? How many is that?'

'Douzaine,' Harris said. 'Dozen, douzaine. Douze, douze.'

'It is the same,' Madame Dupont said. 'Isn't that so often the case? They are so alike, French and English. Sometimes there is hardly any difference at all, really.'

'French is more beautiful—'

'Oh! no. English is very beautiful too.' Sea-light from the wide hot bay sparkled on Madame Dupont's spectacles as she lifted her face. 'The family Bayard has gone, I see. They have rearranged the tables.'

Harris, with his back to the room, could not see the comings and goings of French families. They were reflected for him in the flashing glasses, the brief arrested pauses of neat lean jaws, the way the silver lobster pincers were held, delicately or with surprise or with a certain stern reproval and expectancy, over a pile of pink-brown shell and whisker.

'I believe they are going to put that family – no, they are not. Thank Heaven.'

'Which family?'

'Blanche. The big fat man in the blue-striped shirt and the white cap that he always forgets to take off in the dining-room.'

After the langoustine that day there were small *filets de Sole Dieppoise* and after that *navarin d'agneau* with tender olive peas. The sun was a blinding silver on the bay. Big blue sardine boats, with blood-bronze sails, came round the distant point of pine and rock with deceptive grace, running quickly out of sight into port. Across the bay an almost complete circle of sand, dead white, lay below blue-black pine woods like a crust of salt left by tide and baked to a dazzling fierceness by wind and sun.

By the time he reached the *navarin* Harris was quite sleepy. It was the same, he discovered, every day. Lunch began at twelve o'clock and every day he was determined to walk, afterwards, along the little coast road under the pines to find out for himself what lay on and about that dazzling curve of sand across the bay. Every day lunch with Jean-Pierre and Madame Dupont went on, with much laughter and sucking of grapes and coffee, until two o'clock, and after it he went to sleep in the sun.

At one-thirty Madame Dupont said, 'It is very queer the table is not occupied. I find it very queer.'

'Monsieur Harris is going to sleep,' the boy said. 'His eyes are shutting!'

'Oh! no, no, no. Wide awake. Thinking.'

'Too much langoustines!'

'They have put special flowers on the table,' Madame Dupont said. 'Roses and things. Nice ones.'

'Monsieur Harris is asleep! He's not listening.'

'I find it very queer,' Madame Dupont said. 'Special flowers and nobody coming.'

'The flowers are always for Americans,' Harris said. 'They will insist on ice-water and plain salad and make a fuss.'

'Fuss, fuss?' the boy said. 'What's that? What's fuss?'

'It's what you are,' Madame Dupont said. 'Fuss fuss!'

'Fuss fuss!' he said.

Madame Dupont, not speaking, began to wash a branch of blue-black grapes in her finger bowl, holding it just under her chin, letting it swing there. Slowly, almost dreamily, she took off the wet grapes with her slender fingers, one by one, pressing them into her mouth, stones and skin and all, with neat and elegant squirts.

'You must not look,' she said, 'but the new people are just coming now.'

Harris idly began to wash a bunch of grapes too. In the water the dark skins gathered crusts of little pearls. The grapes were always sweet and delicious, he found, but sometimes in the early pears and peaches there were to be found, to the boy's amusement, trundling fat maggots, pear-cream or peach-rose according to the flesh from which they unrolled, and Madame Dupont, in horror, covered her twinkling glasses with her hands.

Today, in the boy's slim green pear, there were no maggots, and Madame Dupont's eyes were alert and free.

'I thought it looked for a moment like Monsieur Bazin from St Germain and his wife,' she said. 'He is a man of the same build.'

'Not Americans?'

'Oh! no, no. French. An elderly man and a girl.'

'Nice?' he said. 'The girl.'

A grape lay for a second in the centre of Madame Dupont's lips, delicately poised.

'A beauty.'

As the grape slid into Madame Dupont's mouth, to be sucked and champed and swallowed swiftly away, she said:

'Can I describe her for you?' and went on, not waiting for an answer: 'Very dark. No colour. Big brown eyes. And quite a big girl – big and round, with nice arms and hands.' She broke off another grape. 'About twenty-two.'

'And him?'

'She's wearing a white sun dress with a red coat that slips off. She's putting a flower into his buttonhole.'

'What is he like?'

'A real French papa. He's a little short-sighted I think. He seems to find it hard to read the menu.'

'Perhaps he is long-sighted instead,' Harris said and Madame Dupont, looking hastily down under her glasses, washing grape-stained hands in the finger bowl, seemed for the first time a little confused.

'I have a feeling I have seen him somewhere before,' she said. 'Jean-Pierre, you must wash your hands. Quickly. Wash them. We must go.'

'Fuss fuss!' he said.

'Thanks to you he is learning English too quickly,' she said. 'Are you coming too?'

'Yes,' he said. 'I am going to walk across the bay.'

'On your stomach? or swimming?' she said and once again the three of them, the boy with imp-bright eyes, Madame Dupont no longer severe or confused, laughed gaily together.

'He's asleep!' the boy said. 'His eyes are shut! He's asleep already.'

'Quiet!' she said. 'Walk nicely from the dining-room.'

'Tell me about the war,' the boy said.

'No,' he said. 'Nothing to tell. I must walk across the bay.'

All afternoon he slept, as usual, in the sun.

When he woke, about five o'clock, the wind had turned a little northward, breaking straight through the small gap from the open sea. It stirred even the sheltered bay into a surface of jagged glass, a dark and wonderful indigo, with flouncing edges of salt-white foam. The air was so much cooler that he woke with a sudden start, the wind quite cold across his shoulders, where his wound scar, almost invisible now on dark sea-browned flesh, felt tight and dead.

He dressed and began to walk, as he had always promised himself, up the road that went along the bay. For about half a mile there were little hotels, each with its own small red-tented *plage*, a few villas with shutters pulled down on geranium-filled verandahs against the sun, and then four or five *pensions,* shuttered too and noiseless behind walls of sea-bent cypresses. Between them a few boats lay beached, half-buried in thick white sand; and then the shore, at last, was clear, all pine and slate-blue rock and dune-grass, with the road winding thinner and thinner up the bay.

Here and there a cove of rock, a miniature bay, pushed the road further inland, so that the sea was suddenly not visible over humps of bracken and pine. He began to see that the fine long curve of road was a deception. It would take hours, half a day, perhaps more, to walk the long circle to the point. Sand blew in sharp tedious whirls under the pines and a sound of shaken boughs, somewhere between a moan and a whine, not summery at all, was almost ugly in the cooling afternoon.

He was glad to be on the clear treeless road again, where he could feel sun. And then, abruptly, on a rise of rock, the road ended altogether. It shot upwards over the little rise, ending in barricades of wire and petrol cans and old sea-worn notices that had once spelled *'Danger: Pont coupé'* in brighter red.

Beyond, a narrow estuary, tidal, filling now with the scum of incoming sea, cut him off from the higher coast, and he stood looking down at what remained of the bridge, two lines of old black tooth-stumps, crusted by weed and mussels in the sand. The estuary gave on to a little bay, sheltered from the west by a point of rock, with scattered pools: and then beyond again the repeated dazzling dunes of sand.

He sat down, lazy in the strong sea-air, glad to be cheated of the walk along the coast. He had not come to France for walking; he was happy to absorb sea and sun and sand, eat a thousand *langoustes,* a thousand *langoustines,* and sleep, with no one to worry him, every day. He had been shot down over Lorient a day or two before invasion began. He had been wounded in the left shoulder; and now it produced a curious deflective sort of action in his arm, so that he travelled crab-wise when swimming. Partisans had taken care of him for a week or two, grim, high-spirited and very kind, and his first thought, after the war, had been to come back to them. He had wandered, later, all through the coast country about here, trying to find his unit in a countryside littered with abrupt, tired, severe notices saying 'No: we do *not* know where your unit is.' All of it now seemed a million years away.

He would not have known the girl coming up the road, five minutes later, if it had not been for Madame Dupont's description of her: a white sun-dress with a red coat that could be slipped off. She had taken off the coat and was carrying it in her hand.

She too stood looking down at the little estuary, the bay, and the remains of the bridge; the wind filling and beating the skirt of her dress, so that she held it down with her free hand.

'The bridge is cut,' he said. He spoke in French and for a moment she did not reply.

Then she said, with a curious repetitive flatness that he could not explain as either ironical or bored:

'Yes: the bridge is cut.'

She stared across the bay, lips full, thrust outward, almost pouting. It was true, as Madame Dupont said, that she was a big girl, big and round, with sallow skin and fine full arms; but her eyes, like her voice, were flat and unresponsive. Sea-light seemed to have pulled over the deep brown pupils a thin opaque blind.

He stood for a second or two not knowing what to say and then he remarked that, below, the little bay was very beautiful.

Yes, it was very beautiful, she said: flatly again, as if, perhaps, it were a stretch of corrugated iron.

There was probably a road round the estuary, he said, if she thought of walking on; and she said:

Yes, there was probably a road round the estuary: as if neither she nor anyone could possibly care.

Quite suddenly she turned and began to walk back down the road to the hotel. He watched her for some minutes and then began to walk back too. Half-way there the wind blew cool again, whining and moaning under the pines, and the girl put on the little scarlet coat as she walked along.

That evening the *patron* came to the table, as he always did, and said, 'Tonight, sir, Mister Harris m'sieu, we have on the *menu* to eat a nice potage, a broth, and then some local fish cooked *en fenouille,* and afterwards a piece of meat, bifteck, cooked in butter. It is all right? You find it?'

He would find it excellent, Harris answered, and at the bifteck Madame Dupont said:

'The girl is all alone. She is wearing quite a nice dress, dark blue and white. It goes well with that dark hair of hers.'

'You have butter on your chin, Monsieur Harris,' Jean-Pierre said, and Harris licked the running butter away with his tongue.

'Their name is Michel. I found it from Madame. He is something in automobiles in Paris. Quite well off, I think, too.'

'Are they married?'

'They are father and daughter.'

'Then why do you suppose the father isn't here tonight?'

'Because he has gone to Paris,' Madame Dupont said. 'He is like so many other gentlemen. He has *affaires* in Paris and he will come here, no doubt, for the *wickend.*'

'Have you seen him before?'

'I don't know,' Madame Dupont said. 'I am not sure. Somehow there is a little feeling I have seen him somewhere.'

In the evenings there was nothing to do but sit on the terrace and, in the darkness, almost always warm but hardly ever without a stir of wind, watch the awakening of lights across the bay. The long sea-strong days made Harris very sleepy and by ten o'clock, most evenings, he was too tired to keep awake and fell asleep at once, on the top floor, in his small attic bed. In the hotel *salon* games of bridge between staid French pairs, at tables of green baize, went on until midnight; and in the bar below plaintive French songs, on records, with dancing, beat into the wave-lapped night air for an hour or two longer.

That night he did not fall asleep. With sunset the bristling wind across the bay had died. In the still air the gramophone from below thumped like the heavy throbbing of a sardine boat setting out to open sea.

It seemed as if, for an hour, the same tune was played over and over again. He got up and looked at his watch. He shook it several times to make sure that half past nine, and not, as he thought, half past ten, was the time it showed. Across the bay, at the headland, a navigation light flashed green and red, and below, on the terrace, there was still a noise of spoons in coffee saucers.

It suddenly came to him that, in a moment of sleepiness, he had made a mistake of an hour in the time. He dressed and went downstairs. There was much knitting by French mesdames in the lounge, and outside, under arbours of plane-leaves, a few people were still drinking, served by a waiter who in moments of idleness stared out at a dreamy milk-calm sea. In the bar a few others were dancing, the windows open for air, the gramophone filling the room with the beat of the same hot sweet tune he had heard upstairs.

In the bar he found the girl: but not dancing.

She was sitting alone on a high stool at the bar, playing with a few dark-golden grains of sugar in a coffee spoon.

'Would you dance?' he said.

She held up her arms, not speaking, without a smile. The sleeves of her dress, dark blue, were long, ending in cuffs that clipped together with small white shells. The stuff of the dress was some light crêpe-like material through which, as they danced, he could feel her skin, smooth and blood-warm and unencumbered. She danced mechanically, smoothly, staring over his shoulder: either as if she were deep in thought or not thinking at all. He asked her once if she knew the name of the French tune that now, as before, the gramophone kept playing over and over again, but she shrugged her shoulders, whether because she did not understand or because she did not know he never discovered.

After the third or fourth dance he experienced a curious feeling. A latent boredom, a kind of soft fungus of drowsiness rising from the same dance, the same tune, the same mechanical rhythm of her body – as if she had done all this and done it as silently, as beautifully and as efficiently with a hundred men like him before – began to creep up through his mind. He felt it over-hot in the little bar. He began to dislike the haunting repetitive little tune. A smell of sea-air, fresh and salt, came in lightly through the open window, and suddenly he felt he wanted to be outside, watching the bay and its lights, walking by the sea.

'Shall we walk?' he said.

Her response to the idea of walking was exactly as it had been to the idea of dancing. Not speaking, again without a smile, she walked in her anonymous way into the darkness ahead of him. He followed her and, side by side, they began to walk along the

little curving esplanade. For a time street lights at regular intervals lit up bright purple and scarlet beds of verbena and geraniums, rows of striped bathing huts, blue and brown boats upturned on white sand.

And then, soon, the last of the light had gone. The dark sea,
a white fringe of miniature summer waves, a few dark rocks in
white sand: it was all wonderfully quiet after the bright noises
of the bar.

Half a mile farther on they stopped by the sea-wall and looked
out to where, over the bay, it was possible now to see the lights
of the lower port, the green and scarlet flashes of navigation
points, the trail of a sardine fleet making for open water. He
watched for a few moments and then, casually, he turned to
kiss her. He thought for a moment he had made a hasty and
blundering attempt at it because, as he came close to her, she
turned her face away. And then suddenly he knew that she was
simply offering her cheek, lightly and formally, in the conventional French way.

'Not that way,' he said and began to turn her towards him,
kissing her full on the mouth. He felt a great start of quickened
response flare up through her body that, from her breast downward, seemed to have nothing covering it but the flimsy crêpe-
like stuff of the dress.

Like one of the navigation lights pricking the darkness, the
start of her body flared up and went out again. She seemed to kill
it and then hold herself away.

He stood for some moments tracing with one finger, slightly
puzzled, the line of her long arm and the bare curve of one shoulder. She had taken up a half-crouching attitude, leaning forward
on the wall, looking at the sea.

'How long do you stay here?' he said.

'Until the hot weather is finished. It is very hot in Paris now.

'Do you live in Paris?'

'I live in Paris.'

'Do you like it here?' he said. 'Do you swim?'

'Yes: I swim.'

There was something increasingly curious, he thought, about
that repeated formality, the flashing start of feeling, the sudden
ending of it, the holding away. He felt that behind it, behind all
the soft correctness of tone, a disturbed moment of high feeling,

of anguish in heat or even anger, might suddenly flare out if he touched her again.

'Perhaps you would like to swim tomorrow?' he said. 'With me.'

'I would like it. Thank you.'

'What time? At half past ten? Before lunch?'

'Before lunch: yes.'

He began to explain to her about the sand in front of the hotel. The wash of tide covered it with unpleasant contours of sea-weed and a species of ugly splintered grey shell. By noon crowds of feet had turned it into a mess. It was better to bathe some distance up the shore and now he suddenly remembered the smaller bay, at the estuary, where the bridge was broken, that he had seen that afternoon.

'Would you come there?' he said. 'It's better.'

'Yes: I will come there,' she said.

For more than half the way back to the hotel she had nothing else to say. He did not kiss her again. At a turn in the esplanade a brief curl of wind, like some afterthought from the breezy afternoon, caught her long hair and blew it, intensely black and beautiful, across her face. She stopped to pin it back; and standing there, in the half-light of the first esplanade lamp forty yards away, she addressed him for the first time with a question of her own.

'How long do you stay here?'

He laughed.

'As long as the money lasts.'

'You don't know?'

'No.'

He had not given it serious thought. He had been able to bring about seventy pounds – all that was left of his precious magnificent gratuity, all he had. After that had gone he hadn't a penny, not a prospect, not the remotest idea of a plan or a job.

'When there's no more money you go home?'

'That's it.'

'You must be careful with your money.'

In the morning they lay in the sun, below dunes of scorching sand, beyond the estuary. A wind had risen with customary freshness after sunrise and it seemed to keep off the heat of a brilliant day. But it was the wind, he knew, that burnt; and he was torn between telling her to cover her body for comfort's sake and letting her leave it there, magnificent and full, breast and loins held in nothing but simple triangles of sea-green, long hair blue-black on her full ripe shoulders, so that he could take his fill of watching it.

Finally he reached for her sun-wrap. She was lying full-stretched on sea-whitened sand, her skin almost as pale. 'You ought to put this on,' he said. 'The sun will burn you.'

She turned over, her flanks picking up star-like grains of sand, one breast dipping and taking up with its heavy tautness a coat of the same shimmering particles of whiteness; and in a moment he felt himself fired and trembling and began to kiss her. Her mouth, now, came full to him at once, without hesitation. Her hair fell across his face and with a long slow arm she brushed it away and then let the arm curl across his back. He felt the five needles of her fingers nicking down the bone of his spine, clench-ed, holding him in still frenzy.

An afternoon of indigo and snow-white brilliance blew in exhilarating bursts of wind that flowered into occasional running whirlwinds of sand. Above the dunes there was a tossing and continuous murmur of pines. Waves lashed with glittering and exciting brilliance at the rocks of the small point and sometimes it was too hot, and then too cool, to lie on naked sand in the sun.

That afternoon he discovered her name; it was Yvonne, but he did not trouble about the rest. Michel or something, Madame Dupont had said. It was Friday; and he said something, just before they went back to the hotel, about her father coming back for the weekend. Whether, in the crash of waves and the general dazzling exhilaration of sea and sun and wind, she did not hear quite what he said, or whether she was really not listening or not wanting to listen, he did not know. But it was not until they were walking back along the road that she answered him:

'Yes: he is coming back tomorrow.'

'Until when?'

'He will go back to Paris on Monday.'

He remembered the little short-sighted dapper man who could not read the menu; the flower in the buttonhole; a certain touch of obedient filial care about her attitude towards him at table. And it did not surprise him when she said:

'I will have to be with him. He likes me to be with him. All the time.'

'I understand.'

That evening they danced in the bar and walked, afterwards, along dark calm sands. Under stars of tense brilliance, to a barely audible splash of tiny waves, she kissed him several times; and said:

'Please don't talk to me when he is here. It isn't for long. Two days. But he likes to walk with me. And play cards in the evenings. You know. That sort of thing.'

'I know,' he said. That night, as she put it, it did not seem very long.

Next day, for lunch, there were again langoustines. He ate six. Saturday, for some reason, was always a disappointing day for food, with dishes that seemed scratched up and tired; and Jean-Pierre set up a commotion of mocking:

'Monsieur Harris doesn't eat his food! Monsieur Harris doesn't eat his food! How many langoustines?'

'I think I'm getting tired of langoustines.'

'When you take things on your plate you have to eat them!'

Madame Dupont flashed her spectacles:

'I see the girl's father has come back. She always puts a flower in his buttonhole.'

He did not turn to look; and Jean-Pierre said:

'If you don't eat your langoustines you can't come to the *pardon* tomorrow.'

'It is the greatest *pardon* of all tomorrow,' Madame Dupont said. 'It's a wonderful thing. You should see it. You should come with us.'

'Please!' the boy said. 'Please!'

'We are hiring a car,' Madame Dupont said. 'There will be plenty of room for you if you care to come.'

There was nothing else to do; and he spent most of Sunday roaming about with the boy and the governess on a high crowded hill full of the shrieks of a fair-ground and the droning of unending priestly incantations. All day a great throng of surplices swarmed about a big grey church like fat, flapping moths. Bishops in yellow robes led a whole hillside of peasant faces in moaning and singing and ceaseless prayer. At the foot of the hillside drunken orgies started between alley-ways of fair-stalls, in cider-booths, and peasants reaped rich harvests from car-parks in paddocks and stubble fields. From the top of the hill a vast bay of sand, clear and superbly cleansed by weedless tides, stretched curving away against miles of bright blue ocean.

And looking at it, thinking of the other, smaller bay, of the girl and her body taking to it like a magnet the golden grains of sand, he felt pained by an ache of sudden anguish for her. He was smitten with grey loneliness, made worse by the dry wearying incantations, the shrill callings down from heaven. He felt sickened by people. He wanted no one near him but the girl, on the burning shore or in the calm darkness of the other bay.

That afternoon Madame Dupont bought many hideous tinsel statuettes of saints and Jean-Pierre ate *pommes frites* from a paper bag and at five o'clock they drove home.

Always, on Sundays, the hotel was crowded. French boys played accordions, and sometimes guitars, with loud sweet tunes, on the esplanade. The gramophone blared all day from the bar.

He gave up the idea of drinking about nine o'clock and decided to go to bed. As he passed the *salon* he stopped and stood looking in through the partially curtained dividing windows. A few games of cards were being played. Lights fell across litters of cards and small piles of money on green baize tables and he saw the girl, upright, neutral-faced, very quiet, playing with her father; but whether she was bored, or tired, or simply unusually circumspect in her black Sunday evening dress he did not know. It struck him that, in these few moments, she hardly looked at her partner, dapper with his long amber cigarette holder, the flower in his buttonhole and his general French air of being the spruce shrewd successful man.

It was during that week, towards the end, that she saw, as they bathed, the scar on Harris' shoulder. It began a conversation not, as it turned out, so much about him as about herself.

Some time before this he had discovered that Madame Dupont had been wrong about her age; she had, perhaps, allowed for the fact that big supple girls are sometimes younger than they seem.

She was, after all, twenty-seven; and the conversation, for that reason, did not surprise him quite so much.

'I have been married,' she said.

With an unpleasant choking sensation in his throat he lay looking at the sky. A sardine boat, chugging seawards about the point, seemed to travel for several miles before she spoke again.

'During the war,' she said. 'The scar reminded me. I wanted to tell you in any case.'

'There was no need to tell me.'

'You would have to find out.'

She seemed suddenly, because of this remark, to speak more easily. The sardine boat cleared the point, quickening up its engines in a stabbing series of coughing barks that broke sharply across the water.

'It was just for a day or two,' she said. 'That's all.'

'The war?'

'Yes: a partisan.' She spoke quickly. 'Two or three nights of love – and then, out – pouff!—'

She did not go on, and now as he turned to her, looking at her face, he found it unexpectedly pained and hard, embittered almost to giving the illusion of being old.

'There was no need to tell this,' he said.

'You would find out in time,' she said, and all of a sudden he felt all the fire of wanting her leap back, a sick central needle of pain. Her body, golden-grained with sand, rolled itself over to him, heavy with emotion, quivering to touch. 'You would know,' she said. 'You would have to know.'

The days of the middle week, in this way, mounted like a castle in sand. By the estuary, under hot white dunes, and then in the evenings, along the deserted shore, to the sound of tiny waves that were not more than spilled echoes, the structure of it, hot and frenzied and delicate, was raised up. And each time the week-end, like the sea, swept in and bore it away.

By each Monday he felt that a dark ugly hole had been torn in his existence. Not merely had the bright insubstantial castle gone. Her other existence, like the sea, had torn deep under it, leaving only a ravaged, lacerating hole of loneliness. He began to hate the dapper, card-playing flower-fop of a father who punctually came down every Saturday to perform, in his neat and neutrally precise way, the shattering extinction of everything beautiful the week had built up. He thought she hated it too.

On the following Friday, for the first time for several weeks, a squally wind brought an afternoon and then an evening of lashed cold rain. A squally touch of winter seemed suddenly to rip across the upturned tables of the terraces. In an hour or two summer, like a sea-wrecked castle too, had been ripped away.

In the bar they had the customary dance or two, her body warm-pressed and supple against him as they went round and round to the familiar steel-worn tunes. But tonight, because of rain, the bar was full. Rain lashed at the windows and there would be no walking, he knew, to places made familiar by love along the deserted sand.

It seemed as if she too was thinking of this:

'You could come to my room,' she said.

For a moment in the bedroom, before undressing, she went to the window to make sure that it was shut and to pull the long chenille curtains. She could not find the cord that pulled the curtains together, and for the space of half a minute she put on the light.

There, by the window, a coat stand held her father's hat and a crisp neat suit of cream alpaca he always wore when walking the esplanade, arm in arm with the girl, silver-headed walking stick jauntily swinging, on Sunday afternoons.

She saw him look at it. 'He left them here to be cleaned,' she said.

At intervals he lay listening to cold rain beating with light flashes on the sea-exposed window beyond the heavy curtains. To his surprise, some time later, he turned and found her face, as he moved to touch it with his mouth, wet with tears.

'Why are you crying? What is it?' he said. 'What is it?'

'I am thinking of the time when you will be gone,' she said. 'I can't bear that time—'

He held her face with his hands, and as she cried a dark accumulation of all that he felt at each week-end, the dry dead misery of being alone, deprived of her, gave him a sudden bitter foretaste of what he knew, in time, would have to come.

But it was only briefly. It was early August now; there would still be four, even five or six weeks of summer. Then he asked himself what would happen if the weather broke? and once more, afraid and hateful, he listened to the rain beating with its almost wintry harshness across the bay.

'Supposing the summer breaks up?'

'We shall stay now. I have told him I want to stay—' He

could hear by her voice that she had stopped crying. She was restrained and quiet again and his fear of losing her, always uppermost in his mind rather than any thought of going away himself, stopped now too.

In the morning his fear was renewed and twisted round. He discovered, as he paid his weekly bill at the hotel desk, that he had somehow made a miscalculation in his money. At the beginning of his holiday he had seemed to be so rich in traveller's cheques that he had really never bothered to count them carefully. The weeks had stretched deliciously ahead. Now, it seemed, he had ten pounds less than he bargained for.

It meant going home a week, perhaps two weeks, earlier than he had calculated.

She was curiously indifferent about these fears. His Englishness revolted against and was troubled by a calculation that had gone wrong. He was worried by the new post-war fear of having no money in a foreign country.

'By the end of next week I'll have no francs left – nothing at all.'

'I have francs. I can get you francs.'

'But I could never pay them back.'

'Who wants you to pay them back?' she said. 'Who wants it? Who cares?'

In his English way he was bothered by a possible failure to do something correctly. It wasn't exactly a question of dishonesty; it was not quite the game. For her, on the other hand, war had killed the meaning, if she had ever understood it in the same way, of all such phrases. Nobody bothered about that sort of thing any longer.

'I will get you francs at the week-end. All the francs you wish.'

"I couldn't possibly pay you back—'

'Please,' she said. 'All the money in France is black market money. Nobody is honest any longer. Who cares?'

He did not know what to answer.

'Everybody has given up worrying about these things. Everybody has to live—'

And after all, it seemed, when she spoke like that, very easy. She could get a little each week for him. And in that way he could stay on.

'And I want you to stay on,' she said. 'I want it so much. I don't want you to go—'

All the time he felt himself held back by a small irritating matter of pride. It was the old uneasy business of taking money from a woman. Of course people did it; there were times when you had to and perhaps there was, after all, really nothing in it; but it always left a bad taste somehow, a feeling of a man being kept.

'I don't know,' he said. 'Somehow—'

'But it's easy, it's so easy,' she said. 'And if you don't take it you have to go—'

'I know, I know,' he said.

'Then if you know and it's so easy why do you make it so difficult?'

He could not explain. All that he felt about being kept by a woman sounded priggish and adolescent and horribly and smugly English. And yet there was something about being kept—

'I love you,' she said. 'Please do it for that. Please. You will do it for that, won't you?'

Well, all right, he said, he would do it for that. He would do it for love.

And then she had a sudden thought. It seemed to her that for him it was really, after all, nothing but a matter of pride, and she said:

'I will put it in a letter. Every Saturday I will write you a little letter and tell you how I love you and the money will be in it.'

He laughed. 'You think of clever things,' he said. 'Don't you?'

'Only because I love you.'

'The more you love the cleverer you get?' he said, 'is that it?'

'Of course,' she said. 'Every woman knows that is what happens—'

And so every Saturday morning, before breakfast, he would find her letter with the hotel-porter, and inside it enough francs to take him through the week, and with the francs a little note, brief and tender, about how she loved him and how she was happy now because, with the money, he could stay a little longer. He took the note away to read on the shore, before he swam, and in the fine exquisite air he lost his fear.

'The season will soon be ending,' Madame Dupont said. 'There is always a horrible rush about the fifteenth and then by the end of the month it begins to thin out a little.'

'Do you have langoustines in England?' the boy said.

'No: no langoustines in England.'

'You have peaches?'

'Yes: peaches.'

'Yesterday I had a big fat animal in a peach. The biggest one I ever had. Pink like a *langouste*, with a black head—'

'I shall be sick!' Madame Dupont said, and buried her face, with its flashing spectacles, in her hands.

After all the weather had not broken. The single day and night of gusting rain had been followed by skies of pure washed blue, exquisite and brilliant: by afternoons of burning indigo breeziness, bringing a saltiness that Harris could taste on the face of the girl as he touched it with his mouth. Her body had become a deep butter-golden brown in the sun.

By the second week in September he began to experience once again the excruciating fear that soon it would all be over. The blue dishes of langoustines, the shrill voice of Jean-Pierre discovering maggots in the peaches, Madame Dupont's unwearying spectacles; the hot afternoons by the estuary, the earlier darkening evenings along the shore. Not even the week-end dole of francs, delivered with the letter after being squeezed somehow from the changeless dapper parent who came up from Paris with unfailing punctuality every Saturday, could save it much longer.

She too seemed to realise it and along the shore, on a dark humid September evening, said to him:

'I wanted to tell you something about myself,' and went on at once: 'It was about being married—'

Listening, not interrupting her, he watched the many navigation lights flowing emerald and white and crimson across the bay. She, too, after all, it seemed, had been one of his partisans. In four years she had helped nearly two hundred men: English mostly, but colonials too, and in the final year a few Americans.

During all the time she spoke of this there was a flatness in her voice that reminded him of the evening he had first walked with her by the sea. She had once again pulled down that opaque blind between them; as if she were keeping something back.

And then she began to talk, presently, of another man. Not an Englishman this time, but a French boy, a young man from

Orleans, an eager brilliant boy who when war broke out had been studying for a degree in engineering and then, late in the war, had become a partisan too. 'He had a wonderful face,' she kept saying. 'Such wonderful brilliant eyes. So intelligent and beautiful.'

After she had known him a few weeks they had been given an assignment, quite a difficult one, seventy or eighty miles north of Marseilles, and suddenly, under all the impulse of war and the emotion of war, they decided to get married before attempting it. They were married in his own village, somewhere south of Paris, and afterwards they set out on bicycles. That was their honeymoon: sleeping in barns, under haystacks, sometimes in small hotels, sometimes in the houses of other partisans. It had been very beautiful, she said, and as she spoke of it he could hear once again the restrictive quietness of unspent tears in her voice, making it flat and calm.

On the second night of the journey as she bicycled downhill in darkness, she missed the road, crashing the bicycle into a bank, buckling it beyond repair. They hid it in a barn so that he could come back for it. Then they rode on together on one bicycle, she on the crossbar. And all that night the feeling of being close to the young eager boy grew deeper, until in that excited, keyed-up, secret and almost funny situation she felt they were inseparable. Here she spoke again of his face, saying how brilliant and beautiful it was.

And then the cross-bar of the second bicycle broke; and they went on to complete the rest of the assignment on foot, quite successfully as it turned out, except that the boy, going back two days later in the hope of picking up at least one of the bicycles, had himself been picked up by waiting Gestapo.

After three months they sent him back. 'There was not much left of his face,' she said. Her voice had a stony, barren sound. 'I did not know him from his face. It was not there.' He died a week or two later.

Pride and anger and tenderness for her flooded up like her own unspent tears through his heart, confusing and hurting him, so that he could not speak again.

'I did not sleep for a year,' she said. 'I felt I could never sleep again.'

He did not answer.

'Something was taken away and has not come back,' she said.

He wanted in that moment to ask her if there was, perhaps, something of himself that could replace the things, the feelings, the inexplicable something she had lost, but he could not express himself in words. A light run of breeze brought a few sharper, more crested waves across the bay. He heard her say how beautiful the evening was, how you could still imagine it was full summer. For some moments longer he listened to a sardine boat chuffing and coughing away to sea and then to her voice reminding him, at last, still with its dry stony pain, that in a week he would be listening to it all no longer.

'Did you mind that I told you all that?' she said.

'No: I'm glad you told me.'

'Sometimes you make me think of him. The same feeling comes. I'm happy again.'

His own happiness and anguish for her kept him quiet again and after she had said, in a sentence he did not understand and did not ask to have explained, 'There are things that can kill you like that, unless you find someone in their place,' they walked back arm in arm to the hotel.

'One has to live,' she said.

The following day, at lunch, there were more langoustines and Madame Dupont, cracking away with neat relish above a pile of pink-brown shells, stared through her spectacles to where, at the table by the window, the girl was threading the customary flower into the dapper bottonhole.

'It was only today I discovered from Madame Prideaux who he is.'

Before Harris could answer her the *patron* came to the table to say: 'I know you do not like the liver, Monsieur Harris – so if you prefer it we have today for you a piece of meat. A bifteck. If you find it all right?'

'Excellent,' Harris said. 'Thank you.' The *patron* smiled and patted Jean-Pierre on the head and walked away. Madame Dupont stared critically, with a kind of dry prudery, through her spectacles. Jean-Pierre said he would be glad when the peaches came and Madame Dupont, holding the lobster-pincers poised under her chin, said:

'He was at La Baule the summer before the war. With another girl.'

'Another daughter?'

'I remembered him very well the moment Madame Prideaux reminded me.'

The noon wind was springing up, deepening the sea to flashing brilliant indigo, across the bay.

'Daughter?' Madame Dupont said. 'She is somebody's daughter, yes. They are all somebody's daughter.'

In the dining-room there was a swift breath of fish hot in butter, and richly, thickly, with nausea, it clotted Harris's throat.

'It's a fine game,' she said. 'I suppose you find it in England too? I suppose one finds it everywhere.'

He suddenly sent his fish away.

'Nor me!' the boy said. 'Nor me. I hate it!'

'You must eat fish,' Madame Dupont said. 'It gives brains.'

'No!'

'It gives brains, doesn't it, Monsieur Harris? He must eat it.'

'Monsieur Harris doesn't eat it.'

'Monsieur Harris is old enough to please himself what he has and what he doesn't have. Aren't you, Monsieur Harris?'

'Yes,' he said.

'You must eat and grow big and get lots of brains,' she said, 'so that you can please yourself what you do.'

Across the bay the rising breeze from open sea carried deeper sparkling furrows broadside along the shore. A blue sardine boat, like an ark, shone with its climbing crimson sail tightening against the long promontory of blue-black pines.

'After all she has to live,' Madame Dupont said. She smiled with dry tolerance, her mouth twisted, her eyes narrowed like the eyes of the old watchful matriarchs behind her spectacles. 'They all have to live.'

Harris, eating his beefsteak, stared blindly across the bay.

'She knows how to make a fuss of an old man like that. And after all the old man wants to live—'

'Fuss, fuss!' the boy said.

'Quiet!' Madame Dupont said. 'Take what fruit you want, Jean-Pierre, and eat it.'

Harris, staring across the sea, thought of the boy who had died, the something that had been taken away from the girl and that he hoped, in a sense, he might have given back. Suddenly it seemed that the other shore of the bay was very far away. It quivered and receded in the bristling air of noon.

And staring at it he realised that he had never, all this time, been across the bay. He had never been across to the other side. It was too late now and as he sat thinking of the girl's dark hair blowing across her face, the rain beating on the windows and the suit of cream alpaca, pressed and neat, hanging in the bedroom, he remembered the stony barren pain of her face and the things that would kill.

'I have a big one!' the boy said. 'Look! Look! Look at that!'

Harris looked away from the sea to where Jean-Pierre, splitting a gold-pink peach in halves, was prodding with the point of his fruit knife a trundling fat maggot that had fattened on the blood-brown shining heart of flesh.

'Kill it! Kill it!' Madame Dupont said. 'Put it away! Take it out of my sight. I can't bear it! For God's sake put it out of my sight!'

All across the bay the sea flashed with its deep noon beauty and in the dining-room Madame Dupont, quite pale behind her golden spectacles, buried her face in her hands.

She was burning chaff in three big yellow separate heaps as he came across the field. A flame was darting up and along the blue-black edge of each heap like lamp-wick, leaving smoking ash behind.

She stood leaning on the long white handle of a hay-fork, arms firm and crooked, hands just below her chin, eyes rather low on the three smoking heaps, as if she was not really watching him at all. The wind was cold for October. It blew in sudden ugly gusts, switching smoke over grey-yellow stubble in blue flat clouds that turned back and bit each other like dogs at play.

'Could you tell me which is Benacre?' he said.

Deliberately she drew the tines of the hay-fork down the curve of the nearest heap, dragging chaff into fire. From the fresh strip of hot ashes new smoke sprang out and was caught by wind and driven into his face as he stood there waiting for an answer.

'You've come wrong way,' she said. 'This is the back end of it. It's up the hill.'

'Which way would that be?'

'Up the hill,' she said. Her voice was tart and confident. She dragged at hot ash and chaff again, stirring them to smoke. This time she darted a quick look at him to see if he had the sense to move away, but he still stood in the wind, letting the blue cloud drive full at his face.

'You'd better stand over here,' she said, 'if you don't want to get smoke-dried.'

In that way she could see him better. She always looked first at men's hands and she saw that his own were large and long-fingered but rather white. His hair was smooth and dark and brushed well back. That was the second thing she always looked for. She could not bear men with scruffy ill-kept hair that sowed seeds all over the shoulders of their jackets.

'Could I cut across the field?' he said.

'You could,' she said, 'if you want to land in the river. Which way did you come?'

286

'I walked from the station.'

'You should have got the bus and asked,' she said. 'Then they'd have put you down at Benacre.'

'I thought I'd like the walk,' he said.

She plunged the hay-fork into hot ash again, pulling half-burnt cakes of chaff out of the centre of the fire. One of them rolled like a slow fire-ball on to the singed ash-dusted stubble as she said:

'You'd better stand back if you don't want to get your shoes burnt.'

That was the next thing she always looked for. Hands and hair and then shoes. Shoes were the things that had character. You could tell by the way a man laced his shoes or polished them or kept them repaired or even by what shape they were whether he was a careful man or a mean one or just slovenly or vain.

His own were rather like his hair: town shoes, smooth and black and well-kept. They were already dusted by a fine powder of chaff-ash and she looked away in irritation. They were good, clean, well-tended shoes and she was annoyed by the dust on them as she might have been annoyed by the dust of his hair flaking down on his shoulders.

Looking away at the fire, she said:

'You're looking for Jean Godden, aren't you?'

'That's right. How—'

'I'm her sister,' she said. 'I'm Doreen.'

He seemed to look at her for the first time. Her face was flushed under the pale blue eyes with blotches of redness from the bluster of wind and the heat of fire. She had a plain white scarf tied tightly back over her head, giving her hair the impression of being whipped severely and sternly back. Her legs were shapeless in short turn-down gum-boots, like a fisherwoman's, and in denim trousers the colour of light brown cow-hide.

'I wouldn't have known it,' he said.

The wind seemed to blow a shadow of fury across her face. No, you wouldn't have known it, she thought. I'm that much older. Nearly forty. On the shelf, past it: that's what you were thinking. She stabbed at the fire again, moving from one heap to another, rolling fire-balls of chaff about the white-blue see-thing ashes and the running tongues of flame.

'I thought you were coming last Sunday?' she said.

'I was,' he said. 'Then I couldn't get my day off. I had to work the week-end.'

'She waited all day. She didn't know what to do with herself.'

'I had to work,' he said. 'There was no way of letting her know.'

'You couldn't get away with that with some girls,' she said.

With me for instance, she thought.

He was standing too near the fire again and as she pushed past him, almost brushing him with the fork-handle, a turn of wind took all the smoke of the three fires upward in a single spiral column that turned in air and doubled back again, plunging down into the central core of ashes so that they grinned, red and teeth-like, in the fanning wind.

'She knows I'm coming today, doesn't she?' he said.

'I expect so. She doesn't tell me everything.'

She looked up at the sky. Clouds were curling up against each other, low and dirty, not unlike reflections in deeper uglier blue of the descending smoke of the fires.

'The wind's gone up the hill,' she said. 'It'll rain before you know where you are. You'd better get down to Benacre while it's dry.'

'Are you going down?'

'I shall do. In a bit—'

'Then I'll wait for you,' he said.

She swung round and said:

'You needn't wait for me. Get on while you've got the chance. I'm used to it. You can cut across to the gate there—'

'I'd rather wait,' he said. 'I'm in no hurry.'

'That's a compliment to somebody,' she said.

Her eyes, as she turned, were held in a frown. Then it lifted. Smoke blew across her face in a long wriggling just like the ghost of an escaping snake and when it cleared again her eyes were fixed with a sort of thoughtful transparence on the central grinning portions of fire. The glow seemed to consume some of her hardness and she said:

'Weren't you going to stay the night? Where are your things?'

'I left my bag over by the gate,' he said.

'You deserve to get it picked up by somebody then, that's all. There's people going by there all the time. You never know who's about.'

'There's nothing in it to matter much,' he said.

'Oh! well,' she said, 'if that's how you look at it.'

In a moment she was moving again from fire to fire, raking and stabbing, letting in wind that woke the chaff to grinning eyes and bright yellow flags of flame.

'Been threshing?' he said.

She wanted to say 'It looks like it, doesn't it?' then she was unpredictably restrained by something, and she remembered her sister, at home in the kitchen, ironing a brown and yellow dress. She said: 'Oh! weeks ago. We got done early. This was just the day for burning chaff, that's all.'

The dress was tight in the waist and had one of those wide black cummerbunds that women were wearing now. It was full about the hips and the ground-colour was a warm and lively brown, the colour of some autumn leaves, with sprigs of yellow tendril-borne flowers all over it, very delicate and small. It was the sort of dress she could never have chosen for herself. She always went wrong somewhere. The brown would have looked like furniture polish and the yellow crude and brassy, like dandelions.

She hadn't the taste of her sister. Things never came off for her. She hadn't the luck either. She hadn't the way of not seeming to want men, the cool, aloof, irresponsible touch.

'There's a spit of rain,' he said, and she laughed, very short and taunting, for the first time.

'You'll look well if she's not there when you get there,' she said.

'Oh! she'll be there – she said she would.'

'Oh! will she? Supposing she isn't? You take yourself for granted, don't you? You let her down on Sunday.'

'I didn't let her down.'

'Well, something like it. It didn't make her feel any sweeter.'

'What would you do, then?' he said.

'I'd pitchfork anybody out, quick,' she said, 'if they let me down,' and she made the gesture with her fork above the fire, scattering ash and smoke and chaff and a few flapping flames that seemed to turn dark orange, above the ash, in the darkening afternoon.

He did not speak and she turned quickly to see if her taunting had touched him at all. His face was flushed. She felt amused in a confident sort of way about that. His hands were in his trouser's pockets, deep, so that she could not tell if they were clenched or open. Wind had disturbed his hair, raking up a few thin separate strands, exactly like the separations in a feather. His shoes were almost white from dusty ash and she was suddenly uneasy about the changes in the image of him since he had first walked across the field. For a moment she lost all her hard, high taunting composure and she stabbed pointlessly at the fire again and said:

'You mustn't mind me. You mustn't take any notice of me. Do you want to go? You do, don't you?'

Before he answered she heard the first spits of rain falling softly, piff! piff! into the heart of the fires.

'What about the fire?' he said. 'I can wait for you.'

'Oh! it'll burn itself out. It always does. Or the rain'll put it out.'

Her mackintosh and her tea-bag lay behind her. As she turned to pick them up he moved to help her but she was there first, grabbing the coat before he could touch it. Then she slung the tea-bag over her back and sloped the fork over her shoulder.

'Come on, we'd better go,' she said.

Rain in faster spits, sharply hissing as it struck down through the full sepia-orange of surrounding oaks, came out of the west as the two of them walked across the field. She found herself striding with head down, her big feet flat, her eyes looking at his shoes, ash-covered and now rain-pocked, their neatness gone.

'You think she'll be there all right?' he said.

'I expect so. If you're fool enough to come I suppose she'll be fool enough to be there,' she said.

She could not resist that. And supposing she was not there? She always was; she liked the boys, she had all the luck with them. She was pretty enough, with all the taste, for anybody. But supposing she were not, this time? Rain came swishing faster through the dry golden-brown oaks and made impression in her mind of thoughts rushing forward, herded and lost in disjointed confusion. What would she do if she were not there? Put on the green dress with the leather belt? And the flat shoes? And do her hair tightly up, in a coconut?

'Where's your case?' she said.

'Behind the hedge,' he said. With head down against the rain he brought back a small brown week-end case he had left in the shelter of the hedge, by the gate to the field.

'Here, you have this mac,' she said.

'No,' he said. 'No. I'm all right.'

'You've got your best suit on,' she said. 'You'll get it wet through. You'll ruin it. Come on, you have the mac on.'

'No, you. It's yours. You have it.'

'I don't want it,' she said. 'I'm used to it. Come on.'

'I'm all right,' he said.

'Are we going to quarrel over a mac?' she said. 'You've ruined your shoes already.'

Queer how the thought of the ruined shoes upset her. As he looked down at them she put the mac over his shoulders. They were standing in the road now and suddenly rain came beating down in white sheets on the black metal surface, at the same time tearing pale brown clouds of leaves that fell wetly across the slate-blue sky and its lighter drifts of low blue smoke from the fires.

When he spoke again his voice was sharp and annoyed.

'Now give me your tea-bag and hold the mac over your head,' he said. 'Go on. Hold one side while I hold the other. I don't know what we're arguing about. Put the mac over your head. Go on. There's enough for both of us.'

She was quiet. She put the mac over her head and stared down at her big boots slapping in the wet, leaf-printed road, side by side with the neat half-spoilt shoes she liked so much. She did not know what to say and she wished suddenly that it was night-time, with nobody on the road, so that there was no way of seeing her face.

Presently she could bear it no longer and stopped and swung round to look back across the fields at the fires. The wind was blowing chaff and smoke and dust and flame into darkening rain from the three yellow heaps that were like solitary pyres.

'Keep the mac over your head,' he said. 'What are you looking at now?'

'Just the fires,' she said.

'Oh! come on, they'll burn out. You said they would.'

'All right. I know.'

'That's the trouble with some people,' he said. 'They always know. They always think they know.'

She did not answer. She walked with head still further down, watching the two pairs of feet. The rain beating on her lowered face made her feel dry and tired inside. What did she know? What were the sort of things she was supposed to know?

She was a fool and there was nothing, she thought, that she did know – nothing but the falling rain, the queer odour of the mac on her head, the fading smell of fire and smoke and falling leaf, and the chaff driving in the wind.

THE EVOLUTION OF SAXBY

I first met him on a black wet night towards the end of the war, in one of those station buffets where the solitary spoon used to be tied to the counter by a piece of string.

He stood patiently waiting for his turn with this spoon, spectacled and undemonstrative and uneager, in a shabby queue, until at last the ration of sugar ran out and nobody had any need for the spoon any longer. As he turned away he caught sight of me stirring my coffee with a key. It seemed to impress him, as if it were a highly original idea he had never thought of, and the thickish spectacles, rather than his own brown kidney-like eyes, gave me an opaque glitter of a smile.

'That's rather natty,' he said.

As we talked he clutched firmly to his chest a black leather brief-case on which the monogram of some government department had been embossed in gilt letters that were no longer clear enough to read. He wore a little homberg hat, black, neat, the fraction of a size too small for him, so that it perched high on his head. In peace-time I should have looked for a rose in his buttonhole, and in peace-time, as it afterwards turned out, I often did; and I always found one there.

In the train on which we travelled together he settled himself down in the corner, under the glimmer of those shaded bluish lights we have forgotten now, and opened his brief-case and prepared, as I thought, to read departmental minutes or things of that sort.

Instead he took out his supper. He unfolded with care what seemed to be several crackling layers of disused wallpaper. He was evidently very hungry, because he took out the supper with a slow relish that was also wonderfully eager, revealing the meal as consisting only of sandwiches, rather thickly cut.

He begged me to take one of these, saying: 'I hope they're good. I rather think they should be. Anyway they'll make up for what we didn't get at the buffet.' His voice, like all his actions, was uneager, mild and very slow.

I remembered the spoon tied to the counter at the buffet and partly because of it and partly because I did not want to offend him I took one of his sandwiches. He took one too. He said something about never getting time to eat at the department and how glad he would be when all this was over, and then he crammed the sandwich eagerly against his mouth.

The shock on his face was a more powerful reflection of my own. His lips suddenly suppurated with revulsion. A mess of saffron yellow, repulsively mixed with bread, hung for a few moments on the lips that had previously been so undemonstrative and uneager. Then he ripped out his handkerchief and spat.

'Don't eat it,' he said. 'For God's sake don't eat it.' He tore the sandwich apart, showing the inside of it as nothing but a vile mess of meatless, butterless mustard spread on dark war-time bread. 'Give it to me, for God's sake,' he said. 'Give it to me. Please don't have that.'

As he snatched the sandwich away from me and crumpled it into the paper his hands were quivering masses of tautened sinew. He got up so sharply that I thought he would knock his glasses off. The stiff wallpaper-like package cracked in his hands. His handkerchief had fallen to the seat and he could not find it again and in a spasm of renewed revulsion he spat in air.

The next thing I knew was the window-blind going up like a pistol shot and the window clattering down. The force of the night wind blew his hat off. The keen soapy baldness of his head sprang out with an extraordinary effect of nakedness. He gave the revolting yellow-oozing sandwiches a final infuriated beating with his hands and then hurled them far out of the window into blackness, spitting after them. Then he came groping back for his lost handkerchief and having found it sat down and spat into it over and over again, half-retching, trembling with rage.

He left it to me to deal with the window and the black-out blind. I had some difficulty with the blind, which snapped out of my hands before I could fix it satisfactorily.

When I turned round again I had an impression that the sudden snap of the blind had knocked his spectacles off. He was sitting holding them in his hands. He was breathing very heavily. His distraction was intolerable because without the spectacles he really looked like a person who could not see. He seemed to sit there groping blindly, feeble and myopic after his rush of rage.

His sense of caution, his almost fearsome correctness, returned in an expression of concern about the black-out blind. He got up and went, as it were, head-first into his spectacles, as a man dives into the neck of his shirt. When he emerged with the glasses on he realised, more or less sane now, his vision corrected, that I had put up the blind.

'Oh! You've done it,' he said.

A respectable remorse afflicted him.

'Do you think it was seen?' he said. 'I hate doing that sort of thing. I've always felt it rather a point to be decent about the regulations.'

I said it was probably not serious. It was then nearly March, and I said I thought the war was almost over.

'You really think so?' he said. What makes you think that? I've got a sort of ghastly feeling it will last for ever. Sort of tunnel we will never get out of.'

I said that was a feeling everyone got. His spectacles had grown misty again from the sweat of his eyes. He took them off again and began slowly polishing them and, as if the entire hideous episode of the mustard had never happened, stared down into them and said:

'Where do you live? Have you been able to keep your house on?'

I told him where I lived and he said:

'That isn't awfully far from us. We live at Elham Street, by the station. We have a house that practically looks on the station.'

He put on his spectacles and with them all his correctness came back.

'Are you in the country?' he said. 'Really in the country?' and when I said yes he said that was really what he himself wanted to do, live in the country. He wanted a small place with a garden – a garden he could see mature.

'You have a garden?' he said.

'Yes.'

'Nice one?'

'I hope it will be again when this is over.'

'I envy you that,' he said.

He picked up his hat and began brushing it thoughtfully with his coat sleeve. I asked him if he had a garden too and he said:

'No. Not yet. The war and everything – you know how it is.'

He put on his hat with great care, almost reverently.

'Not only that. We haven't been able to find anywhere that really suits my wife. That's our trouble. She's never well.'

'I'm sorry—'

'They can't find out what it is, either,' he said. He remembered his handkerchief and as he folded it up and stuck it in his breast-pocket the combination of handkerchief and homberg and his own unassertive quietness gave him a look that I thought was unexpressibly lonely and grieved.

'We move about trying to find something,' he said, 'but—'

He stopped, and I said I hoped she would soon be well again.

'I'm afraid she never will,' he said. 'It's no use not being frank about it.'

His hands, free now of handkerchief and homberg, demonstrated her fragility by making a light cage in the air. His spectacles gave an impervious glint of resignation that I thought was painful.

'It's one of those damnable mysterious conditions of the heart,' he said. 'She can do things of course. She can get about. But one of these days—'

His hands uplifted themselves and made a light pouf! of gentle extermination.

'That's how it will be,' he said.

I was glad at that moment to hear the train slowing down. He heard it too and got up and began to grope about along the hat-rack.

'I could have sworn I had my umbrella,' he said.

'No,' I said.

'That's odd.' His face tightened. An effort of memory brought back to it a queer dry little reflection of the anger he had experienced about the sandwiches of mustard. He seemed about to be infuriated by his own absent-mindedness and then he recovered himself and said:

'Oh! no. I remember now.'

Two minutes later, as the train slowed into the station, he shook me by the hand, saying how pleasant it had been and how much he had enjoyed it all and how he hoped I might one day, after the war, run over and see him if it were not too far.

'I want to talk to you about gardens,' he said.

He stood so smiling and glassy-eyed and uneager again in

final good-bye that I began too to feel that his lapse of frenzy about the mustard sandwiches was like one of those episodic sudden bomb-explosions that caught you unawares and five minutes later seemed never to have happened.

'By the way my name is Saxby,' he said. 'I shall look for you on the train.'

Trains are full of men who wear homberg hats and carry brief-cases and forget their umbrellas, and soon, when the war was over, I got tired of looking for Saxby.

Then one day, more than a year later, travelling on a slow train that made halts at every small station on the long high gradient below hills of beech-wood and chalk, I caught sight of a dark pink rose floating serenely across a village platform under a homberg hat.

There was no mistaking Saxby. But for a few seconds, after I had hailed him from the carriage window, it seemed to me that Saxby might have mistaken me. He stared into me with glassy preoccupation. There was a cool and formidable formality about him. For one moment it occurred to me to remind him of the painful episode of the mustard sandwiches, and then a second later he remembered me.

'Of course.' His glasses flashed their concealing glitter of a smile as he opened the carriage door. 'I always remember you because you listen so well.'

This was a virtue of which he took full advantage in the train.

'Yes, we've been here all summer,' he said. 'You can very nearly see the house from the train.' This time he had his umbrella with him and with its crooked malacca handle he pointed south-west-ward through the open window, along the chalk hillside. 'No. The trees are rather too dense. In the early spring you could see it. We had primroses then. You know, it's simply magnificent country.'

'How is your wife?' I said.

The train, charging noisily into the tunnel, drowned whatever he had to say in answer. He rushed to shut the window against clouds of yellow tunnel fumes and suddenly I was reminded of his noisy and furious charge at the window in the black-out, his nauseated frenzy about the sandwiches. And again it seemed, like an episodic explosion, like the war itself, an unreality that had never happened.

When we emerged from the tunnel black-out into bright summer he said:

'Did you ask me something back there?'

'Your wife,' I said. 'I wondered how she was.'

The railway cutting at that point is a high white declivity softened by many hanging cushions of pink valerian and he stared at it with a sort of composed sadness before he answered me.

'I'm afraid she's rather worse if anything,' he said. 'You see, it's sort of progressive – an accumulative condition if you understand what I mean. It's rather hard to explain.'

He bent his face to the rose in his buttonhole and seemed to draw from it, sadly, a kind of contradictory inspiration about his wife and her painfully irremediable state of health.

It was rather on the lines of what diabetics had, he said. The circle was vicious. You got terribly hungry and terribly thirsty and yet the more you took in the worse it was. With the heart it was rather the same. A certain sort of heart bred excitement and yet was too weak to take it. It was rather like overloading an electric circuit. A fuse had to blow somewhere and sometime.

Perhaps my failure to grasp this was visible in my stare at the railway cutting.

'You see, with electricity it's all right. The fuse blows and you put in another fuse. But with people the heart's the fuse. It blows and—'

Once again he made the light pouf! of extermination with his hands.

I said how sorry I was about all this and how wretched I thought it must be for him.

'I get used to it,' he said. 'Well, not exactly used to it if you understand what I mean. But I'm prepared. I live in a state of suspended preparation.'

That seemed to me so painful a way of life that I did not answer.

'I'm ready for it,' he said quietly and without any sort of detectable desire for sympathy at all. 'I know it will just happen at any moment. Any second it will all be over.'

There was something very brave about that, I thought.

'Well anyway the war's over,' he said cheerfully. 'That at least we've got to be thankful for. And we've got this house, which is awfully nice, and we've got the garden, which is nicer still.

'You must be quite high there,' I said, 'on the hill.'

'Nearly five hundred feet,' he said. 'It's a stiffish climb.'

I said I hoped the hills were not too much for his wife and he said:

'Oh! she hardly ever goes out. She's got to that stage.'

But the garden, it seemed, was wonderful. He was settling down to the garden. That was his joy. Carnations and phloxes did awfully well there and, surprisingly enough, roses. It was a *Betty Uprichard*, he said, in his buttonhole. That was one of his favourites and so were *Etoile d' Hollande* and *Madame Butterfly*. They were the old ones and on the whole he did not think you could beat the old ones.

'I want gradually to have beds of them,' he said. 'Large beds of one sort in each. But you need time for that of course. People say you need the right soil for roses – but wasn't there someone who said that to grow roses you first had to have roses in your heart?'

'There was someone who said that,' I said.

'It's probably right,' he said, 'but I think you probably need permanence more. Years and years in one place. Finding out what sorts will do for you. Settling down. Getting the roots anchored – you know?'

The sadness in his face was so peculiar as he said all this that I did not answer.

'Have you been in your house long?' he said.

'Twenty years,' I said.

'Really,' he said. His eyes groped with diffused wonder at this. 'That's marvellous. That's a lifetime.'

For the rest of the way we talked – or rather he did, while I did my virtuous act of listening – about the necessity of permanence in living, the wonder of getting anchored down.

'Feeling your own roots are going deeper all the time. Feeding on the soil underneath you,' he said. 'You know? Nothing like it. No desk stuff can ever give you that.'

And then, as the train neared the terminus, he said:

'Look. You must come over. I'd love you to see the place. I'd love to ask you things. I know you're a great gardener. There must be lots you could tell me. Would you come? I'd be awfully grateful if you'd care to come.'

I said I should be delighted to come.

'Oh! good, oh! good,' he said.

He produced from his vest-pocket the inevitable diary with a silver pencil and began flicking over its leaves.

'Let's fix it now. There's nothing like fixing it now. What about Saturday?'

'All right,' I said.

'Good. Saturday's a good day,' he said.

He began to pencil in the date and seemed surprised, as he suddenly looked up, that I was not doing the same.

'Won't you forget? Don't you put it down?'

'I shall remember,' I said.

'I have to put everything down,' he said. 'I'm inclined to forget. I get distracted.'

So it would be two-thirty or about that on Saturday, he said, and his enthusiasm at the prospect of this was so great that it was, in fact, almost a distraction. He seemed nervously uplifted. He shook hands with energetic delight, repeating several times a number of precise and yet confusing instructions as to how to get to the house, and I was only just in time to save him from a spasm of forgetfulness.

'Don't forget your umbrella,' I said.

'Oh! Good God, no,' he said. 'You can't miss it,' he said, meaning the house. 'It's got a sort of tower on the end of it. Quite a unique affair. You can't miss it. I shall look out for you.'

The house was built of white weatherboard and tile and it hung on the steep chalk-face with the precise and arresting effect of having been carved from the stone. The tower of which Saxby had spoken, and which as he said was impossible to miss, was nothing more than a railed balcony that somebody had built on the roof of a stable, a kind of look-out for a better view. That day it was crutched with scaffolding. In the yard below it there were many piles of builders' rubble and sand and broken timber and beams torn from their sockets. A bloom of cement dust lay thick on old shrubberies of lilac and flowing currant, and in the middle of a small orchard a large pit had been dug. From it too, in the dry heat of summer, a white dust had blown thickly, settling on tall yellow grass and apple leaves and vast umbrellas of seeding rhubarb.

There was nowhere any sign of the garden of which Saxby had spoken so passionately.

It took me some time, as he walked with me to and fro between the derelict boundaries of the place, to grasp that this was so. He was full of explanations: not apologetic, not in the form of excuses but, surprisingly, very pictorial. He drew for me a series of pictures of the ultimate shapes he planned. As we walked armpit deep through grass and thistle – the thistle smoking with dreamy seed in the hot air as we brushed it – he kept saying:

'Ignore this. This is nothing. This will be lawn. We'll get round to this later.' Somebody had cut a few desultory swathes through the jungle with a scythe, and a rabbit got up from a seat in a swathe that crackled like tinder as it leapt away. 'Ignore this – imagine this isn't here.'

Beyond this jungle we emerged to a fence-line on the crest of the hill. The field beyond it lay below us on a shelf and that too, it seemed, belonged to him.

Spreading his hands about, he drew the first of his pictures. There were several others, later, but that was the important one. The farther you got down the slope, it seemed, the better the soil was, and this was his rose garden. These were his beds of *Uprichard* and *Madame Butterfly* and *Sylvia* and all the rest. He planned them in the form of a fan. He had worked it out on an arc of intensifying shades of pink and red. Outer tones of flesh would dissolve with graded delicacy through segments of tenderer, deeper pink until they mounted to an inverted pinnacle of rich sparkling duskiness.

'Rather fine,' he said, 'don't you think?' and I knew that as far as he was concerned it actually lay there before him, superbly flourishing and unblemished as in a catalogue.

'Very good,' I said.

'You really think so?' he said. 'I value your opinion terrifically.'

'I think it's wonderful,' I said.

We had waded some distance back through the jungle of smouldering thistle before I remembered I had not seen his wife; and I asked him how she was.

'I fancy she's lying down,' he said. 'She feels the hot weather quite a bit. I think we shall make quite a place of it, don't you?'

He stopped at the point where the grass had been partially mown and waved his hand at the wilderness. Below us lay incomparable country. At that high point of summer it slept for miles in richness. In the hotter, moister valley masses of meadow-sweet spired frothily above its hedgerows, and in its cleared hayfields new-dipped sheep grazed in flocks that were a shade mellower and deeper in colour than the flower.

'It's a marvellous view,' I said.

'Now you get what I mean,' he said. 'The permanence of the thing. You get a view like that and you can sit and look at it for ever.'

Through a further jungle of grass and thistle, complicated at one place by an entire armoury of horseradish, we went into the house.

'Sit down,' Saxby said. 'Make yourself comfortable. My wife will be here in a moment. There will be some tea.'

For the first time since knowing Saxby I became uneasy. It had been my impression for some time that Saxby was a man who enjoyed – rather than suffered from – a state of mild hallucination. Now I felt suddenly that I suffered from it too.

What I first noticed about the room was its windows, shuttered with narrow Venetian blinds of a beautiful shade of grey-rose. They only partially concealed long silk curtains pencilled with bands of fuchsia purple. Most of the furniture was white, but there were a few exquisite Empire chairs in black and the walls were of the same grey-rose tint as the blinds. An amazing arrangement of glass walking-sticks, like rainbows of sweetmeats, was all the decoration the walls had been allowed to receive with the exception of a flower-spangled mirror, mostly in tones of rose and magenta, at the far end. This mirror spread across the entire wall like a lake, reflecting in great width the cool sparkle of the room in which, on the edge of an Empire chair, I sat nervously wondering, as I had done of Saxby's mustard sandwiches, whether what I saw had the remotest connection with reality.

Into this beautiful show-piece came, presently, Mrs Saxby.

Mrs Saxby was an immaculate and disarming woman of fifty with small, magenta-clawed hands. She was dressed coolly in grey silk, almost as if to match the room, and her hair was tinted to the curious shade of blue-grey that you see in fresh carnation leaves. I did not think, that first day, that I had ever met anyone quite so instantly charming, so incessantly alive with compact vibration – or so healthy.

We had hardly shaken hands before she turned to Saxby and said:

'They're coming at six o'clock.'

Saxby had nothing to say in answer to this. But I thought I saw, behind the flattering glasses, a resentful hardening bulge of the kidney-brown eyes.

Not all beautiful women are charming, and not all charming women are intelligent, but Mrs Saxby was both intelligent and charming without being beautiful. We talked a great deal during tea – that is, Mrs Saxby and I talked a great deal, with Saxby putting in the afterthought of a phrase or two here and there.

She mostly ignored this. And of the house, which I admired again and again, she said simply:

'Oh! it's a sort of thing with me. I like playing about with things. Transforming them.'

When she said this she smiled. And it was the smile, I decided, that gave me the clue to the fact that she was not beautiful. Her grey eyes were like two hard pearl buttons enclosed by the narrow dark buttonholes of her short lashes. As with the house, there was not a lash out of place. The smile too came from teeth that were as regular, polished and impersonal as piano keys.

It seemed that tea was hardly over before we saw a car draw up among the rubble outside. In the extraordinary transition to the house I had forgotten the rubble. And now as I became aware of it again it was like being reminded of something unpleasantly chaotic. For some uneasy reason I got to thinking that the inside of the house was Mrs Saxby's palace and that the outside, among the wilderness of plaster and thistle and horse-radish, was Saxby's grave.

The visitors turned out to be a man and wife, both in the sixties, named Bulfield. The woman was composed mainly of a series of droops. Her brown dress drooped from her large shoulders and chest and arms like a badly looped curtain. A treble row of pearls drooped from her neck, from which, in turn, drooped a

treble bagginess of skins. From under her eyes drooped pouches
that seemed once to have been full of something but that were
now merely punctured and drained and flabby. And from her
mouth, most of the time, drooped a cigarette from which she
could not bother to remove the drooping ashes.

Of Bulfield I do not remember much except that he too was
large and was dressed in a tropical suit of white alpaca, with
colossal buckskin brogues.

'Would you like a drink first?' Mrs Saxby said, 'or would you
like to see the house first?'

'I'd like a drink,' Mrs Bulfield said, obviously speaking for
both of them. 'If all the house is as terrific as this it will do me.
It's terrific, isn't it, Harry?'

Harry said it was terrific.

Perhaps because of something disturbing about Saxby's silence
– he sat defiantly, mutinously sipping glasses of gin for almost
an hour with scarcely a word – it came to me only very slowly
that the Bulfields had come to buy the place.

It came to me still more slowly – again because I was troubled
and confused about Saxby's part in it all – that the reason the
Bulfields wanted to buy the house was because they were rising
in the world. They sought – in fact desired – to be injected
with culture: perhaps not exactly culture, but the certain flavour
that they thought culture might bring. After the first World War
Bulfield would have been called a profiteer. During the second
World War it was, of course, not possible to profiteer; Bulfield
had merely made money. Mrs Bulfield must have seen, in magazines and books, perhaps scores of times, pictures of the kind of
house Mrs Saxby had created. She must have seen it as a house
of taste and culture and she had come to regard these virtues
as she might have regarded penicillin. Injected with them, she
would be immunised from the danger of contact with lower circumstances. Immunised and elevated, she could at last live in
the sort of house she wanted without being able to create for
herself but which Mrs Saxby – the sick, slowly expiring Mrs
Saxby – had created for her.

This was as much an hallucination as Saxby's own belief that
his rose-garden was already there in the wilderness. But all
dreams, like fires, need stoking, and for an hour the Bulfields sat
stoking theirs. They drank stodgily, without joy, at a sort of un-

holy communion of whisky. And by seven o'clock Mrs Bulfield was loud and stupefied.

Whether it was the moment Mrs Saxby had been waiting for I don't know, but she suddenly got up from her chair, as full of immaculate and sober charm and vibration as ever, and said:

'Well, would you like to see the rest of the house now?'

'If it's all like this it's as good as done,' Mrs Bulfield said. 'It's absolutely terrific. I think it's perfect – where do you keep the coal?'

Bulfield let out thunderclaps of laughter at this, roaring:

'That's it! – we got to see the coal-hole. We must see that. And the whatsit! – we got to see the whatsit too.'

'I'm sorry, Mrs Bulfield,' Mrs Saxby said. 'Forgive me – perhaps you'd like to see it in any case?'

'Not me. I'm all right,' Mrs Bulfield said. 'I'm like a drain.'

'Coal-hole!' Bulfield said. 'Come on, Ada. Coal-hole! Got to see the coal-hole!'

'You'll excuse us, won't you?' Mrs Saxby said to me, and once again the eyes were buttoned-up, grey and charming as the walls of the house, so pale as to be transparent, so that I could look right through them and see nothing at all beyond.

It must have been a quarter of an hour before Saxby spoke again. He drank with a kind of arithmetical regularity: the glass raised, three sips, the glass down. Then a pause. Then the glass up again, three sips, and the glass down. It seemed to me so like a man determined to drink himself silly that I was intensely relieved when he said:

'Let's get a spot of air. Eh? Outside?'

So we wandered out through the back of the house, and his first act there was to point out to me three or four rose trees actually growing on a wall. A bloom of cement dust covered the scarlet and cream and salmon of the flowers. He regarded them for a few moments with uncertainty, appeared about to say something else about them and then walked on.

His evident determination to say nothing more about one hallucination, that of the rose-garden, prepared me for his reluctance to elaborate or surrender another. This was his illusion of the sick, the expiring Mrs Saxby.

'She'll kill herself,' he said. 'She can't stand up to it. She'll just wear herself down to the bone.'

I refrained from saying anything about how healthy I thought Mrs Saxby seemed to be.

'You know how many houses she's done this to?' he said. 'You want to know?'

I encouraged him and he said:

'Fifteen. We've lived in fifteen houses in twenty years.'

He began to speak of these houses wrathfully, with jealousy and sadness. He spoke with particular bitterness of a house called *The Croft*. I gathered it was a big crude mansion of stone in post-Edwardian style having large bay-windows of indelicate pregnant massiveness pushing out into shrubberies of laurel and a vast plant called a gunnera, a kind of giant's castle rhubarb. 'Like fat great paunches they were, the windows,' he said, 'like great fat commissionaires,' and I could see that he hated them as he might have hated another man.

On one occasion the Saxbys had lived in a windmill. Saxby had spent a winter carrying buckets of water up and down the stairway, eating by the light of hurricane lamps, groping across a dark, stark hillside every morning to catch his train to the office in Whitehall. Then there had been a coastguard's house by the sea. The shore was flat and wind-torn and unembellished by a single feather of tamarisk or sea-holly or rock or weed. Then, because the war came, there were smaller houses: accessible, easy to run, *chic* and clever, sops to the new avidity of war, the new, comfortless servantless heaven for which men were fighting. She roamed restlessly about, looking for, and at, only those places that to other people seemed quite impossible: old Victorian junkeries, old stables, old warehouses, old cart-sheds, a riverside boat-house, bringing to all of them the incessant vibration, the intense metamorphosis of her charm. Her passion for each house was, I gathered, a state of nervous and tearing exultancy. She poured herself into successive transformations with an absorption that was violent. She was like a woman rushing from one amorous orgy to another: hungry and insatiable and drained away.

She had in fact been unfaithful to him for a series of houses; it amounted to that. She had taken love away from him and had given it with discriminate wantonness to bricks and mortar. I do not say she could help this; but that was how I looked at it. She and Saxby had been married rather late. He was reaching the outer boundaries of middle-aged comfort when he first met her.

He had wanted, as men do, a place of his own. He had wanted to come home at night to a decent meal, unassertive kindliness and some sense of permanency. Above all the sense of permanency. He had a touching desire to get his roots down: to plant things, invest in earth, reap the reward of sowing and nurturing things in one place.

He came home instead to that quivering febrile vibration of hers that was so astonishing and charming to other people – people like me – until he could stand it no longer and could only call it a disease. He was really right when he said there was something wrong with her heart. The profundity of its wrongness was perhaps visible only to him. Case-books had no name for her condition or its symptoms or anything else about her – but he had, and he knew it had turned him into a starved wanderer without a home.

That was the second of his pictures: of Mrs Saxby constantly sick with the pressure of transforming another house, too sick to eat, distraught by builders and decorators and electricians and above all by the ferocious impact of herself. 'She's really ill. You don't see it today. She's really ill. She'll kill herself. She lives at that awful pace—'

The third was of himself.

Did I remember the sandwiches, that first night we had met in the train? That was the sort of thing he had to put up with. Could I imagine anything more hideous than that awful bread and mustard? That had been her idea of his supper.

I thought he might well be sick as he spoke of it. And I even thought for a moment I might be sick too. We had again wandered beyond the house into the wilderness of horse-radish and smoking thistle. In the hot late afternoon a plague of big sizzling flies, a fierce blackish emerald turquoise, had settled everywhere on leaves and thistle-heads, in grass mown and unmown. Our steps exploded them. He swung at these repulsive insect-clouds with his hands, trying to beat them off in futile blasphemies that I felt must be directed, really, in their savagery, against Mrs Saxby. I could not help feeling that, in his helpless fury, he wanted to kill her and was taking it out on the flies.

But he was not taking it out on the flies: not his feelings for Mrs Saxby anyway. He took an enormous half-tipsy swipe at a glittering and bloated mass of flies and spat at them:

'Get out, you sickening creepers, get out! You see,' he said to me, 'I wouldn't care so much if it wasn't for the people. She makes all the houses so lovely – she always does it so beautifully – and then she sells them to the most ghastly people. Always the most bloody awful ghastly people. That's what gets me.'

From the house, a moment later, came the sound of Mr Bulfield triumphantly playing with the appurtenances of the whatsit and of Mrs Bulfield, drooping drunkenly from an upstairs window, trumpeting hoarsely in the direction of the rose-garden that was not there:

'Now you've started something. Now you've set him off! He'll spend his life in there.'

And I knew, as Saxby did, that another house had gone.

We met only once more: in the late autumn of that year.

On that occasion we travelled down together, into the country, by the evening train. He seemed preoccupied and did not speak much. I imagined, perhaps, that another house had been begun, that he was off again on his homeless, bread-and-mustard wanderings. But when I spoke of this he simply said:

'The Bulfields haven't even moved in yet. We had some difficulty about another licence for an extension over the stable.'

'How is your wife?' I said.

'She's—'

The word dying was too painful for him to frame. Yet I knew that it was the word he was trying to say to me; because once again, as when I had first met him, he lifted his hands in that little pouf! of sad and light extermination.

'She started another house on the other side of the hill,' he said. 'It was too much for her. After all she can't go on like it for ever—'

After he had got out at the little station I could not help feeling very sorry for him. He had left behind him a queer air of sadness that haunted me – and also, as if in expression of his great distraction, his umbrella.

And because I did not know when I should see him again I drove over, the following afternoon, to the house on the chalk hillside, taking the umbrella with me.

The house stood enchanting in its wilderness of perishing grass and weeds, yellow with the first burning of frost on them, and a maid in a uniform of pale grey-rose – to match, evidently, the exquisite walls of that room in which Bulfield had roared his joy over the coal-hole and the whatsit – opened the door to me.

'Is Mr Saxby in?' I said. 'I have brought the umbrella he left in the train.'

'No, sir,' she said. 'But Mrs Saxby is in. Would you care to see Mrs Saxby?'

'Yes,' I said.

I went in and I gave the umbrella to Mrs Saxby. The day was coolish, with clear fresh sunlight. As I came away she stood for a moment or two at the door, talking to me, the light filling her eyes with delicate illumination, giving her once again that look of being full of charm, of being very alive with an effect of compact vibration – and as healthy as ever.

'I am glad you came over once more,' she said. 'We are moving out on Saturday.'

The dead grasses, scorched by summer and now blanched by frost, waved across the white hillside where the rose-garden should have been.

'I'm afraid it's an awful wilderness,' she said. 'But we never touch gardens. That's the one thing people prefer to do for themselves.'

I drove slowly down the hill in cool sunshine. The country was incomparable. The fires of autumn were burning gold and drowsy in the beeches.

If they seemed sadder than usual it was because I thought of Saxby. I wondered how long he had wanted to be free of her and how long he had wanted her to die. I wondered how many times he had wanted to kill her and if ever he would kill her – or if he would remain, as I fancied he would do, just bound to her for ever.

'He is the young man she met on the aeroplane,' Mrs Carteret said. 'Now go to sleep.'

Outside the bedroom window, in full moonlight, the leaves of the willow tree seemed to be slowly swimming in delicate but ordered separation, like shoals of grey-green fish. The thin branches were like bowed rods in the white summer sky.

'This is the first I heard that there was a young man on the aeroplane,' Mr Carteret said.

'You saw him,' Mrs Carteret said. 'He was there when we met her. You saw him come with her through the customs.'

'I can't remember seeing her with anybody.'

'I know very well you do because you remarked on his hat. You said what a nice colour it was. It was a sort of sage-green one with a turn-down brim—'

'Good God,' Mr Carteret said. 'That fellow? He looked forty or more. He was as old as I am.'

'He's twenty-eight. That's all. Have you made up your mind which side you're going to sleep?'

'I'm going to stay on my back for a while,' Mr Carteret said. 'I can't get off. I heard it strike three a long time ago.'

'You'd get off if you'd lie still,' she said.

Sometimes a turn of humid air, like the gentlest of currents, would move the entire willow tree in one huge soft fold of shimmering leaves. Whenever it did so Mr Carteret felt for a second or two that it was the sound of an approaching car. Then when the breath of wind suddenly changed direction and ran across the night landscape in a series of leafy echoes, stirring odd trees far away, he knew always that there was no car and that it was only, once again, the quiet long gasp of midsummer air rising and falling and dying away.

'Where are you fussing off to now?' Mrs Carteret said.

'I'm going down for a drink of water.'

'You'd better by half shut your eyes and lie still in one place,' Mrs Carteret said. 'Haven't you been off at all?'

'I can never sleep in moonlight,' he said. 'I don't know how it is. I never seem to settle properly. Besides it's too hot.'

'Put something on your feet,' Mrs Carteret said, 'for goodness sake.'

Across the landing, on the stairs and down in the kitchen the moonlight and the white starkness of a shadowless glare. The kitchen floor was warm to his bare feet and the water warmish as it came from the tap. He filled a glass twice and then emptied it into the sink and then filled it again before it was cold enough to drink. He had not put on his slippers because he could not remember where he had left them. He had been too busy thinking of Sue. Now he suddenly remembered that they were still where he had dropped them in the coal-scuttle by the side of the stove.

After he had put them on he opened the kitchen door and stepped outside and stood in the garden. Distinctly, with astonishingly pure clearness, he could see the colours of all the roses, even those of the darkest red. He could even distinguish the yellow from the white and not only in the still standing blooms but in all the fallen petals, thick everywhere on dry earth after the heat of the July day.

He walked until he stood in the centre of the lawn. For a time he could not discover a single star in the sky. The moon was like a solid opaque electric bulb, the glare of it almost cruel, he thought, as it poured down on the green darkness of summer trees.

Presently the wind made its quickening watery turn of sound among the leaves of the willow and ran away over the nightscape, and again he thought it was the sound of a car. He felt the breeze move coolly, almost coldly, about his pyjama legs and he ran his fingers in agitation once or twice through the pillow tangles of his hair.

Suddenly he felt helpless and miserable.

'Sue,' he said. 'For God's sake where on earth have you got to? Susie, Susie – this isn't like you.'

His pet term for her, Susie. In the normal way, Sue. Perhaps in rare moments of exasperation, Susan. He had called her Susie a great deal on her nineteenth birthday, three weeks before, before she had flown to Switzerland for her holiday. Everyone thought, that day, how much she had grown, how firm and full she was getting, and how wonderful it was that she was flying off alone. He only thought she looked more delicate and girlish than ever, quite thin and childish in the face in spite of her lipstick, and he was surprised to see her drinking what he thought were too many glasses of sherry. Nor, in contrast to himself, did she seem a bit nervous about the plane.

Over towards the town a clock struck chimes for a half hour and almost simultaneously he heard the sound of a car. There was no mistaking it this time. He could see the swing of its headlights too as it made the big bend by the packing station down the road, a quarter of a mile away.

'And quite time too, young lady,' he thought. He felt sharply vexed, not miserable any more. He could hear the car coming fast. It was so fast that he began to run back to the house across the lawn. He wanted to be back in bed before she arrived and saw him there. He did not want to be caught like that. His pyjama legs were several inches too long and were wet with the dew of the grass and he held them up, like skirts, as he ran.

What a damn ridiculous situation, he thought. What fools children could make you look sometimes. Just about as exasperating as they could be.

At the kitchen door one of his slippers dropped off and as he stopped to pick it up and listen again for the sound of the car he discovered that now there was no sound. The headlights too had disappeared. Once again there was nothing at all but the enormous noiseless glare, the small folding echoes of wind dying away.

'Damn it, we always walked home from dances,' he thought. 'That was part of the fun.'

Suddenly he felt cold. He found himself remembering with fear the long bend by the packing station. There was no decent camber on it and if you took it the slightest bit too fast you couldn't make it. Every week there were accidents there. And God, anyway what did he know about this fellow? He might be the sort who went round making pick-ups. A married man or something. Anybody. A crook.

All of a sudden he had a terrible premonition about it all. It was exactly the sort of feeling he had had when he saw her enter the plane, and again when the plane lifted into sky. There was an awful sense of doom about it: he felt sure she was not coming back. Now he felt in come curious way that his blood was separating itself into single drops. The drops were freezing and dropping with infinite systematic deadliness through the veins, breeding cold terror inside him. Somehow he knew that there had been a crash.

He was not really aware of running down through the rose-garden to the gate. He simply found himself somehow striding up and down in the road outside, tying his pyjama cord tighter in agitation.

My God, he thought, how easily the thing could happen. A girl travelled by plane or train or even bus or something and before you knew where you were it was the beginning of something ghastly.

He began to walk up the road, feeling the cold precipitation of blood take drops of terror down to his legs and feet. A pale yellow suffusion of the lower sky struck into him the astonishing fact that it was almost day. He could hardly believe it and he broke miserably into a run.

Only a few moments later, a hundred yards away, he had the curious impression that from the roadside a pair of yellow eyes were staring back at him. He saw then that they were the lights of a stationary car. He did not know what to do about it. He could not very well go up to it and tap on the window and say, in tones of stern fatherhood, 'Is my daughter in there? Susan, come home.' There was always the chance that it would turn out to be someone else's daughter. It was always possible that it would turn out to be a daughter who liked what she was doing and strongly resented being interrupted in it by a prying middle-aged stranger in pyjamas.

He stopped and saw the lip of daylight widening and deepening its yellow on the horizon. It suddenly filled him with the sobering thought that he ought to stop being a damn fool and pull himself together.

'Stop acting like a nursemaid,' he said. 'Go home and get into bed. Don't you trust her?' It was always when you didn't trust them, he told himself, that trouble really began. That was when you asked for it. It was a poor thing if you didn't trust them.

'Go home and get into bed, you poor sap,' he said. 'You never fussed this much even when she was little.'

He had no sooner turned to go back than he heard the engine

of the car starting. He looked round and saw the lights coming towards him down the road. Suddenly he felt more foolish than ever and there was no time for him to do anything but press himself quickly through a gap in the hedge by the roadside. The hedge was not very tall at that point and he found himself crouching down in a damp jungle of cow parsley and grass and nettle that wetted his pyjamas as high as the chest and shoulders. By this time the light in the sky had grown quite golden and all the colours of day were becoming distinct again and he caught the smell of honeysuckle rising from the dewiness of the hedge.

He lifted his head a second or so too late as the car went past him. He could not see whether Susie was in it or not and he was in a state of fresh exasperation as he followed it down the road. He was uncomfortable because the whole of his pyjamas were sopping with dew and he knew that now he would have to change and get himself a good rub-down before he got back into bed.

'God, what awful fools they make you look,' he thought, and then, a second later, 'hell, it might not be her. Oh! hell, supposing it isn't her?'

Wretchedly he felt his legs go weak and cold again. He forgot the dew on his chest and shoulders as the slow freezing precipitation of his blood began. From somewhere the wrenching thought of a hospital made him feel quite faint with a nausea that he could not fight away.

'Oh! Susie, for Jesus' sake don't do this any more to us. Don't do it any more—'

Then he was aware that the car had stopped by the gates of the house. He was made aware of it because suddenly, in the fuller dawn, the red rear light went out.

A second or two later he saw Susie. She was in her long heliotrope evening dress and she was holding it up at the skirt, in her delicate fashion, with both hands. Even from that distance he could see how pretty she was. The air too was so still in the birdless summer morning silence that he heard her distinctly, in her nice fluty voice, so girlish and friendly, call out:

'Good-bye. Yes: lovely. Thank you.'

The only thing now, he thought, was not to be seen. He had to keep out of sight. He found himself scheming to get in by the side gate. Then he could slip up to the bathroom and get clean pyjamas and perhaps even a shower.

Only a moment later he saw that the car had already turned and was coming back towards him up the road. This time there was no chance to hide and all he could do was to step into the verge to let it go past him. For a few wretched seconds he stood there as if naked in full daylight, trying with nonchalance to look the other way.

In consternation he heard the car pull up a dozen yards beyond him and then a voice called:

'Oh! sir. Pardon me. Are you Mr Carteret, sir?'

'Yes,' he said.

There was nothing for it now, he thought, but to go back and find out exactly who the damn fellow was.

'Yes, I'm Carteret,' he said and he tried to put into his voice what he thought was a detached, unstuffy, coolish sort of dignity.

'Oh! I'm Bill Jordan, sir.' The young man had fair, smooth-brushed hair that looked extremely youthful against the black of his dinner jacket. 'I'm sorry we're so late. I hope you haven't been worried about Susie?'

'Oh! no. Good God, no.'

'It was my mother's fault. She kept us.'

'I thought you'd been dancing?'

'Oh! no, sir. Dinner with my mother. We did dance a few minutes on the lawn but then we played canasta till three. My mother's one of those canasta fanatics. It's mostly her fault, I'm afraid.'

'Oh! that's all right. So long as you had a good time.'

'Oh! we had a marvellous time, sir. It was just that I thought you might be worried about Susie—'

'Oh! great heavens, no.'

'That's fine, then, sir.' The young man had given several swift looks at the damp pyjamas and now he gave another and said: 'It's been a wonderfully warm night, hasn't it?'

'Awfully close. I couldn't sleep.'

'Sleep – that reminds me.' He laughed with friendly, expansive well-kept teeth that made him look more youthful than ever and more handsome. 'I'd better get home or it'll be breakfast-time. Good night, sir.'

'Good night.'

The car began to move away. The young man lifted one hand in farewell and Carteret called after him:

'You must come over and have dinner with us one evening—'

'Love to. Thank you very much, sir. Good night.'

Cartaret walked down the road. Very touching, the sir business. Very illuminating and nice. Very typical. It was touches like that which counted. In relief he felt a sensation of extraordinary self-satisfaction.

When he reached the garden gate the daylight was so strong that it showed with wonderful freshness all the roses that had unfolded in the night. There was one particularly beautiful crimson one, very dark, almost black, that he thought for a moment of picking and taking upstairs to his wife. But finally he decided against it and left it where it grew.

By that time the moon was fading and everywhere the birds were taking over the sky.

THE MAKER OF COFFINS

Every Sunday evening in summertime she sat at the front window and watched until he came up the hill. Her hands on the horsehair rests of the chair were like pieces of stone-grey paper painted with thin lines of water-colour, palest blue, the skin transparent and the fingers crabbed over the little palms. She always wore a straw hat that had once evidently been purple, the shadows of the trimmings, dark grey, on the mildew grey of the faded, remaining straw.

She sat surrounded by a mass of greenery in brass and china pots, set about on bamboo stands. The curtains in the big bay window were like blankets of red chenille bearing fruitings of soft bobbles down the sides. The old-fashioned gas-brackets over the mantelshelf bore opaque globes of pink and under them were ornaments of twisted yellow glass from which sprouted dead stalks of feathery brown reed and bunches of paper spills. She made the spills for Luther, with her own hands, every Saturday.

Whenever he came round the corner of the long steep hill she always thought that he looked, in his black suit and carrying the black fiddle case, so much like a doctor. Even from that distance the big rough-angled body dwarfed the fiddle case so that it did not look much larger than a doctor's bag. She had in mind particularly Dr Farquharson's bag because it was the bag she had known best. It had brought her the twelve children, beginning with Luther.

The illusion of bag and doctor remained with her through his journey up the hill. He walked with a slight groping roll, big feet splayed out as if he wanted to grip the hill with his toes. She knew he did not roll like that because he was drunk but only because his feet were bad. His feet had always been bad. They had been bad ever since the time he was a child and had grown so fast that she could never afford to buy shoes to catch up with him. In those days he had had to suffer a lot of things in that way because he was the first and times were desperate. She felt keenly that she had never been able to do her best for him. The others had been luckier.

When he came into the room at last it was always with a series of bungling noisy clashes as he tried to find a resting-place for the fiddle case somewhere among the many little tables, the piano, the bookcase and the chairs. He could never find room for the damn fiddle, he thought. The bookcase and the piano were both locked up, polished as glass, and she kept the keys on a chain. He groped among the chairs with bull-like stupor but she never at any time took a great deal of notice of it. He had always been clumsy on his feet. He had been a day or two short of nineteen months before he had started walking at all. She always remembered that, of being so afraid that he would never walk: an awful thing, to have a child so fragile that it never walked.

If she was aware of feeling that the enormous body still enshrined the fragile child she did not reveal it. She turned on him with little grunts of peevish affection that had no effect on him at all.

'It'll be dark before you get up here one of these days.'

'Had a rush job on. Wonder I got finished at all.'

When he had at last disposed of the fiddle he liked to sit by the piano, in the dark patch caused by one end, so that she could not see his face.

'Who was it?' she said. 'Thought you said trade was so bad.'

'So it is. Man in Canal Street. Burying tomorrow.'

'What man?'

'A man named Johnson.'

'Who's he? What name?'

'Johnson. Call him Polly Johnson. Kin to Liz Johnson—'

'Nobody I know.'

The lines of her face would crease themselves in deeper ruts of disapproval. Her mouth would go on muttering without sound for some moments longer while he settled himself by the piano with hot discomfort and perhaps a belch or two.

'You can take your coat off.'

She liked him better with his coat off. It reminded her of the Sundays when all of them were at home, a dinner, all the boys with clean white aprons on, so that the gravy from the Yorkshire pudding did not drop on their chapel suits.

The absence of the coat revealed a man of gross, crusty width, with watery blue eyes starting beerily from a face fired by summer to lines of smouldering bruisy red. His collar-stud pressed brassily on his thick throat and his shirt-sleeves were rolled up above arms massive and blackly haired.

His voice had a yeasty thickness:

'All of 'em gone chapel?'

'Rose and Clarice and Will have gone. Lawrence and Nell went this morning.'

Lawrence and Will were good boys: steady boys, fellows with enough ambition to get good jobs and enough sense to hang on to them when they got them. They were solid, pin-stripe men. She had never had any bother with Will and Lawrence; they never troubled her. They did not approve of Luther, but then, they did not understand him.

'Ain't bin out nowhere this week, I reckon? Too hot for you.'

'Went up to Rose's Thursday,' she said.

'Git the bus?'

'Bus! What d'ya think my legs are for?'

'You wanta git the bus,' he said. 'One o' these days you'll be doing that traipse up there once too much and you'll be dropping down.'

'If I do you'll be there measuring me out 'fore I'm cold,' she said swiftly, 'I'll warrant that.'

'Ah, don't sit there horse-facing so much. You horse-face too much by half.'

'Don't you tell me I horse-face,' she said.

He did not answer. It pained him when she horse-faced at him. He dreaded the day when he would be measuring her out, he thought. His only compensating thought about that was that he would make her something very nice; something really high-class and lovely; something fitting and worthy of the old lady.

She sat there for some time looking like a bone carving, and at last he broke the silence by saying:

'Anything to eat? I could do with a mite o' something.'

'I'll be bound you never got your dinner again, did you?'

'Never had time. Bin at it since daylight.'

'Funny how you get so many jobs a-Sundays,' she said and her nose rose, pointed as a bird's.

Then because he sat there without moving for a second or two longer she said:

'Well: you know where the pantry is. You don't expect me to put it in your mouth for you, do you?'

Daylight was fading a little when he came lumbering back into the room with hunks of jam tart and cheese and bread and cold new potatoes and a slice of cold Yorkshire pudding on a plate. He sat with the plate on his knees. He knew that he had to be careful of the crumbs; he knew she would horse-face if he dropped the crumbs. But the taste of the new potatoes and the cold Yorkshire pudding were the taste of all the summer Sunday evenings of his boyhood and he crammed them in with blind-eyed pleasure, bolting them down, licking thick red lips and wishing to God she had a pint in the house to wash them down.

She muttered at last:

'Anybody'd think you'd never had a mite in your life. Don't she ever get you nothing a-Sundays?'

'Never care whether I get much a-Sundays,' he said.

'It don't look like it,' she said.

That was the worst of his mother, he thought. She couldn't hit it off with Edna. He had given up trying to make her now. It was like trying to turn a mule.

'You can get yourself a spill when you want one,' she said.

Edna was a bit easy-going, he knew, but on the whole he didn't complain. She had let herself go a bit, perhaps, after the last baby. She was a bit sloppy round the middle. Her face was nothing much to write home about but then he wasn't a picture either. The chief thing was she didn't nag him; he really didn't get drunk very much and if he was late at *The Unicorn* on a Sunday she and the children ate the dinner without him and he pacified her with a pint of Guinness afterwards.

By the time he had finished eating it was almost dark and he got up and did the thing he always did, without fail, every Sunday. He lit one of the gas-lamps above the mantelshelf and then, holding his big red face under the light, adjusted the burner until it gave a pure white glow. Then he filled his pipe and lit one of her paper spills from the gas-mantle and put it to his pipe. The flame was sucked down by his red powerful mouth into the pipe bowl until at last he blew out strong blue clouds of smoke that almost smothered him.

As she sat in the window she let the smoke come over to her with her head slightly uplifted, as if it were a cool breeze blowing through the warm airless room in which no window had been open all day. There were three moments she really waited for all evening, and this was the second of them. The first was when she saw him turn, so like a doctor with the fiddle case, at the bottom of the hill. The second was the moment of the gas-lamp, the pure white glow on his face, the great sucked-down flame and the smoke puttering across the room in blue string clouds. It was the smoke above all that she associated with that clumsy massiveness of his and after she smelled it she was aware of the slow dying of cantankerousness inside herself, a softening of all the edges of the day.

When the pipe was really going she knew what he was going to do next. She began unconsciously to finger the keys of the piano and the bookcase that hung on the chain round her neck. That was the third moment: the moment when he reached for the fiddle case and undid it and opened it and took out the bow.

He had begun to play the fiddle when he was seven years old. That had been her ambition for him: a fiddler, a violinist, a great player of the violin in the household. Mr Godbold, who had been a fiddler himself in a great orchestra in Leicester or Birmingham or some other big city up in that part of the world, gave him lessons in his front room, twice a week, after school, at two shillings a time.

'He has fine hands,' Mr Godbold said. 'He will make a fine player. He is slow but in the end he will make a fine player.'

The walls of Mr Godbold's front room were hung with many pictures of Mr Godbold playing the violin as a soloist or in orchestras or at social evenings and smoking concerts. She thought Mr Goldbold, in pieces like *The Spring Song* and excerpts from *Mariana* and *Il Trovatore*, played like an angel, and she thought it would be wonderful if Luther could rise as far as that. The first winter he persevered through many exercises and the second winter he came to his first piece, *Robin Adair*. Most children who learned the piano or the violin went to a Miss Scholes, in the High Street, where they learned *The Bluebells of Scotland* as their first piece and Miss Scholes gave them sixpence for doing so. Mr Godbold did not believe in bribing his pupils; they

worked hard on exercises that were the real foundation of music
and then went straight on to pieces like *Robin Adair*.

Luther stuck at *Robin Adair*. He played it through for a whole
winter and then his hands began to grow. By the time he was
twelve he was a big awkward gargoyle of a boy in whose hands
the violin looked effete and fragile. She thought by that time he
could play beautifully: perhaps not quite as beautifully as Mr
Godbold. Perhaps it only seemed to her almost as beautiful
because he was so very young.

'You want the key?' she said. She took it off the chain and
held it out to him.

The sound of the fifths as he spaced them out on the piano
was, she thought, a most wonderful thing. It was different from
anything else that was ever heard on the piano: those queer,
sharp steps of notes climbing up and starting a trembling on the
air. That was the true violin sound: that wonderful prelude of
quivering that drew out finally into the glassy, soaring singing
of strings.

She had never been very happy about his being a carpenter
and at first she opposed it. It was probably that, she thought,
that had made his hands so large and clumsy, She was certain
the hands of a carpenter could not also be the hands of a violinist; the one could only ruin the other. But his father had said a
man had his living to earn and what was wrong with a man being
a carpenter? 'There was One who was a carpenter and there was
no shame in that,' he said.

'Play the' old un?' Luther said, but she said nothing because
she knew he never began with any other.

The time he took to play through *Robin Adair* always seemed
to go by, perhaps because she shut her eyes, very quickly. It
flew away on the song's own delicacy. He liked to play too with
the pipe in his mouth, so that it seemed as if every scrape of the
bow gave out its own rank cloud of smoke that finally choked
the room with gas-green fog.

After *Robin Adair* he played several other pieces he knew:
The Jolly Miller and *Oh! Dear What Can the Matter Be?* She
thought he played better as he got older; but that, after all, was
only natural. That was only as it should be. He was a man of
over fifty now. He had been playing the same pieces, on the same
violin, for forty years.

'Gittin' dark,' Luther would say, after the third piece. 'Better be gittin' steady on home.'

He sat with the fiddle case on his knee and the pipe and the violin in his right hand, waiting to pack up. There would be just time, he thought, to nip into *The Unicorn* and have a couple of beers, perhaps even three or four beers, before they closed at half-past ten. Old Shady Parker would be there and Bill Flawn and Tom Jaques and Flannel Clarke and they would stand each other a round or two. That would rouse him up nicely and he would go home to Edna happy, belching through the dark summer streets, up and down the hills. Tomorrow he would begin to cut out another coffin. Trade was never what you called good in the summer but someone was always going, unexpected or not, and he mucked along somehow. Damn what the family said. That was good enough for him.

'Better put the key back afore you forgit,' he would say and she would take the key from him and clip it back on the chain

The poise of her hands, held for a second or two about her throat, was a signal that she gave him every Sunday.

'Want me to gie y' another?'

'Have you got time? Don't you hang about if you haven't got time.'

'Plenty o' time.' The big voice was crude and massive as the hands. 'You jes' say and I'll play it. Want another? What's it goin' a-be?'

'Play me the old one,' she would say.

The old one was *Robin Adair*. As he played it she stared beyond the smoky gaslight into spaces empty of shape. She sat ageless and tranquil as if already embalmed among the greenery of fern-pots, before a shroud of blanketing curtains, under a gas-blue summer sky. The harsh sound of the fiddle strings drew out thinner and thinner across the spaces into which she was staring until her eyes went cloudily after them and she was sightless as she listened.

'Ah! y' can't beat th' old uns,' Luther said. 'They take a bit o' beatin'.'

She did not answer. She felt always that she could hear the sound of the strings long after they were silent. They were like the sound of pigeons' voices echoing each other far away in summer trees, and in the sound of them was all her love.

LOVE IN A WYCH ELM

When I was a boy the Candleton sisters, seven of them, lived in a large gabled house built of red brick that gave the impression of having been muted by continual sunlight to a pleasant shade of orange-rose. The front face of it had a high, benign open appearance and I always felt that the big sash windows actually smiled down on the long gravel terrace, the iron pergola of roses and the sunken tennis lawn. At the back were rows of stables, all in the same faded and agreeable shade of brick, with lofts above them that were full of insecure and ancient bedsteads, fire-guards, hip-baths, tennis rackets, croquet hammers, rocking horses, muscle-developers, Indian clubs, travelling trunks and things of that sort thrown out by Mr and Mrs Candleton over the course of their fruitful years.

I was never very sure of what Mr Candleton did in life; I was not even sure in fact if he did anything at all except to induce Mrs Candleton, at very regular intervals, to bear another daughter. In a town like Evensford there were at that time very few people of independent means who lived in houses that had stables at the back. The Candletons were, or so it seemed to me, above our station. There was at one time a story that Mr Candleton was connected with wine. I could well believe this. Like his house, Mr Candleton's face had toned to a remarkably pleasant shade of inflammable rose. This always seemed perhaps brighter than it really was because his eyes were so blue. They were of that rare shade of pale violet blue that always seems about to dissolve, especially in intoxication. This effect was still further heightened by hair of a most pure distinguished shade of yellow: a thick oat-straw yellow that was quite startling and remarkable in a male.

All the Candleton sisters too had their father's pale violet dissolving eyes and that exceptional shade of oat-straw hair.

At first, when they were very small children, it was white and silky. Then as they grew up its characteristic shining straw-colour grew stronger. A stranger seeing them for the first time

324

would have said that they were seven dolls who had been dipped
in a solution of something several shades paler than saffron. The
hair was very beautiful when brushed and as children they all
wore it long.

On hot days in summer Mr Candleton wore cream flannel
trousers with a blue pin stripe in them, a blazer with red and
orange stripes, and a straw hat with a band of the same design.
Round his waist he wore a red silk cummerbund. All his shirts
were of silk and he always wore them buttoned at the neck. In
winter he wore things like Donegal tweeds: roughish, sporting,
oatmeal affairs that were just right for his grained waterproof
shooting brogues. He wore smart yellow gloves and a soft tweed
hat with a little feather in the band. He always seemed to be setting off somewhere, brisk and dandyish and correct, a man of
leisure with plenty of time to spare.

It was quite different with Mrs Candleton. The house was big
and rambling and it might well have been built specially to ac-
commodate Mrs Candleton, who was like a big, absent-minded,
untidy, roving bear. My mother used to say that she got up and
went to bed in a pinafore. It wasn't a very clean pinafore either.
Nor were her paper hair-curlers, which were sometimes still
in her rough unruly black hair at tea-time. She always seemed
to be wearing carpet-slippers and sometimes her stockings would
be slipping down. She was a woman who always seemed to be
catching up with life and was always a day and a half behind

The fact was, I suppose, that with seven children in something
like a dozen years Mrs Candleton was still naturally hazy in some
of her diurnal calculations. Instead of her catching up with life,
life was always catching up with her.

Meals, for example, made the oddest appearances in the
Candleton household. If I went on a school-less day to call on
Stella – she was the one exactly of my own age, the one I knew
best – it was either to find breakfast being taken at eleven-thirty,
with Mr Candleton always immaculate behind the silver toast-
rack and Mrs Candleton looking like the jaded mistress of a rag-
and-bone man, or dinner at half-past three or tea at seven. In a
town like Evensford everybody was rigidly governed by factory
hours and the sound of factory hooters. At various times of the
day silences fell on the town that were a hushed indication that
all honest people were decently at work. All this meant that

breakfast was at seven, dinner at twelve-thirty and tea at half-past five. That was how everybody ate and lived and ran their lives in Evensford: everybody, that is, except the Candletons.

These characteristics of excessive and immediate smartness on the one hand and the hair-curler and pinafore style on the other had been bequeathed by him and Mrs Candletown in almost exactly equal measure to their children. The girls were all beautiful, all excessively dressy as they grew up and, as my mother was fond of saying, not over clean.

'If they get a cat-lick once a week it's about as much as they do get,' was one of her favourite sayings.

But children do not notice such things very acutely and I cannot say that I myself was very interested in the virtues of soap and water. What I liked about the Candletons was not only a certain mysterious quality of what I thought was aristocracy but a feeling of untamed irresponsibility. They were effervescent. When the eldest girl, Lorna, was seventeen she ran off with a captain in the Royal Artillery who turned out to be a married man. I thought it might well have been the sort of thing that would have ruined a girl, temporarily at least, in Evensford, but Stella simply thought it a wild joke and said:

'She had a wonderful time. It was gorgeous. They stayed at a marvellous hotel in London. She told us all about it. I thought Mother would die laughing.'

Of laughing, not shame: that was typical of the Candleton standard, the Candleton approach and the Candleton judgement on such things.

The four eldest girls, two of them twins, were called Lorna, Hilda, Rosa and Freda. This habit of giving names ending in the same letter went on to Stella, with whom I played street-games in winter in front of the gas-lit windows of a pork-pie and sausage shop and games in summer in the Candleton garden and among the muscle-developers and bedsteads of the Candleton loft, and then on to the two youngest, who were mere babies as I knew them, Wanda and Eva. Mrs Candleton's Christian name was Blanche, which suited her perfectly.

It was a common tendency in all the Candleton girls to develop swiftly. At thirteen they were filling out; at fifteen they were splendidly and handsomely buxom and were doing up their hair. Hilda appeared to me to be a goddess of marbled form long before she was eighteen and got engaged to a beefy young farmer who bred prize cattle and called for her in a long open sports car.

Hilda had another characteristic not shared by any of the rest of the family except her mother. She sang rather well. At eighteen she began to have her pleasant, throaty, contralto voice trained. Mr Candleton was a strict Sunday morning churchgoer in pin-stripe trousers, bowler hat and spats, and Hilda went with him to sing in the choir. Her voice was trained by a Mr Lancaster, a rather bumptious pint-size tenor who gave her lessons three evenings a week. It was generally known that Mr Lancaster was, as a singer at any rate, past his best, but it was not long before the engagement between Hilda and the farmer was broken.

At that time Stella and I were nine. I, at least, was nine and Stella, physically, was twelve or thirteen. What I liked about her so much in those days was her utter freedom to come and go as she pleased. Other children had errands to run, confirmation classes to attend, catechisms to learn, aunts to visit, restrictive penances like shoes to clean or knives to rub up with bath-brick.

In the Candleton way she had never anything to do but play, enjoy herself, indulge in inconsequential make-believe and teach me remarkable things about life and living.

'What shall we do? Let's be married. Let's go up to the loft and be married.'

'We were married the day before yesterday.'

'That doesn't matter. You can be married over and over again. Hilda's going to be. Come on, let's be married.'

'All right. But not in the loft. Let's have a new house this time.'

'All right. Let's be married in the wych-elm.'

The Candleton garden extended beyond the stables into a rough orchard of old damson trees, with a few crooked espalier pears. A pepper-pot summer house in rustic work with a thatched roof stood in one corner, almost obliterated by lilac trees. In summer damsons and pears fell into the deep grass and no one picked them up. A sense of honeyed rotting quietness spread under the lurching trees and was compressed and shut in by a high boundary line of old, tapering wych-elms.

Rooks nested in the highest of the elms and when summer thickened the branches the trees were like a wall. The house was hidden and shut away. On a heavy summer day you would hear nothing there but the sound of rooks musing and croaking and fruit falling with a squashy mellow plop on the grass and paths.

Up in the wych-elms the peculiar structure of boughs made a house for us. We could walk about it. We crawled, like monkeys, from tree to tree. In this paradise we stayed for entire afternoons, cocooned with scents, hidden away in leaves. We made tea in ancient saucepans on flameless fires of elm twigs and prepared dinners of potatoes and gravy from fallen pears. And up here, on a soft August afternoon, we were married without witnesses and Stella, with her yellow hair done up for the first time, wore a veil of lace curtains and carried a bunch of cow-parsley.

But before that happened I had caught, only the day before, another glimpse of the Candleton way of living.

I had called about six o'clock in the evening for Stella but although the door of the house was open nobody, for some time at any rate, answered my ring at the bell. That was not at all unusual at the Candleton household. Although it never seemed possible for nine such unmistakable people to disappear without trace it was frequently happening and often I went to the door and rang until I was tired of ringing and then went away without an answer.

I remember once ringing the bell and then, tired of it, peeping into the kitchen. It was one of those big old-fashioned kitchens with an enormous iron cooking range with plate racks above it and gigantic dressers and vast fish-kettles and knife-cleaners everywhere. In the middle of it all Mrs Candleton sat asleep. Not normally asleep, I could see. A quarter-full bottle of something for which I had no definition stood on the table in front of her, together with a glass and, beside the glass, most astonishing thing of all, her false teeth.

Blowsily, frowsily, comfortably, toothlessly, Mrs Candleton was sleeping away the afternoon in her hair-curlers and her pinafore.

But on the evening I called for Stella the kitchen was empty. I rang the bell four or five times and then, getting no answer, stepped into the hall.

'Hullo,' someone said.

That very soft, whispered throaty voice was Hilda's. She was standing at the top of the stairs. She was wearing nothing but her petticoat and her feet were bare. In her hands she was holding a pair of stockings, which she had evidently been turning inside out in readiness to put on.

'Oh! it's you,' she said. 'I thought I heard someone.'

'Is Stella here?'

'They're all out. They've all gone to the Robinsons' for tea. It's Katie's birthday.'

'Oh! I see,' I said. 'Well, I'll come again tomorrow—'

'I'm just going to a dance,' she said. 'Would you like to see my dress? Would you? – come on, come up.'

Standing in the bedroom, with the August sunlight shining on her bare shoulders, through the lace of her slip and on her sensational yellow Candleton hair, she was a magnificent figure of a girl.

'Just let me put my stockings on and then you can see my dress.'

She sat down on the bed to put on her stockings. Her legs were smooth and heavy. I experienced an odd sensation as the stockings unrolled up her legs and then were fastened somewhere underneath the petticoat. Then she stood up and looked at the back of her legs to see if her stockings were straight. After that she smoothed the straps of her petticoat over her shoulders and said:

'Just wait till I give my hair one more brush.'

I shall never forget how she sat before the dressing mirror and brushed her hair. I was agreeably and mystically stunned. The strokes of the brush made her hair shine exactly, as I have said before, like oat-straw. Nothing could have been purer and more shining. It was marvellously burnished and she laughed at me in the mirror because I stood there so staring and speechless and stunned.

'Well, do I look nice? You think I shall pass in a crowd?'

'Yes.'

'That's good. It's nice to have a man's opinion.'

She laughed again and put on her dress. It was pure white, long and flouncy. I remember distinctly the square low collar. Then she put on her necklace. It was a single row of pearls and she couldn't fasten it.

'Here, you can do this,' she said.

She sat on the bed and I fastened the necklace. The young hair at the nape of her neck was like yellow chicken down. I was too confused to notice whether she had washed her neck or not and then she said:

'That's it. Now just a little of this and I'm ready.'

She sprayed her hair, her arms and the central shadow of her bosom with scent from a spray.

'How about a little for you?'

She sprayed my hair and in a final moment of insupportable intoxication I was lost in a wave of wallflowers.

'That's the most expensive scent there is,' she said. 'The most difficult to make. Wallflowers.'

Perhaps it was only natural, next day, as I came to be married to Stella high at the altar of the wych-elms, that I found myself oppressed by a sensation of anticlimax. Something about Stella, I felt, had not quite ripened. I had not the remotest idea as to what it could be except that she seemed, in some unelevating and puzzling way, awkward and flat.

'What do you keep staring at me for?'

'I'm just going to spray you with scent,' I said. 'There – piff! pish! piff—'

'Whatever made you think of that?'

I was afraid to speak of Hilda and I said:

'All girls have to have scent on when they're married.'

'Do I look nice?'

She didn't really look nice. The lace curtain was mouldy in one corner and had holes down one side. I didn't like the odour of cow-parsley. But the soft golden oat-straw hair was as remarkable as ever and I said:

'You look all right.'

Then we were married. After we were married she said:

'Now you have to make love to me.'

'Why?'

'Everybody has to make love when they're married.'

I looked at her in utter mystification. Then suddenly she dropped the cow-parsley and pushed back her veil and kissed me. She held me in an obliterating and momentary bondage by the trunk of the wych-elm, kissing me with such blistering force that I lost my cap. I was rather upset about my cap as it fell in the nettles below but she said:

'Sit down. We're in bed now. We have to be in bed now we're married. It's the first thing people do.'

'Why?'

'Don't you know?'

I did not know; nor, as it happens, did she. But one of the advantages of being born one of a family of seven sisters is that you arrive much earlier at the approximation of the more delicate truths than you do if you are a boy. Perhaps in this respect I was a backward boy, but I could only think it was rather comfortless trying to make love in a wych-elm and after a time I said:

'Let's go and play in the loft now.'

'What with?'

'I don't know,' I said. 'Let's have a change. We've been married an awful lot of times—'

'I know,' she said. 'We'll play with the chest-developers.'

While we played in the loft with the chest-developers she had an original thought.

'I think if I practise a lot with these I shall get fat up top more quickly.'

'You will?'

'I think I shall soon anyway.'

Like Hilda, I thought. A renewed sensation of agreeable and stupefying delight, together with a scent of wallflowers, shot deliciously through me and I was half-way to the realisation of the truth that girls are pleasant things when she said:

'One day, when we're big, let's be really married, shall us?'

'All right.'

'Promise?'

'Yes,' I said.

'You know what you'll be when you're married to me, don't you?' she said.

I couldn't think.

'You'll be a viscount,' she said.

'What's a viscount?'

'It's the husband of a viscountess.'

'How shall I come to be that?'

'Because a viscountess is the daughter of a lord.'

'But,' I said, 'your father isn't a lord.'

'No,' she said, 'but his brother is. He lives in a castle in Bedfordshire. It has a hundred and forty rooms in it. We go there every summer. And when he dies my father will be a lord.'

'Is he going to die?'

'Soon.'

'Supposing your father dies before he does?'

'Oh! he won't,' she said. 'He's the youngest son. The oldest always die first.'

She went on to tell me many interesting things about our life together. Everything in that life would be of silk, she said, like her father's shirts. Silk sheets on the bed, silk pillows, silk tablecloths, silk cushions. 'And I shall always wear silk drawers,' she said. 'Even on week-days.'

Altogether, it seemed, we should have a marvellous life together.

'And we shall drink port wine for supper,' she said. 'Like my father does. He always drinks port wine for supper.'

'Is it nice?'

'Yes,' she said. 'I'm allowed to have it sometimes. You'll like it. You can get drunk as often as you like then. Like my father does.'

'Does he get drunk?'

'Not as often as my mother does,' she said, 'but quite a lot.'

I suppose I was shocked.

'Oh! that's all right,' she said. 'Lords always get drunk. That's why people always say "drunk as a lord." That's the proper thing to do.'

Armed with the chest-developers, we spent an ecstatic afternoon. I was so filled with the golden snobbery of being a viscount that it was a cold and dusty sort of shock when she told me that anyway we couldn't be married for years and years, not until she was fatter, like Hilda was.

The recollection of Hilda, all burnished and magnificent and intoxicating and perfumed, inflamed and inspired me to greater efforts with the chest-developers.

'We must work harder,' I said.

I wanted so much to be a lord, to live in a castle, to drink port wine and to be married to someone with silk drawers that I was totally unprepared for the shock my mother gave me.

'The little fibber, the little story-teller, the little liar,' she said.

'But she said so,' I said. 'She told me.'

'I went to board school with Reggie Candleton,' she said. 'He was in my class. They came from Gas Street.'

Nothing in the world was worse than coming from Gas Street. You could not go lower than Gas Street. The end of the respectable world was Gas Street.

'It's she who had the money,' my mother said. 'Mrs Candleton. Her father was a brewer and Reggie Candleton worked there. He was always such a little dandy. Such a little masher. Always the one for cutting such a dash.'

I decided it was wiser to say nothing about the prospect of marrying, or about Stella's urgent efforts with the chest-developers, or the silk drawers.

'All top show,' my mother said. 'That's what it is. All fancy fol-di-dols on top and everything dropping into rags underneath. Every one of them with hair like a ten-guinea doll and a neck you could sow carrots in.'

I don't suppose for a moment that Stella remembers me; or that, on an uncomfortable, intimate occasion, we were married in a wych-elm. It is equally unlikely that Hilda remembers me; or that, with her incomparable yellow hair, her white dance dress, her soft blonde flesh and her rare scent of wallflowers, she once asked me to give her my opinion as a man. I believe Stella is married to a bus-conductor. The rest of the Candletons have faded from my life. With the summer frocks, the summer straw-hats and the summer flannels, the cummerbunds, the silk shirts, the elegant brogues, the chest-developers and the incomparable yellow hair they have joined Mr Candleton in misty, muted, permanent bankruptcy.

Love in a wych-elm is not an easy thing; but like the Candletons it is unforgettable.

LET'S PLAY SOLDIERS

The yellow strings of laburnum flower had already faded that afternoon when I stood on sentry for the 1st Battalion Albion Street Light Infantry and Mrs Strickland came out of her kitchen door wearing a sack apron and a man's check cap pinned on her spindly curling rags by a long black hat pin and started shaking mats against the garden fence, not three yards from the tent made of split sacks and old lace curtains where we of the battalion held councils of war before going into battle.

Upstairs across the yard Mrs Rankin was sitting at a window with a bottom like a pumpkin hanging over the sill, huffing energetically on glass already as pure as crystal and then scrupulously polishing the vapour off again with a spotless yellow rag.

The face of Mrs Rankin, smooth and clean as porcelain, looked as if it had been polished too but the face of Mrs Strickland, like her curl-ragged hair, had nothing but greyness in it, a dopey salty greyness at the same time hard so that the skin looked like scoured pumice stone.

I was only six at the time and still a private; but I thought I detected a smell of parsnip wine in the air. Mangled dust and shreds of coco-matting rose in dense brown clouds as Mrs Strickland beat the decaying mats against the fence but I stood unshakably at attention under the laburnum tree, head up, eyes straight ahead, right hand firmly on the umbrella we were using as a rifle because Jeddah Clarke, our Captain, had the air gun, the only other weapon we possessed.

I knew that if I stood firm on guard and didn't flinch and saluted properly and challenged people and didn't let them pass until they gave the password, I might become, in time, a lance-corporal. There was nothing on earth I wanted more than to be a lance-corporal: except perhaps to kill a soldier.

'I wisht Albie was here,' Mrs Strickland said. 'I wisht Albie was here.'

It wasn't only that morning that her voice had that pumice-dry melancholy in it. It was always there, like the curling rags.

Sometimes Mrs Strickland didn't take out the curling rags until after Bill Strickland came home for his bloater tea at six o'clock and sometimes she didn't take them out at all.

'Ain't got a spare Daisy Powder, gal, I reckon?'

Mrs Strickland, staring with diffused and pleading eyes through the dust she had raised, groping up towards the sumptuous pumpkin of Mrs Rankin on the window sill, ran a dreary hand several times across her aching brow.

'Ain't got nivry one left,' Mrs Rankin said. 'You had the last one yisty.'

Daisies were a brand of headache powder guaranteed to refresh and free you from pain in five minutes. Mrs Strickland was taking them all day.

'Ain't Bill a-workin' then?'

'Bad a-bed. Can't lift 'isself orf the piller. I wisht Albie was here.'

I knew Albie couldn't be there. Albie, who was eighteen, a private too like me, was in France, fighting the Germans. I liked Albie; he had a ginger moustache and was my friend. Every other day or so I asked Mrs Strickland if and when Albie was going to become a lance-corporal, but somehow she never seemed to think he was.

'Ain't you got nivry one tucked away, gal, somewheer?'

'Nivry one,' Mrs Rankin said. 'Nivry one.'

Despair wrapped Mrs Strickland's face in a greyer, dustier web of gloom.

'Me 'ead's splittin'. It'll split open. I wisht Albie was here.'

'Won't the boy nip and get y' couple? Ask the boy.'

Mrs Strickland, seeming to become aware of me for the first time, turned to my impassive sentinel figure with eyes of greyest supplication.

'Nip down the shop and fetch us a coupla Daisies, there's a good boy. Nip and ask your mother to lend us a thrippenny bit, there's a good boy. I left me puss upstairs.'

It was funny, my mother always said, how Mrs Strickland was always leaving, losing or mislaying her purse somewhere.

'And a penn'orth o' barm too, boy, while you're down there. I gotta make a mite o' bread, somehow,' she called up to Mrs Rankin. 'Aain't got a mite in the place, gal. Not so much as a mossel.'

Mrs Rankin, who would presently be hurrying down to the yard to scour and white-wash the kitchen steps to blinding glacier whiteness and who, as my mother said, almost polished the coal before putting it on the fire, merely turned on Mrs Strickland a rounder, blanker, completely unhelpful pumpkin.

I didn't move either; I was on guard and Jeddah Clarke said you could be shot if you moved on guard.

'Nip and ask your mother to lend us a thrippenny bit, boy. Tanner if she's got it, boy—'

'I can't go, Mrs Strickland. I'm on sentry,' I said. 'I'll get shot.'

'Kids everywhere,' Mrs Strickland said, 'and nivry one on 'em to run of arrant for you when you want. I wisht Albie was here.'

Mrs Strickland dragged the decaying mats to the middle of the yard. The smell of parsnip wine went with her and she called up to Mrs Rankin:

'Ain't got 'arf a loaf I can have for a goin' on with gal, I reckon? Jist till the baker gits here? Jist 'arf? Jist the top?'

'You want one as'll fit on the bottom I lent you the day afore yisty? or will a fresh 'un do?'

Fiery, tempestuous white curls seemed to fly suddenly out of Mrs Strickland's mournful, aching head.

'What's a matter wi' y'? Askt y' a civil question, dint I? Askt y' civil question. What's a matter wi' y' all of a pop?'

'Sick on it,' Mrs Rankin said. 'About sick to death on it.'

'Go on, start maungin'! Start yelpin'!'

'Yelpin',' yelpin'?' Ain't got nothing to yelp about, I reckon, have I? When it ain't bread it's salt. When it ain't salt it's bakin' powder. Enough to gie y' the pip. When it ain't—'

'Keep on, keep on!' Mrs Strickland said. 'It'll do your fat gullet good. And me with 'im in bed. And the damn war on. And Albie not here.'

Suddenly she dropped the mats, picked up a bucket from the kitchen drain and started beating and rattling it like a wargong. In a flash Mrs Rankin's pumpkin darted through the window, dragging the sash down behind it. Behind the crystal glass Mrs Rankin's face remained palely distorted, mouthing furiously.

Down below in the yard, Mrs Strickland rattled the bucket again, shaking her curling rags, and yelled:

'Mag, mag. Jaw, jaw. That's all folks like you are fit for. Mag, jaw, mag, jaw—'

Mrs Rankin's face, ordinarily so polished and composed, splintered into uncontrollable furies behind the glass as Mrs Strickland started to fill the bucket with water from the stand-pipe in the yard.

In a second Mrs Rankin had the window up with a shrilling squeak of the sash and was half leaping out:

'And don't you start your hanky-pankies. Don't you start that! – I oiled and polished my door!—'

An arc of white water struck Mrs Rankin's back door like a breaker. Mrs Rankin slammed down the window and started beating the panes with her fists. Mrs Strickland screamed that she wisht Albie was here, Albie would let some daylight into somebody, and threw the bucket with a crashing roll across the yard.

A moment later a bedroom window shot open in the Strickland house and an unsober chin of black stubble leaned out and bawled:

'What the bloody 'ell's going on down there? If you two don't shut your yawpin' chops I'll come down and lay a belt acrosst the pair on y'—'

'I wisht Albie was here!' Mrs Strickland said. 'I wisht Albie was here!'

Drearily she slammed away into the house and after that it was silent for some minutes until suddenly from the street beyond the yard I could hear the inspiring note of war cries. A minute later the first battalion Albion Street Light Infantry came triumphantly pounding down the path between the cabbage patches, led by Jeddah Clarke, carrying the air-gun, Wag Chettle, bearing the standard, a red handkerchief tied to a bean-pole, and Fred Baker, beating a drum he had had for Christmas.

Fred and Jeddah were actually in khaki uniforms. Jeddah, besides the air-gun, wore a bandolier across his chest with real pouches and two clips of spent cartridges; Fred had a peaked khaki cap on, with the badge of the Beds & Bucks Light Infantry on one side and that of the Royal Welch Fusiliers on the other. At that time the Fusiliers were billeted in the town and we had an inspired admiration for them because they kept a white goat as mascot. The goat ate anything you gave it, even cigarettes.

What now surprised me about the battalion was not its air of triumph but its size. Usually it was no more than eight strong. Now it was twenty. Those bringing up the rear were even flying a second flag. It was a square of blue-and-white football shirt. I caught the gleam of a second and even a third air-gun and then suddenly Jeddah Clarke, our Captain, raised his air-gun and yelled:

'Gas Street are on our side! They're in the battalion! Gas Street have come in with us! Charge!'

We all cheered madly and charged. The little hairs of my neck stuck up in pride, excitement and admiration as we thundered dustily into the summer street outside.

'Charge!' we all shouted. 'Charge! Capture 'em! Charge!'

Heady with thought of battle, we wheeled like thunder into Winchester Street: completely unnoticed by a milk float, two bakers' carts, a chimney sweep on a bicycle and two women pushing prams.

'Charge!' I yelled, and was stunned to hear the blast of a bugle, suddenly blown at my side by a boy named Charley Fletcher, who was in the Lads' Brigade.

This new note, defiant above the roll of Fred Baker's drum, had us all in a frenzy of battle just as we surged past a railway dray loading piles of bulky leather outside a factory, where the crane swung out from its fourth storey door like a gallows and dropped its thirty-feet of rippling chain down to the shining hot pavement below.

'Charge!' I yelled, bringing up the rear with the umbrella under my arm and pointing it forward as if it had a bayonet in the end, exactly as I had seen in pictures of soldiers charging from the trenches. There was nothing we didn't know about soldiers and the trenches. We knew all about Vimy Ridge, Ypres, Hill 60 and Verdun too. We had seen them all in pictures.

The voice of our Captain, Jeddah Clarke, tore the air with fresh challenge as we whipped out of Winchester Street into Green's Alley. Continually Charley Fletcher's bugle ripped the quiet of the afternoon to shreds with raucous notes that were almost hysterical, rallying both us and the reinforcements of Gas Street, and I wondered suddenly where we were going and where the attack would be made.

Jeddah, yelling, told us all a moment later:

'Down to The Pit! We'll git 'em in The Pit!'

My heart went absolutely icy, turned sour and dropped to my stomach.

The Pit was a terrible place. You never went to The Pit. No one ever did. If you did you never came out alive. The people there, who lived in sordid back-to-back hovels with sacks at the windows, captured you, tied you up, locked you in satanic privies and let you suffocate to death. If they didn't do that they starved you, took away all your clothes and sold you naked in slavery. They were the most awful people in the world. People like Mrs Strickland were respectable by comparison. They were always dirty, drunk and fighting. They were always stinking and they were full of bugs and fleas.

I suddenly wanted to turn back, stand guard in the cabbage patch and dream quietly about being a lance-corporal one day.

'Charge!' everyone yelled. 'Charge! Git the stones ready!'

Out of Green's Alley we swung on the tide of battle into The Jetty, a narrow track of dried mud and stone. There the triumphant column broke up for a moment or two and we began to hack stones from the dust with the heels of our boots. By this time my legs and knees were shaking: so much so that all I could hack out were two pebbles and the stopper of a broken beer bottle. But Fred Baker, seeing this, took pity on me and armed me with half a brick.

The bugle sounded again, shrill as a cornet.

'Air-guns in front!' Jeddah yelled. 'Git ready when I say charge!'

We thundered on. We had been joined now by a butcher's boy on a bicycle and for some reason I found myself clinging to his saddle. Suddenly in the excitement the butcher's boy started pedalling madly and I could hardly keep up with the column as it pounded along.

Less than a minute later we were facing the jaws of The Pit. They were nothing more than a gap between two rows of derelict gas-tarred fences but beyond them I could see the little one-storey hovels with sacks at their windows, the horrible squat brick prisons of outdoor privies and a few dirty flags of shirt on a washing line.

It was impossible for my heart to turn cold a second time; it was frozen stiff already. But the paralysis that kept it stuck at the pit of my stomach now affected my legs and I stopped running.

This, as it turned out, was a purely instinctive reaction. Everyone else had stopped running too.

'Charge!' someone yelled and this time it was not our Captain, Jeddah.

The order came from behind us and as we turned in its direction we found ourselves the victims of the oldest of all battle manoeuvres. We were being attacked in the rear.

This time my eyes froze. The Pit Brigade stood waiting for us: eight or ten of them, headed by a black-mouthed deaf-mute armed with five-foot two-pronged hoe. Another had an ugly strip of barrel hoop sharpend up like a sword and another a catapult with a black leather sling big enough to hold an egg. He was smoking a cigarette. Two others were manning a two-seater pram armoured with rusty plates of corrugated iron and this, we all realised, was an armament we did not possess. It was the first tank we had encountered.

The deaf-mute started showing his black teeth, gurgling strange cries. He made vigorous deaf-and-dumb signs with his hands and the snarling faces about him jabbered. The entire Pit Brigade, older, bigger, dirtier and better armed than we were, stood ready to attack.

It was too late to think about being a lance-corporal now and a moment later they were on us.

'Charge!' everyone shouted from both sides. 'Charge!' and we were locked in an instant clash of bricks, stones, catapults, flags, sticks and air-guns that would not fire. Above it all the unearthly voice of the deaf mute gurgled like a throttled man, mouthing black nothings.

I threw my brick. It fell like the legendary sparrow through the air. Someone started to tear the coat off my back and I thrashed madly about me with the umbrella. I could see our two flags rocking ship-mast fashion in the centre of battle and Charley Fletcher using the bugle as a hammer. The two-pronged hoe fell like a claw among us and the armour plates fell off the pram-tank as it ran into Fred Baker and cut his legs, drawing first blood.

Soon we actually had them retreating.

'We're the English!' I heard Jeddah shouting. 'We're the

English! The Pit are the bloody Germans,' and this stirring cry
of patriotism roused us to fresh thrills of battle frenzy.

'We're the English!' we all yelled. 'We're the English!'

Suddenly as if a trap door had opened the Pit Brigade, under
sheer weight of pressure, fell backward into the jaws of The Pit,
hastily slamming the door behind them as a barricade and
leaving outside a single stray soldier armed with a rusty flat iron
suspended on a piece of cord and dressed as a sergeant of the
Royal Artillery, complete with spurs and puttees.

Cut off from the tide of battle, this soldier gave several rapid
and despairing looks about him, dropped the flat iron and bolted
like a hare.

'Prisoner!' Jeddah yelled. 'Prisoner! Git him! Take him
prisoner!'

In a moment Fred Baker, Charley Fletcher and myself were
after him. We caught him at the top to The Jetty. At first he
lay on his back and kicked out at us with the spurs, spitting at
the same time, but soon I was sitting on his face, Fred Baker on
his chest and Charley Fletcher, who was the eldest, on his legs.
For a long time he kept trying to spit at us and all the time there
was a strong, putrid, stinking, funny smell about him.

We kept him prisoner all afternoon. Then we decided to strip
him. While Fred and I sat on his face and chest Charley unrolled
the puttees and took off the spurs.

'You always have spoils of war when you take prisoners,'
Charley explained. 'Soldiers call it a bit of buckshee.'

We spent some time arguing about how the buckshee should
be divided and finally Charley was awarded the puttees, because
he was the eldest, and Fred Baker and I each had a spur. Having the spur was even better than being a lance corporal and I
couldn't remember ever having had anything that made me feel
more proud.

It was almost evening before Jeddah and the rest of the Battalion got back, fifty strong, from telling of our victory in far
places, in Lancaster Street, Rectory Street, Bedford Row, King's
Lane and those parts of the town who could not be expected to
hear of our triumph other than by word of mouth and from us.

'We still got the prisoner, Captain,' we said. 'What shall we
do with him?'

'Shoot him,' Jeddah said.

Orders were orders with Jeddah and we asked if we could have the air-gun.

He handed it over.

'I leave it to you,' Jeddah said. He was now wearing a forage cap, three long service stripes, a leather belt and a Welch black flash he had captured. 'Charge!'

The sound of returning triumph from the fifty-strong battalion had hardly died away before we set to work to shoot the flat-iron boy.

First of all we made him stand up by the fence, among a pile of junk and nettles. By this time we had tied his hands and legs with the cord off the flat-iron and had taken off his shoes so that he found it hard to run. But he still spat at us as he stood waiting to be shot and he still had that funny, sickening smell.

Fred Baker shot him first. The unloaded air-gun made a noise rather like a damp squib. Then Charley Fletcher shot him and the gun made a noise like a damp squib a second time. Then I shot him and as I did so I made a loud, realistic noise that was more like the crack of a bursting paper bag. I aimed between the eyes of the flat-iron boy as I shot and I was very thrilled.

'Now you're dead,' we said to him. 'Don't you forget. Don't you move – you're dead. You can't fight no more.'

He didn't look very dead when we left him but we knew he he was. We told the Captain so when we rejoined the battalion in Gas Street, Fred Baker blowing the bugle and wearing the artillery puttees, Charley Fletcher and I taking turns to carry the air-gun and both of us waving a spur.

Jeddah was drunk with victory. 'Tomorrow we're goin' to charge The Rock!' he said. The Rock was even worse than The Pit but now none of us was appalled and all of us cheered. There was no holding us now.

'We'll kill 'em all!' Jeddah said. 'We'll burn ole Wag Saunders at the stake.' Wag was their Captain. 'Just like Indians. We'll win 'em. We ain't frit. Who are we?'

'We're the English!' we yelled.

It was already growing dark when I trotted home through the streets with my spur. In the back yard there were no lights in Mrs Rankin's neat, white-silled windows and in Mrs Strickland's house all the blinds were drawn although all the lights were on.

'Where have you been all this long time?' my father said.

He sat alone in the kitchen, facing a cold rice pudding. My father was very fond of cold rice pudding but tonight he did not seem to want it. Under the green gaslight the brown nutmeg skin of it shone unbroken.

'Fighting with our battalion,' I said.

I told him how the battle had been won and how I had captured the spur.

'That spur doesn't belong to you,' he said. 'Tomorrow morning you must take it back.'

I felt sick with disappointment and at the way grown-up people didn't understand you.

'Can I keep it just for tonight?'

'Just for tonight,' he said. 'But you must take it back tomorrow.'

Then I remembered something and I told him how the boy I'd got it from was dead.

'How is that?' he said. 'Dead?'

'We shot him.'

'Oh! I see,' he said. 'Well: tomorrow you go and find the dead boy and give him back his spur.'

Looking round the kitchen I now remembered my mother and asked where she was.

'She's with Mrs Strickland,' my father said. 'Mrs Rankin's with her too. I expect you noticed that all the blinds were drawn?'

I said I had noticed and did it mean that someone was dead?

'It's your friend – your friend Albie's not going to come back,' my father said.

After that my father didn't seem to want to speak very much and I said:

'Could I go and play in the tent until mother comes home?'

'You can go and play in the tent,' he said.

'With a candle?' I said. 'It's dark now outside.'

'Take a candle if you like,' he said.

I took a candle and sat in the tent all by myself, looking at my spur. It was shaped something like a handcuff to which was attached a silver star. The candlelight shone down on the spur with wonderful brilliance and as I looked at it I remembered the voices of Mrs Strickland and Mrs Rankin squabbling with bitterness over a loaf of bread in the afternoon and how Mrs Strickland wisht that Albie would come back, and now I listened again for their voices coming from the outer darkness but all I could hear was the voice from the afternoon:

'I wisht Albie was here. I wisht Albie was here.'

There is nothing much you can do with a solitary candle and a single spur. The spur can only shine like silver and the candle-light with a black vein in the heart of it.

Early next morning I took the spur back to The Pit. I ran all the way there and I was glad that no one saw me. The sun was coming up over the gas-tarred fences, the little hovels, the privies and the washing lines and all I did was to lay the spur on a stone in the sunlight, hoping that someone would come and find it there.

I ran all the way home, too, as hard as I could: afraid of the enemy we had conquered and the soldier I had killed.

THE WATERCRESS GIRL

The first time he ever went to that house was in the summer, when he was seven, and his grandfather drove him down the valley in a yellow trap and all the beans were in flower, with skylarks singing so high above them in the brilliant light that they hung trembling there like far-off butterflies.

'Who is it we're going to see?' he said.

'Sar' Ann.'

'Which one is Sar' Ann?'

'Now mek out you don' know which one Sar' Ann is,' his grandfather said, and then tickled the flank of the pony with the end of the plaited whip – he always wanted to plait reeds like that himself but he could never make them tight enough – so that the brown rumps, shorn and groomed for summer, quivered like firm round jellies.

'I don't think I've ever seen her,' he said.

'You seen her at Uncle Arth's,' his grandfather said. 'Mek out you don't remember that, and you see her a time or two at Jenny's.' He pronounced it Jinny, but even then the boy couldn't remember who Jinny was and he knew his grandfather wouldn't tell him until he remembered who Sar' Ann was and perhaps not even after that.

He tried for some moments longer to recall what Sar' Ann was like and remembered presently a square old lady in a porkpie lace cap and a sort of bib of black jet beads on a large frontal expanse of shining satin. Her eyes were watering. She sat on the threshold of a house that smelled of apples and wax polish. She was in the sun, with a lace-pillow and bone bobbins in a blue and ivory fan on her knees. She was making lace and her hands were covered with big raised veins like the leaves of cabbages when you turned them upside down. He was sure that this was Sar' Ann. He remembered how she had touched his hands with her big cold cabbagy ones and said she would fetch him a cheesecake, or if he would rather have it a piece of toffee, from the cupboard in her kitchen. She said the toffee was rather sugary

345

and that made him say he preferred the cheese-cake, but his grandfather said:

'Now don't you git up. He's ettin' from morn to night now. His eyes are bigger'n his belly. You jis sit still,' and he felt he would cry because he was so fond of cheese-cake and because he could hardly bear his disappointment.

'She's the one who wanted to give me cheese-cake,' he said, 'isn't she?'

'No, she ain't,' his grandfather said. 'That's your Aunt Turvey.'

'Then is she the one who's married to Uncle Arth? Up the high steps?' he said.

'Uncle Arth ain't married,' his grandfather said. 'That's jis the widder-woman who looks after him.'

His Uncle Arth was always in a night-shirt, with a black scarf round his head. He lived in bed all the time. His eyes were very red. Inside him, so his grandfather said, was a stone and the stone couldn't go up or down but was fixed, his grandfather said, in his kitney, and it was growing all the time.

The stone was an awful nightmare to him, the boy. How big was it? What sort of stone was it? he would say, a stone in the kitney?

'Like a pibble,' his grandfather said. 'Hard as a pibble. And very like as big as a thresh's egg. Very like bigger'n that by now. Very like as big as a magpie's.'

'How did it get there?'

'You're arstin' on me now,' his grandfather said. 'It'd be a puzzle to know. But it got there. And there it is. Stuck in his kitney.'

'Has anybody ever seen it?'

'Nobody.'

'Then if nobody's ever seen it how do they know it's there?'

'Lean forward,' his grandfather said. 'We're gittin' to Long Leys hill. Lean forward, else the shafts'll poke through the sky.'

It was when they climbed slowly up the long wide hill, already white with the dust of early summer, that he became aware of the beans in flower and the skylarks singing so loftily above them. The scent of beans came in soft waves of wonderful sweetness. He saw the flowers on the grey sunlit stalks like swarms of white, dark-throated bees. The hawthorn flower was nearly over and was turning pink wherever it remained. The singing of the sky-larks lifted the sky upward, farther and farther, loftier and loftier, and the sun made the blue of it clear and blinding. He felt that all summer was pouring down the hill, between ditches of rising meadowsweet, to meet him. The cold quivering days of coltsfoot flower, the icy-sunny days of racing cloud-shadow over drying ploughland, the dark-white days of April hail, were all behind him, and he was thirsty with summer dust and his face was hot in the sun.

'You ain't recollected her yit, have you?' his grandfather said.

They were at the top of the hill now and below them, in its yellow meadows, he could see a river winding away in broad and shining curves. He knew that that river was at the end of the earth; that the meadows, and with them the big woods of oak and hornbeam and their fading dusty spangles of flower, were another world.

'Take holt o' the reins a minute,' his grandfather said. He put on the brake a notch and the brake shoes scraped on the metal tyres. The boy held the thin smooth reins lightly between his fingers, the way he had been taught to do. He sat forward on the high horse-hair cushions and looked down the long black tram-lines of the dead level reins to the brown pony's ears and felt himself, for one moment, high on the hill, to be floating in air, level with all the skylarks above the fields below.

'I'll jis git me bacca going,' his grandfather said. 'We'll be there in about a quartern of hour. You keep holt on her steady.'

He wanted to say to his grandfather that that was a funny word, quartern; his schoolteacher never used that word; and then as he turned he saw the brown, red-veined face softened by the first pulls of tobacco. All the mystery of it was dissolved in a blue sweet cloud. Then his grandfather began coughing be-cause the bacca, he said, had gone down wrong way and was tiddling his gills. His eyes were wet from coughing and he was laughing and saying:

'You know who she is. She's the one with the specs like glarneys.'

Then he knew. She was a little woman, he remembered clearly now, with enormous spy-glass spectacles. They were thick and round like the marbles he played with. She was always whisking about like a clean starched napkin. He had seen her at Uncle

Arth's and she had jolted Uncle Arth about the bed with a terrible lack of mercy as she re-made his pillows, smacking them with her lightning hands as if they were disobedient bottoms. The colossal spectacles gave the eyes a terrible look of magnification. They wobbled sometimes like masses of pale floating frog-spawn. He didn't like her; he was held in the spawn-like hypnotism of the eyes and dared not speak. She had a voice like a jackdaw's which pecked and mocked at everybody with nasty jabs. He knew that he had got her mixed up somehow and he said:

'I thought the one with the glass eye was Aunt Prunes.'

'Prudence!' his grandfather said. 'They're sisters. She's the young 'un, Prudence.' He spat in a long liquid line, with off-hand care, over the side of the trap. 'Prunes? – that was funny. How'd you come to git holt o' that?'

'I thought everybody else called her Prunes.'

'Oh! You did, simly? Well, it's Prudence. Prudence – that's her proper name.'

Simly was another funny word. He would never understand that word. That was another word his schoolteacher never used.

'Is she the one with the moustache?'

'God alive,' the man said. 'Don't you say moustache. You'll git me hung if you say moustache. That's your Aunt Prudence you're talking about. Females don't have moustaches – you know that.'

He knew better than that because Aunt Prunes had a moustache. She was a female and it was quite a long moustache and she had, what was more, a few whiskers on the central part of her chin.

'Why doesn't she shave it off?' he said.

'You watch what you're doing,' his grandfather said. 'You'll have us in the duck-pond.'

'How do you spell it?' he said. 'Her name – Prunes?'

'Here, you gimme holt o' the reins now,' his grandfather said. 'We'll be there in five ticks of a donkey's tail.'

His grandfather took the reins and let the brake off, and in a minute the pony was trotting and they were in a world of high green reeds and grey drooping willows by the river.

'Is it the house near the spinney?' he said.

'That's it,' his grandfather said. 'The little 'un with the big chimney.'

He was glad he remembered the house correctly: not because he had ever seen it but because his grandfather always described it with natural familiarity, as if taking it for granted that he had seen it. He was glad too about Aunt Prunes. It was very hard to get everyone right. There were so many of them, Aunt Prunes and Sar' Ann and Aunt Turvey and Uncle Arth and Jenny and Uncle Ben Newton, who kept a pub, and Uncle Olly, who was a fat man with short black leggings exactly like polished bottles. His grandfather would speak of these people as if they were playmates who had always been in his life and were to be taken for granted naturally and substantially like himself. They were all very old, terribly old, and he never knew, even afterwards, if they were ordinary aunts or uncles or great ones or only cousins some stage removed.

The little house had two rooms downstairs with polished red bricks for floors and white glass vases or dried reeds from the river on the mantelpiece. His grandfather and Aunt Prunes and Sar' Ann and himself had dinner in the room where the stove was, and there were big dishes of potatoes, mashed with thick white butter sauce. Before dinner he sat in the other room with his grandfather and Aunt Prunes and looked at a large leather book called *Sunday at Home*, a prize Aunt Prunes had won at Bible Class, a book in which there were sandwiched, between steel-cuts of men in frock coats and sailors in sailing ships and ladies in black bonnets, pressings of dried flowers thin as tissue from the meadows and the riverside. His contemplation of the flat golden transparencies of buttercup and the starry eyes of bull-daisy and the woolly feathers of grass and reed was ravaged continually by the voice of Sar' Ann, the jackdaw, pecking and jabbing from the kitchen:

'There's something there to keep you quiet. That's a nice book, that is. You can look at that all afternoon.'

'You tell me,' Aunt Prunes said softly, 'when you want another.'

He liked Aunt Prunes. She was quiet and tender. The moustache, far from being forbidding, brushed him with friendly softness, and the little room was so hot with sun and cooking that there were beads of sweat on the whiskers which he made the mistake of thinking, for some time, were drops of the cowslip wine she was drinking. His grandfather had several glasses of cowslip wine and after the third or fourth of them he took off his coat and collar.

At the same time Aunt Prunes bent down and took the book away from him and said:

'You can take off your coat too. That's it. That's better. Do you want to go anywhere?'

'Not yet.'

'When you do it's down the garden and behind the elderberry tree.' Her eyes were a modest brown colour, the same colour as her moustache, and there were many wrinkles about them as she smiled. He could smell the sweetish breath, like the yeast his grandmother used for baking, of the fresh wine on her lips, and she said:

'What would you like to do this afternoon? Tell me what you'd like to do.'

'Read this book.'

'I mean really.'

'I don't know.'

'You do what you like,' she said. 'You go down to the back-brook or in the garden or into the spinney and find snails or sticklebacks or whatever you like.'

She smiled delicately, creating thousands of wrinkles, and then from the kitchen Sar' Ann screeched:

'I'm dishing up in two minutes, you boozers. You'd guzzle there till bulls'-noon if I'd let you.'

Bulls'-noon was another word, another strange queer thing he didn't understand.

For dinner they had Yorkshire pudding straight out of the pan and on to the plate, all by itself, as the opening course. Sometimes his grandfather slid slices of the creamy yellow pudding into his mouth on the end of his knife and said he remembered the days when all pudden was eaten first and you had your plate turned upside down, so that you could turn it over when the meat came. Sar' Ann said she remembered that too and she said they were the days and she didn't care what anybody said. People were happier. They didn't have so much of everything but they were happier. He saw Aunt Prunes give a little dry grin whenever Sar' Ann went jabbing on and once he thought he saw her wink at his grandfather. All the time the door of the little room was open so that he could see into the garden with its white pinks and stocks and purple iris flags and now and then he could hear the cuckoo, sometimes near, sometimes far off across the meadows, and many blackbirds singing in endless call and answer in the oak-trees at the end of the garden, where rhubarb and elderberry were in foaming flower together.

'You can hear nightingales too,' Aunt Prunes said. 'Would you like more pudding? You can have more pudding if you want it.'

But his grandfather said again that his eyes were always bigger than his belly and the pudding was put away. 'Ets like a thacker,' his grandfather said and Aunt Prunes said, 'Let him eat then. I like to see boys eat. It does your heart good,' and she smiled and gave him cloudy piles of white potatoes and white sauce from a blue china boat and thin slices of rich beef with blood running out and washing against the shores of his potatoes like the little waves of a delicate pink sea.

'How's Nance and Granny Houghton?' Sar' Ann said, and his grandfather said they were fair-to-mid and suddenly there was great talk of relatives, of grown-ups, of people he didn't know, of Charley and a man he thought was named Uncle Fuggles and Cathy and Aunt Em and Maude Rose and two people called Liz and Herbert from Bank Top. His grandfather, who had begun the meal with three or four glasses of cowslip wine and a glass of beer, now helped himself to another glass of beer and then dropped gravy down his waistcoat. Aunt Prunes had beer too and her eyes began to look warm and sleepy and beautifully content.

Afternoon, cuckoo-drowsy, very still and full of sun, seemed to thicken like a web about him long before the meal was over. He thought with dread of the quietness when all of them would be asleep and he himself in the little room with a big boring book and its rustling transparencies of faded flowers. He knew what it was like to try to move in the world of grown-up sleep. The whisper of the thinnest page would wake them. Night was the time for sleeping and it was one of the mysteries of life that people could also sleep by day, in chairs, in summertime, in mouth-open attitudes, and with snorting noises and legs suddenly jumping like the legs of horses when the flies were bad.

Then to his joy Aunt Prunes remembered and said:

'You know what I said. You run into the garden and have a look in the spinney for nests. Go down as far as the back-brook if you like.'

'That's it,' his grandfather said. 'You'll very like see a moor-hen's or a coot's or summat down there. Else a pike or summat. Used to be a rare place for pike, a-layin' there a-top o' the water—'

'Don't you git falling in,' Sar' Ann said. 'Don't you git them feet wet. Don't you git them gooseberries – they'll give you belly-ache summat chronic—'

'You bring me some flowers,' Aunt Prunes said. 'Eh? – how's that? You stay a long time, as long as you like, and bring me some flowers.'

There were no nests in the spinney except a pigeon's high up in a hazel-tree that was too thin to climb. He was not quite sure about the song of a nightingale. He knew the blackbird's, full and rich and dark like the bird itself and deep like the summer shadow of the closing wood, and with the voices of thrushes the blackbirds' song filled all the wood with bell-sounds and belling echoes.

Beyond the wood the day was clear and hot. The grass was high to his knees and the ground, falling away, was marshy in places, with mounds of sedge, as it ran down towards the back-brook and the river. He walked with his eyes on the ground, partly because of oozy holes among the sedge, partly because he hoped to see the brown ring of a moorhen's nest in the marshier places.

It was because of his way of walking that he did not see, for some time, a girl standing up to her knees in red-ochre mud, among half-floating beds of dark-green cresses. But suddenly he lifted his head and saw her standing there, bare-legged and bare-armed, staring at him as if she had been watching him for a long time. Her brown osier cress-basket was like a two-bushel measure and was slung over her shoulder with a strap.

'You don't live here,' she said.

'No,' he said. 'Do you?'

'Over there,' she said. 'In that house.'

'Which house?' He could not see a house.

'You come here and you can see it,' she said.

When he had picked his way through tufts of sedge to where

she was standing in the bed of cresses he still could not see a
house, either about the wood or across the meadows on the rising
ground beyond.

'You can see the chimney smoking,' she said.

'It's not a house. It's a hut,' he said.

'That's where we live.'

'All the time?'

'Yes,' she said. 'You're sinking in.'

The toes of his boots were slowly drowning in red-ochre
water.

'If you're coming out here you'd better take your shoes and
stockings off,' she said.

A moment or two later his bare feet were cool in the water.
She was gathering cresses quickly, cutting them off with an old
shoe-knife, leaving young sprigs and trailing skeins of white root
behind. She was older than himself, nine or ten, he thought, and
her hair hung ribbonless and uncombed, a brown colour, rather
like the colour of the basket, down her back.

'Can I gather?' he said, and she said, yes, if he knew what
brook-lime was.

'I know brook-lime,' he said. 'Everybody knows brook-lime.'

'Then which is it? Show me which it is. Which is brook-lime?'

That was almost as bad, he thought, as being nagged by Sar'
Ann. The idea that he did not know brook-lime from cress
seemed to him a terrible insult and a pain. He snatched up a
piece in irritation but it did not break and came up instead from
the mud-depths in a long rope of dripping red-black slime, spat-
tering his shirt and trousers.

She laughed at this and he laughed too. Her voice, he thought,
sounded cracked, as if she were hoarse from shouting or a cold.
The sound of it carried a long way. He heard it crack over the
meadows and the river with a coarse broken sort of screech that
was like the slitting of rag in the deep oppressive afternoon.

He never knew till long afterwards how much he liked that
sound. She repeated it several times during the afternoon. In the
same cracked voice she laughed at questions he asked or things
he did not know. In places the water, shallower, was warm on
his feet, and the cresses were a dark polished green in the sun.
She laughed because he did not know that anyone could live by
gathering cresses. He must be a real town boy, she said. There

was only she and her father, she told him, and she began to tell what he afterwards knew were beautiful lies about the way they got up every other day at two in the morning and tramped out to sell cresses in Evensford and Bedford and towns about the valley.

'But the shops aren't open then,' he said and that made her laugh again, cracked and thin, with that long slitting echo across the drowsy meadows.

'It's not in the shops we sell them,' she said. 'It's in the streets – don't you know that? – in the streets—'

And suddenly she lifted her head and drew back her throat and yelled the cry she used in the streets. He had heard that cry before, high and long and melancholy, like a call across lonely winter marshes in its slow fall and dying away, and there was to be a time in his life when it died for ever and he never heard it again :

'Watercree-ee-ee-ee-ee-s! Fresh cre-ee-ee-ee-ee-ee-s! Lovely fresh watercre-ee-ee-ee-ee-ee-s!'

Standing up to his knees in water, his hands full of wet cresses and slimy skeins of roots dripping red mud down his shirt and trousers, he listened to that fascinating sound travelling like a bird-cry, watery and not quite earthly, down through the spinney and the meadows of buttercup and the places where the pike were supposed to lie.

His eyes must have been enormous and transfixed in his head as he listened, because suddenly she broke the note of the cry and laughed at him again and then said :

'You do it. You see if you can do it—'

What came out of his mouth was like a little soprano trill compared with her own full-throated, long-carrying cry. It made her laugh again and she said :

'You ought to come with us. Come with us tomorrow – how long are you staying here?'

'Only today.'

'I don't know where we'll go tomorrow,' she said. 'Evensford, I think. Sometimes we go forty or fifty miles – miles and miles. We go to Buckingham market sometimes – that's forty miles—'

'Evensford,' he said. 'That's where I come from. I could see you there if you go.'

'All right,' she said. 'Where will you be? We come in by *The Waggon and Horses* – down the hill, that way.'

'I'll be at *The Waggon and Horses* waiting for you,' he said. 'What time?'

'You be there at five o'clock,' she said. 'Then I'll learn you how to do it, like this – watercree-ee-ee-ee-ee-ee-ee-s! Fresh cree-ee-ee-ee-ee-ee-ee-s! Lovely fresh watercree-ee-ee-ee-ee-s!'

As the sound died away it suddenly seemed to him that he had been there, up to his knees in water, a very long time, perhaps throughout the entire length of the sultry, sun-flushed afternoon. He did not know what time it was. He was cut off from the world of Aunt Prunes and Sar' Ann and his grandfather, the little house and the white pinks and the gooseberry trees, the big boring book whose pages and dead flowers turned over in whispers.

He knew that he ought to go back and said:

'I got to go now. I'll see you tomorrow though – I'll be there. Five o'clock.'

'Yes, you be there,' she said. She wiped a may-fly from her face with her forearm, drawing water and mud across it, and then remembered something. 'You want some cresses for tea? You can take some.'

She plunged her hands into the basket and brought them out filled with cresses. They were cool and wet; and he thought, not only then but long afterwards, that they were the nicest things perhaps anyone had ever given him.

'So long,' she said.

'So long.' That was another funny expression, he thought. He could never understand people who said so long when they seemed to mean, as he did, soon.

She waved her hands, spilling arcs of water-drops in the sun, as he climbed the stile into the spinney and went back. He did his best to wave in answer, but his shoes and stockings were too wet to wear and his hands were full with them and the cresses. Instead he simply stood balanced for a moment on the top bar of the stile, so that she could see him well and then call to him for the last time:

'Cree-ee-ee-ee-ee-es! Lovely fresh cree-ee-ee-ee-ee-es!'

It was only Aunt Prunes who was not angry with him. His grandfather called him 'A young gallus,' and kept saying, 'Where the Hanover've you bin all the time? God A'mighty, you'll git me hung. I'll be burned if I don't git hung,' and Sar' Ann flew about the kitchen with the squawks of a trapped hen, telling him:

'You know what happens to little boys what git wet-foot? And look at your shirt! They git their death, they catch their death. And don't you know who them folks are? Gyppos – that's all they are. Gyppos – they nick things, they live on other folks. That's the sort of folks they are. Don't you go near such folks again – they'll very like keep you and take you away and you'll never see nobody who knows you again. Then we'll find you in the bury-hole.'

But he was not afraid of that and Aunt Prunes only said:

'You didn't bring me my flowers, did you? I like watercress though. I'm glad you brought the watercress. I can have it with my tea.'

It was late before they could start for home again. That was because his socks and shirt took a long time to dry and his shirt had to have an iron run over it several times in case, Sar' Ann kept saying, his mother had a fit. Before getting up into the trap he had to kiss both Sar' Ann and Aunt Prunes, and for some moments he was lost in the horror of the big globular spectacles reflecting and magnifying the evening sun, and then in the friendliness of the dark moustaches below which the warm mouth smiled and said:

'How would you like to stay with me one day? Just you and me in the summer. Would you?'

'Yes,' he said.

'Then you come and see me again, won't you, soon?'

He said Yes, he would see her soon. But in fact he did not see her soon or later or at any time again. He did not go to that house again until he was grown up. That was the day they were burying her and when the cork of silence that passed over the grave had blown out again he felt he could hear nothing but the gassy voice of Sar' Ann, who was old by then but still with the same fierce roving globular eyes, shrilly reminding him of the day he had gathered cresses.

'I'll bet you would never know her now,' she said, 'that girl, would you? Would you ever know that this was her?'

Then she was by his side and he was talking to her: the girl who had gathered the cresses, the same girl who had called with that screeching, melancholy, marshy cry across the summer afternoon. She was all in black and her hat had a purple feather in the crown. He remembered the little hut and the brown osier basket on her lithe thin shoulders and he asked her where she lived and what she was doing now. 'In the new houses,' she said. 'I'm Mrs Corbett now.' She took him to the garden hedge and pointed out to him blocks of bricks, like the toys of gigantic children, red and raw and concrete fenced, lining the road above the valley. That was the road where he and his grandfather had driven down on that distant summer morning, when the beans were in flower and he had got so mixed with his relatives and had wondered how Aunt Prunes had spelled her name.

'That's us,' she said. She pointed with stout and podgy finger, a trifle nervously but with pride, across the fields. 'The second one. The one with the television. Have you got television?'

'No.'

'You ought to have it,' she said. 'It's wonderful to see things so far away. Don't you think it's wonderful?'

'Wonderful,' he said.

But on the night he drove home as a boy, watching the sky of high summer turn from blue to palest violet and then more richly to purple bronze and the final green-gold smokiness of twilight, he did not know these things. He sat still on the cushions of the trap, staring ahead. The evening was full of the scent of bean flowers and he was searching for early stars.

'Shall we light the lamps?' he said.

And presently they lit the lamps. They too were golden. They seemed to burn with wonderful brightness, lighting the grasses of the roadside and the flowers of the ditches and the crowns of fading may. And though he did not know it then they too were fading, for all their brightness. They too were dying, along with the things he had done and seen and loved: the little house, the cuckoo day, the tender female moustaches and the voice of the watercress girl.

THE COWSLIP FIELD

Pacey sat on the stile, swinging her legs and her cowslip-basket.

Pacey, he thought, was by far the littlest lady he had ever seen. She had very thick dumpy legs and black squashy button boots and a brown felt hat under which bright blue eyes roamed about like jellyfish behind large sun-shot spectacles. On her cheek, just under her right eye, was a big furry brown mole that looked like the top of a bullrush that had been cut off and stuck there.

Pacey was nice, though. He liked Pacey.

'How far is it now to the cowslip field, Pacey?' he said.

'A step or two furder yit,' Pacey said.

'It's not *furder*,' he said. 'It's *further*.'

'Oh! is't?' Pacey said. 'All right, it's *further*. I never knew such a boy for pickin' me up afore I'm down.'

'And it's not *afore*,' he said. 'It's *before*.'

'Oh! is't?' Pacey said. 'All right, *before* then. I never knowed sich a boy for whittlin' on me—'

'And it's not *on*,' he said. 'It's *of*—'

'Here,' Pacey said, 'for goodness' sake catch holt o' the cowslip-basket and let me git down and let's git on. Else we'll never be there afore bull's-noon.'

When Pacey jumped down from the stile her legs sank almost to the top of her button boots in meadow grasses. She was so thick and squatty that she looked like a duck waddling to find the path across the field.

In that field the sun lay hot on sheets of buttercups. Soon when he looked at Pacey's boots they were dusty yellow faces, with rows of funny grinning eyes. At the end of the field rolled long white hedges of hawthorn, thick and foamy as the breakers he had once seen at the seaside, and from a row of sharp green larches, farther on, he heard a cuckoo call.

It was past the time when the larches had little scarlet eye-lashes springing from their branches but he still remembered them.

'Pacey,' he said, 'why do the trees have—'

'Jist hark at that cuckoo,' Pacey said. 'Afore long it'll charm us all to death.'

'Pacey,' he said, 'why don't cowslips grow in this field?'

'Because it ain't a cowslip field,' Pacey said, 'don't you know that? Don't you know the difference between a cowslip field and a buttercup field? If you don't it's time you did. Now you jis run on and git to the next stile and sit there quiet and wait fer me.'

From the next stile he sat and watched Pacey waddling down the slope of the field, between dazzling sheets of buttercups, under a dazzling high blue sky. In the wide May morning she looked more than ever like a floundering little duck, funnier, tinier than ever.

'Pacey,' he said, 'will you ever grow any bigger?'

'Not unless me luck changes a lot more'n it's done up to yit.'

'Will I grow any bigger?'

' 'Course you will.'

'Well then, why won't you?'

'Hark at that cuckoo,' Pacey said. 'If it's called once this morning, it's called a thousand times.'

In the next field brown and white cows were grazing and Pacey took his hand. Some of the cows stood at a pond, over their hocks in water, flicking flies from their white-patched brown rumps in the sun. All across the field there were many ant-hills and Pacey let him run up and down them, as if they were switchbacks, always holding his hand.

Her own hands were rough and clammy and warm and he liked them.

'What do the ants do in their ant-hills all the time, Pacey?' he said.

'They git on with their work,' Pacey said, ' 'ithout chattering so much.'

As they passed the pond he could smell the thick warm odours of may-bloom and fresh dung that the cows had dropped and mud warming in the sun. All the smell of rising summer was in the air. The tips of a few bulrushes, so brown and so like Pacey's mole, were like the last tips of winter, half-strangled by rising reeds.

Then somehow he knew that the next field was the cowslip field and he suddenly broke free of Pacey's hand and ran jumping over the last of the ant-hills until he stood on a small plank bridge that went over a narrow stream where brook-lime grew among bright eyes of wild forget-me-not.

'Pacey, Pacey, Pacey!' he started shouting. 'Pacey!'

He knew he had never seen, in all his life, so many cowslips. They covered with their trembling orange heads all the earth between himself and the horizon. When a sudden breeze caught them they ducked and darted very gently away from it and then blew gently back again.

'We'll never gather them all before it's dark, Pacey,' he said, 'will we?'

'Run and git as many as you can,' Pacey said. 'It won't be dark yit awhile.'

Running, he tripped and fell among cowslips. He did not bother to get to his feet but simply knelt there, in a cowslip forest, picking at the juicy stems. All the fragrance of the field blew down on him along a warm wind that floated past him to shake from larches and oaks and hedges of may-bloom a continuous belling fountain of cuckoo calls.

When he turned to look for Pacey she too was on her knees, dumpier, squattier than ever, filling her hands with golden sheaves of flower.

'Pacey, what will we do with them all?' he said. 'What will we do with them all?'

'Mek wine,' Pacey said. 'And I wouldn't be surprised if it were a drop o' good.'

Soon he was running to Pacey with his own sheaves of flower, putting them into the big brown basket. Whenever he ran he buried his face in the heads of flower that were so rich and fragrant and tender. Then as he dropped them into the basket he could not resist dipping his hands into the growing mound of cowslips. They felt like little limp kid gloves. They were so many soft green and yellow fingers.

'The basket'll soon be full, Pacey,' he said. 'What will we do when the basket's full?'

'Put 'em in we hats,' Pacey said. 'Hang 'em round we necks or summat.'

'Like chains?'

'Chains if you like,' Pacey said.

Soon the basket was almost full and Pacey kept saying it was bloomin' hot work and that she could do with a wet and a wind.

From a pocket in her skirt she took out a medicine bottle of milk
and two cheese cakes and presently he and Pacey were sitting
down in the sea of cowslips, resting in the sun.

'The basket's nearly full,' he said. 'Shall we start making
chains?'

'There'll be no peace until you do, I warrant.'

'Shall we make one chain or two chains?'

'Two,' Pacey said. 'I'll mek a big 'un and you mek a little
'un.'

As he sat there threading the cowslip stalks one into another,
making his chain, he continually looked up at Pacey, peering in
her funny way, through her thick jelly spectacles, at her own
cowslip chain. He noticed that she held the flowers very close to
her eyes, only an inch or two away.

'Pacey,' he said, 'what makes the sky blue?'

'You git on with your chain,' Pacey said.

'Who put the sky there?'

'God did.'

'How does it stay up there?'

Pacey made a noise like a cat spitting and put a cowslip stalk
into her mouth and sucked it as if it were cotton and she were
threading a needle.

'How the 'nation can I thread this 'ere chain,' she said, 'if you
keep a-iffin' and a-whyin' all the time?'

Squinting, she peered even more closely at her cowslips, so
that they were now almost at the end of her nose. Then he remembered that that was how she sang from her hymn-book on
Sundays, in the front row of the choir. He remembered too how
his mother always said that the ladies in the front row of the
choir sat there only to show off their hats and so that men could
look at them.

'Have you got a young man, Pacey?' he said.

'Oh! dozens,' Pacey said. 'Scores.'

'Which one do you like best?'

'Oh! they're like plums on a tree,' Pacey said. 'So many I don't
know which one on 'em to pick.'

'Will you get married, Pacey?'

Pacey sucked a cowslip stalk and threaded it through another.

'Oh! they all want to marry me,' Pacey said. 'All on 'em.'

'When will you?'

'This year, next year,' Pacey said. 'When I git enough plum-stones.'

'Why do you have to have plum-stones?'

'Oh! jist hark at that cuckoo all the time,' Pacey said. 'Charming us to death a'ready. How's your chain?'

His chain was not so long as Pacey's. She worked neatly and fast, in spite of her thick stumpy fingers. Her chain was as long as a necklace already, with the cowslips ruffled close together, but his own was not much more than a loose golden bracelet.

'Thread twothri more on it,' Pacey said, 'and then we can git we hats filled and go home to dinner.'

When he looked up again from threading his last two cowslip stalks he saw that Pacey had taken off her brown felt hat. Her uncovered hair was very dark and shining in the sun. At the back it was coiled up into a rich, thick roll, like a heavy sausage. There seemed almost too much hair for her stumpy body and he stared at it amazed.

'Is that all your hair, Pacey?' he said.

'Well, it's what they dished out to me. I ain't had another issue yit.'

'How long is it?' he said. 'It must be very long.'

'Prit near down to me waist.'

'Oh! Pacey,' he said.

As he finished threading his cowslip chain and then joined the ends together he sat staring at Pacey, with her dark hair shining against the blue May sky and her own cowslip chain lying like a gold-green necklace in her lap.

'Does your hair ever come down?' he said, 'or does it always stay up like that?'

'Oh! it comes down a time or two now and agin.'

'Let it come down now.'

'It's time to go home to dinner,' Pacey said. 'We got to git back—'

'Please, Pacey,' he said. 'Please.'

'You take your hat and git it filled with cowslips and then we can go—'

'Please,' he said. 'Then I can put my chain on top of your head and it'll look like a crown.'

'Oh! you'd wheedle a whelk out of its shell, you would,' Pacey said. 'You'd wheedle round 'Im up there!'

As she spoke she lifted her face to the blue noon sky so that her spectacles flashed strangely, full of revolving light. A moment later she started to unpin the sausage at the back of her head, putting the black hairpins one by one into her mouth. Then slowly, like an unrolling blind, the massive coil of her hair fell down across her neck and shoulders and back, until it reached her waist.

He had never seen hair so long, or so much of it, and he stared at it with wide eyes as it uncoiled itself, black and shining against the golden cowslip field.

'That's it,' Pacey said, 'have a good stare.'

'Now I've got to put the crown on you,' he said.

He knelt by Pacey's lap and reached up, putting his cowslip chain on the top of her head. All the time he did this Pacey sat very still, staring towards the sun.

'Now yours,' he said.

He reached up, draping Pacey's own longer necklace across her hair and shoulders. The black hair made the cowslips shine more deeply golden than before and the flowers in turn brought out the lights in the hair.

Pacey sat so still and staring as he did all this that he could not tell what she was thinking and suddenly, without asking, he reached up and took off her spectacles.

A strange transformed woman he did not know, with groping blue eyes, a crown on her head and a necklace locking the dark mass of her hair, stared back at him.

'Well, now I suppose you're satisfied?'

'You look very nice, Pacey,' he said. 'You look lovely. I like you.'

'Well, if you're satisfied let's git ready and start back,' Pacey said, 'or else I be blamed if we shan't miss we dinners.'

Hastily, half-blindly, she started to grope with her hands towards her hair.

'And put my specs back on!' she said. 'You took 'em off. Now put 'em back. How the 'nation do you think I can see 'ithout them?'

'It's not *'ithout*,' he said. 'It's *without*.'

'Oh! *without* then! But put 'em back!'

By the time they began to walk back home his hat was full of cowslips. Pacey's brown felt hat was full too and the basket was brimming over with the flowers that were so like tender, kid-gloved fingers.

At the plank across the stream, as Pacey set down the basket and rested for a moment, he turned and looked back. Once again, as before, the cowslips seemed to stretch without break between himself and the bright noon sky.

'There's just as many as when we came,' he said. 'We didn't make any difference at all, Pacey. You'd think we'd never been, wouldn't you?'

Suddenly, with a cry, Pacey seized him and picked him up, swinging him joyfully round her body and finally holding him upside down.

'Up, round and down!' Pacey said. 'Now what can you see?'

'London!'

Pacey laughed loudly, swinging him a second time and then setting him on his feet again.

When he tried to stand still again he found that the world too was swinging. The cowslip field was rolling like a golden sea in the sun and there was a great trembling about Pacey's hair, her necklace and her little crown of gold.

GREAT UNCLE CROW

Once in the summer time, when the water-lilies were in bloom and the wheat was new in ear, his grandfather took him on a long walk up the river, to see his Uncle Crow. He had heard so much of Uncle Crow, so much that was wonderful and to be marvelled at, and for such a long time, that he knew him to be, even before that, the most remarkable fisherman in the world.

'Masterpiece of a man, your Uncle Crow,' his grandfather said. 'He could git a clothes-line any day and tie a brick on it and a mossel of cake and go out and catch a pike as long as your arm.'

When he asked what kind of cake his grandfather seemed irritated and said it was just like a boy to ask questions of that sort.

'Any kind o' cake,' he said. 'Plum cake. Does it matter? Carraway cake. Christmas cake if you like. Anything. I shouldn't wonder if he could catch a pretty fair pike with a cold baked tater.'

'Only a pike?'

'Times,' his grandfather said, 'I've seen him sittin' on the bank on a sweltering hot day like a furnace, when nobody was gittin' a bite not even off a bloodsucker. And there your Uncle Crow'd be a-pullin' 'em but by the dozen, like a man shellin' harvest beans.'

'And how does he come to be my Uncle Crow?' he said, 'if my mother hasn't got a brother? Nor my father.'

'Well,' his grandfather said, 'he's really your mother's own cousin, if everybody had their rights. But all on us call him Uncle Crow.'

'And where does he live?'

'You'll see,' his grandfather said. 'All by hisself. In a little titty bit of a house, by the river.'

The little titty bit of a house, when he first saw it, surprised him very much. It was not at all unlike a black tarred boat that had either slipped down a slope and stuck there on its way to launching or one that had been washed up and left there in a flood. The roof of brown tiles had a warp in it and the sides were mostly built, he thought, of tarred beer-barrels.

The two windows with their tiny panes were about as large as chessboards and Uncle Crow had nailed underneath each of them a sill of sheet tin that was still a brilliant blue, each with the words 'Backache Pills' in white lettering on it, upside down.

On all sides of the house grew tall feathered reeds. They enveloped it like gigantic whispering corn. Some distance beyond the great reeds the river went past in a broad slow arc, on magnificent kingly currents, full of long white islands of water-lilies, as big as china breakfast cups, shining and yellow-hearted in the sun.

He thought, on the whole, that that place, the river with the water-lilies, the little titty bit of a house, and the great forest of reeds talking between soft brown beards, was the nicest place he had ever seen.

'Anybody about?' his grandfather called. 'Crow! – anybody at home?'

The door of the house was partly open, but at first there was no answer. His grandfather pushed open the door still farther with his foot. The reeds whispered down by the river and were answered, in the house, by a sound like the creek of bed springs.

'Who is't?'

'It's me, Crow,' his grandfather called. 'Lukey. Brought the boy over to have a look at you.'

A big gangling red-faced man with rusty hair came to the door. His trousers were black and very tight. His eyes were a smeary vivid blue, the same colour as the stripes of his shirt, and his trousers were kept up by a leather belt with brass escutcheons on it, like those on horses' harness.

'Thought very like you'd be out a-pikin',' his grandfather said.

'Too hot. How's Lukey boy? Ain't seed y' lately, Lukey boy.'

His lips were thick and very pink and wet, like cow's lips. He made a wonderful erupting jolly sound somewhat between a belch and a laugh.

'Comin' in it a minute?'

In the one room of the house was an iron bed with an old red check horse-rug spread over it and a stone copper in one corner and a bare wooden table with dirty plates and cups and a tin kettle on it. Two osier baskets and a scythe stood in another corner.

Uncle Crow stretched himself full length on the bed as if he was very tired. He put his knees in the air. His belly was tight as a bladder of lard in his black trousers, which were mossy green on the knees and seat.

'How's the fishin'?' his grandfather said. 'I bin tellin' the boy—'

Uncle Crow belched deeply. From where the sun struck full on the tarred wall of the house there was a hot whiff of baking tar. But when Uncle Crow belched there was a smell like the smell of yeast in the air.

'It ain't bin all that much of a summer yit,' Uncle Crow said. 'Ain't had the rain.'

'Not like that summer you catched the big 'un down at Archer's Mill. I recollect you a-tellin' on me—'

'Too hot and dry by half,' Uncle Crow said. 'Gits in your gullet like chaff.'

'You recollect that summer?' his grandfather said. 'Nobody else a-fetching on 'em out only you—'

'Have a drop o' neck-oil,' Uncle Crow said.

The boy wondered what neck-oil was and presently, to his surprise, Uncle Crow and his grandfather were drinking it. It came out of a dark-green bottle and it was a clear bright amber, like cold tea, in the two glasses.

'The medder were yeller with 'em,' Uncle Crow said. 'Yeller as a guinea.'

He smacked his lips with a marvellously juicy, fruity sound. The boy's grandfather gazed at the neck-oil and said he thought it would be a corker if it was kept a year or two, but Uncle Crow said:

'Trouble is, Lukey boy, it's a terrible job to keep it. You start tastin' on it to see if it'll keep and then you taste on it again and you go on tastin' on it until they ain't a drop left as 'll keep.'

Uncle Crow laughed so much that the bed springs cackled underneath his bouncing trousers.

'Why is it called neck-oil?' the boy said.

'Boy,' Uncle Crow said, 'when you git older, when you git growed-up, you know what'll happen to your gullet?'

'No.'

'It'll git sort o' rusted up inside. Like a old gutter pipe. So's you can't swaller very easy. Rusty as old Harry it'll git. You know that, boy?'

'No.'

'Well, it will. I'm tellin', on y'. And you know what y' got to do then?'

'No.'

'Every now and then you gotta git a drop o' neck-oil down it. So's to ease it. A drop o' neck-oil every once in a while – that's what you gotta do to keep the rust out.'

The boy was still contemplating the curious prospect of his neck rusting up inside in later years when Uncle Crow said: 'Boy, you go outside and jis' round the corner you'll see a bucket. You bring handful o' cresses out on it. I'll bet you're hungry, ain't you?'

'A little bit.'

He found the watercresses in the bucket, cool in the shadow of the little house, and when he got back inside with them Uncle Crow said:

'Now you put the cresses on that there plate there and then put your nose inside that there basin and see what's inside. What is't, eh?'

'Eggs.'

'Ought to be fourteen on 'em. Four-apiece and two over. What sort are they, boy?'

'Moor-hens'.'

'You got a knowin' boy here, Lukey,' Uncle Crow said. He dropped the scaly red lid of one eye like an old cockerel going to sleep. He took another drop of neck-oil and gave another fruity, juicy laugh as he heaved his body from the bed. 'A very knowin' boy.'

Presently he was carving slices of thick brown bread with a great horn-handled shut-knife and pasting each slice with summery golden butter. Now and then he took another drink of neck-oil and once he said:

'You get the salt pot, boy, and empty a bit out on that there saucer, so's we can all dip in.'

Uncle Crow slapped the last slice of bread on to the buttered pile and then said:

'Boy, you take that there jug there and go a step or two up the path and dip yourself a drop o' spring water. You'll see it. It comes out of a little bit of a wall, jist by a doddle-willer.'

When the boy got back with the jug of spring water Uncle Crow was opening another bottle of neck-oil and his grandfather was saying: 'God a-mussy man, goo steady. You'll have me agooin' one way and another—'

'Man alive,' Uncle Crow said, 'and what's wrong with that?'

Then the watercress, the salt, the moor-hens' eggs, the spring water, and the neck-oil were all ready. The moor-hens' eggs were hard-boiled. Uncle Crow lay on the bed and cracked them with his teeth, just like big brown nuts, and said he thought the watercress was just about as nice and tender as a young lady.

'I'm sorry we ain't got the gold plate out though. I had it out a-Sunday.' He closed his old cockerel-lidded eye again and licked his tongue backwards and forwards across his lips and dipped another peeled egg in salt. 'You know what I had for my dinner a-Sunday, boy?'

'No.'

'A pussy-cat on a gold plate. Roasted with broad-beans and new taters. Did you ever heerd talk of anybody eatin' a roasted pussy-cat, boy?'

'Yes.'

'You did?'

'Yes,' he said, 'that's a hare.'

'You got a very knowin' boy here, Lukey,' Uncle Crow said. 'A very knowin' boy.'

Then he screwed up a big dark-green bouquet of watercress and dipped it in salt until it was entirely frosted and then crammed it in one neat wholesale bite into his soft pink mouth.

'But not on a gold plate?' he said.

He had to admit that.

'No, not on a gold plate,' he said.

All that time he thought the fresh watercress, the moor-hens' eggs, the brown bread-and-butter, and the spring water were the most delicious, wonderful things he had ever eaten in the world. He felt that only one thing was missing. It was that whenever his grandfather spoke of fishing Uncle Crow simply took another draught of neck-oil.

'When are you goin' to take us fishing?' he said.

'You et up that there egg,' Uncle Crow said. 'That's the last one. You et that there egg up and I'll tell you what.'

'What about gooin' as far as that big deep hole where the chub lay?' grandfather said. 'Up by the back-brook—'

'I'll tell you what, boy,' Uncle Crow said, 'you git your grandfather to bring you over September time, of a morning, afore the steam's off the winders. Mushroomin' time. You come over and we'll have a bit o' bacon and mushroom for breakfast and then set into the pike. You see, boy, it ain't the pikin' season now. It's too hot. Too bright. It's too bright of afternoon, and they ain't a-bitin'.'

He took a long rich swig of neck-oil.

'Ain't that it, Lukey? That's the time, ain't it, mushroom time?'

'Thass it,' his grandfather said.

'Tot out,' Uncle Crow said. 'Drink up. My throat's jist easin' orf a bit.'

He gave another wonderful belching laugh and told the boy to be sure to finish up the last of the watercress and the bread-and-butter. The little room was rich with the smell of neck-oil, and the tarry sun-baked odour of the beer-barrels that formed its walls. And through the door came, always, the sound of reeds talking in their beards, and the scent of summer meadows drifting in from beyond the great curl of the river with its kingly currents and its islands of full blown lilies, white and yellow in the sun.

'I see the wheat's in ear,' his grandfather said. 'Ain't that the time for tench, when the wheat's in ear?'

'Mushroom time,' Uncle Crow said. 'That's the time. You git mushroom time here, and I'll fetch you a tench out as big as a cricket bat.'

He fixed the boy with an eye of wonderful, watery, glassy blue and licked his lips with a lazy tongue, and said:

'You know what colour a tench is, boy?'

'Yes,' he said.

'What colour?'

'The colour of the neck-oil.'

'Lukey,' Uncle Crow said, 'you got a very knowin' boy here. A very knowin' boy.'

After that, when there were no more cresses or moor-hens' eggs or bread-and-butter to eat, and his grandfather said he'd get hung if he touched another drop of neck-oil, he and his grandfather walked home across the meadows.

'What work does Uncle Crow do?' he said.

'Uncle Crow? Work? – well, he ain't – Uncle Crow? Well, he works, but he ain't what you'd call a reg'lar worker—'

All the way home he could hear the reeds talking in their beards. He could see the water-lilies that reminded him so much of the gold and white inside the moor-hens' eggs. He could hear the happy sound of Uncle Crow laughing and sucking at the neck-oil, and crunching the fresh salty cresses into his mouth in the tarry little room.

He felt happy, too, and the sun was a gold plate in the sky.

THE ENCHANTRESS

Nearly fifty years ago I knew her as a rather plump, fair-skinned child with eyes of brilliant hyacinth blue and long ribbonless blonde hair that hung half way down her back in curls.

Her mother was a gaunt, hungry faced, prematurely aged woman who, with sickly yellow eyes sunk far into her head behind steel-rimmed spectacles, treadled feverishly all day and half the night at a sewing machine, in a black dress and apron, closing boot uppers, in the dirty window of a little house in one of the narrow yards we used as short cuts at the railway end of the town. Her father was an ex-pug grown coarse and fat who worked little, boozed a lot and spent most of his time in a pub called *The Waterloo*, re-telling for friends and strangers alike the story of how – incredibly as a light-weight – he had won impermanent fame and a silver belt as a champion twenty years before.

On Sundays her mother skulked furtively to Methodist Chapel, wearing a black dress that might well have been the one she worked in, an old black straw hat without trimmings and black button boots worn badly down at the heel, looking like the poorest of the poor. In a town like Evensford, where boots and shoes are made, even the poor have no way of acquiring public derision more swiftly than to be seen in boots or shoes that need heeling badly. It is not merely a point of honour not to do such things; it incurs a sharp communal scorn. But no one felt either scorn or derision for Mrs Jackson. Nor did anyone ever seem to know the cause of her state of perpetual mourning, but as the years went past I guessed – correctly – that it was not mourning at all. She was merely saving for Bertha.

The yard in which they lived was no more than a slum alley eight or nine feet wide and only those who lived there knew what went on behind the narrow backways that, bounded by fearsome little privies on either side, were no more than naked asphalt squares from which the fences had been ripped down. That

372

stretch of the town, low down by the station, was called The Pit. To come from The Pit was the social equivalent of having leprosy. Sometimes a deaf mute, a scrawny wild-eyed man of thirty or so, stood guarding the upper end of it, making the noises of a caged animal and spitting at passers-by. It was a place of loafers playing crown-and-anchor under smoky walls, of yelling women in perpetual curling rags and men's caps who leered down to *The Waterloo* with beer jugs in their hands and made twice-weekly visits, with rattling prams, to pop-shops.

On Mondays Bertha's mother went to the pop-shop too; on Saturdays she redeemed whatever she had pawned. It is my guess that she went about in apparently perpetual mourning only because whatever clothes she otherwise possessed were in almost eternal pawn. And they were there because of Bertha.

Even as early as these days they started calling Bertha the princess. At ten she was already big for her age. She had already a clean, splendid sumptous bloom about her. Her eyes were most wonderfully clear and brilliant, with a great touch of calm and candid pride about them. Her hair was magnificent. It is quite common to see young girls with hair of palest bleached yellow and of extraordinary lightness in texture, but Bertha was the only child I ever saw whose hair was the colour of thistledown and of exactly the same lovely insubstantial airy quality.

She was always beautifully dressed. It used to be said that her mother, sitting up into the small hours or surreptitiously working on Sunday afternoons, made all her dresses for her, but years later I met a woman, one of two sisters, the proprietress of a very good class dress shop at the other end of the town, who said:

'Oh! no. Bertha's clothes all came from here. We made them for her, my sister and I. And her underclothes. I suppose it would surprise you to know that that child never had anything but pillow lace on her petticoats? And always paid for.'

At thirteen she already looked like a girl of sixteen or seventeen. She was tall, with full sloping shoulders and a firm high bust. Her legs were the sort of legs that make men turn round in the street, at least once if not twice, and she had a certain languid way of swinging her arms, with a backward graceful pull, as she walked. All this time her mother sat at the little window in the yard, treadling with sick desperation, almost insanely, at the sewing machine, and her father sat in *The Waterloo*, working his way through the chronicles of his history as a light-weight. You never saw them together.

At fourteen she put her hair up. There was a good deal of it – it had been her mother's eternal pride never to cut it at all – and now, not so light in colour, though still very blonde and airy in texture, it made her seem an inch or two taller, giving her better proportions.

By this time she was working in a boot factory. In those days women went to work in the oldest clothes they could find, pretty shabbily sometimes and often in the sort of thin black apron that Bertha's mother wore, but Bertha went to the factory exactly as she had previously gone to school: with her own impeccable quality, beautifully, fastidiously dressed.

Already, by now, she looked like a young woman of twenty and already, people began to say, you could see all the old, eternal danger signs. It was only a question of time before girls of sensational early maturity found themselves in trouble, disgraced and tasting the fruits of bitter unlearned lessons. Girls of fourteen who went out of their way to look like women of twenty, dealing in the deliberate coinage of voluptuous attractions, had only themselves to blame if they bought what they asked for. The time had come for Bertha's fall.

Just under three years later she astounded everybody by suddenly getting married – quite undisgraced – to a retired leather dresser with a modest income, a most respectable Edwardian house enclosed by an orchard of apple and pear trees and a taste for driving out in a landau, in straw hat and cream alpaca suit, on summer afternoons.

William James Sherwood was a neat, courteous, decorous man of the old school, very gentlemanly and of quiet habits; and the whole thing was a sensation. No one could say how it happened.

'But she comes from The Pit!' they said. 'She's from The Pit! From *there*. And seventeen. How do you suppose it happened? What possessed him?'

When a man of seventy marries a girl of seventeen who is remarkably mature, fastidious and beautiful for her age it never seems to occur to anyone that all that has possessed him is a firm dose of taste, enterprise and common sense. Consequently it did not occur to anyone that William Sherwood might have made, in Bertha, a good bargain for himself.

'But she's from The Pit!' they kept saying. 'She works in a factory. And the way she walks. The way she fancies herself. She isn't his kind. She can't be. Look who she comes from – the poorest of the poor. Her mother scraping and saving at shoe-work, her old man cooked every day in *The Waterloo*.'

Presently Bertha was to be seen driving out with William James Sherwood in a landau on fine summer afternoons. By the way she sat there, upright, composed, holding a parasol over her head, one hand resting lightly and decorously on the side of the carriage, you could have supposed that she had rarely done anything else but drive in landaus for the better part of her seventeen years. But there was something else still more surprising and more interesting about her. She looked supremely content and happy.

For the next three years she went on matching herself, her ways and her appearance to William James Sherwood. She behaved more like a woman contentedly settled in her middle thirties who had been born and brought up in a quiet country house, of good family, than a girl still in her teens who had been brought up in The Pit, on pawn-shop bread. Sometimes in summer you would see her not only driving out in the landau but walking, quietly, slowly and in thoughtful conversation, with William James Sherwood, in the orchard of apples and pears. They looked like a couple locked in the most harmonious tranquillity. It was easy to see that he was fond of her. His ways had obviously become her ways. In the swiftest and most unobtrusive fashion the daughter of The Pit, the child of the coarse ex-pug, had become a good wife, leaving all trace of any other self behind.

Then suddenly, when she was twenty, James William Sherwood slipped from a ladder while pruning a pear-tree, fell to a concrete path below and died of a haemorrhage two days later.

'Now watch her,' everybody said. 'She's got what she wanted. Now watch her let it rip. Now watch her slide.'

Sherwood died in January. One very hot oppressive evening in the following July I was walking slowly through the town, up to the tennis club, when a low green open sports car cut a corner as I was crossing, almost killed me and then roared away through

rapid changes of gears and the guttural grind of twin exhausts. I
had just time to catch sight of a man named Tom Pemberton at
the wheel, and a very fair, bare-headed girl with one arm round
his neck, before the car cut another corner and disappeared.

It was some minutes before it came to me that the girl was
Bertha, and the fact that I hadn't recognised her instantly was
due to an interesting thing. Bertha had bobbed her hair. Twenty
minutes later I walked into the tennis club and found her playing
tennis with Pemberton and a man named Saunders and another
girl whose name I can't remember. Saunders was a rather surly,
dark-eyed man of great virility who played tennis well above the
local average and Pemberton, though a fool in all other respects,
was as polished and fluent a player as you ever get in an ordinary
club.

I was still trying to recover from my astonishment that Bertha
was playing as well as any of them – in fact from my astonishment that she could play tennis at all – when I saw that Tom
Pemberton had been drinking. Though not actually drunk, he
threw the ball in the air several times and missed it and once,
missing a smash, he fell headlong into the net and lay underneath it cursing and giggling. Every time he did something of
this kind Bertha started giggling too.

It was plain, presently, to see that Saunders was tiring of this
and soon they were exchanging, hotly, some words about a ball
being on the wrong side of the line. Pemberton, I thought, was
less drunk than stupid. But Saunders was not the kind of man
who took any kind of argument very lightly and presently, surly
as a mongrel, he hit a ball deliberately high over the shrubberies
and into the street beyond.

The next thing I realised was that Pemberton was walking off
the court, followed by a cool, racy, slightly haughty Bertha who
looked, I thought, more striking than ever. But this was not what
impressed me, at that moment, most powerfully.

What impressed me so much was that she had trained herself
to Pemberton's pattern. She no longer looked like a woman
nestling down into the contentment of her middle thirties.
Though she was now a widow she looked, with her close-bobbed
hair, severe twentyish tennis frock, her low waist and short skirt
that showed her magnificent legs to superb advantage, like a
careless wild-headed girl of seventeen.

Five minutes later they were roaring away in Pemberton's sports car and older members of the club began to say, prophetically as it turned out, that Pemberton would kill himself before he was much older. And I actually heard her scream – with delight, not fear – as the car skidded round a bend.

I never cared much for Pemberton or indeed for men of Pemberton's upbringing, outlook and class. Tom was the only son of a wealthy boot-manufacturer who lived in a house of hideous château-like design surrounded by large conservatories with occasional diamonds of coloured glass in them. He had no need to be anything but empty headed and the father encouraged the condition by ceaseless indulgence with sports cars, open cheques, expensive suits and the ready payment of court fines whenever, as so often happened, Tom ran the sports car into lamp-posts, trees or even other sports cars. Drunk or sober, he always looked pitifully handsome, vacant, vain and without direction.

It occurred to me – I don't know why – that Bertha, who had married so unexpectedly and quietly into the gentility of James William Sherwood's septuagenarian household behind the pear-trees, was the very person to dispossess him of these unlikeable characteristics. I was wrong.

It was many years indeed before I grasped that Bertha never dispossessed anybody of anything. The truth about Bertha was in fact very slow in coming to me. All I thought I saw in the incident of the tennis club was a girl who, consorting with an idiot, had caught a rash of idiocy. It was too early for me to know that the same characteristics that had turned her temporarily into a decorous wife for an elderly gentleman were the very same as those that were now turning her into a flapper of loud clipped speech, skirts above her knees and a taste for wild parties at dubious clubs on riversides. Grieflessly, swiftly and with not the slightest pressure on the nerves of conscience she had slipped out of the part of widow as easily as she might have slipped out of one of her petticoats, taking on the new tone, new pattern and new outlook of another man.

About a year later Tom Pemberton, driving his car home very late and very fast one night in a thunderstorm, with Bertha at his side, crashed into a roadside tree for the last time.

By one of those strange tricks that surround violent and accidental death Pemberton was terribly mutilated while Bertha, thrown clear, landed with miraculous gentleness on grass, dazed but unbruised, as if she had slid gently down a helter-skelter at a fair.

Only a few weeks later a great scandal broke out in the town.

Bertha, by this time, had gone back to live with her mother in The Pit. It might have been supposed that the few hundred pounds James William Sherwood had left her would have revolutionised life behind the dark little front window and the treadle sewing machine. Nothing of the kind had happened. The sick, yellow-eyed figure went on treadling as desperately as ever; in *The Waterloo* the ex-pug unfolded to all who would listen his tale of light-weight triumphs; and Bertha, splendid and well dressed as ever, went back to the factory.

Two or three days after the death of Tom Pemberton a young curate named Ormsby-Hill called to see Bertha in The Pit, bearing the conventional condolences of the clergy and hoping, after the crash and its mutilations, that all was well as could be expected. Clergymen have a strange habit of calling on their sheep at awkward times and Ormsby-Hill, getting no answer at the front door of the house, which no one ever used anyway, went round to the back, among the miserable naked yards, just after six o'clock. The ex-pug, by that time, was already in *The Waterloo*, and Bertha's mother, free for a few minutes after the long day of treadling, was out doing shopping.

Bertha, big arms and chest bare in a sleeveless chemise, was at the kitchen sink, washing away her factory grime.

'Oh! come in if you can get in,' she said. She clearly remembered the young curate at Tom Pemberton's funeral. 'I'm afraid the kitchen's in a mess. Can you find a chair in the living room?'

Ormsby-Hill sat down in the little living room while Bertha, entirely unaffected, finished washing and drying herself in the kitchen. It was never very clear to me, nor I think to anyone else, why Ormsby-Hill had entered the church. He was in all ways the complete opposite of the young curate of convention. Big, bovine, sensuous-lipped, fond of beer and rugby football, he belonged to that class of clergymen, not I think so common now, who thought godliness should be muscular and the way to heaven a hearty free for all. He thought the gospel went down much better from clergymen who offered it while dressed in tweeds rather than dog collars, with pints of foaming ale in their hands rather than crucifixes and by means of sportsmen's services, sometimes actually held in pubs, where the congregation was roughly addressed as 'chaps.'

That evening he had gone to The Pit in trepidation, with some idea that Bertha was a wild bad girl. Nobody liked going down to The Pit if they didn't have to and Ormsby-Hill had been deliberately sent there on a distasteful errand by a vicar too squeamish to stomach the sordid alleyway of privies, louts playing crown-and-anchor on the asphalt and the deaf-mute keeping guard for a stray policeman at the top of the yard.

His surprise at seeing Bertha was very great. His surprise at hearing her voice for the first time was even greater.

With Tom Pemberton it had become a shrill, empty, fun-at-any-price sort of voice; during her marriage to James William Sherwood it had been a decorous, sympathetic toned-down voice of charm and understanding.

When Ormsby-Hill heard it for the first time it was a smooth, throaty voice, easy and rather casual: as if she had already decided what voice he would like her to have.

'I'll slip upstairs and put on a dress if you don't mind waiting,' she said. 'I won't be five minutes. I have to be at the dressmakers by seven anyway.'

When she came down, about five minutes later, she was wearing a sleeveless yellow dress with a low neck and a very short skirt and with it white cotton gloves and white high-heeled shoes. She was very fond of white and yellow clothes and once or twice later I used to see her in this dress. It was tight and smooth across her thighs and so short that it showed her pretty rounded knees to great advantage. She hardly ever wore a hat in those days – she really didn't need to because the fine close-trimmed blonde hair was shaped exactly like a hat itself – and the low-cut neck of the dress, in the fashion of the time, showed a deep curve of soft low breast, the skin clear, unblemished and wonderfully smooth.

When Ormsby-Hill saw her come downstairs into the dingy little living room he forgot almost at once what he had come to say to her. She was already drawing on her gloves and she said:

'I'm awfully afraid I shall have to go. My dressmaker closes at half-past seven and I have to have this fitting. I don't know which way you're going back, but it's only in the High Street, this shop, if you'd like to walk that way.'

Walking down the yard, out of The Pit, he managed to repeat a few words of conventional condolence about Tom Pemberton, asking her at the same time how she herself was.

'It was very sad,' she said, 'but I don't remember much about it.'

'I believe you also suffered another unfortunate bereavement,' he said.

'Yes,' she said. 'Some time ago.'

By the time they were out in the street she was talking easily, lightly and readily of something else, quite unperturbed and sometimes laughing. She had a laugh that had a kind of spring to it. It uncoiled suddenly and lightly, ending in a series of high shimmering notes, merrily, like repeated echoes.

And as he walked with her that evening through a High Street still crowded with late shoppers Ormsby-Hill could hardly bring himself to believe that he was with a young woman who had lost a husband and a lover in so short a time. Nor was there the slightest sign of the wild, bad girl he had expected. He felt indeed that he had never met anyone quite so pleasant to talk to, to look at or to listen to. Above all he couldn't believe – it was simply incomprehensible – that she had been born, bred and shaped in The Pit. It made his head rock with wonder that she had come, so golden and impeccable and pleasant, from that sordid rat-hole.

He fell in love with her at once, with abandonment, quite blindly, and she let him fall in love for precisely the same reason as she had let James William Sherwood and Tom Pemberton fall in love: because she liked it.

The scandal warmed and mounted quickly. It was one thing for a young curate to be seen in occasional conversation with a good-looking girl or even to dance with her at one of those decorous functions by which the church, in the nineteen-twenties, had begun to try to lure youth back into the grace of the fold; but it was quite another for Ormsby-Hill to be seen waiting for her at the factory door, often at the dinner hour and almost always at night, and then walking home to The Pit with her through the rushing crowds of shoemakers hungrily herding homewards on foot or on bicycles.

'He comes of such a good family. He went to Oxford. His mother lives in a big house in Wiltshire. And Bertha – from The Pit. From *there! What do you suppose the vicar thinks?* And his mother? He doesn't wear the dog-collar very often, does he? I suppose he's ashamed.'

Ormsby-Hill, strangely, was not ashamed. He existed boldly, for an entire autumn, a winter and part of the following spring, in a state of suspended enchantment. And Bertha in turn rewarded him as she had rewarded James William Sherwood and Tom Pemberton: with the sort of affection that moulds itself on the pattern of the receiver. If it is possible to imagine her as being sensuous in well-cut tweeds that was how she looked that autumn, winter and spring. And she looked like that and dressed like that for a sound simple reason: because Ormsby-Hill loved her and because he wanted her to. She also went to church, though her mother was a Methodist and went to chapel, and watched him take part in the services and listened to him preaching and reading the lessons. She took on also some of his accent, slightly Oxford, his phrases and his muscular mannerisms. She was sometimes to be seen in country pubs outside the town, drinking from large tankards of draught ale, laughing with ravishing heartiness and saying such things as:

'Darling, how could you? You're too, too awful. You're really shame-making, honestly you are. Really shy-making. All right, pet, let's have another. Why not?'

Suddenly, in the June of that year, there was no longer a Rev. Ormsby-Hill in the town, though down in Cornwall, in a remote rocky village isolated on the coast, a new congregation was getting ready to welcome a new curate in September.

'One dead. One killed. One disgraced,' people said. 'Who's she going to ruin next?'

Nobody seemed to understand that, down in The Pit, it was not Bertha's place to give an answer.

I, in part, gave it instead.

She was now, like the century, in her twenties. It was the bright, gay, desperate time. There was much dancing.

She was always the central figure at dances, seldom wearing

the same dress twice, always strikingly golden, elegant, friendly, in demand. Perhaps the friendliness was the nicest thing about her. She never refused the clumiest lout a quick-step. She waltzed on equal terms with youth, age, undergraduates, shoe-hands, golfers, shooting men, clerks, masters of fox-hounds, always beautifully companionable, at ease, talking whatever language they spoke to her.

And presently, the following summer, she was even dancing with me.

It was a very hot sultry evening in early July and some of the men, after the habit of the twenties, were wearing blazers and white flannels. Most of the girls were in light silk or satin frocks and the doors and windows of the dance hall were all wide open and you could see the blue brilliant evening beyond.

I had just decided to disentangle myself from the hot sea-crab embraces of a *Paul Jones* when suddenly the music stopped and I found myself, by pure accident, facing Bertha, almost isolated on that corner of the floor.

She smiled and at once raised her bare golden arms towards me. Both the smile and the gesture might have been those between two old friends, though we had in fact never even spoken before.

She was dressed, that evening, in striking oyster-coloured silk. The dress was short and sleeveless, in the fashion of the day, and she had matching gloves and shoes. Her eyes, naturally very blue, seemed to catch in reflection all the brilliance of the evening outside, so that they appeared to be deep violet in colour. Her hair looked as if she had spent most of the day brushing it and she had now begun to let it grow a little longer again, so that it hung down in the shape of a casque.

She danced superbly. But what really struck me, in that hot, saxophonic scrum of pounding feet, was not her dancing. It was her coolness. Sweat was pouring heavily from the faces of all the men and now and then you could see across the back of a girl's dress the large wet ham-print of a hand.

Bertha's arms and hands were, by contrast, as cool as porcelain cups dipped in spring water.

'Enjoying it?' I said.

'Oh! awfully,' she said, 'aren't you?'

I confessed I felt it rather warm and then she said:

'I hear you've started to become a writer.'

'Oh?' I said. 'Who told you that?'

'As a matter of fact I read an article of yours the other day,' she said. 'About flowers. I cut it out because I liked it so much.'

After that it was impossible not to be happily at ease with her, friendly and greatly flattered. To my dismay the music stopped almost immediately. The dance had ended. She immediately gave me a wonderful smile of thanks and I had the presence of mind to ask her if she would like some ice-cream and if she would have the next dance with me.

'Of course,' she said. 'How nice of you.'

Over the ice-cream, which we took outside to eat, she said:

'About those flowers. They weren't from our part of the country, were they?'

'Most of them.'

'But the orchids? – I didn't know we had orchids in this country. Do they grow here – the wild ones you said were like greeny white butterflies?'

'In Longley Spinneys,' I said, 'just outside the town.'

'Honestly?'

She licked the last of her ice-cream from the spoon and looked at me with, I thought, an air of disbelief.

'You don't believe it,' I said.

'Oh! I don't want you to think that,' she said. 'Please.'

I have always found that women are frequently most incredulous when you tell them the truth. I have also always been, all my life, a person governed by the swiftest, if sometimes the most foolish, impulses.

'If you don't believe me I'll take you to see them,' I said. 'They're in bloom now.'

'Oh! that's lovely,' Bertha said. 'When should we go?'

'Now,' I said.

The wide dark blue eyes did not look in the least surprised. It was only when I suddenly remembered that I was talking to a girl whose late habit had been to ride both in landaus and in cars of fast sporting design that I was aware of a stupid object standing in the way of what I had just proposed.

'Damn,' I said. 'I forgot I'd only got my bicycle.'

Her reply was typical.

'What's wrong with a bicycle?' she said. 'I haven't got mine but I could ride on the back of yours.'

Suddenly I knew I had made the first of several new discoveries about Bertha. I knew now that she was not merely beautiful, sumptuous, companionable and physically delightful. She had an altogether wonderful innocence about her.

'Come on, let's go,' she said. 'Before we change our minds.'

'All right,' I said, 'but you ride the bike and I'll step it on the back. In case you soil your dress or tear your stockings.'

There are an infinite number of ways of making love to a girl for the first time but the approach from the back of a bicycle, on a hot half-dark summer night is, I suppose, not among the most common of them.

The road to Longley Spinneys is a fairly flat one and the actual business of bicycling was not hard for Bertha. It was I who had the difficult job of keeping my balance on the back and at first I rode with my hands on her bare cool shoulders.

'Are my hands heavy for you up there?' I said. 'Say if they are.'

'Just a little heavy.'

I put my hands round her waist.

'Is that better?'

'Much better.'

As we rode I could smell the fragrance of hay from summer meadows, the lightest of scents from hedge-roses and from somewhere farther off, in the hot darkness, the deeper, thicker breath of limes. By the time we were coasting down the last small incline to the spinneys, in that soundless intoxicating air, my hands were holding her breasts. They were firm and corsetless and my mouth was resting against her bare smooth shoulder.

It was the most exquisite bicycle ride ever undertaken, but as we stood by the wood-side she made no comment on any of these happenings. They were perfectly natural to her. Soon I started to kiss her. I let my hands run over the cool sumptuous skin of her shoulders. In exquisite suspense, with closed eyes, I forgot the orchids. I thought she had forgotten them too but at last, in a low voice, she aroused me from a daze.

'What about these flowers? These orchids?' she said. 'Or did you just invent them?'

I took her into the spinneys. It was still not fully dark; but presently, under the ashlings, we came upon the first of the orchids, rare, fragile, milk-green winged, the ghostliest of flowers. The scent of them was overpoweringly sweet, too sweet, un-English, almost tropical, on the calm night air. 'You must have extraordinary eyes to see them in the dark,' she said. 'Or does the scent guide you?' I had no answer to make to her and for the second or third time, with trembling intoxication, I stopped under a tree, took her in my arms and kissed her. The acquiescence of her body was sensational in its quietness. There was not a murmur in the spinneys, the fields, the sky or the hedgerows about us. I could hear only in my own mind the echo of some words of a poem that had been haunting me since waking and that the later saxophonic pounding cries, the bicycle ride and the orchids had driven temporarily away:

> *Dear love, for nothing less than thee*
> *Would I have broke this happy dream.*

She stood, dream-like herself, for a few moments as insubstantial as the flowers she was holding, while I quoted to her with ardent quietness Donne's words about excess of joy. She listened not only as if she had been used all her life to hearing young men quote verse to her at night, in summer woods, but also as she must have listened to those other accents, the accents of James William Sherwood, Tom Pemberton, Ormsby-Hill and the rest, charmingly ready, now, to take on mine.

When at length I finished with the last line I could remember,

> *Enter these arms, for since thou thoughtst it best*
> *Not to dream all my dream, let's act the rest,*

she laughed softly, throatily, and said:

'Did you write all that? It's lovely.'

'No,' I said and I told her who had written it. 'Three hundred years ago.'

'He was a man who knew about things,' she said. 'Like you with your flowers.'

We rode home, hours later, in a darkness no less sultry for the pink light breaking in the east, the paling stars and a thin rising dew. Towards the end of the journey a few birds had already begun a light July chorus and once a leveret skimmed across in front of the bicycle, almost throwing us, so that I clutched harder, half in self-preservation, at her body. She was even then so acquiescent, so friendly and so full of her own apparent excess of joy that she actually half-turned her head a few moments later and kissed me as we rode.

Presently I took her as far as The Pit in order to say, in the rapidly rising dawn, the tenderest of good-byes.

'Tomorrow night?'

'I'm awfully sorry. I can't tomorrow,' she said. 'I'm going out with George Freeman.'

I felt as if I had been hit rudely and ferociously with the bicycle.

'But Bertha—'

'I'm going out with George three nights a week,' she said, 'but I'd love to come with you on the others. I would – I love the way you talk. I loved that poetry. I want to hear all about you and your writing.'

It was hard to believe she was still in her early twenties. It was harder still to believe that she could forsake my own particular excess of joy, the verse, the summer woods and the green-ghost orchids for George Freeman, a muscular flat-capped skittles player who drove a brewers' dray.

A few days later my father started to admonish me.

'I hear you've been seen with that Bertha Jackson girl.'

I started to protest.

'Oh! yes, I know,' he said. 'I daresay she *is* all right. She may be. *But that sort of girl can easily trap you.* You understand?'

There was really not much need to understand.

'Probably a good thing,' my father said, 'that you're going to live in London soon.'

A few weeks afterwards, bearing a sheaf of torn, tender memories that already seemed as delicate and hauntingly insubstantial as the milk-green orchids, the ghostliest of flowers, I went to live away from home.

Seventeen years later I stood before the desk of my commanding officer, who had sent for me with some urgency and now said:

'Didn't you tell me once, old boy, that you came from the Nene valley? Isn't that your native country? Evensford?'

When I said that it was he went on:

'Good show. I think I've got a bright idea for a powerful piece for you. The Yanks have carved out a hell of a great bomber airfield just outside Evensford. Wouldn't it be nice if you went down and looked at it and wrote a nostalgic piece about it? – the revolution of war, the bomb that blew your childhood scene sky-high and that sort of thing? You get it? It would please the Americans.'

I said I thought I got it and he turned with eagerness to a pile of papers.

'A chap named Colonel Garth F. Parkington, it seems, is Station Commander,' he said, 'and H.Q. at Huntingdon say he's the nicest sort of bloke to deal with. Spend as long as you like up there. Absorb the atmosphere. I'll lay everything on.'

A day later I was driving northward, up to my native country. It was early summer. Gipsies were camping about their fires outside a strawberry field that I passed and just inside the field a line of women and children in light cotton dresses were gathering the berries and putting them into white chip baskets. One of the prettier of the girls, a blonde, seeing my uniform, waved her hand to me, laughing, showing clean white teeth, her hands red with strawberry stain. Farther along the road a field of wheat had already the lovely grey-blue sheen of pre-ripeness on the stiff straight ears and I could hear, all along the hedgerows, whenever I opened the car window, the song of yellow-hammers chipping with monotony at the heart of the sunny afternoon.

Something about the fair-haired girl waving her hand to me from the strawberry field made me remember Bertha. Seventeen years is a longish time and my hair had begun to go grey.

Then presently, as I drove along, I found myself trying to remember the number of times I had heard her name in seventeen years. It was perhaps half a dozen. Someone, I forget who, had once told me that she was seeing a great deal of a prominent follower of the Pytchley; that she was much in the swim at flat race meetings and point-to-points. Someone else thought she was a hostess in a sea-side hotel. At least two people thought she had gone to live in London but when I mentioned this to another he said: 'Don't believe it. Bertha's still there, up at Evensford. Still the same as ever. Still going strong.'

About three o'clock I found myself in a completely strange,

foreign country. Only by stopping the car, getting out and identifying, through some minutes of amazed reorientation, a slender stone church steeple I had known since boyhood, could I recognise that I had reached, in fact, the frontiers of my native land. Three great hangars, like monstrous brooding night-bats, succeeded in saving from moon-mountain barrenness an otherwise naked sky-line. In brilliant sunshine a perimeter track curled across bare grass like a quivering bruising strip of steel. Like black, square-faced owls, Flying Fortresses everywhere rested on land where, as a boy, I had searched for sky-larks' eggs, walked in tranquillity on summer Sunday evenings with my family and gathered cowslips in exalted spring-times.

Over everything swept the unstopped thundering prop-roar of engines warming up and dead in the heart of it a giant water-tank, like a Martian ghoul on stilts, strode colossus-wise across the sky. This was the country through which, on a July night, I had bicycled with Bertha, first put my hands with lightness on her breasts and talked to her of dreams and joy's excesses in terms of ghost-green orchid flowers.

A few minutes later I was with Colonel Parkington, a likeable Nordic giant with many ribbons, an immaculate tunic and trousers of expensive light pink whip-cord who felt it imperative, every few moments, to call me old boy.

'Sit down, old boy.' A telephone rang on his desk. He picked it up. 'Be right with you, old boy.' A voice began crackling in the telephone. 'Hell. No. Blast. Hell, Christ no.' A second telephone rang. The colonel did not pick it up. 'But what the flaming hell! What does Washington know? Through channels, for Christ's sake? Hell! It takes a century.' The second telephone kept ringing and Colonel Parkington, not picking it up, started shouting into the first. 'Always channels. Always channels. They think of nothing but channels. This is an operational station. Dammit, I can't wait! Where do they think this goddam war is being fought? In Albuquerque or where?'

He slammed down the telephone. The second telephone stopped ringing for ten seconds and then, as if taking breath, started again. Colonel Parkington picked it up, put his hand over the mouthpiece and said to me with polite, genuine sorrow:

'Look, old boy. This goes on all day. Every day. It's hell. I tell you what. Go get yourself fixed up with a room. The lieutenant out there will fix you up. Then show up at six o'clock at my house down the road. We're having a little party – about fifty folks, cocktails. I want you to meet my wife. She's English too. O.K.? See you then, old boy.'

Thunder was muttering ominously along the eastern sky-line as I walked down the road soon after six o'clock but its gathering rages were like the squeakings of sick mice compared with the already raucous bawlings coming out of the big Victorian red-brick house that the Colonel had taken for himself about a mile from the bomber station.

Inside, in the big lofty Victorian rooms, it seemed that an army of giant locusts had settled. The species was mainly a laughing one. Between its laughter it sucked at glasses, ate ice-cream, blew smoke, gnawed at small brown sausages and yelled.

In this maelstrom I sought refuge behind an ancient hat-rack, where a young lieutenant with many ribbons, pale flight-weary eyes and a glass beer-mug in his hand, had already forestalled me. The beer-mug was filled with what seemed to be port wine and the lieutenant, staring up from it, started calling me Bud.

'Hullo, Bud, what's the uniform?'

'Royal Air Force.'

'Is it? For Christ's sake.'

Drinking deeply at the port, he wiped his mouth across the back of his hand, staring the uniform up and down.

'Forgot to put your ribbons on, Bud.'

I explained that I had not only no ribbons to put on but that, so far, I had done nothing whatever to deserve any ribbons.

'Hell, that's terrible,' he said. 'Don't look right without ribbons.'

He drank again. I surveyed the smoky locust scene, looking for Colonel Parkington. As I searched unsuccessfully through the crowded gnawing faces the young lieutenant, mouth wet with port, spoke with terse, unsober bitterness of the day's events above Stettin.

'Damn dirty trip,' he kept saying. 'A helluva damn stinking dirty trip.'

'Do you know if Colonel Parkington is here?' I said.

'Sure.'

He too surveyed the scene, peering with difficulty from under lids that were closing down on the eyes' weary dilations.

'Don't see him though.'

'Which is Mrs Parkington?'

Before he could answer a girl came up. She had the fair small-featured elegance that is so common to girls in that part of England and she heard my question.

'That's her,' she said. 'Over at the top end of the room. In the black and silver dress. By the fireplace.'

'Probably the colonel's there too,' the lieutenant said. 'How's things? How's the shape?' he said to the girl, catching her by the shoulder, and I moved away.

Half way across the room I stopped. The colonel's personal lieutenant, the one who had arranged my room, stupefied by the sight of a guest without a drink in his hand and thinking perhaps that I had halted in stupefaction too, as in fact I had, dragged me solicitously aside to a long table where mess orderlies were serving drinks from a barricade of ice-buckets.

'Please have what you like, sir,' he said. 'I'm sorry. I didn't see you come in. The colonel's not here yet. He had a rush call to H.Q. at five.'

An orderly poured me a drink. I bore it away through the crowd of faces and stood by a wall. I stood there a long time, alone, sipping the drink, watching Mrs Parkington.

There was no mistaking that fine yellow hair. Bertha was wearing it rather long now, almost down to her shoulders, in the war-time fashion, and it matched with its curled brushed smoothness the long close line of the black and silver dress that made her appear even taller than she was. The dress, as always, was low-cut, showing the strong smooth bosom, and she was wearing rather large pear-shaped earrings, black, probably of jet, that quivered every now and then like shining berries as she tossed back her head, laughing.

She was surrounded, on all sides, by young officers in uniform. There were, I noticed, no other women near. With native good sense they had clearly retreated, fearful of being overshadowed by a sumptuous, glittering, popular mountain.

At intervals her laugh rang out clear, merry and golden. I hesitated for a long time about moving over towards her but at last I started, setting down my empty glass on a window sill outside which I could see the far blue violence of summer lightning striking the sky above the black hangars on the hill.

I did not get very far. For a second time the horrified lieutenant, alarmed by the sight of a single drinkless guest, stopped me and begged:

'Let me get you something, sir. They're not looking after you. The colonel said to be sure to look after you. We don't get so many visits from you boys.'

He disappeared and I stood for three or four minutes longer within hearing distance of Bertha, waiting for the drink. She spoke, I now discovered, with a slight American accent, just clipped enough to be charming.

'Oh! it's all channels, channels,' I heard her say. 'Nothing but channels. It's like Garth says – you'd think they were fighting the war in Albuquerque or somewhere. For goodness' sake what does Washington know?'

The young officers about her laughed with that particular brittle brand of laughter that young officers reserve for occasions when brass-hats, governments or cabinet officials are mentioned and one, younger, more good-looking and more tipsy than the rest, gazed with fondness at her bosom, as if almost ready to plant a kiss there, and said:

'Good for Bertha. My God, we should send Bertha back home as special envoy. She'd knock 'em dead.'

A moment later my drink arrived. I listened to her laughing and talking for a few moments longer, watching the earrings quiver like black berries against the long yellow hair and then at last, feeling unarmed for the encounter, I moved away.

As I walked back up the road lightning struck with explosive blue tributaries, fierce and jagged, all about the woodless skyline. I walked slowly in the hot air, carrying my cap, and if I was sad it was not so much because of Bertha, gay and sumptuous as ever, but because, remembering James William Sherwood and Tom Pemberton, I feared that the night's ominous storminess might contain in it the fires of other premonitions.

I need not, as it happened, have worried at all.

The war was hardly over before I was filled with unbearable longings to travel again, to feel what France smelled like and to see flowers blooming about the classical stones of Italy, in fierce sunlight, about the vineyards, high above the lakesides.

These things were still not easy and it was already a year later when I met a man who promptly scorned them, told me of experiences that had given him equal, easier pleasures and said:

'France? Why bother with France? You've got it all in Jersey. No currency nonsense. Everybody speaks English. Pretty good food. And this hotel – I'll write the name of this hotel down for you.'

Jersey is not France; nor are the Channel Islands the hills of Tuscany. I listened with unenraptured patience and with that glassiness of eye that, my friends tell me, draws down over my pupils whenever I grow dreamy or bored.

'There. That's it. You can mention my name if you like – but the great thing is to get hold of this woman. The hostess there.'

I am, I am bound to confess, afraid of hotels with hostesses.

'I'd better write her name down too,' he said. 'Because she's the one. She'll do anything for you. You mustn't forget her. Mrs Jackson Parkington.'

Over my eyes two little blinds of boredom had drawn themselves down. Suddenly, with explosive revelation, they snapped up again.

'What's she like?' I said.

'Terrific,' he said. 'Blonde. Long hair. Early forties, I should say, but it's hard to tell. Figure of a young girl. Gorgeous dancer. Beautiful clothes. Easy with everybody. Able to talk to anybody, on any level, about anything, at any time.'

'English?'

'Sort of,' he said. 'Well, actually yes, I suppose. She was married to an American Air Force Colonel, they say, but it's all over now. Usual story. Divorced. Came out of it pretty comfortably, I understand. Just does the hostess thing for fun.'

I tried to think of one or two more questions I might possibly ask about Bertha, but my friend swept me away in waves of greater eagerness, saying:

'You go there. You'll never regret it. That's the way to make a hotel go – get a woman like that in. If there's anything she can possibly do to make you happy she will. Somehow she's got the knack of making everybody happy.'

'I'll think about it,' I said.

I did think about it; and for the first time there was, about Bertha, something I found not easy to forgive. It was not like Bertha to be pompous. Her body, her mind, her ways and her generosity were those of an enthralled innocence. I could not see her growing grand; I could not think of her, somehow, as rising too high in the world, half way as it were to being a duchess, calling herself Mrs Jackson Parkington. But it was a little thing; and I was glad, really, she was still making people happy.

It was another five years, nearly six, before I saw my Italian mountains, deep-fissured and burnt by late August heat, the lakes below them oiled in blue-rose calm, the little cream clustered towns melting like squat candles into the water, the pink and pale yellow oleanders blooming below the vines.

Even this, after a few days, was too much for me. I found I could not sleep in the fierce, hot, mosquito nights of the lakeside and presently I moved to a village up a valley, half way to the mountains.

In cooler exquisite mornings I walked about the rocks, stopped at little *caffès* for glasses of cold red wine and looked at the mountain flowers. In August there were not many flowers but sometimes on the paths, on the roads and outside the *caffès* little girls would be selling bunches of pink wild cyclamen, like small rosy butterflies, full of fragile loveliness before they drooped in the heat of noon.

'But what flowers are they? Could you tell me what flowers they are?'

At the corner of a mountain road I came, one morning, on a man and a woman buying bunches of the small pink cyclamen from a mute Italian child.

'But don't you know what flowers they are?' The man spoke in Italian, the woman in English. As I passed them the man gave the child a hundred lire note, but she stepped back, still mute, black eyes wide, like a dog frightened. 'Are they violets?' the woman said. 'Don't you know?'

In the white dust of the road the child started shuffling her bare feet. The woman opened her handbag, felt in it and started to offer the child another hundred lire note but suddenly the child, dropping her mouth with a cry, was away down the dust of the hillside.

'Sweet,' the woman said. 'What a pity.'

She closed her handbag. It was white, shaped like a little elegant drum. Her costume, of thinnest silk, was white too. Her shoes, earrings and necklace were also white and she was carrying white gloves in her hands.

I turned from some four yards up the hillside.

'The flowers are wild cyclamen,' I said.

'Oh! really?' she said. Thank you. How clever of you to know.'

The man, who was dressed in a thin Italian suit of lavender with darker stripings, raised a white hat in my direction. Underneath it the head was handsome, distinguished and nuttily bald.

'Cyclamen,' she said to him. 'Wild cyclamen.'

'Ah! yes,' he said. 'Ah! yes. That is so. That is the word I was trying to think of.' He spoke now in English. 'Thank you, sir.'

In a suspense I found I could not break with words I stood trying to take in the immaculate picture, all white and gold, the legs perfectly exquisite, the bosom firm and uplifted, the eyes of intensely clear, hyacinth brightness, of Bertha framed at the age of fifty against the mountainside. If from that distance she gave me any sign of recognition I did not detect it and presently, with a short wave of the hand, I turned and walked up the road.

Ten seconds later a figure came panting up behind me.

'Sir. Signor. It was most very kind of you to say the name of the flower. My wife is delighted. She thanks you very much.' He took off his hat again, revealing the sun-browned head, smiled in a distinguished way and shook hands. 'We are in the Hotel Savoia. By the bridge. If you have time will you take an *apéritif* with us, perhaps, this night?'

'It's very kind of you,' I said, 'but I'm leaving this afternoon.'

'Ah! too bad,' he said. 'Too bad. Too much pity. If you should change your mind my name is Count Umberto Pinelli. Please ask for me.'

He turned, lifted his hand and in a few seconds had joined her down the hillside. There, for a moment, she too lifted her hand.

'Thank you so much!' she called. 'Very, very kind of you. I do appreciate it. I never know about flowers.'

She smiled. Her hair shone with brilliance, with no trace of grey, against the fierce Italian sky. Her shoulders were as firm, sloping and impressive as the mountains. The cyclamen were pink and delicate in her hands.

And since I was in Italy and since I could think, as I stood there remembering a gaunt, yellow-eyed, prematurely ageing woman feverishly treadling at a sewing machine, of no reason to do otherwise, I smiled back to her and bowed in answer.

'Not at all,' I said. 'Enchanted.'

Clara Corbett, who had dark brown deeply sunken eyes that did not move when she was spoken to and plain brown hair parted down the middle in a straight thin line, firmly believed that her life had been saved by an air warden's anti-gas cape on a black rainy night during the war.

In a single glittering, dusty moment a bomb had blown her through the window of a warden's post, hurling her to the wet street outside. The wind from the bomb had miraculously blown the cape about her face, masking and protecting her eyes. When she had picked herself up, unhurt, she suddenly knew that it might have been her shroud.

'Look slippy and get up to Mayfield Court. Six brace of partridges and two hares to pick up—'

'And on the way deliver them kidneys and the sirloin to Paxton Manor. Better call in sharp as you go out. They're having a lunch party.'

Now, every rainy day of her life, she still wore the old camouflaged cape as she drove the butcher's van, as if half fearing that some day, somewhere, another bomb would blow her through another window, helplessly and for ever. The crumpled patterns of green-and-yellow camouflage always made her look, in the rain, like a damp, baggy, meditating frog.

Every day of his life, her husband, Clem, wore his bowler hat in the butcher's shop, doffing it obsequiously to special customers, revealing a bald, yellow suet-shining head. Clem had a narrow way of smiling and argued that war had killed the meat trade.

Almost everyone else in that rather remote hilly country, where big woodlands were broken by open stretches of chalk heathland covered with gorse and blackthorn and occasional yew trees, had given up delivering to outlying houses. It simply didn't pay. Only Clem Corbett, who doffed his hat caressingly to customers with one hand while leaving the thumb of his other on the shop scales a fraction of a second too long, thought it worth while any longer.

'One day them people'll all come back. The people with class. Mark my words. The real gentry. They're the people you got to keep in with. The pheasant-and-partridge class. The real gentry. Not the sausage-and-scragenders.'

Uncomplainingly, almost meekly, Clara drove out, every day, in the old delivery van with a basket or two in the back and an enamel tray with a few bloody, neatly-wrapped cuts of meat on it, into wooded, hilly countryside. Sometimes in winter, when the trees were thinned of leaves, the chimneys of empty houses, the mansions of the late gentry, rose starkly from behind deep thick beechwoods that were thrown like vast bearskins across the chalk. In summer the chalk flowered into a hill garden of wild yellow rock-rose, wild marjoram, and countless waving mauve scabious covered on hot afternoons with nervous darting butterflies.

She drove into this countryside, winter and summer, camouflaged always by the gas-cape on days of rain, without much change of expression. Her meek sunken eyes fixed themselves firmly on the winter woods, on the narrow lanes under primroses or drifts of snow, and on the chalk flowers of summer as if the seasons made no change in them at all. It was her job simply to deliver meat, to rap or ring at kitchen doors, to say good morning and thank you and then to depart in silence, camouflaged, in the van.

If she ever thought about the woods, about the blazing open chalkland in which wild strawberries sparkled, pure scarlet, in hot summers, or about the big desolate mansions standing empty among the beechwoods, she did not speak of it to a soul. If the mansions were on day to be opened up again, then they would, she supposed, be opened up. If people with money and class were to come back again, as Clem said they would, once more to order barons of beef and saddles of lamb and demand the choicest cuts of venison, then she supposed they would come back. That was all.

In due course, if such things happened, she supposed Clem would know how to deal with them. Clem was experienced, capable and shrewd, a good butcher and a good business man. Clem knew how to deal with people of class. Clem, in the early days of business, had been used to supplying the finest of everything, as his father and grandfather had done before him, for house parties, shooting luncheons, ducal dinners, and regimental messes. The days of the gentry might, as Clem said, be under a temporary cloud. But finally, one day, class would surely triumph again and tradition would be back. The war might have half killed the meat trade, but it couldn't kill those people. They were there all the time, as Clem said, somewhere. They were the backbone, the real people, the gentry.

'Didn't I tell you?' he said one day. 'Just like I told you. Belvedere's opening up. Somebody's bought Belvedere.'

She knew about Belvedere. Belvedere was one of those houses, not large but long empty, whose chimneys rose starkly, like tombs, above the beechwoods of winter-time. For six years the army had carved its ashy, cindery name on Belvedere.

'See, just like I told you,' Clem said two days later, 'the gentleman from Belvedere just phoned up. The right people are coming back. We got an order from Belvedere.'

By the time she drove up to Belvedere, later that morning, rain was falling heavily, sultrily warm, on the chalk flowers of the hillsides. She was wearing the old war-time cape, as she always did under rain, and in the van, on the enamel tray, at the back, lay portions of sweetbreads, tripe, and liver.

High on the hills, a house of yellow stucco frontage, with thin iron balconies about the windows and green iron canopies above them, faced the valley.

'Ah, the lady with the victuals! The lady with the viands. The lady from Corbett, eh?' A man of forty-five or fifty, in shirtsleeves, portly, wearing a blue-striped apron, his voice plummy and soft, answered her ring at the kitchen door.

'Do come in. You are from Corbett, aren't you?'

'I'm Mrs Corbett.'

'How nice. Come in, Mrs Corbett, come in. Don't stand there. It's loathsome and you'll catch a death. Come in. Take off your cape. Have a cheese straw.'

The rosy flesh of his face was smeared with flour dust. His fattish soft fingers were stuck about with shreds of dough.

'You arrived in the nick, Mrs Corbett. I was about to hurl these wretched things into the stove, but now you can pass judgment on them for me.'

With exuberance he suddenly put in front of her face a plate of fresh warm cheese straws.

'Taste and tell me, Mrs Corbett. Taste and tell.'

With shyness, more than usually meek, her deep brown eyes lowered, she took a cheese straw and started to bite on it.

'Tell me,' he said, 'if it's utterly loathsome.'

'It's very nice, sir.'

'Be absolutely frank, Mrs Corbett,' he said. 'Absolutely frank. If they're too revolting say so.'

'I think—'

'I tell you what, Mrs Corbett,' he said, 'they'll taste far nicer with a glass of sherry. That's it. We shall each have a glass of pale dry sherry and see how it marries with the cheese.'

Between the sherry and the cheese straws and his own conversation she found there was not much chance for her to speak. With bewilderment she watched him turn away, the cheese straws suddenly forgotten, to the kitchen table, a basin of flour, and a pastry board.

With surprising delicacy he pressed with his fingers at the edges of thin pastry lining a brown shallow dish. Beside it lay a pile of pink peeled mushrooms.

'This I know is going to be delicious,' he said. 'This I am sure about. I adore cooking. Don't you?'

Speechlessly she watched him turn to the stove and begin to melt butter in a saucepan.

'*Croûte aux champignons,*' he said. 'A kind of mushroom pie. There are some things one knows one does well. This I love to do. It's delicious – you know it, of course, don't you? Heavenly.'

'No, sir.'

'Oh, don't call me sir, Mrs Corbett. My name is Lafarge. Henry Lafarge.' He turned to fill up his glass with sherry, at the same time fixing her with greyish bulbous eyes. 'Aren't you terribly uncomfortable in that wretched mackintosh? Why don't you throw it off for a while?'

The voice, though not unkindly, shocked her a little. She had never thought of the cape as wretched. It was a very essential, useful, hard-wearing garment. It served its purpose very well, and with fresh bewilderment she pushed it back from her shoulders.

'Do you think I'm a fool?' he said. 'I mean about this house? All my friends say I'm a fool. Of course it's in a ghastly state, one knows, but I think I can do things with it. Do you agree? Do you think I'm a fool?'

She could not answer. She felt herself suddenly preoccupied, painfully, with the old brown dress she was wearing under the gas-cape. With embarrassment she folded her hands across the front of it, unsuccessfully trying to conceal it from him.

To her relief he was, however, staring at the rain. 'I think it's letting up at last,' he said. 'In which case I shall be able to show you the outside before you go, You simply must see the outside, Mrs Corbett. It's a ravishing wilderness. Ravishing to the point of being sort of almost Strawberry Hill. You know?'

She did not know, and she stared again at her brown dress, frayed at the edges.

Presently the rain slackened and stopped and only the great beeches overshadowing the house were dripping. The sauce for the *croûte aux champignons* was almost ready, and Lafarge dipped a little finger into it and then thoughtfully licked it, staring at the same time at the dripping summer trees.

'I'm going to paint most of it myself,' he said. 'It's more fun, don't you think? More creative. I don't think we're half creative enough, do you? Stupid to allow menials and lackeys to do all the nicest things for us, don't you think?'

Pouring sauce over the mushrooms, he fixed on her an inquiring, engaging smile that did not need an answer.

'Now, Mrs Corbett, the outside. You must see the outside.'

Automatically she began to draw on her cape.

'I can't think why you cling to that wretched cape, Mrs Corbett,' he said. 'The very day war was over I had a simply glorious ceremonial bonfire of all those things.'

In a cindery garden of old half-wild roses growing out of matted tussocks of grass and nettle, trailed over by thick white horns of convolvulus, he showed her the southern front of the house with its rusty canopies above the windows and its delicate iron balconies entwined with blackberry and briar.

'Of course at the moment the plaster looks frightfully leprous,' he said, 'but it'll be pink when I've done with it. The sort of pink you see in the Mediterranean. You know?'

A Virginia creeper had enveloped with shining tendrilled greed the entire western wall of the house, descending from the roof in a dripping curtain of crimson-green.

'The creeper is coming down this week,' he said. 'Ignore the creeper.' He waved soft pastry-white hands in the air, clasping and unclasping them. 'Imagine a rose there. A black one. An enormous deep red-black one. A hat rose. You know the sort?'

Again she realised he did not need an answer.

'The flowers will glow,' he said, 'like big glasses of dark red wine on a pink tablecloth. Doesn't that strike you as being absolute heaven on a summer's day?'

Bemused, she stared at the tumbling skeins of creeper, at the rising regiments of sow-thistle, more than ever uncertain what to say. She began hastily to form a few words about it being time for her to go when he said: 'There was something else I had to say to you, Mrs Corbett, and now I can't think what it was. Terribly important too. Momentously important.'

A burst of sunshine falling suddenly on the wet wilderness, the rusting canopies and Clara's frog-like cape seemed abruptly to enlighten him. 'Ah – hearts,' he said. 'That was it.'

'Hearts?'

'What's today? Tuesday. Thursday,' he said, 'I want you to bring me one of your nicest hearts.'

'One of my hearts?'

He laughed, again not unkindly. 'Bullock's,' he said.

'Oh! Yes, I see.'

'Did you know,' he said, 'that hearts taste like goose? Just like goose-flesh?' He stopped, laughed again, and actually touched her arm. 'No, no. That's wrong. Too rich. One can't say that. One can't say hearts like goose-flesh. Can one?'

A stir of wind shook the beech boughs, bringing a spray of rain sliding down the long shafts of sunlight.

'I serve them with cranberry sauce,' he said. 'With fresh peas and fresh new potatoes I defy anyone to tell the difference.'

They were back now at the kitchen door, where she had left her husband's basket on the step.

'We need more imagination, that's all,' he said. 'The despised heart is absolutely royal, I assure you, if you treat it properly—'

'I think I really must go now, Mr Lafarge,' she said, 'or I'll never get done. Do you want the heart early?'

'No,' he said, 'afternoon will do. It's for a little evening supper party. Just a friend and I. Lots of parties, that's what I shall have. Lots of parties, little ones, piggy ones in the kitchen, first.

Then one big one, an enormous house-warmer, a cracker, when the house is ready.'

She picked up her basket, automatically drawing the cape round her shoulders and started to say, 'All right, sir. I'll be up in the afternoon—'

'Most kind of you, Mrs Corbett,' he said. 'Good-bye. So kind. But no "sir" – we're already friends. Just Lafarge.'

'Good-bye, Mr Lafarge,' she said.

She was halfway back to the van when he called, 'Oh, Mrs Corbett! If you get no answer at the door you'll probably find me decorating.' He waved soft, pastry-white hands in the direction of the creeper, the canopies, and the rusting balconies. 'You know – up there.'

When she came back to the house late on Thursday afternoon, not wearing her cape, the air was thick and sultry. All along the stark white fringes of chalk, under the beechwoods, yellow rock-roses flared in the sun. Across the valley hung a few high bland white clouds, delicate and far away.

'The creeper came down with a thousand empty birds' nests,' Lafarge called from a balcony. 'A glorious mess.'

Dressed in dark blue slacks, with yellow open shirt, blue silk muffler, and white panama, he waved towards her a pink-tipped whitewash brush. Behind him the wall, bare of creeper, was drying a thin blotting-paper pink in the sun.

'I put the heart in the kitchen,' she said.

Ignoring this, he made no remark about her cape, either. 'The stucco turned out to be in remarkably good condition,' he said. 'Tell me about the paint. You're the first to see it. Too dark?'

'I think it's very nice.'

'Be absolutely frank,' he said. 'Be as absolutely frank and critical as you like, Mrs Corbett. Tell me exactly how it strikes you. Isn't it too dark?'

'Perhaps it is a shade too dark.'

'On the other hand one has to picture the rose against it,' he said. 'Do you know anyone who grows that wonderful black-red rose?'

She stood staring up at him. 'I don't think I do.'

'That's a pity,' he said, 'because if we had the rose one could judge the effect – However, I'm going to get some tea. Would you care for tea?'

In the kitchen he made tea with slow, punctilious ritual care.

'The Chinese way,' he said. 'First a very little water. Then a minute's wait. Then more water. Then another wait. And so on. Six minutes in all. The secret lies in the waits and the little drops of water. Try one of these. It's a sort of sourmilk tart I invented.'

She sipped tea, munched pastry, and stared at the raw heart she had left in a dish on the kitchen table.

'Awfully kind of you to stop and talk to me, Mrs Corbett,' he said. 'You're the first living soul I've spoken to since you were here on Tuesday.'

Then, for the first time, she asked a question that had troubled her.

'Do you live here all alone?' she said.

'Absolutely, but when the house is done I shall have masses of parties. Masses of friends.'

'It's rather a big house for one person.'

'Come and see the rooms,' he said. 'Some of the rooms I had done before I moved in. My bedroom for instance. Come up-stairs.'

Upstairs a room in pigeon grey, with a deep green carpet and an open french window under a canopy, faced across the valley.

He stepped out on the balcony, spreading enthusiastic hands.

'Here I'm going to have big plants. Big plushy ones. Petunias. Blowzy ones. Begonias, fuchsias, and that sort of thing. Opulence everywhere.'

He turned and looked at her. 'It's a pity we haven't got that big black rose.'

'I used to wear a hat with a rose like that on it,' she said, 'but I never wear it now.'

'How nice,' he said, and came back into the room, where suddenly, for the second time, she felt the intolerable dreariness of her brown woollen dress.

Nervously she put her hands in front of it again and said:

'I think I ought to be going now, Mr Lafarge. Was there something for the weekend?'

'I haven't planned,' he said. 'I'll have to telephone.'

He stood for a moment in the window, looking straight at her with a expression of sharp, arrested amazement.

'Mrs Corbett,' he said, 'I saw the most extraordinary effect just now. It was when I was on the ladder and we were talking about the rose. You were standing there looking up at me and your eyes were so dark that it looked as if you hadn't got any. They're the darkest eyes I've even seen. Didn't anyone ever tell you so?'

No one, as she remembered it, had ever told her so.

The following Saturday morning she arrived at the house with oxtail and kidneys. 'I shall have the kidneys with *sauce madère*,' he said. 'And perhaps even *flambés*.'

He was kneading a batch of small brown loaves on the kitchen table, peppering them with poppy seeds, and he looked up from them to see her holding a brown-paper bag.

'It's only the rose off my hat,' she said. 'I thought you might like to try—'

'Darling Mrs Corbett,' he said. 'You dear creature.'

No one, as she remembered it, had ever called her darling before. Nor could she ever remember being, for anyone, at any time, a dear creature.

Some minutes later she was standing on the balcony outside his bedroom window, pressing the dark red rose from her hat against the fresh pink wall. He stood in the cindery wilderness below, making lively, rapturous gestures.

'Delicious, my dear. Heavenly. You must see it. You simply must come down!'

She went down, leaving the rose on the balcony. A few seconds later he was standing in her place while she stood in the garden below, staring up at the effect of her dark red rose against the wall.

'What do you feel?' he called.

'It seems real,' she said. 'It seems to have come alive.'

'Ah! but imagine it in another summer,' he said. 'When it will be real. When there'll be lots of them, scores of them, blooming here.'

With extravagant hands he tossed the rose down to her from the balcony. Instinctively she lifted her own hands, trying to catch it. It fell instead into a forest of sow-thistle.

He laughed, again not unkindly, and called, 'I'm so grateful, darling Mrs Corbett. I really can't tell you how grateful I am. You've been so thoughtful. You've got such taste.'

With downcast eyes she picked the rose out of the mass of sow-thistle, not knowing what to say.

Through a tender August, full of soft light that seemed to reflect back from dry chalky fields of oats and wheat and barley just below the hill, the derelict house grew prettily, all pink at first among the beeches. By September, Lafarge had begun work on the balconies, painting them a delicate seagull grey. Soon the canopies were grey, too, hanging like half sea-shells above the windows. The doors and windows became grey also, giving an effect of delicate lightness to the house against the background of arching, massive boughs.

She watched these transformations almost from day to day as she delivered to Lafarge kidneys, tripe, liver, sweetbreads, calves' heads, calves' feet, and the hearts that he claimed were just like goose-flesh.

'Offal,' he was repeatedly fond of telling her, 'is far too underrated. People are altogether too superior about offal. The eternal joint is the curse. What could be more delicious than sweetbreads? Or calf's head? Or even chitterlings? There is a German recipe for chitterlings, Mrs Corbett, that could make you think you were eating I don't know what – some celestial, melting manna. You must bring me chitterlings one day soon, Mrs Corbett dear.'

'I have actually found the rose too,' he said one day with excitement. 'I have actually ordered it from a catalogue. It's called *Château Clos de Vougeot* and it's just like the rose on your hat. It's like a deep dark red burgundy.'

All this time, now that the weather had settled into the rainless calm of late summer, she did not need to wear her cape. At the same time she did not think of discarding it. She thought only with uneasiness of the brown frayed dress and presently replaced it with another, dark blue, that she had worn as second-best for many years.

By October, when the entire outside of the house had become transformed, she began to feel, in a way, that she was part of it. She had seen the curtains of creeper, with their thousand bird's nests, give way to clean pink stucco. The canopies had grown from bowls of rusty green tin to delicate half seashells and the balconies from mere paintless coops to pretty cages of seagull grey. As with the fields, the beechwoods, the yellow rock-roses running across the chalk and the changing seasons she had hardly any way of expressing what she felt about these things. She could simply say, 'Yes, Mr Lafarge, I think it's lovely. It's very nice, Mr Lafarge. It's sort of come alive.'

'Largely because of you, dear,' he would say. 'You've inspired the thing. You've fed me with your delicious viands. You've helped. You've given opinions. You brought the rose for the wall. You've got such marvellous instinctive taste, Mrs Corbett dear.'

Sometimes too he would refer again to her eyes, that were so dark and looked so straight ahead and hardly moved when spoken to. 'It's those wonderful eyes of yours, Mrs Corbett,' he would say. 'I think you have a simply marvellous eye.'

By November the weather had broken up. In the shortening rainy days the beeches began to shed continuous golden-copper showers of leaves. Electric light had now been wired to the outer walls of the house, with concealed lamps beneath the balconies and windows.

She did not see these lights switched on until a darkening afternoon in mid November, when Lafarge greeted her with an intense extravagance of excitement.

'Mrs Corbett, my dear, I've had an absolute storm of inspiration. I'm going to have the house-warmer next Saturday. All my friends are coming and you and I have to talk of hearts and livers and delicious things of that sort and so on and so on. But that isn't really the point. Come outside, Mrs Corbett dear, come outside.'

In the garden, under the dark, baring trees, he switched on the lights. 'There, darling!'

Sensationally a burst of electric light gave to the pink walls and feather-grey canopies, doors, windows, balconies, a new, uplifting sense of transformation. She felt herself catch her breath.

The house seemed to float for a moment against half-naked trees, in the darkening afternoon, and he said in that rapturously plummy voice of his, 'But that isn't all, dear, that isn't all. You see, the rose has arrived. It came this morning. And suddenly I had this wild surmise, this wonderful on-a-peak-in-Darien sort of thing. Can you guess?'

She could not guess.

'I'm going to plant it,' he said, 'at the party.'

'Oh yes, that will be nice,' she said.

'But that's not all, dear, that's not all,' he said. 'More yet. The true, the blushful has still to come. Can't you guess?'

Once again she could not guess.

'I want you to bring that rose of yours to the party,' he said. 'We'll fix it to the tree. And then in the electric light, against the pink walls—'

She felt herself catch her breath again, almost frightened. 'Me?' she said. 'At the party?'

'Well, of course, darling. Of course.'

'Mr Lafarge, I couldn't come to your party—'

'My dear,' he said, 'if you don't come to my party, I shall be for ever mortally, dismally, utterly offended.'

She felt herself begin to tremble. 'But I couldn't, Mr Lafarge, not with all your friends—'

'Darling Mrs Corbett. You are my friend. There's no argument about it. You'll come. You'll bring the rose. We'll fix it to the tree and it will be heaven. All my friends will be here. You'll love my friends.'

She did not protest or even answer. In the brilliant electric light she stared with her dark diffident eyes at the pink walls of the house and felt as if she were under an arc-light, about to undergo an operation, naked, transfixed, and utterly helpless.

It was raining when she drove up to the house on Saturday evening, wearing her cape and carrying the rose in a paper bag. But by the time she reached the hills she was able to stop the windscreen-wipers on the van and presently the sky was pricked with stars.

There were so many cars outside the house that she stood for some time outside, afraid to go in. During this time she was so nervous and preoccupied that she forgot that she was still wearing the cape. She remembered it only at the last moment, and then took it off and rolled it up and put it in the van.

Standing in the kitchen, she could only think that the house was a cage, now full of gibbering monkeys. Bewildered, she stood staring at trays of glasses, rows of bottles, many dishes of decorated morsels of lobster, prawns, olives, nuts, and sausages.

As she stood there a woman came in with a brassy voice, a long yellow cigarette holder, and a low neckline from which melon-like breasts protruded white and hard, and took a drink from a tray, swallowing it quickly before taking the entire tray back with her.

'Just float in, dear. It's like a mill-race in there. You just go with the damn stream.'

Cautiously Mrs Corbett stood by the door of the drawing-room, holding the rose in its paper bag and staring at the gibbering, munching, sipping faces swimming before her in smoky air.

It was twenty minutes before Lafarge, returning to the kitchen for plates of food, accidentally found her standing there, transfixed with deep immobile eyes.

'But darling Mrs Corbett! Where have you been? I've been telling everyone about you and you were not here. I want you to meet everyone. They've all heard about you. Everyone!'

She found herself borne away among strange faces, mute and groping.

'Angela darling, I want you to meet Mrs Corbett. The most wonderful person. The dearest sweetie. I call her my heart specialist.'

A chestless girl with tow-coloured hair, cut low over her forehead to a fringe, as with a basin, stared at her with large, hollow, unhealthy eyes. 'Is it true you're a heart specialist? Where do you practise?'

Before Clara could answer a man with an orange tie, a black shirt and a stiff carrot beard came over and said, 'Good lord, what a mob. Where does Henry get them from? Let's whip off to the local. That woman Forbes is drooling as usual into every ear.'

Excuseless, the girl with hollow eyes followed him away. Lafarge too had disappeared.

'Haven't I seen you somewhere before? Haven't we met? I rather fancied we had.' A young man with prematurely receding, downy yellow hair and uncertain reddish eyes, looking like a stoat, sucked at a glass, smoked a cigarette, and held her in a quivering, fragile stare.

'Known Henry long? Doesn't change much, does he? How's the thing getting on? The opus, I mean. The great work. He'll never finish it, of course. Henry's sort never do.'

It was some time before she realised what was wrong with the fragile uncertain eyes. The young man spilt the contents of his glass over his hands, his coat, and his thin, yellow snake of a tie. He moved away with abrupt unsteadiness and she heard a crash of glass against a chair. It passed unnoticed, as if a pin had dropped.

Presently she was overwhelmed by hoglike snorts of laughter followed by giggling, and someone said, 'What's all this about a rose?'

'God knows.'

'Some gag of Henry's.'

A large man in tweeds of rope-like thickness stood with feet apart, laughing his hoglike laugh. Occasionally he steadied himself as he drank and now and then thrust his free hand under a heavy shirt of black-and-yellow check, scratching the hairs on his chest.

Drinking swiftly, he started to whisper, 'What's all this about Henry and the grocer's wife? They say she's up here every hour of the day.'

'Good lord, Henry and what wife?'

'Grocer's, I thought – I don't know. You mean you haven't heard?'

'Good lord, no. Can't be. Henry and girls?'

'No? You don't think so?'

'Can't believe it. Not Henry. He'd run from a female fly.'

'All females are fly.'

Again, at this remark, there were heavy, engulfing guffaws of laughter.

'Possible, I suppose, possible. One way of getting the custom.'

She stood in a maze, only half hearing, only half awake. Splinters of conversation sent crackling past her bewildered face like scraps of flying glass.

'Anybody know where the polly is? Get me a drink while I'm gone, dear. Gin. Not sherry. The sherry's filthy.'

'Probably bought from the grocer.'

Leaning against the mantelpiece, a long arm extended, ash dropping greyly and seedily down her breast, the lady with the yellow cigarette holder was heard, with a delicate hiss, to accuse someone of bitchiness.

'But then we're all bitches, aren't we,' she said, 'more or less? But she especially.'

'Did she ever invite you? She gets you to make up a number for dinner and when you get there a chap appears on the doorstep and says they don't need you any more. Yes, actually!'

'She's a swab. Well, poor Alex, he knows it now.'

'That's the trouble, of course – when you do know, it's always too bloody late to matter.'

Everywhere the air seemed to smoke with continuous white explosions. Soon Clara started to move away and found herself facing a flushed eager Lafarge, who in turn was pushing past a heavy woman in black trousers, with the jowls of a bloodhound and bright blonde hair neatly brushed back and oiled, like a man.

'There you are, Mrs Corbett. You've no drink. Nothing to eat. You haven't met anybody.'

A man was edging past her and Lafarge seized him by the arm.

'Siegfried. Mrs Corbett, this is my friend Siegfried Pascoe. Siegfried, dear fellow, hold her hand. Befriend her while I get her a drink. It's our dear Mrs Corbett, Siegfried, of heart fame.' He squeezed Mrs Corbett's arm, laughing. 'His mother called him Siegfried because she had a Wagner complex,' he said. 'Don't move!'

An object like an unfledged bird, warm and boneless, slid into her hand. Limply it slid out again and she looked up to see a plump creaseless moon of a face, babyish, almost pure white under carefully curled brown hair, staring down at her with pettish, struggling timidity. A moment later, in a void, she heard the Pascoe voice attempting to frame its syllables like a little fussy machine misfiring, the lips loose and puffy.

'What do you f-f-f-feel about Eliot?' it said.

She could not answer; she could think of no one she knew by the name of Eliot.

To her relief Lafarge came back, bearing a glass of sherry and a plate on which were delicate slices of meat rolled up and filled with wine-red jelly. 'This,' he told her, 'is the heart. Yes, your heart, Mrs Corbett. The common old heart. Taste it, dear. Take the fork. Taste it and see if it isn't absolute manna. I'll hold the sherry.'

She ate the cold heart. Cranberry sauce squeezed itself from the rolls of meat and ran down her chin and just in time she caught it with a fork.

The heart, she thought, tasted not at all unlike heart and in confusion she heard Lafarge inquire, 'Delicious?'

'Very nice.'

'Splendid. So glad—'

With a curious unapologetic burst of indifference he turned on his heel and walked away. Five seconds later he was back again, saying, 'Siegfried, dear boy, we shall do the rose in five minutes. Could you muster the spade? It's stopped raining. We'll fling the doors open, switch on the lights, and make a dramatic thing of it. Everybody will pour forth—'

He disappeared a second time into the mass of gibbering faces, taking with him her glass of sherry, and when she turned her eyes she saw that Siegfried Pascoe too had gone.

'What on earth has possessed Henry? They say she's the butcher's wife. Not grocer's after all.'

'Oh, it's a gag, dear. You know how they hot things up. It's a gag.'

She set her plate at last on a table and began to pick her way through the crush of drinkers, seeking the kitchen. To her great relief there was no one there. Suddenly tired, hopelessly bewildered and sick, she sat down on a chair, facing a wreckage of half-chewed vol-au-vents, canapés, salted biscuits and cold eyes of decorated egg. The noise from the big drawing-room increased like the hoarse and nervous clamour rising from people who, trapped, lost, and unable to find their way, were fighting madly to be free.

Out of it all leapt a sudden collective gasp, as if gates had been burst open and the trapped, lost ones could now mercifully find their way. In reality it was a gasp of surprise as Lafarge switched on the outside lights, and she heard it presently followed by a rush of feet as people shuffled outwards into the rainless garden air.

Not moving, she sat alone at the kitchen table, clutching the rose in the paper bag. From the garden she heard laughter bursting in excited taunting waves. A wag shouted in a loud voice, 'Forward the grave-diggers! On with the spade-work!' and there were fresh claps of caterwauling laughter.

From it all sprang the sudden petulant voice of Lafarge, like a child crying for a toy, 'The rose! On, my dear, the rose! Where *is* the rose? We can't do it without the rose.'

Automatically she got up from the table. Even before she heard Lafarge's voice, nearer now, calling her name, she was already walking across the emptied drawing-room, towards the open french windows, with the paper bag.

'Mrs Corbett! Mrs Corbett! Oh, there you are, dear. Where did you get to? What a relief – and oh, you poppet, you've got the rose.'

She was hardly aware that he was taking her by the hand. She was hardly aware, as she stepped into the blinding white light of electric lamps placed about the bright pink walls, that he was saying, 'Oh, but Mrs Corbett, you must. After all, it's your rose, dear. I insist. It's all part of the thing. It's the nicest part of the thing—'

Vaguely she became aware that the rose tree, spreading five fanlike branches, was already in its place by the wall.

'Just tie it on, dear. Here's the ribbon. I managed to get exactly the right-coloured ribbon.'

From behind her, as she stood under the naked light, tying the rose to the tree, she was assailed by voices in chattering boisterous acclamation. A few people actually clapped their hands and there were sudden trumpeted bursts of laughter as the wag who had shouted of grave-diggers suddenly shouted again, 'Damn it all, Henry, give her a kiss. Kiss the lady! Be fair.'

'Kiss her!' everyone started shouting. 'Kiss her. Kiss! Kiss, Henry! Kiss, kiss!'

'*Pour encourager les autres!*' the wag shouted. 'Free demonstration.'

After a sudden burst of harsh, jovial catcalls she turned her face away, again feeling utterly naked and transfixed under the stark white lights. A second later she felt Lafarge's lips brush clumsily, plummily across her own.

Everyone responded to this with loud bursts of cheers.

'Ceremony over!' Lafarge called out. He staggered uncertainly, beckoning his guests housewards. 'Everybody back to the flesh-pots. Back to the grain and grape.'

'Henry's tight,' somebody said. 'What fun. Great, the kissing. Going to be a good party.'

She stood for some time alone in the garden, holding the empty paper bag. In an unexpected moment the lights on the pink walls were extinguished, leaving only the light from windows shining across the grass outside. She stood for a few moments longer and then groped to the wall, untied the rose and put it back in the paper bag.

Driving away down the hillside, she stopped the van at last and drew it into a gateway simply because she could think of no other way of calming the trembling in her hands. She stood for a long time clutching the side of the van. In confusion she thought of the rose on the wall, of hearts that were like goose-flesh, and of how, as Clem said, the gentry would come back. Then she took her cape and the paper bag with its rose out of the van.

When she had dropped the paper bag and the rose into the ditch she slowly pulled on the old cape and started to cry. As she cried she drew the cape over her head, as if afraid that some-one would see her crying there, and then buried her face in it, as into a shroud.

Colonel Gracie, who had decided to boil himself two new-laid eggs for lunch, came into the kitchen from the garden and laid his panama hat on top of the stove, put the eggs into it and then, after some moments of blissful concentration, looked inside to see if they were cooking.

Presently he sensed that something was vaguely wrong about all this and began to search for a saucepan. Having found it, a small blue enamel one much blackened by fire, he gazed at it with intent inquiry for some moments, half made a gesture as if to put it on his head and then decided to drop the eggs into it, without benefit of water. In the course of doing this he twice dipped the sleeve of his white duck jacket into a dish of raspberry jam, originally put out on the kitchen table for breakfast. The jam dish was in fact a candlestick, in pewter, the candle part of which had broken away.

Soon the Colonel, in the process of making himself some toast, found himself wondering what day it was. He couldn't be sure. He had recently given up taking *The Times* and it was this that made things difficult. He knew the month was July, although the calendar hanging by the side of the stove actually said it was September, but that of course didn't help much about the day. He guessed it might be Tuesday; but you never really knew when you lived alone. Still, it helped sometimes to know whether it was Tuesday or Sunday, just in case he ran short of tobacco and walked all the way to the village shop only to find it closed.

Was it Tuesday? The days were normally fixed quite clearly in his mind by a system of colouration. Tuesday was a most distinct shade of raspberry rose. Thursday was brown and Sunday a pleasant yellow, that particularly bright gold you got in sunflowers. Today seemed, he thought, rather a dark green, much more like a Wednesday. It was most important to differentiate, because if it were really Wednesday it would be not the slightest use his walking down to the shop to get stamps after lunch, since Wednesday was early closing day.

There was nothing for it, he told himself, but to semaphore his friend Miss Wilkinson. With a piece of toast in his hand he set about finding his signalling flags, which he always kept in a cupboard under the stairs. As he stooped to unlatch the cupboard door a skein of onions left over from the previous winter dropped from a fragile string on the wall and fell on his neck without alarming him visibly.

One of the flags was bright yellow, the other an agreeable shade of chicory blue. Experience had shown that these two colours showed up far better than all others against the surrounding landscape of lush chestnut copse and woodland. They were clearly visible for a good half mile.

In the army, from which he was now long retired, signalling had been the Colonel's special pigeon. He had helped to train a considerable number of men with extreme proficiency. Miss Wilkinson, who was sixty, wasn't of course quite so apt a pupil as a soldier in his prime, but she had nevertheless been overjoyed to learn what was not altogether a difficult art. It had been the greatest fun for them both; it had whiled away an enormous number of lonely hours.

For the past five weeks Miss Wilkinson had been away, staying on the south coast with a sister, and the Colonel had missed her greatly. Not only had there been no one to whom he could signal his questions, doubts and thoughts; he had never really been quite sure, all that time, what day it was.

After now having had the remarkable presence of mind to put an inch or two of water into the egg saucepan the Colonel set out with the flags to walk to the bottom of the garden, which sloped fairly steeply to its southern boundary, a three foot hedge of hawthorn. Along the hedge thirty or forty gigantic heads of sunflower were in full flower, the huge faces staring like yellow guardians across the three sloping open meadows that lay between the Colonel and Miss Wilkinson, who lived in a small white weatherboard house down on the edge of a narrow stream. Sometimes after torrential winter rains the little stream rose with devastating rapidity, flooding Miss Wilkinson, so that the Colonel had to be there at the double, to bale her out.

In the centre of the hedge was a stile and the Colonel, who in his crumpled suit of white duck looked something like a cadaverous baker out of work, now stood up on it and blew three sharp blasts on a whistle. This was the signal to fetch Miss Wilkinson from the kitchen, the greenhouse, the potting shed, or wherever she happened to be. The system of whistle and flag suited both the Colonel and Miss Wilkinson admirably, the Colonel because he hated the telephone so much and Miss Wilkinson because she couldn't afford to have the instrument installed. For the same reasons neither of them owned either television or radio, the Colonel having laid it down in expressly severe terms, almost as if in holy writ, that he would not only never have such anti-social devices in the house but that they were also, in a sense, degenerate: if not immoral.

Miss Wilkinson having appeared in her garden in a large pink sun hat and a loose summery blue dress with flowers all over it, the Colonel addressed her by smartly raising his yellow flag. Miss Wilkinson replied by promptly raising her blue one. This meant that they were receiving each other loud and clear.

The day in fact was so beautifully clear that the Colonel could actually not only see Miss Wilkinson in detail as she stood on the small wooden bridge that spanned the stream but he could also pick out slender spires of purple loosestrife among the many tall reeds that lined the banks like dark green swords. Both he and Miss Wilkinson, among their many other things in common, were crazy about flowers.

Having given himself another moment to get into correct position, the Colonel presently signalled to Miss Wilkinson that he was frightfully sorry to trouble her but would she very much mind telling him what day it was?

To his infinite astonishment Miss Wilkinson signalled back that it was Thursday and, as if determined to leave no doubt about it, added that it was also August the second.

August? the Colonel replied. He was much surprised. He thought it was July.

No, no, it was August, Miss Wilkinson told him. Thursday the second – the day he was coming to tea.

The Colonel had spent the morning since ten o'clock in a rush of perspiring industry, cleaning out the hens. The fact that he was going to tea with Miss Wilkinson had, like the precise date and month, somehow slipped his mind.

'You hadn't forgotten, had you?'

'Oh! no, no, I hadn't forgotten. Had an awfully long morning, that's all. Would you mind telling me what time it is now?'

In the clear summer air the Colonel could distinctly see the movement of Miss Wilkinson's arm as she raised it to look at her watch. He himself never wore a watch. Though altogether less pernicious than telephone, television and radio, a watch nevertheless belonged, in his estimation, to that category of inventions that one could well do without.

'Ten to four.'

Good God, the Colonel thought, now struck by the sudden realisation that he hadn't had lunch yet.

'I was expecting you in about ten minutes. It's so lovely I thought we'd have tea outside. Under the willow tree.'

Admirable idea, the Colonel thought, without signalling it. What, by the way, had he done with the eggs? Were they on the boil or not? He couldn't for the life of him remember.

'Do you wish any eggs?' he asked. 'I have heaps.'

'No, thank you all the same. I have some.' It might have been a laugh or merely a bird-cry that the Colonel heard coming across the meadows. 'Don't be too long. I have a surprise for you.'

As he hurried back to the house the Colonel wondered, in a dreamy sort of way, what kind of surprise Miss Wilkinson could possibly have for him and as he wondered he felt a sort of whisper travel across his heart. It was the sort of tremor he often experienced when he was on the way to see her or when he looked at the nape of her neck or when she spoke to him in some specially direct or unexpected sort of way. He would like to have put this feeling into words of some kind – signalling was child's play by comparison – but he was both too inarticulate and too shy to do so.

Half an hour later, after walking down through the meadows, he fully expected to see Miss Wilkinson waiting for him on the bank of the stream under the willow-tree, where the tea-table, cool with lace cloth, was already laid. But there was no sign of her there or in the greenhouse, where cucumbers were growing on humid vines, or in the kitchen.

Then, to his great surprise, he heard her voice calling him from some distance off and a moment later he saw her twenty yards or so away, paddling in the stream.

'Just remembered I'd seen a bed of watercress yesterday and I thought how nice it would be. Beautifully cool, the water.'

As he watched her approaching, legs bare and white above emerald skim of water-weed, the Colonel again experienced the tremor that circumvented his heart like a whisper. This time it was actually touched with pain and there was nothing he could say.

'Last year there was a bed much farther upstream. But I suppose the seeds get carried down.'

Miss Wilkinson was fair and pink, almost cherubic, her voice jolly. A dew-lap rather like those seen in ageing dogs hung floppily down on the collar of her cream shantung dress, giving her a look of obese friendliness and charm.

'The kettle's on already,' she said. 'Sit yourself down while I go in and get my feet dried.'

The Colonel, watching her white feet half-running, half-trotting across the lawn, thought again of the surprise she had in store for him and wondered if paddling in the stream was it. No other, he thought, could have had a sharper effect on him.

When she came back, carrying a silver hot water jug and teapot, she laughed quite gaily in reply to his query about the surprise. No: it wasn't paddling in the stream. And she was afraid he would have to wait until after tea before she could tell him, anyway.

'Oh! how stupid of me,' she said, abruptly pausing in the act of pouring tea, 'I've gone and forgotten the watercress.'

'I'll get it, I'll get it,' the Colonel said, at once leaping up to go into the house.

'Oh! no, you don't,' she said. 'Not on your life. My surprise is in there.'

Later, drinking tea and munching brown bread and butter and cool sprigs of watercress dipped in salt, the Colonel found it impossible to dwell on the question of the surprise without uneasiness. In an effort to take his mind off the subject he remarked on how good the sunflowers were this year and what a fine crop of seeds there would be. He fed them to the hens.

'I think it's the sunflowers that give the eggs that deep brown colour,' he said.

'You do?' she said. 'By the way did you like the pie I made for you?'

'Pie?'

With silent distress the Colonel recalled a pie of morello cherries, baked and bestowed on him the day before yesterday. He had put it into the larder and had forgotten that too.

'It was delicious. I'm saving half of it for supper.'

Miss Wilkinson, looking at him rather as dogs sometimes look, head sideways, with a meditative glint in her eye, asked suddenly what he had had for lunch? Not eggs again?

'Eggs are so easy.'

'I've told you before. You can't live on eggs all the time,' she said. 'I've been making pork brawn this morning. Would you care for some of that?'

'Yes, I would. Thank you. I would indeed.'

From these trivial discussions on food it seemed to the Colonel that a curious and elusive sense of intimacy sprang up. It was difficult to define but it was almost as if either he or Miss Wilkinson had proposed to each other and had been, in spirit at least, accepted.

This made him so uneasy again that he suddenly said:

'By the way, I don't think I told you. I've given up *The Times.*'

'Oh! really. Isn't that rather rash?'

'I don't think so. I'd been considering it for some time actually. You see, one is so busy with the hens and the garden and all that sort of thing that quite often one gets no time to read until ten o'clock. Which is absurd. I thought that from time to time I might perhaps borrow yours?'

'Of course.'

The Colonel, thinking that perhaps he was talking too much, sat silent. How pretty the stream looked, he thought. The purple loosestrife had such dignity by the waterside. He must go fishing again one day. The stream held a few trout and in the deeper pools there were chub.

'Are you quite sure you won't feel lost without a paper? I think I should.'

'No, no. I don't think so. One gets surfeited anyway with these wretched conferences and ministerial comings and goings and world tension and so on. One wants to be away from it all.'

'One mustn't run away from life, nevertheless.'

Life was what you made it, the Colonel pointed out. He preferred it as much as possible untrammelled.

Accepting Miss Wilkinson's offer of a third cup of tea and

another plate of the delicious watercress he suddenly realised
that he was ravenously hungry. There was a round plum cake
on the table and his eye kept wandering back to it with the poig-
nant voracity of a boy after a game of football. After a time
Miss Wilkinson noticed this and started to cut the cake in readiness.

'I'm thinking of going fishing again very soon,' the Colonel said.
'If I bag a trout or two perhaps you might care to join me for
supper?'

'I should absolutely love to.'

It was remarks of such direct intimacy, delivered in a moist,
jolly voice, that had the Colonel's heart in its curious whispering
state again. In silence he contemplated the almost too pleasant
prospect of having Miss Wilkinson to supper. He would try his
best to cook the trout nicely, in butter, and not burn them. Perhaps he would also be able to manage a glass of wine.

'I have a beautiful white delphinium in bloom,' Miss Wilkinson
said. 'I want to show it you after tea.'

'That isn't the surprise?'

Miss Wilkinson laughed with almost incautious jollity.

'You must forget all about the surprise. You're like a small
boy who can't wait for Christmas.'

The Colonel apologised for what seemed to be impatience and
then followed this with a second apology, saying he was sorry
he'd forgotten to ask Miss Wilkinson if she had enjoyed the long
visit to her sister.

'Oh! splendidly. It really did me the world of good. One gets
sort of ham-strung by one's habits, don't you think? It's good
to get away.'

To the Colonel her long absence had seemed exactly the opposite. He would like to have told her how much he had missed
her. Instead something made him say:

'I picked up a dead gold-finch in the garden this morning.
It had fallen among the sea kale. Its yellow wing was open on one
of the grey leaves and I thought it was a flower.'

'The cat, I suppose?'

'No, no. There was no sign of violence at all.'

Away downstream a dove cooed, breaking and yet deepening
all the drowsiness of the summer afternoon. What did one want
with world affairs, presidential speeches, threats of war and all

those things? the Colonel wondered. What had newspapers ever given to the world that could be compared with that one sound, the solo voice of the dove by the waterside?

'No, no. No more tea, thank you. Perhaps another piece of cake, yes. That's excellent, thank you.'

The last crumb of cake having been consumed, the Colonel followed Miss Wilkinson into the flower garden to look at the white delphinium. It's snowy grace filled him with an almost ethereal sense of calm. He couldn't have been, he thought, more happy.

'Very beautiful. Most beautiful.'

'I'm going to divide it in the spring,' Miss Wilkinson said, 'and give you a piece.'

After a single murmur of acceptance for this blessing the Colonel remained for some moments speechless, another tremor travelling round his heart, this time like the quivering of a tightened wire.

'Well now,' Miss Wilkinson said, 'I think I might let you see the surprise if you're ready.'

He was not only ready but even eager, the Colonel thought.

'I'll lead the way,' Miss Wilkinson said.

She led the way into the sitting room, which was beautifully cool and full of the scent of small red carnations. The Colonel, who was not even conscious of being a hopelessly untidy person himself, nevertheless was always struck by the pervading neatness, the laundered freshness, of all parts of Miss Wilkinson's house. It was like a little chintz holy-of-holies, always embalmed, always the same.

'Well, what do you say? There it is.'

The Colonel, with customary blissful absent-mindedness, stared about the room without being able to note that anything had changed since his last visit there.

'I must say I don't really see anything in the nature of a surprise.'

'Oh! you do. Don't be silly.'

No, the Colonel had to confess, there was nothing he could see. It was all exactly as he had seen it the last time.

'Over there. In the corner. Of course it's rather a small one. Not as big as my sister's.'

It slowly began to reach the blissfully preoccupied cloisters of the Colonel's mind that he was gazing at a television set. A cramping chill went round his heart. For a few unblissful moments he stared hard in front of him, tormented by a sense of being unfairly trapped, with nothing to say.

'My sister gave it to me. She's just bought herself a new one. You see you get so little allowed for an old one in part exchange that it's hardly worth—'

'You mean you've actually got it permanently?'

'Why, yes. Of course.'

The Colonel found himself speaking with a voice so constricted that it seemed almost to be disembodied.

'But I always thought you hated those things.'

'Well, I suppose there comes a day. I must say it was a bit of a revelation at my sister's. Some of the things one saw were absorbing. For instance there was a programme about a remote Indian tribe in the forests of South America that I found quite marvellous.' The Colonel was stiff, remote-eyed, as if not listening. 'This tribe was in complete decay. It was actually dying out, corrupted—'

'Corrupted by what? By civilisation my guess would be.'

'As a matter of fact they were. For one thing they die like flies from measles.'

'Naturally. That,' the Colonel said, 'is what I am always trying to say.'

'Yes, but there are other viewpoints. One comes to realise that.'

'The parallel seems to me to be an exact one,' the Colonel said.

'I'm afraid I can't agree.'

There was now a certain chill, almost an iciness, in the air. The ethereal calm of the afternoon, its emblem the white delphinium, seemed splintered and blackened. The Colonel, though feeling that Miss Wilkinson had acted in some way like a traitor, at the same time had no way of saying so. It was all so callous, he thought, so shockingly out of character. He managed to blurt out:

'I really didn't think you'd come down to this.'

'I didn't come down to it, as you so candidly put it. It was simply a gift from my sister. You talk about it as if I'd started taking some sort of horrible drug.'

'In a sense you have.'

'I'm afraid I disagree again.'

'All these things are drugs. Cinemas, radio, television, telephone, even newspapers. That's really why I've given up *The Times*. I thought we always agreed on that?'

'We may have done. At one time. Now we'll have to agree to differ.'

'Very well.'

A hard lump rose in the Colonel's throat and stuck there. A miserable sense of impotence seized him and kept him stiff, with nothing more to say.

'I might have shown you a few minutes of it and converted you,' Miss Wilkinson said. 'But the aerial isn't up yet. It's coming this evening.'

'I don't think I want to be converted, thank you.'

'I hoped you'd like it and perhaps come down in the evenings sometimes and watch.'

'Thank you, I shall be perfectly happy in my own way.'

'Very well. I'm sorry you're so stubborn about it.'

The Colonel was about to say with acidity that he was not stubborn and then changed his mind and said curtly that he must go. After a painful silence Miss Wilkinson said:

'Well, if you must I'll get the pork brawn.'

'I don't think I care for the pork brawn, thank you.'

'Just as you like.'

At the door of the sitting room the Colonel paused, if anything stiffer than ever, and remarked that if there was something he particularly wanted he would signal her.

'I shan't be answering any signals,' Miss Wilkinson said.

'You won't be answering any signals?'

An agony of disbelief went twisting through the Colonel, imposing on him a momentary paralysis. He could only stare.

'No: I shan't be answering any signals.'

'Does that mean you won't be speaking to me again?'

'I didn't say that.'

'I think it rather sounds like that.'

'Then you must go on thinking it sounds like that, that's all.'

It was exactly as if Miss Wilkinson had slapped him harshly in the face; it was precisely as if he had proposed and been rudely rejected.

'Good-bye,' he said in a cold and impotent voice.

'Good-bye,' she said. 'I'll see you out.'

'There's no need to see me out, thank you. I'll find my way alone.'

Back in his own kitchen the Colonel discovered that the eggs had boiled black in the saucepan. He had forgotten to close the door of the stove. Brown smoke was hanging everywhere. Trying absentmindedly to clear up the mess he twice put his sleeve in the jam dish without noticing it and then wiped his sleeve across the tablecloth, uncleared since breakfast-time.

In the garden the dead gold-finch still lay on the silvery leaf of sea kale and he stood staring at it for a long time, stiff-eyed and impotent, unable to think one coherent simple thought.

Finally he went back to the house, took out the signalling flags and went over to the stile. Standing on it, he gave three difficult blasts on the whistle but nothing happened in answer except that one of two men standing on the roof of Miss Wilkinson's house, erecting the television aerial, casually turned his head.

Then he decided to send a signal. The three words he wanted so much to send were 'Please forgive me' but after some moments of contemplation he found that he had neither the heart nor the will to raise a flag.

Instead he simply stood immovable by the stile, staring across the meadows in the evening sun. His eyes were blank. They seemed to be groping in immeasurable appeal for something and as if in answer to it the long row of great yellow sunflower faces, the seeds of which were so excellent for the hens, stared back at him, in that wide, laughing, almost mocking way that sunflowers have.

LOST BALL

'I often wonder if you couldn't do it by holding your breath for five minutes,' the girl said. 'I suppose that would be the most painless way.'

For some distance inland, in places unprotected by the sea-white shoulders of long sand-dunes, the shore had invaded the golf-course, giving wide stretches of it a sandy baldness from which hungry spears of grass sprang wirily, like greyish yellow hairs.

In other places the winds of old winters had thrown up pebbles, some grey, some brown, some like mauve oval cakes of soap, but most of them pure chalk white, water-smoothed to the perfection of eggs laid in casual clutches by long-vanished birds.

It was somewhere among the eggs that Phillips had lost his golf ball. He was always losing one there. They were so damn difficult to see and when it happened over and over again it was enough to drive you mad.

'They're so hellishly expensive too,' he said. That was why he had come back to search for the second time through the summer evening, after almost everyone else was either cheerfully gathered in the club-house or had long since gone home. 'I mean it makes the whole thing—'

'When did you lose it?'

'This morning. About half-past eleven. Of course I couldn't stop then. Still playing. I suppose you weren't here about that time, were you?'

'I've been here all day.'

'I mean I suppose you didn't see or hear anything about that time? I wondered if you might perhaps have—'

'Not a sound.'

Every Sunday morning he played eighteen holes with the same three fellows: Robinson, Chalmers and Forbes. He supposed they had played like that for ten, perhaps twelve years, at any rate ever since the war, except when they played in competitions,

425

when of course they were paired with other people and it wasn't quite the same.

'You couldn't have hit it into the sea, could you?' she said. He looked at her sharply. She was still lying exactly where he had first stumbled across her and in the same position: curved and reclined pale bare arms clasped at the back of her brown hair, her entire body crumpled into the white sandy lap of dune.

On her face, in which the eyes were remarkably dark and inert, as if she were half asleep as she contemplated the sky, he thought the expression of deep indifference amounted almost to contempt. Young people often looked like that and he supposed she was only nineteen or twenty.

He felt faintly annoyed too. Lately a lot of people had been using the golf course for any old thing: parking cars, picnics, courting in the sand dunes, exercising dogs and that sort of caper. The committee had tried hard to stop it several times but it was damn difficult with the shore and the course so often merging into one.

Moreover it was a good fifty or sixty yards from the middle of the fairway to the dunes and then another forty or fifty to the sea.

'Into the sea?' he said. 'Half a minute, I'm not that bad.'

'I should have thought it would have been quite a feat to have hit it into the sea.'

Quite obviously she hadn't a clue about the game; which when you came to think of it was rather remarkable in these days, when so many women hit the ball as hard as a man.

'Well, I'm going to have another look,' he said. 'I'm going to find the damn thing if it kills me.'

Still contemplating the sky, still in that same half-sleepy, crumpled position, she said:

'If it hasn't killed you in five minutes I'll help you look for it.'

He walked away without answering. Among the hollows of the dunes the evening air was still warm. Thick white sand sucked his shoes down and from the sea came one of those liquid summer breeezes that you thought were so pleasant until they tired you.

As he walked about the shore scattered clutches of pebbles, like white eggs, continually bobbed up to deceive him, so much so that once or twice he was on the point of running to pick up his ball.

He always hated the idea of losing a ball. Quite apart from the expense it was a point of honour. Once before he had come back three evenings running to find a ball that other fellows would have given up as a bad job. He had had the luck to find three of someone else's too: which simply went to show that it didn't pay to give up.

After another twenty minutes of slogging about the dunes he suddenly felt quite tired. He was beginning to put on weight: not so much weight as either Chalmers or Forbes, both of whom had a belly, but more than Robinson, who was fifty-five, three years older than he was.

When he got back to the dune where the girl was he found her half sitting up, her knees bent. On one knee she was smoothing with slow strokes of her hand a square of silver paper. The brilliance of the smooth tin-foil in the evening sun made him realise for the first time the exact colour of her dress. He had simply thought it to be brown. Now he saw that it was really a blend of two colours: of dark rose-brown and purple shot together.

Under the dress the shape of her knees was graceful. The tips of her toes were buried in the sand. The way she smoothed the silver paper was merely mechanical. She was not really looking at it at all.

'Found it?'

'No,' he said. 'I'll probably have to come back tomorrow. It's enough to drive you to drink, or suicide, or both. I don't know.'

'As bad as that?'

'Irritating. Maddening.'

She was still smoothing the silver paper and yet not looking at it. A breeze caught the paper and crackled it upward, like the flutter of a wing, and she pinned it down on her knee again with one finger, quite casually, as if bored.

'Mind if I ask you something?' she said.

'No. What?'

'How would you go about it?'

For a moment he was mystified and then realised, with abrupt surprise, what she was talking about.

'Oh! here, wait a minute,' he said, 'it hasn't got quite as far as that.'

'Oh! hasn't it? I thought you said it had.'

'Well, hardly. I mean it's one of those things everybody says—'

'But supposing it did?'

He felt a chill of distaste run over him. Abruptly he looked at the western horizon and thought that there might be still another hour in which to search for the ball before twilight came down.

It was then that she said:

'I often wonder if you couldn't do it by holding your breath for five minutes. I suppose that would be the most painless way?'

Got to find that damn ball somehow, he thought. He had been on the point of sitting down for five minutes' rest but now he found himself prickling with impatience instead.

'I suppose you wouldn't help me look?' he said. 'There isn't a lot more daylight—'

'If you like. I don't mind.'

As she got to her feet he saw that her dark brown hair, very ruffled, was starred everywhere with dry white sand. She seemed not to notice it. Nor did she even bother to shake it out.

Suddenly, as she climbed up to the grassy crest of the dune, he was captured by the grace of her bare legs, the skin a fine pure cream under the brown-purple skirt. With astonishment he found himself really looking at her for the first time. She was rather tall, shapely and no longer crumpled.

She was what the fellows at the club would call nifty; she was what Freddy Robinson, in his heavy, waggish way, would refer to as a *petite morçeau de tout droit*.

Suddenly from the top of the dune she turned, looking towards the sea. For some moments her eyes looked quite hollow and there was no answer for him when he said:

'You'll have to watch out for the pebbles. Especially the white ones. They're the ones that trick you.'

He was never more than ten or a dozen yards from her as they walked about the dunes. The sun, falling as a coppery-orange disc into a rippled milk-blue sea, gradually stained sand and grass and pebbles with a flush of fire. The marine blue thorns of sea-thistle were touched with sepia rose. Her dress turned a sombre purple against her bare cream legs and arms.

'Have to give it up,' he called at last. 'Afraid it's no go. Just have to come back tomorrow, that's all.'

Once again there was no answer. She was simply walking with unbroken dreamy indifference across shadowy, smouldering sand.

'Can I give you a lift or something?' he said. 'My car's at the club-house. No distance at all.'

Again there was no answer; but suddenly he saw her stoop, straighten slowly up again and then hold up her hand.

'Is this it?'

He actually started running. When he reached her she was holding the ball, exactly like a precious egg, in the palm of her hand.

'My God, it is,' he said. 'My God, what a bit of luck.'

He felt extraordinarily excited. He had a ridiculous impulse to shake her by the hand.

'My God, what a bit of luck,' he kept saying. 'Nearly dark. What a bit of luck.'

In the excitement of grasping the ball he was unaware that she had already started to walk away.

'Are you off?' he said. 'Where are you going? Which way?'

She walked along the beach without pausing or looking back.

'Just back to where I was sitting. I dropped my piece of silver paper.'

He found himself almost running after her.

'Saved me a shilling too,' he said. 'I can tell you that.'

'Oh?' she said. 'Is that all they cost?'

He laughed. 'Oh! Good God, no. Didn't mean that. I meant we have a sort of kitty – the four of us, I mean, the chaps I play with. Every time we lose a ball we put a bob in.'

'Why?'

'Sort of fine. Amazing how it adds up.'

'What do you do with it when it adds up?'

'Buy more balls.' He laughed again. 'That's where the fun starts.'

'Fun?'

She was walking more slowly now. The folds of her purplish skirt were touched with copper. The sea burned with small metallic waves.

'You see we have a draw. Sort of lottery. Lucky number. Chap who gets the lucky number gets the balls.'

'I don't get it.'

'Suppose it's the old thrill – the kick you get out of any gamble. Something for nothing.'

She started to look about her, as if not quite certain about the exact place where she had left her silver paper on the beach.

'You see what I mean, don't you?' he said. 'You might never lose a ball for a couple of months and then wham! you hit the jack-pot. That's when it's fun – when you see the faces of the other chaps.'

'I see.'

'Of course it might be you next time.' He laughed again. 'But so far I've been damn lucky. Struck it three times out of five. Fred Chalmers is the one – never had it once. Worth anything to see his face – livid, I tell you. Livid isn't the word.'

He laughed yet again and suddenly she let out a quick startled cry.

'Oh! my silver paper's gone.'

He didn't bother to answer. A vivid picture of Fred Chalmers' furious face lit up the air between sea and beach with a heartening glow.

'The wind must have taken it,' she said. 'I'd had it all day.'

In the failing light she stood staring thoughtfully down at the hollow her body had made in the sand.

'It isn't so important, is it?' he said. The ball felt hard and secure as he pressed it in his hand and put it in his pocket. 'I'm afraid I must be going. What about you? Coming along?'

'No. I think I'll stay a little longer.'

'Getting dark.'

'It always does some time.'

She took a few light half-running steps down the beach, as if she had seen the silver paper. A fragment of dying light bounced from a breaking wave. A few spreading phosphorescent tongues of foam lapped the sand.

'Sure you won't change your mind and come and have a drink?'

'No thanks. I'll stay a bit longer. I want to find my piece of silver paper.'

'Really? Why?'

She was walking away now, face towards the sunset but slightly downcast.

'I just do. I'll just cover the water-front a few more times.

'You know that song? *I cover the Water-front?*'

He thought he heard her sigh; she might suddenly have been holding her breath.

'Can't say I do.'

'Nice song. *"I cover the Water-front. I'm watching the sea. Oh! When will my love come back to me—"*'

She was already too far away for him to hear the rest of the song. Her figure was black against the last thin running bars of copper above the sea.

'Afraid you won't stand much chance of seeing anything now, will you?' he called.

He got no answer. He looked briefly at her figure, the darkening sand and the lapping phosphorescent tongues of foam and then started to walk up the slope of the beach towards the dunes.

The evening wind was fresher there. The grey-yellow hairs of dune-grass were pressed close against smoothed ridges of sand. A leaf or two of sea-thistle rattled sharply.

Caught among hairs of grass, the square of silver paper rattled too.

'Wrong way,' he started saying aloud. 'Looking the wrong way!'

He was half-way down to the beach, waving the silver paper, before he realised ruddenly what he was doing.

'Here, I've got your piece of paper,' he was already saying. 'I've found it—'

A second later he stopped speaking and pulled up sharp, glancing round at the same time as if someone might possibly be listening.

Then suddenly he realised what an awful damn fool he was making – absolute damn fool. He looked hastily along the shore in the gathering darkness to make quite sure that the girl had not heard him running back with that ridiculous piece of paper. Why the hell could it be all that important to her? What on earth could anyone possibly want with that?

It was time he stopped fooling around and got back to the club-house and talked to the chaps and bought himself a whisky, he thought – perhaps two.

He started up the slope towards the dunes again, screwing up the silver paper into a little ball as he went. At the ridge he turned for a second time and looked back.

The shore was quite empty. He threw down the silver ball among the pebbles that were so like clutches of eggs laid by long-vanished birds and didn't even bother to watch where it fell.

Looking finally towards the last copper straws of sunset cloud, he started suddenly to congratulate himself. 'Just as well not to chase your luck too far,' he thought. 'Might get caught up with something funny. Anyway, you got your ball back, old boy. Be satisfied.'

He listened again for a sound of her voice or her footsteps coming back. But all he could hear was the sound of wind and tide rising and halting and falling in little bursts along the darkening shore.

It was exactly as if the sea sometimes held its breath and then broke into a little fragile, broken song.

THELMA

The place where she was born was eighty miles from London. She was never to go to London in all her life except in dreams or in imagination, when she lay awake in the top bedroom of the hotel, listening to the sound of wind in the forest boughs.

When she first began to work at *The Blenheim Arms* she was a plump short girl of fourteen, with remarkably pale cream hands and a head of startling hair exactly the colour of autumn beech leaves. Her eyes seemed bleached and languid. The only colour in their lashes was an occasional touch of gold that made them look like curled paint brushes that were not quite dry.

She began first as a bedroom maid, living in and starting at five in the morning and later taking up brass cans of hot shaving water to the bedrooms of gentlemen who stayed over-night. These gentlemen – any guest was called a gentleman in those days – were mostly commercial travellers going regularly from London to the West country or back again and after a time she got to know them very well. After a time she also got to know the view from the upper bedroom windows very well: southward to the village, down the long wide street of brown-red houses where horses in those days were still tied to hitching posts and then westward and northward and eastward to the forest that sheltered the houses like a great horseshoe of boughs and leaves. She supposed there were a million beech-trees in that forest. She did not know. She only knew, because people said so, that you could walk all day through it and never come to the other side.

At first she was too shy and too quiet about her work in the bedrooms. She knocked on early morning doors too softly. Heavy sleepers could not be woken by the tap of her small soft hands and cans of hot water grew cold on landings while other fuming frowsy men lay awake, waiting for their calls. This early mistake was almost the only one she ever made. The hotel was very old, with several long back stair-cases and complicated narrow passages and still more flights of stairs up which she had to lug, every morning to attic bedrooms, twenty cans of water. She soon learned that it was stupid to lug more than she need. After two mornings she learned to hammer hard with her fist on the doors of bedrooms and after less than a week she was knocking, walking in, putting the can of hot water on the wash-stand, covering it with a towel and saying in a soft firm young voice:

'Half-past six, sir. You've got just an hour before your train.'

In this way she grew used to men. It was her work to go into bedrooms where men were frequently to be startled in strange attitudes, half-dressed, unshaved, stupid with sleep and sometimes thick-tongued and groping. It was no use being shy about it. It was no use worrying about it either. She herself was never thick-tongued, stupid or groping in the mornings and after a time she found she had no patience with men who had to be called a second time and then complained that their shaving water was cold. Already she was speaking to them as if she were an older person, slightly peremptory but not unkind, a little vexed but always understanding

'Of course the water's cold, sir. You should get up when you're called. I called you twice. Do you expect people to call you fifty times?'

Her voice was slow and soft. The final syllables of her sentences went singing upward on a gentle and inquiring scale. It was perhaps because of this that men were never offended by what she had to say to them even as a young girl and that they never took exception to remarks that would have been impertinent or forward in other girls.

'I know, Thelma,' they would say. 'That's me all over, Thelma. Never could get the dust out of my eyes. I'll be down in five shakes – four and a half minutes for the eggs, Thelma. I like them hard.'

Soon she began to know not only the names of travellers but exactly when they had to be called, what trains they had to catch and how they liked their eggs boiled. She knew those who liked two cans of shaving water and a wad of cotton wool because they always cut themselves. She was ready for those who groped to morning life with yellow eyes:

'Well, you won't be told, sir. You know how it takes you. You take more than you can hold and then you wonder why you feel like death the morning after.'

'I know, Thelma, I know. What was I drinking?'
'Cider most of the time and you had three rum and ports with Mr Henderson.'
'Rum and port! – Oh! my lord, Thelma—'
'That's what I say – you never learn. People can tell you forty times, can't they, but you never learn.'

Once a month, on Sunday, when she finished work at three o'clock, she walked in the forest. She was very fond of the forest. She still believed it was true, as people said, that you could walk through it all day and never come to the farther side of it but she did not mind about that. She was quite content to walk some distance into it and, if the days were fine and warm, sit down and look at the round grey trunks of the countless shimmering beeches. They reminded her very much of the huge iron-coloured legs of a troupe of elephants she had once seen at a circus and the trees themselves had just the same friendly sober air.

When she was eighteen a man named George Furness, a traveller in fancy goods and cheap lines of cutlery, came to stay at the hotel for a Saturday night and a Sunday. She did not know quite how it came about but it presently turned out in the course of casual conversation that Furness was quite unable to believe that the nuts that grew on beech-trees were just as eatable as the nuts that grew on hazel or walnut trees. It was a silly, stupid thing, she thought, for a grown man to have to admit that he didn't know about beech-nuts.

'Don't kid me,' Furness said. 'They're no more good to eat than acorns.'

For the first time, in her country way, she found herself being annoyed and scornful by someone who doubted the truth of her words.

'If you don't believe me,' she said, 'come with me and we'll get some. The forest is full enough of them. Come with me and I'll show you – I'll be going there tomorrow.'

The following say, Sunday, she walked with Furness in the forest, through the great rides of scalded brilliant beeches. In the October sunshine her hair shone in a big coppery bun from under the back of her green straw Sunday hat. Furness was a handsome, light-hearted man of thirty-five with thickish lips and dark oiled hair and a short yellow cane which he occasionally swished, sword-fashion, at pale clouds of dancing flies. These flies, almost transparent in the clear October sun, were as light and delicate as the lashes of Thelma's fair bleached eyes.

For some time she and Furness sat on a fallen tree-trunk while she picked up beech-nuts, shelled them for him and watched him eat them. She did not feel any particular sense of triumph in having shown a man that beech-nuts were good to eat but she laughed once or twice, quite happily, as Furness threw them gaily into the air, caught them deftly in his mouth and said how good they were. His tongue was remarkably red as it stiffened and flicked at the nuts and she noticed it every time. What was also remarkable was that Furness did not peel a single nut himself. With open outstretched hand and poised red tongue he simply sat and waited to be fed.

'You mean you really didn't know they were good?' she said.

'To tell you the honest,' Furness said, 'I never saw a beech-tree in my life before.'

'Oh! go on with you,' she said. *'Never?'*

'No,' he said. 'Honest. Cut my throat. I wouldn't know one if I saw one anyway.'

'Aren't there trees in London?'

'Oh! plenty,' Furness said. 'Trees all over the place.'

'As many as this?' she said. 'As many as in the forest?'

'Oh! easy,' Furness said, 'only more scattered. Scattered about in big parks – Richmond, Kew, Hyde Park, places like that – miles and miles. Scattered.'

'I like to hear you talk about London.'

'You must come up there some time,' he said. 'I'll show you round a bit. We'll have a day on the spree.'

He laughed again in his gay fashion and suddenly, really before she knew what was happening, he put his arms round her and began to kiss her. It was the first time she had ever been kissed by anyone in that sort of way and the lips of George Furness were pleasantly moist and warm. He kissed her several times again and presently they were lying on the thick floor of beech-leaves together. She felt a light crackle of leaves under her hair as George Furness pressed against her, kissing her throat, and then suddenly she felt afraid of something and she sat up, brushing leaves from her hair and shoulders.

'I think we ought to go now,' she said.

'Oh no,' he said. 'Come on. What's the hurry, what's the worry? Come on, Thelma, let's have some fun.'

'Not here. Not today—'

'Here today, gone tomorrow,' Furness said. 'Come on, Thelma, let's make a little hay while the sun shines.'

Suddenly, because Furness himself was so gay and light-hearted about everything, she felt that perhaps she was being over-cautious and stupid and something made her say:

'Perhaps some other day. When are you coming back again?'

'Well, that's a point,' he said. 'If I go to Bristol first I'll be back this way Friday. If I go to Hereford first I'll stay in Bristol over the week-end and be back here Monday.'

Sunlight breaking through thinning autumn branches scattered dancing blobs of gold on his face and hands as he laughed again and said:

'All right, Thelma? A little hay-making when I come back?'

'We'll see.'

'Is that a promise?'

'We'll see.'

'I'll take it as a promise,' he said. He laughed again and kissed her neck and she felt excited. 'You can keep a promise, Thelma, can't you?'

'Never mind about that now,' she said. 'What time shall I call you in the morning?'

'Call me early, mother dear,' he said. 'I ought to be away by six or just after.'

She could not sleep that night. She thought over and over again of the way George Furness had kissed her. She remembered the moist warm lips, the red gay tongue flicking at beech-nuts, and how sunlight breaking through thinning autumn branches had given a dancing effect to his already light-hearted face and hands. She remembered the way he had talked of promises and making hay. And after a time she could not help wishing that she had done what George Furness had wanted her to do. 'But there's always next week-end,' she thought. 'I'll be waiting next week-end.'

It was very late when she fell asleep and it was after half-past six before she woke again. It was a quarter to seven before she had the tea made and when she hurried upstairs with the tray her hands were trembling. Then after she had knocked on the door of George Furness' bedroom she went inside to make the first of several discoveries. The bed was empty and George Furness had left by motor-car.

Only a few years later, by the time she was twenty-five, almost every gentleman came and went by motor-car. But that morning it was a new and strange experience to know that a gentleman did not need to go by train. It was a revolution in her life to find that a man could pay his bill overnight, leave before breakfast and not wait for his usual can of shaving water.

All that week, and for several weeks afterwards, she waited for George Furness to come back. She waited with particular anxiety on Fridays and Mondays. She found herself becoming agitated at the sound of a motor-car. Then for the few remaining Sundays of that autumn she walked in the forest, sat down in the exact spot where George Furness had thrown beech-nuts into the air and caught them in his red fleshy mouth, and tried intensely to re-experience what it was like to be kissed by that mouth, in late warm sunlight, under a million withering beech-leaves.

All this time, and for some time afterwards, she went about her work as if nothing had happened. Then presently she began to inquire, casually at first, as if it was really a trivial matter, whether anyone had seen George Furness. When it appeared that nobody had and again that nobody even knew what Furness looked like she found herself beginning to describe him, explain him and exaggerate him a little more. In that way, by making him a little larger than life, she felt that people would recognise him more readily. Presently there would inevitably come a day when someone would say 'Ah! yes, old George. Ran across him only yesterday.'

At the same time she remained secretive and shy about him. She did not mention him in open company. It was always to some gentleman alone, to a solitary commercial traveller sipping a late night whisky or an early morning cup of tea in his bedroom, that she would say:

'Ever see George Furness nowadays? He hasn't been down lately. You knew him didn't you?'

'Can't say I did.'

'Nice cheerful fellow. Dark. Came from London – he'd talk

to you hours about London, George would. Used to keep me fascinated. I think he was in quite a way up there.'

And soon, occasionally, she began to go further than this:

'Oh! we had some times, George and me. He liked a bit of fun, George did. I used to show him the forest sometimes. He didn't know one tree from another.'

One hot Sunday afternoon in early summer, when she was twenty, she was walking towards the forest when she met another commercial traveller, a man in hosiery named Prentis, sauntering with boredom along the roadside, flicking at the heads of buttercups with a thin malacca cane. His black patent leather shoes were white with dust and something about the way he flicked at the buttercups reminded her of the way George Furness had cut with his cane at dancing clouds of late October flies.

'Sunday,' Prentis said. 'Whoever invented Sunday? Not a commercial, you bet. If there's one day in the week I hate it's Sunday – what's there to do on Sundays?'

'I generally walk in the forest,' she said.

Some time later, in the forest, Prentis began kissing her very much as George Furness had done. Under the thick bright mass of leaves, motionless in the heat of afternoon, she shut her eyes and tried to persuade herself that the moist red lips of Furness were pressing down on hers. The recaptured sensation of warmth and softness excited her into trembling. Then suddenly, feeling exposed and shy in the open riding, she was afraid that perhaps someone from the hotel might walk past and see her and she said:

'Let's take the little path there. That's a nice way. Nobody ever goes up there.'

Afterwards Prentis took off his jacket and made a pillow of it and they lay down together for the rest of the afternoon in the thick cool shade. At the same time Prentis' feet itched and he took off his shoes. As he did so and she saw the shoes white with summer dust she said:

'You'd better leave them with me tonight. I'll clean them nicely.'

And then presently, lying on her back, looking up at the high bright mass of summer leaves with her bleached far-off eyes, she said:

'Do you like the forest? Ever been in here before?'

'Never.'

'I love it here,' she said. 'I always come when I can.'

'By yourself?'

'That would be telling,' she said.

'I'll bet you do,' he said. He began laughing, pressing his body against her, stringing his fingers like a comb through her sharp red hair. 'Every Sunday, eh? What time will you bring the shoes?'

Presently he kissed her again. And again she shut her eyes and tried to imagine that the mouth pressing down on hers was the mouth of George Furness. The experience was like that of trying to stalk a butterfly on the petal of a flower and seeing it, at the last moment, flutter away at the approach of a shadow. It was very pleasant kissing Prentis under the great arch of beech-leaves in the hot still afternoon. She liked it very much. But what she sought, in the end, was not quite there.

By the time she was twenty-five she had lost count of the number of men she had taken into the forest on Sunday afternoons. By then her face had broadened and begun to fill out a lot. Her arms were fleshy and her hips had begun to stand out from her body so that her skirts were always a little too tight and rode up at the back, showing the hem of her underclothes. Her feet, from walking up and down stairs all day, had grown much flatter and her legs were straight and solid. In the summer she could not bear to wear her corsets and gradually her figure became more floppy, her bust like a soft fat pillow untidily slept in.

Most of them who came to spend a night or two at the hotel were married men, travellers glad of a little reprieve from wives and then equally glad, after a week or two on the road, to go back to them again. She was a great comfort to such men. They looked forward through dreary days of lugging and unpacking sample cases to evenings when Thelma, pillowy and soft, with her soothing voice, would put her head into their bedrooms and say:

'Had a good week, sir? Anything you want? Something you'd like me to get for you?'

Many of them wanted Thelma. Almost as many of them were content simply to talk with her. At night, when she took up to their bedrooms hot jugs of cocoa, tots of whisky, pots of tea or in winter, for colds, fiery mugs of steaming rum and cinnamon, they liked her to stay and talk for a while. Sometimes she simply stood by the bedside, arms folded over her enlarging bosom, legs a little apart, nodding and listening. Sometimes she sat on the edge of the bed, her skirt riding up over her thick knees, her red hair like a plaited bell-rope as one of the travellers twisted it in his hands. Sometimes a man was in trouble: a girl had thrown him over or a wife had died. Then she listened with eyes that seemed so intent in their wide and placid colourlessness that again and again a man troubled in loneliness gained the impression that she was thinking always and only of him. Not one of them guessed that she was really thinking of George Furness or that as she let them twist her thick red hair, stroke her pale comforting, comfortable arms and thighs or kiss her unaggressive lips she was really letting someone else, in imagination, do these things. In the same way when she took off her clothes and slipped into bed with them it was from feelings and motives far removed from wantonness. She was simply groping hungrily for experiences she felt George Furness, and only George Furness, ought to have shared.

When she was thirty the urge to see George Furness became so obsessive that she decided, for the first and only time in her life, to go to London. She did not really think of the impossibility of finding anybody in so large a place. She had thought a great deal about London and what it would be like there, with George Furness, on the spree. Lying in her own room, listening to the night sounds of a forest that was hardly ever really still all through winter and summer, she had built up the impression that London, though vast, was also composed in large part of trees. That was because George Furness had described it that way. For that reason she was not afraid of London; the prospect of being alone there did not appal her. And always at the back of her mind lay the comforting and unsullied notion that somehow, by extraordinary chance, by some unbelievable miracle, she would run into George Furness there as naturally and simply as if he were walking up the steps of *The Blenheim Arms.*

So she packed her things into a small black fibre suit-case, asked for seven days off, the only holiday she had ever taken in her life, and started off by train. At the junction twelve miles away she had not only to change trains but she had also to wait for thirty-five minutes for the eastbound London train. It was midday on a warm oppressive day in September and she decided to go into the refreshment room to rest and get herself an Eccles cake, of which she was very fond, and a cup of tea. The cakes in fact tempted her so much that she ordered two.

Just before the cakes and the tea arrived at her table she became uneasily aware of someone looking at her. She looked round the refreshment room and saw, standing with his foot on the rail of the bar, beside a big blue-flamed tea-urn, a man she knew named Lattimore, a traveller in novelty lines for toy-shops and bazaars. Lattimore, a tallish man of thirty-five with fair receding hair and a thick gold signet ring on the third finger of his right hand, was drinking whisky from a tumbler.

She was so used to the state and appearance of men who took too much to drink that she recognised, even at that distance across the railway refreshment room, that Lattimore was not quite sober. She had seen him drunk once or twice before and instinctively she felt concerned and sorry for him as he picked up his glass, wiped his mouth on the back of his free hand and then came over to talk to her.

'Where are you going, Mr Lattimore?' she said.

'Down to the old *Blenheim*,' he said. 'Where are *you*?'

She did not say where she was going. In the few moments before her cakes arrived she looked at Lattimore with keen pale eyes. The pupils of his own eyes were dusky, ill-focused and beginning to water.

'What is it, Mr Lattimore?' she said.

'Blast and damn her,' he said. 'Blast her.'

'That isn't the way to talk,' Thelma said.

'Blast her,' he said. 'Double blast her.'

Her cakes and tea arrived. She poured herself a cup of tea.

'A cup of this would do you more good than that stuff,' she said.

'Double blast,' he said. He gulped suddenly at the glass of whisky and then took a letter from his pocket. 'Look at that, Thelma. Tell us what you think of that.'

It was not the first time she had read a letter from a wife to a husband telling him that she was finished, fed up and going away. Most of that sort of thing, she found, came right enough in the end. What she chiefly noticed this time was the postmark on the envelope. The letter came from London and it reminded her suddenly that she was going there.

'Have one of these Eccles cakes,' she said. 'You want to get some food inside you.'

He fumbled with an Eccles cake. Flaky crumbs of pastry and loose currants fell on his waistcoat and striped grey trousers. To her dismay he then put the Eccles cake back on the plate and, after a pause, picked up her cake in mistake for his own. Something about this groping mistake of his with the cakes made her infinitely sad for him and she said:

'You never ought to get into a state like this, Mr Lattimore. It's awful. You'll do yourself no good getting into this sort of state. You're not driving, are you?'

'Train,' he said. 'Train.' He suddenly drained his whisky and, before she could speak, wandered across the refreshment bar to get himself another. 'Another double and what platform for Deansborough?' he called. He banged his hand on the counter and then there was a sudden ring of breaking glasses.

Ten minutes later she was sitting with him in the train for Deansborough, going back home, his head on her shoulder. It was warm and oppressive in the carriage and she opened the window and let in fresh air. The wind blowing on his face ruffled his thinning hair and several times she smoothed it down again with her hands. It came to her then that she might have been smoothing down the hair of George Furness and at the same time she remembered London, though without regret.

'What part of London do you come from?' she said.

'Finchley.'

'That isn't near the parks is it?' she said. 'You don't ever run across a man named George Furness, do you?'

The little local train was rattling slowly and noisily between banks of woodland. Its noises rebounded from trees and cuttings and in through the open window so that for a moment she was not quite sure what Lattimore was saying in reply.

'Furness? George? Old George? – dammit, friend of mine. Lives in Maida Vale.'

She sat staring for some time at the deep September banks of woodland, still dark green from summer, streaming past the windows. The whisky breath of Lattimore was sour on the sultry air and she opened the window a little further, breathing fast and deeply.

'When did you see him last?' she said.

'Thursday – no, Wednesday,' he said. 'Play snooker together every Wednesday, me and George.'

Within a month the leaves on the beeches would be turning copper. With her blood pounding in her throat, she sat thinking of their great masses of burning, withering leaf and the way, a long time before, George Furness had held out his hand while she peeled nuts for him and then watched him toss them into the air and catch them on his moist red tongue.

'How is he these days?' she said.

'Old George? – same as ever. Up and down. Up and down. Same as ever.'

Once again she stared at the passing woodlands, remembering. Unconsciously, as she did so, she twisted quietly at the big signet ring on Lattimore's finger. The motion began to make him, in his half-drunk state, soothed and amorous. He turned his face towards her and put his mouth against her hair.

'Ought to have married you, Thelma,' he said. 'Ought to have put the ring on you.'

'You don't want me.'

'You like the ring?' he said. 'You can have it.' He began struggling in groping alcoholic fashion to take the ring off his finger. 'Have it, Thelma – you put it on.'

'No,' she said. 'No.' And then: 'How was George Furness when you saw him last Wednesday?'

He succeeded suddenly in taking the ring from his finger and began pressing it clumsily on one of her own.

'There y'are, Thelma. You put it on. You wear it. For me. Put it on and keep it, Thelma. For me.'

The ring was on her finger.

'How was George?' she said.

'Getting fat,' he said. 'Can't get the old pod over the snooker table nowadays. Rest and be thankful – that's what they call George.'

Half sleepy, half drunk, Lattimore let his head slip from her shoulder and the mass of her thick red hair down to the shapeless comforting pillow of her bosom and she said:

'What's he travel in now? The same old line?'

'Same old line,' he said. 'Furniture and carpets. Mostly carpets now.'

She realised suddenly that they were talking of quite different things, quite different people. She was listening to a muddled drunk who had somehow got the names wrong. She stared for a long time at the woods rushing past the rattling little train. There was no need to speak. Lattimore was asleep in her bosom, his mouth open, and the ring was shining on her finger.

Next day Lattimore did not remember the ring and she did not give it back. She kept it, as she kept a great many other things, as a memento of experiences that men liked to think were services she had rendered.

A drawer in the wardrobe in her bedroom was full of these things. She hardly ever used them: handkerchiefs, night-dress cases and bits of underwear from travellers in ladies' wear, bottles of perfume and powder, night-dresses and dress-lengths of satin, necklaces of imitation pearl and amber; presents given for Christmas, her birthday or for a passing, comforting week-end.

Some of the men who had given them came back only once or twice and she never saw them again. They changed jobs or were moved to other districts. But they never forgot Thelma and travellers were always arriving to say that they had seen Bill Haynes and Charlie Townsend or Bert Hobbs only the week before and that Bill or Charlie or Bert wished to be remembered. Among themselves too men would wink and say 'Never need be lonely down at *The Blenheim*. What do you say, Harry? Thelma always looks after you,' and many a man would be recommended to stay there, on the edge of the forest, where he would be well looked after by Thelma, rather than go on to bigger towns beyond.

By the time she was forty she was not only plumper and more shapeless but her hair had begun to show the first cottony signs of grey. There was nothing she disliked more than red hair streaked with another colour and from that time onwards she began to dye her hair. Because she could never shop anywhere except in the village or at most in Chippingham, the junction, twelve miles away, she never succeeded in getting quite the right shade for her hair. The first dye she used was a little too yellow and gave her hair the appearance of an old fox fur. One day the shop in the village ran out of this dye and sold her something which, they said, was the nearest thing. This shade made her hair look as if stained with a mixture of beetroot and bay rum. It was altogether too dark for her. Later when the shop got in its new supplies of the yellow dye she uneasily realised that neither tint was suitable. The only thing that occurred to her to do then was to mix them together. This gave a strange gold rusty look to her hair and something in the dye at the same time made it much drier, so that it became unnaturally fuzzier and more difficult to manage than it had been.

The one thing that did not change about her as she grew older was the colour and appearance of her eyes. They remained unchangeably bleached and distant, always with the effect of the mild soft lashes being still wet with a touch of gold paint on them. While the rest of her body grew plumper and older and greyer the eyes remained, perhaps because of their extreme pallor, very young, almost girlish, as if in a way that part of her would never grow up.

It was these still pale, bleached, unnaturally adolescent eyes that she fixed on a man named Sharwood more than ten years later as she took him a tray of early morning tea and a newspaper on a wet late October morning, soon after she was fifty. During the night torrents of rain had hurled through the miles of beeches, bringing down great flying droves of leaves. Through the open bedroom window rain had poured in too on the curtains and as Thelma reached up to shut the window she said:

'Not much of a morning to be out, sir. Which way are you off today?'

'London,' he said.

There was no need for him to say any more. Purposely she fussed a little with curtains and then casually, in the same slow, upward-singing voice, asked the inevitable question:

'London? I suppose you never run into George Furness up there?'

Sharwood, a middle-aged man who travelled mainly in woollen goods, put three lumps of sugar into his tea, stirred it and then said:

'As a matter of fact I was thinking of asking you the same question.'

'Me?'

'Funny thing,' Sharwood said, 'it was George who recommended me here.'

Her heart began racing, fast and heavily, as it had done on the warm afternoon with Lattimore, drunk in the train.

'Ran across him up in Glasgow about a month ago.' Sharwood said. 'You knew he was up there, didn't you? – I mean had been. Been up there for thirty years – settled there. Even got himself a bit of a Scotch accent on the way.'

'No, I didn't know,' she said. 'I never only saw him the once.'

She did not know quite why she should admit, for the first and only time, that she had seen him only once, but by now she was so transfixed and overwrought that she hardly knew what she was saying.

'I know,' Sharwood said. 'He told me. It's been all those years ago, he said, but if you go to *The Blenheim Arms* ask if Thelma's still there. She'll look after you.'

She locked her hands together to prevent them quivering too hopelessly and he said:

'That was the last time he was ever down this way. He moved up to Glasgow the next week. Heard of a good job there with a big wholesale firm of cloth people and there he stopped.'

Sharwood paused, drank his tea and stared over the rim of the cup to the October rain slashing on the window beyond.

'He'd have been up there just thirty-five years if he'd lived till November.'

Her heart seemed to stop its racing.

She did not know what to say or do. Then after a moment Sharwood said:

'Hand me my wallet off the wash-stand, will you? I've got a cutting about him. Clipped it out of *The Glasgow Herald*.'

She stood staring for a few moments longer at the newspaper cutting that Sharwood handed her across the bed. The face of George Furness stared back at her from a photograph and she said simply:

'I don't think he's changed a lot, do you?'

'Same as ever,' Sharwood said. 'You'd have known him anywhere.'

That afternoon, although it was a mid-week afternoon, she left *The Blenheim Arms* about three o'clock, walked up the road and into the forest. The rain had stopped about noon and now it was a day of racing sea-bright cloud, widening patches of high blue sky and a wind that broke from the beeches an endless stream of leaves.

She walked slowly down the long riding. She stopped for a few moments at the place where she and George Furness had eaten beech-nuts and where, some years later, she had tried for the first of many times to recapture the moment with another man. She picked up a few beech-nuts and made an attempt to peel them but the summer that year had been rainy and cool and most of the husks she broke were empty.

Finally she walked on and did something she had never done before. Slowly, in brightening sunlight, through shoals of drenched fallen leaves, she walked the entire width of the forest to the other side. It was really, after all, not so far as people had always lead her to believe.

By the time she reached the open country beyond the last of the enormous beeches the sky had been driven almost clear of cloud. The sun was warm and brilliant and as she sat down on a bank of leaves at the forest edge she could feel it burning softly on her face and hands.

After a time she lay down. She lay there for two hours, not moving, her frizzed foxy hair blown against wet leaves, her bleached pale eyes staring upwards beyond the final rim of forest branches to where the sky, completely clear now of cloud, was almost fierce with high washed blue light in the falling afternoon.

That night she did not sleep much. The following night she was restless and there was a sharp, drawing pain in her back whenever she breathed a little hard. The following afternoon the doctor stood by her bed and said, shaking his head, joking with her:

'Now, Thelma, what's all this? What have you been up to? It's getting cool at night this time of year.'

'I sat down in the forest,' she said. 'That's all. I lay down for a while.'

'You know, Thelma,' he said, 'you're getting too old for lying down in the forest. You've got a good warm bed, haven't you?'

'I like the forest.'

'You're really getting too old for this sort of thing,' he said. 'Now be a good girl and take care of yourself a little better.

You've had your fling – we all know – but now you'll have to take care a little more. Understand?'

She made no sign that she understood except for a slight flicker of her thin pale gold lashes.

'There comes a time,' the doctor said.

She died five days later. On the coffin and on the graveside in the church-yard that lay midway between the village and the forest there were a great many wreaths. Many gentlemen had remembered her, most of them individually, but someone had had the idea of placing a collecting box on the bar of *The Blenheim Arms* so that casual callers, odd travellers passing, could put into it a few coppers or a shilling or two and so pay their last respects.

A good deal of money was collected in this way and because so many people, mostly men, had contributed something it was impossible to indicate who and how many they were. It was thought better instead to put on the big round wreath of white chrysanthemums only a plain white card.

'Thelma. R.I.P.,' it said. 'Loved by all.'

MRS EGLANTINE

Every morning Mrs Eglantine sat at the round bamboo bar of the New Pacific Hotel and drank her breakfast. This consisted of two quick large brandies, followed by several slower ones. By noon breakfast had become lunch and by two o'clock the pouches under and above Mrs Eglantine's bleared blue eyes began to look like large puffed pink prawns.

'I suppose you know you've got her name wrong?' my friend the doctor said to me. 'It's really Eglinton. What makes you call her Eglantine?'

'She must have been rather sweet at some time.'

'You think so?' he said. 'What has Eglantine got to do with that?'

'The Sweet-briar,' I said, 'or the Vine, or the twisted Eglantine.'

For a woman of nearly fifty Mrs Eglantine wore her blue lined shorts very neatly. Her legs were brown, well-shaped and spare. Her arms were slim and hairless and her nails well-manicured. She had pretty delicate ears and very soft pale blue eyes. Her hair, though several shades too yellow, was smooth and always well-brushed, with a slight upward curl where it fell on her tanned slender shoulders.

Her only habit of untidiness was that sometimes, as she sat at the bar, she let one or both of her yellow sandals fall off. After that she often staggered about the verandah with one shoe on. and one in her hand; or with both shoes off, carrying them and saying:

'Whose bloody shoes are these? Anybody know whose bloody shoes these are?'

Soon, when she got to know me a little better, she would slap one of her sandals on the seat of the bar-stool next to her and say:

'Here, England, come and sit here.' She always called me England. 'Come and sit down and talk to me. I'm British too. Come and sit down. Nice to meet someone from the old country in this lousy frog-crowd. What do you make of Tahiti?'

I had never time to tell her what I thought of Tahiti before, licking brandy from her lips, she would say something like:

'Swindle. The big myth. The great South-sea bubble. The great South-sea paradise. Not a decent hotel in the place. All the shops owned by Chinks. Everybody bone-lazy. Takes you all day to cash a cheque at the bank. Hot and dirty. Still, what else do you expect with the Froggies running the show?'

Presently, after another brandy or two, she would begin to call me dear.

'You've seen the travel posters, haven't you, dear? Those nice white sands and the Polynesian girls with naked bosoms climbing the palms? All a myth, dear. All a bloody swindle. All taken in the Cook Islands, hundreds of miles away.'

Talking of the swindle of white sands and Polynesian girls she would point with her well-kept hands to the shore:

'Look at the beach, dear. Just look at it. I ask you. Black sand, millions of sea-eggs, thousands of those liverish-looking sea-snakes. Coral island, my foot. I can bear most things, England, but not black sand. Not a beach that looks like a foundry yard.'

It was true that the beaches of Tahiti were black, that the sea, where shallow, was thick with sea-eggs and at low tide with creatures looking like inert lumps of yellow intestine. But there were also shoals of blue and yellow fish, like delicate underwater sails, with sometimes a flying fish or a crowd of exquisite blue torpedoes flashing in bluest water.

It occurred to me that something, perhaps, had made her ignore these things.

'How long have you been here now?' I said.

'Ever been to Australia?' she said. 'That's the place for beaches. Miles of them. Endless. You've seen the Cook Islands? White as that. Me? Six months, dear. Nearly seven months now.'

'Why don't you take the sea-plane and get out,' I said, 'if you hate it so much?'

'Long story, England,' she said. 'Bloody complicated.'

Every afternoon she staggered away, slept in her room and re-appeared about six, in time for sunset. By that time she had changed her shorts for a dress, generally something very simple in cotton or silk that, from a distance or behind, with her brief lean figure, made her look attractive, fresh and quite young.

I noticed that, in the evening, she did not go at once to the bar. For perhaps ten minutes or a quarter of an hour she would stand in silence at the rail of the verandah, gazing at the sunset.

The sunsets across the lagoon at Tahiti, looking towards the great chimneys of Moorea, are the most beautiful in the world. As the sun dips across the Pacific the entire sky behind the mountains opens up like a blast furnace, flaming pure and violent fire. Over the upper sky roll clouds of scarlet petal, then orange, then yellow, then pink, and then swan-white as they sail away, high, and slowly, over the ocean to the north. In the last minutes before darkness there is left only a thunderous purple map of smouldering ash across the sky.

'It's so beautiful, England dear,' she said to me. 'God, it's so beautiful it takes your breath away. I always want to cry.'

Once or twice she actually did cry but soon, when sunset was over and the enormous soft southern stars were breaking the deep black sky, she would be back to brandy and the bar. Once again her eyes would take on the appearance of swollen prawns. One by one her shoes would fall off, leaving her to grope barefooted, carrying her shoes about the verandah, not knowing whose they were.

'Sweet people,' she said once. 'Very sweet people, you and Mrs England. Good old England. That's a sweet dress she has on. What would you say, Mrs England, if you wanted to marry someone here and they wouldn't let you?'

She laughed. From much brandy her skin was hot and baggy. Her eyes, looking as if they were still in tears from the sunset, could no longer focus themselves.

'A Froggy too,' she said, 'which I call damn funny. Rather a nice Froggy too.'

Her voice was thick and bitter.

Rather funny? she said. 'I come all this way from Australia. to meet him here and then find they've sent him to New Caledonia. Administrative post. Administrative trick, dear, see?'

I said something about how simple it was, nowadays, to fly from one side of the Pacific to the other, and she said:

'Can't get permission, dear. Got to get permission from the

Froggies to go to Froggy territory,' she went on. 'Of course
he'll come back here in time.'

I said something about how simple it was to wait here, in
Tahiti, where she was, and she said:

'Can't get permission, dear. Got to get permission from the
Froggies to stay in Froggy territory. Froggy red tape, dear. Can't
stay here, can't go there. Next week my permit expires.'

I made some expression of sympathy about all this and she
said:

'All a trick, dear. Complete wangle. His father's a friend of
the governor. Father doesn't like me. Governor doesn't like me.
Undesirable type, dear. Divorced and drink too much. Bad
combination. British too. They don't want the British here.
Leaves more Tahitian girls for the Froggies to set up fancy house
with.'

There were, as my friend the doctor said, only two general
types in Tahiti: those who took one look at the island, wanted
to depart next day and never set eyes on it again; and those who,
from the first moment, wanted to stay there for ever. Now I had
met a third.

'Going to make my last appeal for an extension of my permit
tomorrow,' Mrs Eglantine said. 'Suppose you wouldn't like to
write it for me, would you, England dear? It'll need to be bloody
well put, that's sure.'

'Where will you go?' I said. 'If you have to go?'

'Nearest British possession, dear. Cook Islands. Wait there.'

The Cook Islands are very beautiful. Across a long, shallow,
sharkless lagoon flying-boats glide down between soft fringes
of palm and purest hot white coral sand. At the little rest-house,
by the anchorage, the prettiest and friendliest of Polynesian
girls serve tea and cakes, giggling constantly, shaking back their
long loose black hair.

'Yes, it's very lovely,' I said. 'You couldn't have a better place
to go than that. That's a paradise.'

'And a dry one,' she said, 'in case you didn't know it. Worse
than prohibition. They allow you a bottle of something stronger
than lime-juice once a month, dear, and you even need a permit
for that.'

We left her under the moth-charged lights of the verandah
groping for her shoes.

'*Dormez bien,* dears,' she said. 'Which is more than I shall do.'

'She must have been very pretty once,' my wife said.

'She's pretty now,' I said, 'sweet and rather pretty.'

Five days later she flew out with us on the morning plane. Half way to the Cook Islands I brought her breakfast and she said, as she knocked it back, 'Bless you, England dear.'

In the lagoon, by the anchorage, a little crowd of Polynesians, mostly women and girls, sat under the shade of palm-trees, out of the pure blistering heat of white coral sand, singing songs of farewell to a young man leaving by the plane.

The songs of Polynesia have a great sadness in them that is very haunting. A few of the women were weeping. Then at the last moment a girl rushed on bare feet along the jetty towards the waiting launch, wringing her hands in sorrow, her long hair flying, bitterly weeping final words of good-bye.

On the scalding white coral beach, under the palms, Mrs Eglantine was nowhere to be seen. And presently, as the launch moved away, I could no longer hear the songs of sad farewell or the haunting voice of the girl who was weeping. But only, running through my head, haunting too:

'The Sweet-briar, or the Vine, or the twisted Eglantine.'